VOODOO
SHANGHAI

VOODOO
SHANGHAI

Kristi Charish

A KINCAID STRANGE NOVEL

VINTAGE CANADA

VINTAGE CANADA EDITION, 2020

Copyright © 2020 Kristi Charish

Published by Vintage Canada,
a division of Penguin Random House Canada Limited, in 2020.
Distributed in Canada by Penguin Random House Canada Limited, Toronto.

Vintage Canada with colophon is a registered trademark.

www.penguinrandomhouse.ca

Library and Archives Canada Cataloguing in Publication

Title: Voodoo Shanghai : a Kincaid Strange novel / Kristi Charish.

Names: Charish, Kristi, author.

Identifiers: Canadiana (print) 20190137363 | Canadiana (ebook) 20190137398 |
ISBN 9780345815927 (softcover) | ISBN 9780345815934 (HTML)

Classification: LCC PS8605.H3686 V67 2020 | DDC C813/.6—dc23

Text and cover design by Five Seventeen

Cover images: (woman) © John Fedele / Getty Images;
(powder) © RedGreen / Shutterstock.com;
(swamp) © Krystian Piątek / Unsplash

Printed and bound in Canada

2 4 6 8 9 7 5 3 1

Penguin
Random House
VINTAGE CANADA

For anyone who's been ghosted
and wondered why

CHAPTER 1

JOSS PAPER BLUES

I closed my eyes as I stood in the bone-chilling November night, willing the heady, sandalwood-cored incense burning in my pentagram to distract me from the twelve Singaporean mourners as they let out another concerted wail of despair.

Nope. No good.

Despite the relaxing fragrance of the joss sticks—the scent of burning spices and wood, the warmth of the smoke against the crisp night air—it was no use. Not even the soothing incense could help me focus as the circus of a funeral unfolded.

I winced as another puff pastry hit me in the back of the head, throwing my concentration off once again.

Goddamnit . . .

"You don't understand!" cried Mrs. Young, an attractive fifty-something Singaporean woman. I'd challenge anyone to peg her a day over thirty-five. She slumped into a cushioned lawn chair, her black mourning dress striking an artful balance between sexy and elegant as its crinoline-lined skirt flared out. The Youngs' house staff had carted dozens of the chairs into the Seattle botanical gardens earlier this afternoon, especially for this evening's event.

"She won't let us sleep more than a few hours—she's relentless!" Mrs. Young said, fixing pleading, red-rimmed eyes on me. Despite her impeccably made-up face, she hadn't been able to conceal her grief.

I took that as a good sign that the grief was genuine, at least to some degree. I supposed that put the Youngs on the better side of my usual clientele for this sort of thing.

We all winced as another dish smashed to the frost-covered ground near our feet, originating from my pentagram of chrysanthemums just an arm's throw away. The flowers were an elaborate piece of trickery devised especially for this evening's event. It was November and the real beds of chrysanthemums were long dead, the tops shrivelled and pinched off by gardeners weeks ago. But, as the Youngs had said when they hired me, that was what twenty-four-hour, all-seasons florists were for . . . and twenty-four-hour caterers, and twenty-four-hour delivery people . . .

My pentagram of chrysanthemums was punctuated with strategically placed incense to keep, well—

There was yet another, louder crash as an entire table loaded with Singaporean delicacies was overturned, and then a young woman's scream pierced the air. "*Mommy? Mommy*! I can hear you!" the young woman shouted.

Mrs. Young collapsed into another round of sobs, covering her face with her hands. Mr. Young, looking just as sleep-deprived and out of sorts, placed a supportive hand on his wife's shoulder before fixing his own red-rimmed, grief-stricken eyes on me. The image he cut now was a far cry from the composed business professional who had contacted me in desperation a week before.

"You have to do something," he pleaded.

Well, at least the three of us were in general agreement on that small detail. Now, if I could just get them on board with the rest of it . . .

"*Mommy? Daddy?* I'm serious! Get over here, right now, and let me out!" The shout was followed by another table overturning and the sound of stamping feet.

Goddamnit. She was making a mess of my pentagram. If only the Youngs had listened to me about the funerary tables—I'd told them the elaborate layout wouldn't— *Damn it!*

I ducked just in time to miss an airborne egg tart. It skirted my hair, almost clocking me.

—wouldn't suit the occasion and would only add ammunition . . .

The egg tart landed at Mrs. Young's feet, and she lifted her tear-streaked face from her hands and fixed her sullen eyes on me. "*Please*, Kincaid Strange. Can you *please* make Astrid behave?" she whispered.

I closed my eyes and nodded as a breeze blew more of the thick joss smoke my way, its soothing warmth mixing with the icy night air, and I braced for another round with Astrid.

Oh gods, zombies and ghosts, let the joss smoke stay my temper. Seriously, I really need the help right now.

As if in answer to my plea, a pastry hit me in the cheek. I wiped whipped cream and chocolate icing off my face.

Well, so much for the universe helping me mend broken family relationships . . .

"I'll take care of it," I told the Youngs. I turned on my heel and strode back to my pentagram of Chinese incense and white chrysan-themums less than ten feet away. It held one Astrid Young, the recently deceased twenty-one-year-old daughter of the wealthy and powerful Young family, currently summoned as a zombie for the evening by yours truly and throwing the mother of all temper tantrums.

"Astrid," I called out. "I'm coming back in to talk." I reined in my own temper and ducked as another puff pastry sailed towards my head and the mourners let out another choreographed wail. Another hothead at this seance wouldn't help one damn bit.

An imported troupe of professional mourners, fresh chrysan-themum blooms purchased from what had to be every high-end florist in downtown Seattle, pastries and other delicacies flown in from a Paris bistro Astrid had been fond of, joss incense sticks specially blessed by the monks from a Buddhist monastery the Youngs supported . . .

An awful lot of money and trouble could have been saved if I'd been able to run this seance in the privacy of their own garden.

Then again, after meeting Astrid's ghost this evening, it was probably for the best that I hadn't raised her anywhere near her family home.

For that matter, was I ever glad I'd gone with a zombie and not a ghost, as the Youngs had requested. After less than a minute of meeting the recently deceased Astrid, I'd patted myself on the back. Zombies are physical, more easily contained . . .

"No more pastries, Astrid, I mean it!" I called out as I carefully eased myself over the chrysanthemums and joss smoke. The white blooms were only now starting to freeze and crack in the evening chill. There was only so much the portable heaters could do to keep the cold at bay—and the Otherside from the summoning didn't help.

A pork bun, still warm and smelling of spices and delicious roast pork, hit me in the face.

Your fault for asking, Kincaid. I swear to god, though, if she throws another one of those at me again, I'm going to start eating her funerary offerings.

We'd see how she liked that.

Though she was trying, Astrid couldn't cross my barrier of chrysanthemums and joss smoke—no normal ghost or zombie could. Chrysanthemums repulse the dead, which is probably why they were historically used as a funeral flower in Asia.

But that didn't stop her from throwing things across.

I ducked as a teacup sailed my way this time, full to the brim.

"Nope, not done yet," I said under my breath. Needless to say, the story the Youngs had spun me about Astrid's ghost's violent tendencies had flagged some serious safety and poltergeist concerns . . .

Whatever it had been that led to Astrid's premature demise— the Youngs' parenting, Astrid's disposition, her love affair with fast cars or some unholy mix of the three—what I was faced with now was a desperately spoiled and angry zombie unlike any I'd come across before.

And so here we were at the botanical gardens, complete with imported mourners, the best designer funerary finery money could buy and the distraught Youngs. A funerary shrine erected for Astrid, or her zombie at any rate, so she wouldn't feel "threatened" by the confrontation.

I was grateful that her family had refused to cremate their daughter's remains, a common practice for Buddhist families. Otherwise I'd be dealing with an angry ghost. A very angry ghost. Maybe even a poltergeist—and they've been known to break out of pentagrams.

I strode to the centre of the pentagram where a beautiful young woman stood, every muscle in her dead body balled up and tense with anger and fury. She was just out of her teens. Even as a corpse, she was stunning. Her milky, porcelain complexion was a shade or two paler, her eyes had dulled to a murky, watery brown, but her black hair was still shining—no doubt in part due to the hairdresser Mrs. Young had flown in from Singapore for the sole purpose of attending Astrid.

"I already told you, I don't want to talk to you," Astrid shouted as I kept coming.

I ignored her. She couldn't hurt me, not really, not inside my own pentagram and sporting my bindings. Where the hell had things gone so wrong for Astrid? She'd led the life of a modern-day princess, the cherished only daughter of an obscenely wealthy and not unkind family. Her birth, unlike my own, was probably a joyous occasion with all the accoutrements rich people have for that sort of thing.

"I'm warning you, get away from me!" She grabbed a bottle of Dom Pérignon.

I mean, Astrid could have been *anything* she wanted. An actress, a model, a businesswoman at one of her parents' many companies.

"It's no use, Astrid. We are going to have a conversation. A civil one, so can you stop— *Shit!*" I ducked behind an overturned table as the Dom sailed my way. This was getting ridiculous.

"Last chance, Astrid!" I shouted, and tapped into the Otherside I still had stored from the raising. I eased myself around the table. Thankfully, Astrid had run out of culinary projectiles.

"Do you have any idea *who I am?*" She turned to face her parents. "*Mommy! Daddy!*"

Yeah, I'm starting to think that's where a lot of your problems started myself.

"Make the awful practitioner go away!"

I thought I heard Mrs. Young renew her sobs, but it was hard to tell over the mourners. Crying was standard at these funerary proceedings, the Youngs had assured me, but the wailing, hair pulling and shaking fits were an extra expense, completely worth it for their precious daughter.

The Youngs didn't respond to her cries. It's so refreshing when people take my professional advice seriously. I crossed my arms and tapped my foot. "There's an easy way and a hard way to do this, Astrid," I said.

Not getting the reaction she'd hoped for from her parents, Astrid fixed her watery brown eyes on me. They turned a reddish orange, and more than one of her zombie bindings flared.

Oh, that was not a good sign . . . My Otherside sight firmly in place, I concentrated on my wayward socialite, looking beyond the bindings I'd set to animate her corpse all the way to the ghost trapped and temporarily tangled amongst them.

Astrid's ghost flickered between the normal, dim Otherside gold of a ghost and the bright, anger-fuelled, blinding orange gold of a poltergeist, courtesy of the Otherside her anger siphoned across the barrier every time she had a spectacular temper tantrum. Like she was about to do now.

"Stop that," I warned, holding my ground lest I give Astrid the wrong idea . . . Despite what my five-foot-three, slip-of-nothing frame suggested, I was *not* weak. Astrid's ghost was most definitely exhibiting some serious poltergeist tendencies—hurtling objects towards unsuspecting staff, scaring guests off—*safe-ishly* contained in the zombie bindings for now.

Poltergeists are an intriguing type of ghost once you get past the violence and mayhem. For the most part, ghosts can't do much this side of the barrier. Oh, they can move the odd thing around, even turn on radios or TVs and possess the occasional pay phone, but it takes a hell of a lot of effort, and the more they try to affect the world of the living, the faster they burn out.

But a poltergeist is a different beast entirely. Poltergeists are typically the ghosts of evil and wretched people—the ones who have no regret over the horrible things they did in life. Scratch that, they regret not having caused more damage. The only thing their souls derive pleasure from is making the living utterly miserable. Bonus points if you manage to kill someone—and trust me, they are a damnably clever bunch when it comes to murder. They tend towards spontaneous carnage; patience and planning aren't their strong suit. Though I've seen enough cleverly laid traps—bricks above doors, oil spilled at the top of a flight of stairs—to know that when they put their dead and vengeful minds to it, just about anything is possible.

Gideon, the ghost of an evil sorcerer and my recent teacher, had been an eye-opening lesson in just what the dead can get away with when they put their minds to it. And time is something the dead have on their hands.

But poltergeists are the ghosts of people who were *bad*, *evil*. Unrepentant souls whose first love is causing pain—emotional, physical, take your pick. Serial killers, criminals, occasionally politicians and lawyers . . . those are the kinds of people who become poltergeists.

Unlike a poltergeist, Astrid had moments of lucidity and could hold a semi-civil conversation, though those moments were quickly disappearing as the anger took over . . .

By all accounts, Astrid had been a selfish, spoilt bitch, but she wasn't evil—she'd had no interest in hurting people. As a ghost, she wasn't really interested in hurting anyone either; otherwise she'd have dumped scalding tea over my head, not thrown puff pastries.

Could someone be so spoilt, so selfish, so obsessed with self-gratification, that it drove them to become a poltergeist?

"You call these pork buns!" Astrid screamed, grabbing one from the ground.

A philosophical question for another day . . .

"Oh, hell!" I dodged another onslaught of Singaporean delicacies. They sailed over the chrysanthemums and joss sticks and rained down on the troupe of mourners instead. I had to hand it to them, they were as professional as Astrid's mother claimed—they didn't miss a beat or a wail as they gracefully dodged and swerved around the flying pastries.

Damn it, zombies were usually so obedient when I raised them. I'd never actually had a zombie I'd summoned put up a fight.

"Don't say I didn't warn you," I whispered as I grabbed hold of Astrid's bindings and drained the anger off. And Astrid stopped, just as she'd been about to throw another bottle of Dom at her parents.

Shock stilled her features and she fixed her eyes on me. "You! How dare you?"

"Yeah, yeah, you're a very important ghost, yada, yada, I've heard it before. Now, like I said earlier, we're going to sit down and have a civilized conversation about your ghostly activities—"

But Astrid wasn't done. Not by a long shot. She turned to the audience whose numbers she knew she had.

"*Mommy, Daddy,*" she intoned with a practised mix of sorrowful begging and whining. "How *could* you?"

Normally, I'm all for letting the dead vent at their still-living relatives, but in Astrid's case? "Astrid," I warned. "Talk to me, not your—"

"How could we what?" Mrs. Young cried out.

Goddamnit. And there we went, talking to the zombies. Not even my good clients could follow one simple rule . . .

I mean, what is it about talking to zombies when the practitioner tells you not to? Is there some kind of Otherside lure the dead use to rope their family members into an argument they can't possibly win?

Don't argue with the dead. The dead don't change. They're set in their patterns. You won't win, it's like the house in poker.

"You know exactly what you did!" Astrid reached for another pork bun, but I stopped her with a quick tug on her bindings.

"Astrid, stop!" I shouted, and clapped my hands. Zombies, four-line and five-line alike, respond to sounds, scents and bright lights, and combining them works even better.

Astrid's childish affectations vanished as the Otherside flashed with her broiling anger again. "What did you do?!" Astrid hissed at her mother, ignoring me. "I specifically asked for the new Louis Vuitton bag three weeks ago!"

Oh, dear god . . . Please tell me this entire debacle was not over Astrid not getting the right joss paper offering . . .

Joss paper referred to the elaborate gifts—clothing, money, houses, cars, designer bags, all in paper form—that families could purchase and burn for their loved ones. The idea was that the burning would send the gifts across the barrier for the dead to use, in the same way that the funerary offerings were for the dead to eat.

Every culture has its own beliefs regarding the afterlife and what awaits them on the Otherside. While I personally find Christians have the most vague, depressing and dark versions—purgatory and hell—the Chinese and Japanese have an outright delightful version. Not unlike the ancient Egyptians, the Chinese envision an afterlife that isn't too far off from our own world—a ghost world, where money, food and material possessions are necessary. These items are left out or burned in special shrines that families believe their dearly departed frequently visit.

Most ghosts don't have their own personal set mirror to cross the barrier with, but if they do make it across, they are certainly able to eat and drink the things from life they most craved. I'd seen Nate and other ghosts that frequented Lee's bar, Damaged Goods, put back enough pints of beer to prove that.

But burning joss paper was an interesting possibility. At least theoretically, it might send items, or the manifestations of them, across the barrier for the intended ghosts to use—or believe they could use. Not that ghosts like to talk about what goes on behind the barrier, leaving the living to their own suppositions and meditation on what matters when you're dead. I supposed that was probably for the best.

"But we sent you the Louis Vuitton bag last week! The new one from the limited edition collection. The Joss Edition, specially made for you! Do you have any idea what it cost to have the joss paper bag done by hand on rush?" Mrs. Young cried.

Sparks of Otherside flickered around Astrid, drawn by her anger like mosquitoes to bare skin. I was having trouble now siphoning off all the anger-fuelled Otherside.

"Astrid!" I clenched my teeth as Astrid bucked against the bindings and ran to the edge of the pentagram, in defiance of every one of my guidelines.

"You sent me the red one!" Astrid screamed, pointing a waxy finger at her mother. "I specifically asked for the blue. You did that on purpose to humiliate me!"

Shit. I grabbed hold of Astrid's bindings, ready to really reel her in if push came to shove.

"Astrid, he wouldn't make the bag in blue! It only comes in red! He had the leather specially produced for a very exclusive run."

"It goes with nothing I own!" Astrid shrieked.

Woah boy. I dug my feet into the frosty grass and mud as Astrid lunged towards her mother.

I mean, I'd raised Astrid as a four-line zombie, so technically I was the one in control . . . of her physical body. I couldn't control her mind. I *could* compel her to behave—I'd had to do it before, but . . . well, there were ethical issues I had with that. I was fine with stopping a zombie from moving. The body at this point was a loaner—from me. I was calling the shots and I was also responsible for any zombie I raised. Now, compelling them to *do* or *tell me* things? That was eerily close to what soothsayers did, and that was an ethical grey area I tried to avoid. Screwing around with ghosts' souls traumatizes them. The only thing they have left is their free will. Taking that away from them . . .

"Astrid," Mrs. Young said. "That simply isn't true. It goes perfectly with the wardrobe I just sent you."

"You mean those cheap, knock-off joss papers?" Astrid scoffed. "Don't think I didn't notice, Mother. I was humiliated when my servants brought over those hand-me-downs!"

"Aiya!" Mrs. Young shouted back, now irate. "That wardrobe was entirely couture! Do you know how hard it was to convince the designers to hand-draw all those dresses? And don't get me started on the food you've been requesting! Oysters and caviar—the caviar is out of season, and you know it!"

"You were also supposed to send me a new Ferrari!"

"Absolutely out of the question!" her father said, now drawn into the fray. "You and your fast cars have brought this family enough disgrace. No more sports cars! I forbid it!"

Astrid vibrated through the lines I was holding as she bunched up her fists.

"Could everyone take a good ten steps back from the pentagram? Please?" I managed.

"You're just upset you can't control me anymore—"

"Control you?" Mr. Young shouted back. "Is that what you call this? We should have controlled you much more! Or do you not even remember how you died—the shame, the dishonour?"

Whatever composure Astrid had dissolved. She bucked against my zombie conditions, wrenching the reins of Otherside. I just about fell flat on my face as she lunged for her father. She made it to the edge of the chrysanthemum pentagram, her face contorted in rage. "How could you say such things to your poor dead daughter!"

Another snort from Mrs. Young as she crossed her arms. "Poor dead daughter? What about your poor mother? You'll never give me grandchildren—"

"Ah! And now we see why you're really here, Mother! This is all about you! Make Alex have grandchildren if you want them so badly."

"Alex will never give me grandchildren the way he cavorts around London with that horrible Tang girl!" Mrs. Young said.

Oh boy, here we go again . . . Whoops! I was almost dragged off my feet as Astrid swiped for her mother—but the barrier stopped her hand mid-slap.

Astrid looked at her fingers, momentarily shocked. Then she turned her reddening eyes on me. The Otherside that had been fuelling my pentagram started a slow creep towards her, drawn in by her uncontrolled anger. Just how it would behave for a poltergeist. Strange, firefly flickers of Otherside began to collect around her.

Okay, that was it. As they say in the famous Alice Cooper zombie song, no more Mister Nice Practitioner.

Time to pull out the big guns . . .

"How dare—" Astrid started.

"Oh, for the love of god, will you put a sock in it?" I shouted back, and reached for one of the thin Otherside lines that ran down her throat and controlled her vocal cords. Deftly, I tied it in a knot. Compelling the dead to shut up wasn't in my repertoire, but tying their mouths shut so I could get a word in edgewise? Totally okay with that.

Astrid opened her mouth, but not a peep came out. She reached for her throat with a mixture of shock and surprise.

"Now," I said, "about that conversation."

Astrid's lip curled into a snarl and she took two steps towards me. I was ready for that too. While she reached for my neck, I tied off the lines to her muscles.

She froze in place, staring down at her feet.

I sighed a cold breath. Now that was done.

Holding the Otherside reins tight, I walked right up to Astrid until my own face was inches from hers, close enough I could smell the formaldehyde preservative that mingled with a perfume of jasmine and roses. "What the *hell* is your problem?" I asked.

Astrid's eyes widened and her mouth opened in shock. Her lips snapped open and shut, but though she tried valiantly to speak, all she managed was to look like an angry goldfish gulping for air.

I realized I was probably the first person in her life or afterlife who had ever challenged her.

I crossed my arms until Astrid stopped gulping and turned her full attention on me.

A little more brute force than I liked to get to this point, but since we were here . . .

I straightened and tweaked my new blazer. "Astrid, allow me to introduce myself. I'm Kincaid Strange. Have you heard of me?"

Astrid's eyes widened and she nodded. I was happy to see that her eyes had shifted from poltergeist red back to a more natural, watery brown, the bright gold flickers of Otherside gone.

"Good. Here's the deal. In a moment I will loosen the bindings on your mouth so you can speak. I don't want to hear any shouting, whining, screaming. If anything comes out of your mouth besides answers to my questions, I'll tie your tongue in a knot. Literally. Got it?"

After she once again gulped and realized it was no use, she nodded.

As promised, I loosened my hold on her—not completely, though. I really didn't trust her not to throw any more food at me.

Astrid promptly collapsed in a heap on the cold, frost-covered grass and broke into sobs.

I whistled as I took stock of the thousands and thousands of dollars of damage Astrid had caused in a half-hour. Out of the four tables, only one was conspicuously untouched by Astrid's tantrum. On it was a small copper brazier lit with a small gas flame, and beside it sat the most elaborate collection of joss papers I'd ever seen. There was the money—copper, gold and silver—but also the papier mâché versions of designer clothes, handbags, a miniature dog, a larger, doll-sized paper version of a beachside villa complete with a paper doll cast of servants and a driver, sitting in a papier mâché Rolls Royce. I noted that the high-powered sports cars Astrid had been so fond of were conspicuously absent.

Probably for the best . . .

All right, Kincaid, time to get to the bottom of the Youngs' haunting problem and prevent Astrid from becoming the unholy poltergeist terror that her stomping, designer-clad, undead foot is promising . . .

Astrid sniffled and sat up. She picked up one of the discarded puff pastries, gingerly dusting it off before popping it in her mouth, all the while watching me warily.

"Okay, Astrid, I think we need to get a couple ground rules going," I said, still holding the reins of her zombie bindings as I took a seat across from her on the frosted grass. Not able to resist any longer, I picked up a pork bun, still steaming. I brushed it off and took a generous bite. The pork filling was everything the smells wafting my way had promised.

"First," I said, stopping before a second bite, "and without any yelling, I need you to explain to me why exactly you decided to trash your parents' dinner party last Monday."

She frowned and gave me a queer look. "Those are for the dead," she said, pointing at my half-eaten bun. "The living aren't supposed to eat them."

I shook my head. "My zombie policy is you launch your food, then it's mine." If Astrid had just shown some restraint before dumping all the tea, we'd be having an outright civilized conversation. "Now," I said, steering things back on track, "am I right in assuming all this haunting over the past two weeks—the screaming, the shouting, the ruined dinner parties—is all because your mother sent you the wrong joss paper bag?"

Astrid glared but didn't comment.

The security footage the Youngs had shown me was spectacular, to say the least. Not many new ghosts could flip an entire table, let alone one for twelve while it was loaded with food and surrounded by dinner guests. Everyone had run for their lives, including the visiting Singapore ambassador, who had twisted his knee tripping over one of the rugs in the mayhem.

Astrid might not have died as true poltergeist material, but if her habits didn't change fast . . .

I'd seen enough weird Otherside feats these past two months to know how bad things could get.

Somewhat subdued, Astrid stared at the ground and mumbled something under her breath.

I held my hand to my ear. "What was that?"

She lifted her head. "I said, it wasn't just over a bag." I caught Astrid shooting furtive glances at her parents.

Hmmm. Initially I thought all the anger was over losing her life so young—lost opportunities, a life barely lived . . .

"Mr. and Mrs. Young? Would you mind?" I said, and nodded sheepishly towards the pathway where the mourners were congregating.

I waited until they were out of earshot before turning back to Astrid.

"Why are you haunting your parents? Go," I said, selecting a puff pastry this time.

Astrid scoffed. "I can't believe this—I make a handful of requests for clothes, shelter and food to get me through my existence—"

"Ah!" I held up my finger. She stopped talking without me having to pull the Otherside reins, so to speak. "Nice try." I hadn't bothered to bring the file for this one. I didn't need it. "But the stunt you pulled at your father's business party wasn't a request for food and designer clothing—and they already gave you four houses for the Otherside, including the beach house which is sitting there waiting to burn. And don't get me started on the funerary food! You're hands down the best-fed ghost from here to Beijing. That party fiasco was a full-on haunting. What I want to know is, *why*?"

Her lips trembled as if she might burst into tears again. "Their poor daughter is left to wander the Otherside and they're upset about a little dinner party—"

"You caused a stampede. You're lucky the Singapore ambassador wasn't trampled. And let's not mention the pot of tea you dumped. You could have really hurt someone, including your parents. You know, the ones who feed you and burn you all your joss?"

Astrid glared but remained silent.

Now that was interesting . . .

I glanced over my shoulder to where Astrid's parents were standing watching me try to reason with their dead, spoilt-rotten daughter.

I turned back to her and sighed, grabbing another of her pork buns from the ground.

"All right, look, your folks are out of earshot and the only person you're performing for is *me*." I pointed at my chest, driving home the point. "I have no stake in any of this, so there really isn't any point in lying."

Astrid snorted. "Why, because you're my friend?"

"No," I said, shrugging. "Because I really couldn't give a flying—"

"It's not fair!" she shouted. Then, remembering her promise not to shout, she covered her mouth. The dead might get away with a lot, but they have a hell of a time breaking their own word.

I let the slip slide. "Astrid, I meet a lot of ghosts and zombies in my line of work whose deaths were really, absolutely, truly unfair." I lowered my head and levelled a serious stare at her. "You're *not* one of them."

Her fist clenched around a pork bun.

"Ah." I held up my hand before she could let the anger take hold again. "Astrid, let's try this. How about you explain to me just what exactly was unfair about your death. Because between drag racing your new Ferrari down the wrong side of a freeway—"

"Lots of my friends race and don't die!"

"Yes, but they also don't usually get their boyfriends to go down on them while they're doing it. And while I admire the feminist implication—seriously, can you honestly say you're surprised you ended up dead? Your boyfriend—or whatever he was—survived, by the way, if you care. It's a miracle the only person who died was you."

Astrid sat stock-still.

"Look, Astrid, you didn't deserve to die. No one deserves to die before their twenty-first birthday, so in a sense you're right—it's not fair. But somewhere in there you must realize that you're responsible. No one *made* you get behind the wheel of that car and race. You could have stayed home watching movies or spent your parents' money visiting every club in Seattle or taking their private jet to Bora-Bora. *Your* actions led to your death. And as much as it pains me to say this to anyone, in the grand scheme of things, that makes it fair." I pointed at her parents. "Everyone this side of the barrier has to live with the consequences of *your* actions. And part of that is determining what it's going to take to stop you from haunting your parents. They're not responsible for this."

Okay, little fib there, which I don't like doing to the dead. I was willing to put fifty-fifty blame on her parents for the fact that this was apparently the first time Astrid had ever heard the word no . . . but this wasn't supposed to be a therapy session.

I got to the point. "What do we need to do to get the haunting to go away?"

Astrid's eyes welled up. "I'm lonely!"

Now . . . out of all the things Astrid could have said, that one hadn't even been on my radar.

As I watched, Astrid covered her face with her hands and started to sob.

I checked to see if her parents had noticed the change in Astrid's composure, but they avoided my eyes.

I sighed and shuffled so I was sitting down beside, not across from, her. Maybe therapy would be the order of the day.

"Look—" I started.

"I'm always lonely—I've always been lonely! You have *no* idea how it was—is," Astrid said, lifting her face from her hands. The carefully applied makeup was now streaked with her tears. Her deathly pallor was more obvious. But the poltergeist anger was gone as well, evaporated into the cold night air.

"My entire life has been nothing but loneliness. All people like you see is the money. 'Poor little rich girl,'" she pantomimed, "'has so much money all she can do is go out on shopping sprees and crash cars.' The money isn't a reward—it's a curse!" A fresh round of tears trickled down her face. "All my life, money has been a replacement, a placeholder my parents used to raise me. Our daughter needs attention? Well, hire a nanny! She wants friends now to play with? Off to boarding school! Astrid's depressed and failed all her courses? Well, send her to Paris on the family jet for fashion week, that should cheer her up!" Her face twisted with despair. "Everything and everyone in my life bought and paid for! I have no friends—I barely have parents. All I've been is an inconvenience." She reached over and plucked an egg tart from the ground and held it up for me to see. "Why, my parents have spent more time on me since I've been haunting them than they did in twenty-one years." A flicker, just a flicker of red-tinged Otherside burned behind her eyes. "And now they've gone and hired *you* to make this little problem go and disappear? Not this time. I'm not going anywhere!" She clenched her fists, the knuckles turning a shade whiter.

I sighed again and shook my head. What the hell did someone say to that? I mean, I was the last person on the planet to be offering family counselling. My own family issues were as numerous as Astrid's speeding tickets. I had issues with victim blaming, courtesy of watching my mother never stand up for herself in front of my father, including the day he pushed her down a flight of stairs and killed her. I had *issues*. Life wasn't fair—Astrid was just another twenty-something who had deluded herself into thinking that the universe owed her something. She'd been given more than a fair shot. And instead of getting help, she'd gone and blown everything.

And there I went with the victim blaming again. Goddamnit . . .

I took a deep breath. I had been hired to help Astrid. I was getting paid to help Astrid, like so many of the people her parents had hired before me.

Why not actually try to help for a change? Instead of trying to just make the problem go away—or sweep it under a very, very expensive rug.

"Look, you're right. That sucks."

She stopped her crying and looked up at me, wary.

"And you're right—I'm being paid a lot of money to convince you to stop haunting them."

I watched as the flash of anger dissipated behind her eyes, and it might have been my imagination, but I thought the gold glitter of anger-fuelled Otherside dissipated as well.

"So if, at the end of this conversation, you decide you want to continue haunting your parents for the remainder of your afterlife, go right ahead."

A flicker of irritation. She'd been here before, I'd wager, with plenty of counsellors over her troubled years. "*But?*" she said.

I nodded. "*But*, you're going to sit there for the next five minutes and listen to me explain what the consequences of the decision you make today will be. All the consequences. And then you can decide whatever the hell you like. Deal?"

She hesitated, but only for a moment, before nodding.

I tried not to shiver against a gust of wind that smelled of overturned soil and dead plants. For the second time that evening, I wished that Astrid had left the tea alone. At least the mourners had switched from distracting wails to a low chant, perhaps having deduced their distraction would impede rather than help.

"Ghosts don't have a lot of sway this side of the barrier," I started. "You can throw a few things around, scare a few people, even make things turn cold. But that's about it. It's scary for a couple months and then people either get used to it or—I don't know, move out?" I shrugged. "There are a couple of unpleasant things we can do to the ghost. Exorcisms and ghost bindings—but people usually don't bother. Eventually the ghost runs out of steam and fades away. But angry ghosts? Now, those are different beasts entirely."

Astrid was watching me carefully now.

I continued. "A ghost who is angry has power—the Otherside likes anger, as you've clearly discovered. Personally? I think Otherside feeds off anger, or maybe it's the other way around and anger feeds off Otherside?" I shook my head. "Either way, an angry ghost is a dangerous ghost."

"I want to be powerful," Astrid said, her voice barely a whisper. "I want to make them listen—and see me. I want to be an angry ghost."

I nodded. "And that's where we have a problem, Astrid, because a ghost who feeds off anger is a poltergeist." I gave her my full stare and threw more than a little Otherside behind it. "And while I don't exorcise ghosts like you, I have no problem doing it to a poltergeist."

More tears ran down her face. "Why can't you just leave me alone? I don't mean anyone harm—I promise I won't hurt anyone. I only want to make them listen. I'm so lonely, and they were getting on with their lives until I started ruining their dinner parties. This time, they can't send me away."

I shook my head. "I can't let you be, Astrid, because poltergeists, no matter how the anger starts out—regret, fear, a natural tendency towards cruel intent, or lashing out at the injustice of it all, like you are—they all end up the same: as evil, mean-spirited ghosts who only exist to cause pain and mischief. Who don't think twice about killing people."

More tears fell as the pleading look on her face turned to defeat. For the first time since meeting her, I felt sorry for her.

I shook my head. "Maybe for a year—maybe for a month or two, sure, you'd keep to your word not to hurt anyone. It's not a bad theory—ghosts don't change, they can't change. But the anger? It *consumes* ghosts, Astrid. It consumes your soul like a fire eats up kindling, until all that's left is a poltergeist's blackened, burned-out core. The other parts of you? The parts that aren't always angry, that don't scream for revenge? That only want your parents to spend time with you?" I made a disappearing gesture with my hands. "Poof, gone. All that's left is that anger. And if you thought having your parents trying to manage you was bad, imagine having that anger consuming you, controlling you, for as long as your soul lives—and for a poltergeist, it can be a long, long time."

Astrid wetted her lips. "Everything has a price."

"Trust me, Astrid, this is one that's not worth paying." I stood up and let Astrid get a full look at just how much Otherside I was batting. "You think it's lonely now? Wait until the only thing you have for company is the anger. It's your choice, Astrid." She cowered as I let a flare of Otherside brush up against her bindings. "I'm not going to stop you haunting your parents—not yet—but the day you become a full-fledged poltergeist?"

Astrid wrapped her arms around her legs and let out another sob. She was possibly the most unhappy ghost I'd ever encountered.

I sighed and crouched down in front of her. Ghosts don't change, that's true, but they retain their decision-making ability. It's within their power to try to make up for the mistakes they made while they were living. They just aren't particularly inclined to do it.

"Astrid?" I said. "You're right. Life wasn't fair. Your parents made you very unhappy—I can relate to that. Really, you have no idea how. But the bad decisions that ended your life were yours and yours alone. You can't go back and change things, but this time, for once, you can avoid a bad decision that will ruin what afterlife you have left. You don't get a lot of choices on the Otherside. Don't throw this one away."

She lifted her head. "I didn't want to die," she said, her lip quivering as she stared at the brazier and the collection of joss paper fit for a royal princess.

It might have been the most honest thing she'd said all night. I took a quick peek at her bindings. The flares and firefly sparks of poltergeist-like Otherside were gone now. I hoped for good, but only time would tell.

Damn you and your soft heart, Kincaid Strange. I sighed and broached a topic I was loath to discuss on US soil. "Normally I wouldn't say this, but, considering your parents, there are options. Singapore, Thailand and China all allow . . ." I gestured at her current form, not wanting to say "five-line zombie" out loud. "The permits are expensive, but I'm sure your parents—"

Astrid stopped me with an emphatic shake of her head, her black hair cascading around her pale face. "No—no, I'm happy where I am," she said decisively.

Well, that was interesting. Not for the first time, I wondered what really went on in the land of the dead.

She wiped her face and did her best to recompose her corpse. "Tell Mommy and Daddy I'll stop haunting them," she said in a quiet voice. "They don't have to cancel their party this weekend. I'll stay away."

I nodded, though it struck me that this could just be the pattern of Astrid's life, of fighting then backing down, then rebounding and fighting all over again.

I really didn't want to be back in three months having to exorcise an unrecognizable Astrid poltergeist from her parents' home . . .

"What if I suggest to your parents that what you really are is lonely, that what you want is for them to spend time with you, once a week or so? Actually sit down and talk to you. You can tell them how things are going on the Otherside."

She nodded absently again, still defeated, but I hoped the wheels were turning.

Astrid, for all her loneliness, had an awful lot of joss to spend on the Otherside courtesy of her parents. If she applied herself, she could make friends—well, eventually. Invite them to her beach house and let them try on her clothes. In the meantime, she could even patch things up with her parents.

Feeling hopeful, I headed for the barrier of incense and chrysanthemums to see what I could work out with the Youngs.

"Wait!" Astrid cried out.

I turned to find her still huddled on the ground, her arms wrapped around her legs, but now she was rocking herself.

"I've changed my mind," she said. "Don't tell them about the loneliness."

"Astrid—" I started.

But Astrid only continued to shake her head and stared at the joss paper offerings still ready to burn on the table. "Mommy won't know what to do with it. Tell her I made all the fuss over the new Louis Vuitton bag. I want it in blue. I know it's not made in blue, but I want her to get them to make it for me anyway."

"Astrid," I tried again, and my hope sank. "That's not going to hel—"

She looked away from the joss paper and back up at me, with a flash of anger. "You don't know *anything* about me or my family. You've been paid to do as you're told, so do it." The anger dissipated as she turned her attention back to the joss paper. "The Louis Vuitton bag in blue and I'll stop haunting them."

She was making a mistake. I knew it, she probably knew it. But she was right—at the end of the day, I was the hired help. Brought in to stop her haunting, not to fix her family. Without another word, I left Astrid in a heap. Why oh why was it that the dead were so damn set in their ways?

I crossed my pentagram and Mr. and Mrs. Young met me halfway.

"Did you speak to my daughter? What has she said?" Mrs. Young asked me in a rush.

For a moment I thought, really thought, about telling them the truth.

"Will she stop haunting us?" her father asked desperately.

"Ah, yeah, she's . . ." I trailed off as the two of them watched me with their earnest expressions. Not *what's wrong?* or *how is she?* or *why?* but had I made the problem go away?

Astrid was right. I had no sense of the tangled lines that worked between their family, in life or death. Unlike the Otherside lines that often make the dead an open book, in the real world the lines that run between people can be very hard to discern.

"Yeah, Astrid has agreed to stop haunting you. She has made one request," I said, and told them about the designer bag.

The Youngs and mourners departed, and I headed back to where Astrid had recomposed herself and was standing, waiting for me.

She lifted her chin as I approached. "What did you tell them?" she asked.

I shook my head. "That you wanted the blue Louis Vuitton bag. You're right, Astrid, I have no idea what you and your family have going on."

She nodded and cleared her throat. "I'm ready to go back now," she said.

I tapped the Otherside I'd been holding in my head when I'd first raised her this evening and reached for the loose ends of her tethered bindings. "Remember what I said about poltergeists, Astrid, and about not wasting your chance." I grabbed the tethers and readied myself to unravel her.

But before I could pull them, a slow, sad smile played on Astrid's lips. "Ah, but do ghosts ever really change, Kincaid Strange? We all have our fates."

A four-line zombie going on about fate and the meaning of death was as sure a sign as anything that Astrid was ready to go back in the ground . . .

"Just hold still, Astrid, this will be over fast."

"You know, they talk about you on the Otherside. Quite a bit. Would you like to know what they say?"

I won't lie. I stalled, only for the briefest moment, at the idea that Astrid might be telling the truth, that she really did know something, even if just a snippet. What did the Seattle dead say about me to each other? Did they hate me, or was I just a footnote in their conversations? It was a question I sometimes lay in bed at night wondering about, and now Astrid was offering an answer.

But I knew why she was offering. What the dead really want out of the living is to hold their attention. And that wasn't a rabbit hole I was stupid enough—or desperate enough—to travel down.

"Goodbye, Astrid," I said. "And remember your promise about the haunting or you'll be seeing me again real soon." And with that, before she could slip another word in edgewise, I pulled the threads.

Astrid held my eyes until the very last moment, when her ghost separated from her body. It may have been my imagination, but for a moment, as her ghost hung suspended over her corpse in the November chill, I could have sworn she winked at me. And then she was gone and her body collapsed to the ground, lifeless again, like a well-dressed rag doll.

I shook my head and turned away, waving to the attendants the Youngs had kept on hand to return Astrid to the family crypt. Goddamnit, I was letting her get to me, feeling more pity than Astrid deserved.

Maybe the Youngs did have it right. Maybe it was less about cajoling her and more about getting her to let the living be.

Speak of the devils . . .

"You did it," Mrs. Young cried, grasping my hands in gratitude. "That's the best she's behaved in months!"

I forced myself to give them a terse smile and handed over a mirror from my new leather satchel. I'd purchased the satchel for carrying documents and permits, something that fit on my bike but was most definitely not a backpack.

"You can talk to her through here. The instructions are taped to the back along with a china marker." It was simple and fairly secure. They could write Astrid messages and talk to her face to face, but Astrid couldn't cross over. "Don't encourage her to cross the barrier, and this is the last designer bag. I mean it, you need to stop giving in to her demands. I'm not suggesting it won't be hard, but it'll be better for all of you in the long run."

They both nodded emphatically and thanked me a handful more times. Mr. Young even pressed an envelope into my hand—unnecessary as they'd already paid me, wiring money to a bank account I'd recently opened on Nate and Aaron's advice. I told them to call me if any more problems arose with Astrid, and sincerely hoped they wouldn't. The Youngs had been nice to me, hadn't argued over my tactics or money—a level of co-operation I often didn't get from clients. Whatever I thought of their misguided parenting, I really did hope I could save them the pain and heartache of being haunted for eternity by their own poltergeist daughter.

Still, I couldn't help but sigh as I headed for my bike, leaving the Youngs as they were thanking the mourners who had been waiting patiently—and, most importantly, *quietly*—at the edge of my frost-wilted chrysanthemum pentagram for their turn to be paid. The rest of the Youngs' staff dutifully finished burning the joss paper offerings for Astrid and deftly cleaned up the mess. Despite their gratitude, the evening had ended on a depressing note. Could families really change? Even the living ones? From my own experience, I was dubious.

The quiet of the cemetery unnerved me after Astrid's shouts and the wailing of the mourners had filled it for the better part of the last hour.

I shivered as I reached my Honda Hawk and threw my leather motorcycle jacket over my blazer.

Yes, I'd worn a blazer.

I wasn't dead. *I* was still living. *I* could still learn from my mistakes. Appearances matter because people make snap judgments. I had a hefty and generous retainer from the Youngs in my bank account to prove it. They'd only ever met the new "professional" me.

I'd paired the expensive blazer with dark jeans and tasteful flats—which, leaning against my red 1990 Honda Hawk GT 650, still in desperate need of a paint job, I slid off, and replaced with my motorbike boots.

As I drove out of the cemetery, I couldn't quite shake the feeling that it wasn't the last I'd be seeing of Astrid.

The afterlife is often a repetitive, vicious circle for the dead of making the same mistakes they'd made in their lives, over and over again. Astrid had spent a lifetime—albeit a brief one—employing a litany of manipulative tricks to get her way. There was no reason to think she'd stop now.

Well, maybe that was for the best. I could keep tabs on her. The last thing the world needed was another violent ghost floating around.

There were enough around already.

As I rode along, I felt my phone buzz in my pocket. I was close to a twenty-four-hour coffee shop I liked, so I pulled over. People didn't call at this hour unless it was an emergency, and my hands were freezing. They could do with a cup of coffee.

It was a text from Nate. I opened it. The dead didn't contact me at this time unless it was an emergency either . . .

Well, okay, Nate contacted me for a laundry list of unnecessary things, but he usually did that through a mirror and left the phone for the emergencies.

It was short and to the point:

Asshole is here. He is pissed. He says to tell you he's waiting.

Fantastic. Of course, the one ghost to whom I was contractually obligated to give my undivided attention was at this very moment sitting in my kitchen.

I slid the phone back inside my jacket pocket and, with great regret, abandoned the coffee shop line right as I reached the register. I mouthed, "Sorry," to the guy behind the counter, though he really didn't appear to care.

I gunned my bike down First towards my warehouse flat. Where none other than Gideon was waiting for me.

Yup. Ghosts don't change. And Gideon, for all his ghostly powers, was exactly what he had been the day he'd been burned at the stake.

A pissed-off, half-evil, *highly* demanding sorcerer.

Like all the dead, what he wanted was my time. But unlike most ghosts, Gideon rarely respected my boundaries.

CHAPTER 2

THE UNGRATEFUL DEAD

I manoeuvred my bike into the lobby turned art gallery and immediately spotted Nathan, hovering behind a garish pastel-pink-skinned, yellow-haired My Little Pony centaur sculpture, which, for some unfathomable reason, the artist had decided would not be complete without a horse's erect, equally pastel-pink, penis. Well, at least Nate wasn't hiding behind the other sculpture in my lobby, the trio of Care Bears huddled around a trash can fire smoking what looked suspiciously like crack . . .

Nate looked exactly as he had the day he died: brown shag haircut, red Converse runners, ripped blue jeans, a yellow *Don't Worry, Be Happy* T-shirt, and a red buffalo plaid flannel shirt he'd never actually worn tied around his waist. The only difference was that his perpetually twenty-something face was creased with worry. Something I did not often see.

"K, Gideon is upstairs," he whispered, floating over to my bike, shooting furtive looks around the lobby as if worried the very act of speaking Gideon's name might conjure the ghost.

It wasn't an unreasonable concern. "Did he say what he wanted?" I asked as Nate followed me into the elevator.

"I don't know, K. After he stared daggers at me and asked, 'Where's Kincaid?' I sent you a message and hightailed it the fuck out of there!"

His sarcasm didn't escape me as I shut the freight elevator door.

I sighed as we headed up to the third-floor apartment. I lived in a converted warehouse by the Seattle docks. It was old, originally used for sugar- and rum-running in the 1800s; the boats had sailed right in where the cargo could be unloaded away from prying eyes. It wasn't until 1950 that they filled in the slough with concrete and converted the warehouse into studio apartments. The one feature they'd left intact was the freight elevator, which I was partial to because it let me take my bike upstairs. No, I don't trust my neighbours.

The proximity to the water kept property values low, with a high chance of hauntings. Instead of buyers, the building attracted a revolving and seemingly endless roster of artists and musicians. The kinds of artists who think homeless, crack-smoking Care Bears and well-endowed manifestations of children's toys are profound, not the indulgent spectacle they are. This explained the makeshift gallery. The artists needed somewhere to stash their rejected work once they'd finished making the art gallery rounds.

"By the way, how'd the seance go?" Nate asked as the elevator gears ground and pulled the car upwards.

I shook my head at him. "A story for another day." He looked at me strangely and I added, "It went fine—they were happy and paid."

Nate kept his eyes and attention fixed on the elevator door. "Good work, by the way, for not dressing like an off-duty stripper."

"*Nate*," I warned as the elevator clanged to a stop at the third floor. I lifted the gate and pushed my bike out.

Nate shot a wary look down the hall but didn't leave the freight car.

"Come on, Nate. Time to gird your paranormal loins."

"Ah, yeah. About that, delivering the warning is as far as I dare to tread towards the evil sorcerer."

I rolled my eyes. Nate wasn't really terrified of Gideon, but he was wary, and rightfully so. After Nate had accidentally stolen a body that Gideon had coveted, well, despite Nate being innocent, Gideon wasn't exactly forgiving.

"Fine. Go. Play fly on the wall," I said, and with that, Nate vanished.

I pushed my bike down the concrete floor towards my place near the end of the hall. Our landlord had finally torn out the ripped and stained hallway carpet and I wondered if he was planning on leaving the concrete or putting in some form of flooring.

I was willing to bet on the bare concrete.

I put the kickstand down to free up both hands to deal with the lock. There's something comforting about having to wrestle with the lock every time I get home, even when it sticks to the point where I start to swear. Aaron had threatened to fix it more than once. I'd never let him. I figure having a door lock that hard to open means it must be hard to pick. There's security in a door that's hard to open on a good day—*with* the key.

Besides, Aaron gave up the right to fix my door months ago.

I'd made it through my cursing script of "Goddamn stupid" to "Open the hell up" when the lock clicked, apparently of its own volition, and my front door flew open. Violently. I winced at the crunch of the door handle smacking the drywall inside.

I glared at the ghost that appeared in the doorway, blocking my way.

Gideon looked as if he had died in his late twenties, perhaps early thirties, though I'd been unable to confirm it. For all I knew, living sorcerers might have a spell for eternal youth. Gideon might have been over a hundred when they'd burned him at the stake in medieval Denmark. Regardless of his actual age when he died, Gideon's sorcery had allowed him to survive for a thousand years as a ghost—something that should be impossible. Most ghosts last 150 years at the most, and zombies don't fare much better, the oldest only reaching 300 or so.

Gideon was an anomaly, and in more ways than the incredible power he wielded and his uncanny ghostly longevity. Whereas other ghosts only ever appear in the clothing of their time, conjuring items that are familiar, things they wore every day, Gideon bucked that trend spectacularly. Tonight, for example, he appeared in jeans and a modern leather jacket and runners.

His pale skin was made paler by death, and his hair—a close-cropped blond in life, I imagined—was dusted with a telltale ghost grey.

Only his eyes veered from the ghost-grey colouring. Ghost-grey blue on a good day, they turned an ominous, glittering black when the sorcerer's ghost was irritated, angry, impatient or just felt he'd been slighted.

. . . Exactly the glittering black shade they were right now.

I manoeuvred my bike through the door and Gideon. He moved, though reluctantly. Shaking my head, I took my sweet time putting my Hawk in its resting place and setting the kickstand. I imagined Nate had slunk back into my apartment, somewhere out of sight.

I nodded towards the new door handle–shaped dent in the entranceway wall. "Seriously, was that called for?" I said, not bothering to hide my own irritation as I peeled off my leathers. "It left a mark."

I must have caught Gideon off guard, because for a moment his eyes shifted back to ghost-grey blue and he frowned at the dented drywall with mild curiosity, as if he was surprised that the door flying open might have caused the damage. And then the glittering black eyes were back and fixated on me.

"You were taking too long. And why on earth don't you get the door lock fixed?"

I sighed. Yet another man telling me what I should and shouldn't do with my front door . . . Goddamnit . . . I gestured for him to move out of my way. He acquiesced.

I walked right past him, dropping my new satchel on the couch and hanging my blazer on the coat rack before heading into the kitchen. After a late night November ride, I was in desperate need of a warm-up.

"I needed you half an hour ago," Gideon continued, following me.

"And I was working." I methodically filled my kettle and selected a smoky black chai—a small, recent splurge I'd allowed myself from my recent paycheques.

"Where are the mirror bindings I asked you to complete?"

"Is that what this is about?" I shook my head and took my time measuring the spiced black tea into my new iron pot.

"You were supposed to have those for me today," Gideon said. "I've been looking for an hour. Where are they?"

I took a deep breath and closed my eyes.

I'd discovered over my lessons and work with Gideon these past few weeks that he was not a ghost of patience. As in none at all. For the first few lessons I'd cowered at his outbursts, but I'd discovered that a better tactic was to call him on it. Otherwise he'd walk all over me, so to speak.

It was as if Gideon didn't *realize* he was being an asshole.

He wasn't upset that I wasn't here when he showed up; he was upset that he couldn't find the three mirrors he'd had me working on. I cringed reflexively, the way I did any time I thought about Gideon's most recent homework assignment. The three mirrors were complicated pieces, a mix of bindings and symbols cherry-picked from different schools of practitioning and then layered over one another. I still wasn't certain what their purpose was, but a number of the symbols gave me a big fat hint. They were commands—compulsions, to be more specific. The kinds that ghost binders and soothsayers use as the bread and butter of their trade. I'd also discovered the mirrors leaked Otherside, a trail of which had drawn Nate in with a reluctant fascination that reminded me of the Tetris-style jewel games I see people obsessing over on their phones, usually while ignoring their companion sitting across the table.

"Your impatience is pathological," I said, bracing myself and tightening my grip on the teapot's iron handle as I swirled the tea egg in the boiling water. I couldn't help it. Every time I thought about who Gideon might be making the mirrors for and what they planned to do with them . . .

"*Where* are they?" he said, and the temperature in the kitchen dropped a few degrees. I shuddered as a teacup shot across the counter and shattered on the linoleum floor.

. . . I counted to three as I stood there, motionless, and waited for my tea to steep, doing my absolute damnedest to ignore the broken cup, though I would have liked nothing better than to throttle Gideon.

A revelation I'd had since working with Gideon was that, though he was prone to physical outbursts that mimicked those of poltergeists, they were never aimed at me—not since the unfortunate strangling incident with my hair dryer cord that had been a serious . . . misunderstanding, and a case of mistaken identity.

Oh, the ghost's outbursts were violent in nature and designed to get my attention, but not aimed at *me*. Rather, they were aimed at the world of the living.

"Kincaid?" Gideon asked. I concentrated on my brewing tea.

I think Gideon had been dead so long he no longer understood the true effect of these small acts of kitchenware violence. The disruptions, the noise, the destruction. The violence was all just a part of his repertoire now. One of the only ways he *could* interact with the living and count on predictable results.

"*Kincaid?*" Gideon said, his eyebrows narrowing, a slight warning to his voice now.

I understood his actions, even sympathized with them—but it didn't make them okay. I *abhorred* Gideon's outbursts. They disgusted me on a visceral level. But yelling and shouting back only fed the fire. I'd had the revelation two weeks ago when Gideon and I had got into another screaming match. He'd said some things, I'd said some things . . .

Over a disagreement on the best way to set a mirror.

It was a circle, a pattern of repetition that ghosts are destined to repeat. A pattern of anger my own parents had fallen into and repeated, over and over, a sickness that settled in and escalated.

A pattern Gideon had been entrenched in for almost a thousand years with who knew *how* many practitioners.

Not that that excused the son-of-a-bitch ghost, not one bit.

Tea finally steeped—or steeped enough, considering the ghost behind me—I started to fill my mug from the teapot, slowly, keenly aware of how close behind me Gideon was hovering by the Otherside chill running down my back.

Yeah, this was going to be a hard habit to break.

"Most of my apprentices over the centuries have shown me some form of deference. . . ."

One, two, three. I counted all the way to ten and refused to look at the shattered cup on the floor.

If I had to work with Gideon for the next two years, *minimum*, then for my own sanity I needed to stop his tantrums. He was going to learn that throwing and breaking things wasn't the way to make me work faster—that they had quite the opposite effect, in fact. I'd grown up with enough violence to last a lifetime, thank you very much.

" . . . or made some attempt at camaraderie," he added. "I'd even say some went so far as the effort of exchanging civil greetings and conversation—"

Nine, ten . . .

"—and yet here you are, still refusing to retrieve what's rightfully mine, *Apprentice*."

The way he said *apprentice*—it just about did me in. But instead of yelling, I forced myself to turn around and face him. I took a long, deep sip of the chai, letting the delicious mix of cinnamon and other spices warm me from the inside out.

Gideon simmered but kept silent.

I took another sip of my tea as I watched him, my face carefully neutral until the chill in the kitchen abated and I could no longer see my breath condense.

"Come on," I said when I gauged Gideon's temper had dissipated as much as it would. Tea still in hand, I headed for my front closet.

I opened the door and pulled out a mid-sized package, wrapped not with paper but with two old, grey army blankets, ones that I had infused with Otherside. Gideon had started teaching me to inscribe Otherside on objects beyond mirrors, and we'd begun with cloth.

It was tricky. Unlike a smooth, reflective surface such as metal or glass, the Otherside didn't like to stick to cloth. It tended to slide off. I had to be nimble, and it'd taken me a few tries. I unwrapped the Otherside-infused blankets and removed the three ornate, silver-framed antique mirrors Gideon had been after. Then I held the blankets out for the ghost to inspect. He took one of them, turning them over and examining them with his translucent hands.

"The mirrors leak Otherside," I explained. "Nate could barely keep his hands off them, and being so close to the bay—"

"You didn't want ghosts stumbling in here searching for the source, so you created an obfuscation cloak of sorts, to dampen the mirrors' pull," he finished for me, and added quietly, "So that's why I couldn't find them." Gideon *tsk*ed to himself as he laid out the two blankets, appearing deep in thought as he continued to examine the identical bindings I'd created on each of them.

I shrugged and crossed my arms over my chest, conscious of Gideon's scrutiny. "I needed two to dampen the Otherside spillover," I said as he walked around the two blankets, frowning.

Still silent, he moved on to the mirrors.

"Like I said, they leak," I repeated. "I wasn't certain if it was a mistake on my end or—"

Gideon shook his head this time, and without looking up said, "No, there was no mistake. They leak Otherside by design."

"*Shit.*" I blurted it out before I could stop myself, almost spilling my tea on the floor. "I *knew* it. I am making ghost traps, aren't I?"

Gideon made a face at my crass vocabulary, as he called it. "By design, yes, they leak Otherside, but not for the purpose you surmised." He glanced back up from the blankets and mirrors. All traces of his earlier anger were gone. "You understand pressure valves, yes? Never mind—of course you do, you boil enough tea."

"Water, actually."

"Mirrors like these, tempered with a touch of sorcery, tend to build pressure, and it needs to release. It's a very common side effect of warping Otherside then giving it means to stay in contact with the barrier."

Like mirrors did. Now that was intriguing. "They off-gas?"

Gideon inclined his head. "I should have mentioned that the mirrors behave like an attractant," he said almost absent-mindedly— for Gideon at least. "I forget how much Maximillian omitted in your training."

"That the mirrors you told me to make might turn my place into a ghost beacon?" I snorted. "Really? You think that might have been an important detail? Gideon, what if a poltergeist had shown up?"

But Gideon, still examining the blankets, waved my concerns off with a ghostly hand. "Nothing would have come of it. I've set enough wards to fend off wandering ghosts and poltergeists."

I nearly choked on a mouthful of tea. "*What?*" The ghost had set wards around what? My place? The building? "Where exactly?"

"The locations are inconsequential. I'll show you another time, when we get to warding spaces." As if sensing my displeasure, Gideon glanced up. "And it was a necessity. Sorcery attracts many of the dead. It was the only way to ensure that everyone but your own ghost knows to stay away."

Unbelievable . . . I made a mental note to tell Nate he'd graduated from "thief" to "my own ghost." He'd get a kick out of that.

"And though the attractant quality of the Otherside off-gas is an unintentional by-product, I suppose it's why so many soothsayers prefer this version of their . . ." He trailed off. "Tool," he finally settled on.

Gideon knew very well what I thought of soothsayers and their trade.

"This," he said, gesturing at my blanket, "is clever, especially as we haven't covered obfuscation bindings yet." He levelled his ghost-grey eyes on me. "Explain to me how you believe it works."

"Ah, well . . ." Despite myself, I couldn't help but enjoy our strategy discussions. In all the years I'd worked with Max, he'd never once asked me how I came up with my more creative bindings and solutions, only berated me for taking what he'd perceived as short-cuts. In contrast, Gideon seemed to have an appreciation of my ingenuity, as he called it.

If there was a peace point in our lessons, that was it.

"I can only get basic bindings to stick to cotton and linen. Wool is easier to work with for complicated bindings."

"You wouldn't be my first apprentice to prefer dead animal material to plant."

Okay, that was not the image I wanted wool to conjure . . . "*But* since the amount of Otherside leaking out was minimal, I figured a basic siphon for Otherside would do the trick."

Gideon glanced up at me. "That would be nowhere near strong enough."

"Which is why I added five." I pointed to the five separate circular bindings I'd added to each wool blanket. Each one filtering a small amount of Otherside back across the barrier. "I still had some residue that made it through, but the second blanket—"

"Solved that problem." Gideon nodded to himself. "Simple, but surprisingly effective in this instance." He turned his attention back to the three mirrors I'd been working on, nodding at them. "The work is adequate for the clients purchasing these. One of them is local, and I would like you to deliver it in person, but not with the cloak." He shot me a sideways glance, one I couldn't quite read. "I don't feel this particular client needs to know about your knack for cobbling together unorthodox bindings. You know the local soothsayer, yes?"

I swallowed, my stomach churning. "Samuel Richan?" I muttered. Yes, I knew who he was.

Samuel Richan was a very successful Seattle art dealer. Late forties, early fifties, not an unattractive man, fashionable, white hair short and carefully groomed, lean, average height and physique. He'd had an uncanny talent for picking art trends ahead of the curve and championing little-known artists who eventually broke out into international and commercial markets. I'd recently—and accidentally—found out why he'd been so successful: it was because he was a soothsayer.

Just like mediums and other practitioners, soothsayers bind Otherside and wrangle ghosts. It's a rare occurrence, but every now and then a ghost gets confused and starts jumping through time, a bit like getting on and off the train without knowing your stop. If you could find one of these ghosts and add direction to its nonsensical jumps, you'd have a hell of a fortune teller—provided, that is, the ghost could find its way back. That's where a soothsayer comes in. Soothsayers bind a ghost's soul to their own skin through Otherside-laced welts. It's an unpleasant business that turns the ghost into little more than a shell, one of the reasons Nate tried so hard to stay under the radar. Soothsaying is the closest thing the paranormal community has to the black arts. I could argue that sorcery isn't innately evil; though it can be used for nefarious purposes, it doesn't exist for that purpose. But soothsaying? The point is to torture ghosts to get what you want. It doesn't get much more dark arts than that . . .

I had a hard time keeping my voice even. "Samuel Richan runs Gallery 6," I said. It was an art gallery near the convention centre, an area where the cost of rent would be astronomical. My one run-in with Richan at Club 9, a month ago, had rapidly devolved into threats. His mostly, telling me things about my future that would send me screaming to my own death and an open threat to bind Nate and hand him over to the highest-bidding record company . . .

I'd avoided Samuel since then.

If Gideon sensed my discomfort, he ignored it. Or didn't care. "Good. Deliver these two by the end of day tomorrow," he said, indicating the mirrors intended for Samuel. "There is no rush and no need to draw attention to yourself. Choose a time when traffic around the gallery is low." He threw me another pointed stare. "If anyone is in the gallery, the mirrors are an artistic endeavour, yes?"

The prospect of seeing Samuel again made my skin crawl, but I nodded. This was part of my new job with Gideon. Saying Gideon was morally nebulous would be putting it mildly. I'd known making deliveries to some of his more . . . unsavoury clients was inevitable. Gideon's services didn't come cheap, and Richan was one of the few who I imagined could afford them.

Why is it always the morally depraved who achieve financial success?

Never mind, I knew the answer to that too . . .

"We'll pick up again tomorrow," Gideon continued. "Five p.m. sharp. In the meantime, read the soothsaying chapters in *Advanced Practitioning Theories*."

More soothsaying? "Gideon—" I tried.

"What?" The sharpness was back, and that pinched expression. The one I imagined Gideon had perfected over his afterlife existence. The same one that promised violence and cruelty.

I sighed. And we'd been doing so well at veering away from violent tendencies . . .

But this time I dug in my heels and stared right back. Soothsaying is the practice of binding ghosts—forcing them to do a practitioner's bidding. Yes, you can do fantastical things with a ghost who can trip through time, giving you stock market tips, but it also drives the ghost completely batshit insane. If you are looking for a way to torture the dead, that is it.

I set my jaw and pushed on, despite the flicker of gold and black in Gideon's eyes. "Can we, I don't know, maybe lay off the evil sooth-sayer stuff—for now, I mean? At least until I've got a better grasp—"

Gideon didn't give me a chance to finish. He let out a long-suffering sigh and turned his attention back to the third mirror. "At what point did we ever agree to call soothsaying evil?" He sounded more annoyed than angry.

For a moment, I was flustered. "I—ah, it's *soothsaying*. The binding of ghosts for nefarious deeds?"

"And who says it's always for nefarious deeds?" Gideon said without looking up.

"Um—everyone? How would you like being bound?"

Gideon *tsk*ed, and I gritted my teeth as it echoed through the Otherside I still held in my head. "I can think of a good many reasons why a ghost would need to be bound. You're naive."

There was only so much I would take from the ghost. "I know exactly what a soothsayer does, thank you very much. Hell, I've even had run-ins with a few—"

Gideon ignored me and headed for the kitchen. He reached my

stove and retrieved one of my frying pans, holding it up . . . The one I used for bacon. It had seen better days . . . and at one point in time had a full coat of Teflon. "So this frying pan is evil."

"What?!"

He held it up over his head with two of his fingers, as if it weighed no more than a feather—which was deceptive. He wasn't actually picking it up—not like we do. He was using Otherside and sorcery to manipulate the world of the living. It always unsettled me just how easily it came to the sorcerer's ghost.

"This frying pan clearly burns as much as it cooks—more so, from the looks of it—probably mixing in all sorts of carcinogens with your food. Therefore, by your account, it must be evil."

Oh, for the love of . . . "Of *course* not. It's a cooking utensil, for Christ's sake. It's not the same thing."

"Ah, so a frying pan is a tool?" Gideon disappeared and reappeared right in front of me. Still holding the frying pan, I noted. He leaned in, his eyes edging towards a more dangerous shade of black than I'd seen in days. "It's *exactly* the same thing," he said, his face inches from mine, the words biting, tinged with Gideon's personal brand of cruelty—and cold. I shivered as the Otherside wafting off him chilled the air.

I wasn't backing down. "At best, soothsaying is a shortcut to torture something you need out of a ghost. At worst, it's a way to enslave them—"

Gideon interrupted me. "Soothsaying is a tool present in any good practitioner's arsenal—nothing more, nothing less. How it's used is at the discretion of the practitioner, and therefore the blame for your perceived good and evil lies with them. An awful lot of people use guns to kill each other, but guns aren't inherently evil."

"And there are a lot of people who would disagree with you on that."

Gideon placed the frying pan on the kitchen table and turned his full attention back on me, eyes narrowed. "But I don't think *you* do. You know as well as I do there are people who deserve to be killed for their actions. You don't think that some ghosts don't deserve a similar fate?"

I swallowed. I could see that Gideon was losing his patience, but before I could stop myself, I said, "I sure as hell can think of one ghost who—"

"Oh, get over yourself, Kincaid! You know I'm not nearly that evil or despicable. I barely rate malcontent on your small world scale. No, your problem is that you hate that I'm right. And you *know* that I'm right. Under the right circumstances, you would have no issue letting someone die for their crimes."

I *knew* I should take a big breath, calm myself and take a step back. "Let's hope I never have to find out."

I could have said more—I wanted to argue. But there were many things Gideon and I would never see eye to eye on. If I picked a battle over every single one . . . In some ways Gideon was like Lee. There were things that were so deeply entrenched in Lee's mind from her old life . . . Gideon, I'd discovered, suffered from a similar blind spot.

I broke eye contact and searched the suddenly interesting floorboards. "Look, I'm not saying I won't do it. All I'm asking for is a break from soothsaying. There has to be something else we can work on—"

"*No.*" He said it with such force and finality I couldn't help but step back, and I silently cursed myself for pushing him. "I'm willing to accommodate your sensibilities to a limited extent. Deliver the mirrors to Richan and make yourself available to work tomorrow evening. Bring the remaining mirror and have the chapters read."

And though the words weren't spoken, a threatening silence hung in the air between us, and the bindings on my wrist, our deal, glowed menacingly.

Or else.

And then, without so much as a goodbye, Gideon dispersed, back to the Otherside or wherever the hell the sorcerer's ghost went.

Well. That had gone well. I refilled my tea and slumped into one of the kitchen chairs that perfectly matched the new table. It, unlike my tea, blazer and satchel, was not a splurge. It was a 1960s red and chrome Arborite number that Nate had found thrown out in an alley. We'd had an "accident" with my previous wooden table courtesy of the wraith that had been stalking Nate. Not only had we flipped it over to use as a barricade, but it had been frozen in the process. The legs had snapped shortly after. In one of his more industrious moments, Nate had decided to replace the table . . .

With something he'd found in an alley.

Nate insisted it was a collector's piece. I wasn't quite buying that. I mean, I'll admit there was a kind of kitsch appeal, and Arborite doesn't chip, though the red surface had faded and the vinyl seats were worn in spots. But, throwaway piece or vintage showroom gem, the table didn't wobble and I didn't think tossing it over or freezing it would put a dent in it. Not that I planned on having any more ghosts stalk my apartment, but after two incidents I like to be prepared.

Besides, its aged quality matched the 1960s linoleum kitchen floor that had turned a permanent yellow sometime in the 1980s and grey with ground-in dust sometime in the 1990s.

And yet my landlord would figure out some way to pocket my deposit.

I folded my arms on the table and lowered my head. Why did I keep letting Gideon get the best of me? Was it fear, or was I letting my temper get in the way of stringing together a coherent and convincing argument? I'd never let Aaron get the best of me like this— not even when I'd first started working for the SPD.

Or was I the one in the wrong this time?

It wasn't that I didn't want to work on ghost binding and soothsaying; the issue was that I didn't think I *could*. Everything about ghost binding made me sick to my stomach. And despite Gideon's arguments, it *was* wrong . . .

I didn't think I could bring myself to make it through another lesson—mentally or physically.

And I still had to deliver the two mirrors to Richan—that was another can of worms.

Why couldn't Gideon get that? No, Gideon got it. The ghost just didn't care.

So absorbed was I in my latest predicament with Gideon, I didn't notice Nate when he returned. Not even when he cleared his throat.

"K?" Nate said.

I didn't lift my head even as I felt the Otherside chill telling me Nate was on my left. I preferred to wallow in my own misery. *Maybe if I don't answer him, he'll take the hint that I want to be left alone . . .*

"Okay, here's the thing, K. I *may* have been eavesdropping."

Nope. Nate was not going to take the hint . . . I raised my head to find Nate sitting across from me, his hands steepled in front of him on the table. The ghost made a face as he searched for the right words.

"And while I don't disagree with anything particular you said, Gideon *scares the shit out of me*." He pronounced each word slowly, as if I were an idiot and not one of the best practitioners on the western seaboard. He turned his steepled hands so the fingers were all pointing at him. "And I *greatly, extremely* question your dedication to keeping us alive— Okay, well, you alive, me not so much, but, you know, continuing my ghostly existence—"

Oh, for Christ's sake . . . "Not this again, Nate." I grabbed my tea mug and headed for the stove. I didn't need this. What I needed was sleep. Where was my hot water bottle?

Nate appeared between me and the kettle.

I ground my teeth. "Nate, out of the way." He knew I wouldn't walk through him. I wasn't going to ghost myself this late at night— it was creepy and I was too damn cold.

Nate held his hands up. "Look, all I'm asking, K, is that you try to be nice to him— Shit! Get back here—"

I wasn't about to pull another globe of Otherside tonight to make Nate move, but I did duck around him. "Seriously, does Gideon have you on his payroll too?" I asked. There was my water bottle. I began filling it with the still-hot kettle water. "I mean, he has no problem buying everyone else off—"

"Of course not!" Nate shouted, something he almost never did. "Jesus, K, I'd never—you know." He scuffed his red, ghostly Converse shoe against the dusty kitchen linoleum and glared at me. He even managed to produce a scuffing sound. Which meant he was being sincere.

I took a deep breath. "Okay, Nate, that was too much. I'm sorry. You would never sell me or yourself out to Gideon. You can't begin to fathom how infuriating that ghost is. He won't *listen* to a damn—"

"K, he's saved both of us! Twice—no, three times now. You from drowning when that crazy poltergeist Anna Bell tied you under the pier *and* Randall's fire, and then me from Cole and . . . well, me."

I leaned against the counter and closed my eyes. It was the one part about my whole arrangement with Gideon that for the life of me I couldn't square away. Gideon was a selfish, usurious ghost—who profited from selling the living and dead the things he knew they couldn't—and wouldn't—refuse. He'd done it to me.

And Nate and I had been tiptoeing around my issues with Gideon for two weeks now. "Nate—" I started. What was I protesting exactly? Gideon or my own damn decisions?

"I mean, what if—and just *consider* this for a second—what if Gideon's not as evil as you think he is? Hunh?"

I shot him a look over my shoulder, and Nate held out his hands once again, as if readying to fend me off. *Me.*

"I mean, he sure as hell doesn't act like a poltergeist," Nate said.

I spun on him. "You just said he scared the crap out of you!"

Nate threw up his hands. "Everyone scares the crap out of me, K!" He started to count off on a translucent hand. "You scare the crap out of me, Gideon scares the crap out of me, Lee scares the crap out of me, and on a really bad fucking day Aaron scares the crap out of me." He shuddered. "It's that whole cop thing. Face it, K, I'm a fucking coward, all right? *But.*" I watched as Nate hedged his answer. "Here's my point. I might be terrified of the fucking sorcerer's ghost, but I don't think he's *actually* evil. I just don't get the whole malicious intent vibe that poltergeists give off, all right? Trust me, I know what evil feels like, and he's not it." Nate paused and levelled his ghost-grey brown eyes at me, pleading. "I don't think you should hold a grudge. I mean, forget the soothsayer thing, you go to every fucking lesson with him like you're going to war, it's like you can't help yourself, and I'm not sure you see—Oh, for fuck's sake, K, come on!" Nate shouted as I grabbed the filled water bottle and headed for my bedroom, only stopping to snatch my bag from the couch.

"It's not up for discussion, Nate."

Nate managed to appear in front of my bedroom doorway and block it. "Why? Why is it not up for discussion? K, you know I have a huge fucking point here. I know I don't make that many of them, but here we are—"

I unleashed all the fury and rage that I felt towards Gideon, all the pent-up anger that I'd been doing my damnedest to keep under wraps while I made it through his lessons. "Because he tried to strangle me! The first memory I have of that damned ghost is him accusing me of stealing and wrapping a hair dryer cord around my neck! Do you have *any* idea what that's like? Do you have any idea how often, how many times in my life, the first contact I have with someone is being accused of something? Because of what I *am*? And now, I need to stand there most nights of the damn week and take more of his crap?" I stood there fuming at Nate. I hadn't been this angry about something in *years*, and it felt so good to let it out.

Nate just stared at me. He was usually an open book, but right now, for the life of me, I couldn't fathom what he was thinking. "Okay, K," he finally said in a quiet voice, and floated away from the door frame, shoving his hands in his jean pockets. "I get it. I don't understand, but I can imagine it really, really sucks. I see the way people treat you. I know you think I don't notice how the cops, clients, even Aaron sometimes treats you, but I do . . ." He trailed off and pursed his lips. "If that's the reason, I can understand the why." He turned one of his rare serious looks on me. "But I don't think that's it. Not all of it, anyway." He searched for words. "I think in this case you and Gideon might have more in common than either of you wants to admit."

I narrowed my eyes at Nate, my often wayward ghost, roommate and arguably my best friend. My sixth sense started tingling. "Nate, what do you know that you're not telling me?"

But Nate, like every other ghost on the Otherside when they have a secret they really can't reveal, skirted a direct answer. He only said, "You can't keep fighting with him. You won't win this one. I don't think either of you will . . ." He trailed off and ran his hand through his hair. "Just find a way to make peace with the terrifying ghost, okay?"

I headed inside my bedroom.

"K?"

I turned around before I managed to shut my door.

"You don't make him angry, K—you terrify him. Think about it," he said, his face still serious. "For all his power, for all the centuries he's been hanging around, a twenty-seven-year-old, mostly self-taught practitioner hid something from him." Nate shook his head. "After all, at the end of the day, he's still a ghost."

I shook my head. "That's . . ." I trailed off. On the surface, it sounded absurd. Gideon was the most powerful practitioner I'd ever met, dead or alive, *period*. But, for all his tricks and sorcery, Gideon was dead, and had been for almost a thousand years. There were connections that the living, people like me, were in touch with that Gideon would never share again.

All of a sudden, Nate's hypothesis didn't seem so ridiculous anymore.

"No one, living or dead, likes to have their limitations pointed out to them, not like that." After a moment Nate added, in a very quiet voice, "You sure as hell don't."

No. I didn't . . .

I sighed and made to close my door. "I'll . . . think about it, all right?"

Nate relaxed. "That's all I ask. Thank you. And now I need beer. I'm going to Lee's." He perked up. "Rumour has it a new ghost is hanging out who's a ringer for Edie Sedgwick." He lowered his voice. "It *might* actually be her."

I sighed. "Fine. Have fun. And pay your bar tab."

"Done!" Nate said, and vanished a little too quickly to convince me of his sincerity.

Battle for another day, I thought as I closed the door and tossed
the hot water bottle under the covers. I swear, sometimes Nate . . .
was Nate. The vintage table, his fear of Gideon—I think it was
the only way he knew how to help. Despite his unreliability and
irresponsible nature over the day-to-day, he was always there when
it mattered.

But contemplating what Nate had said about Gideon would
have to wait for later. Like after about ten hours of sleep in my warm
bed. I slid into track pants and a sweatshirt— I'd shower in the
morning—and crawled under the covers.

Before turning off the lights, I shoved my phone under the pile
of pillows beside me. I had only just found the right angle to rest
my head when I felt and heard the buzz of my cell.

Oh, for . . . now what? I grabbed it in case it was the Youngs.
I doubted Astrid would—or could—get finicky with my guidelines
yet. I didn't think she was strong enough to break her own word,
but I'd been wrong before.

It wasn't the Youngs, though. It was Aaron.

I swore and shoved the phone back under the pillows and closed
my eyes. I knew what the topic would be, what it had been for two
weeks . . .

As per Aaron's usual pattern, it buzzed once more.

He could damn well wait until tomorrow morning like everyone
else, after I'd had my coffee . . . Aaron had stabbed me in the back,
and what's worse, he was unrepentant about it.

Making a mountain out of a molehill my ass—who said that anymore? He had, only earlier this week. And I wasn't . . .

I left Aaron to have a conversation with my polite, if curt, voice
mail.

But, just as I relaxed again, the buzzing resumed.

Oh, damn it all to hell, Aaron . . .

I grabbed my phone and answered. "Aaron," I said, teeth
clenched, ready for a fight. There was a pause.

"Kincaid—" Aaron started, his voice oh so calm, the way it
always was.

No way. "It's late, I'm tired, I'm going to—"

"They found Katy," he rushed, knowing that was all the detail he needed to give me.

My grogginess instantly dissipated. I pushed myself to my elbows and hit the bedside light, wincing at the brightness.

"Where?" I asked, rubbing my eyes. I knew the who. It had to be Katy Price—Martin Dane's last victim—the same one who'd been kidnapped a week after Dane had died. The same Katy everyone had hoped was still alive. "And is she . . ." I let the question trail off, already knowing the answer.

"Dead? Yes. And it's much worse than you're thinking—it's why I need you, Kincaid."

Nausea hit me hard, and not from any Otherside I'd been using.

Martin Dane, the White Picket Fence Killer, had been gunned down outside a gas station two weeks ago. Dane had targeted middle-class suburban families, and after murdering all except one— usually a child—in their own home, he would dress them in 1950s clothes and arrange a macabre dinner party scene. Time after time, bodies were found set up around a fifties Cleaver-style dining room table, bent over empty plates. The surviving child he took with him and, in a demonic game of musical corpses, often killed at his next crime scene, to join the newly dead family at *their* dinner table. He was a monster.

And only last week a new family, the Prices, had been discovered dead in their home, arranged just like the others, in a 1950s vignette, with the child who had still been missing when Dane was shot sitting in their daughter, Katy's, place. It was as if Dane was back from the grave to terrorize all over again. Up until now, there had still been hope that Katy Price would be found alive.

I pushed down my gut reaction to respond to Aaron's plea with an immediate yes.

"Kincaid, I know you already said no, but there's something odd going on. They could really use your expertise."

I sighed. I'd already had a similar discussion last week with Aaron and Captain Marks. Right after the Prices had been found murdered, the captain had asked me to find and bind Dane. I'd given them a resounding no.

"It's kidnapping across state lines, so federal, no? The FBI paranormal units have their own practitioners, Aaron. They're as good as me, if not better. If they haven't tracked down Dane's poltergeist by now, you're probably looking at an accomplice . . ." I trailed off. A living one.

"I know, I know—you need proof there's a ghost or zombie involved—"

"*Ghost.* Since Dane's body was incinerated." The ashes were under lock and key at a secure facility. Just in case some punk-wielding Otherside got creative.

The murder of Katy Price's family, a new vignette and Katy's kidnapping were incriminating evidence that Dane was somehow killing from beyond the grave, but it wasn't *proof.* The fact that no one had caught Dane in the act worked strongly against that theory. Poltergeists aren't known to do anything in half measures, and they love to put on a show, and if the raising done two weeks ago by Liam Sinclair was any indication, Martin Dane was no exception.

Liam Sinclair, a TV celebrity practitioner and star of *The Sinclair After Hour,* had been brought in by the FBI to raise Dane and interrogate him on the whereabouts of the last child he'd taken while he was still alive. In my opinion, Liam had been woefully unqualified—I don't care how many accidental-overdose ghosts he had counselled live on national TV, he was arrogant—and an idiot to think he could handle a serial killer. Sinclair had made the rookie mistake of letting Dane know he was dead, and Dane's zombie had promptly tried to strangle him. *Live,* on TV. The only thing dead serial killers regret is losing out on the chance to kill a few more people, and as Liam was a living, breathing man sitting right across from him with the cameras rolling . . . The feed had been cut when Dane's zombie lunged across the table, grasping for Liam's neck. Liam had managed to release Dane's bindings and hang on to his life, though it had been touch and go for a few minutes.

Now, making a zombie serial killer believe he's still alive and might just get out of this if he co-operates . . . that takes finesse.

Aaron pressed on. "What if I had it? Proof that Dane was involved?"

I paused. If someone had caught Dane on video causing mischief, or even if there was an eyewitness, some kind of irrefutable proof that Dane was continuing to terrorize from six feet under . . .

The answer was still no. "Aaron, I'm not binding Dane." Binding was . . . well, it was a hard no in my books. "If the FBI wants him bound so badly, they can get Sinclair to do it."

"A half-hour tomorrow morning, Kincaid, that's all I'm asking for. There's something odd with Katy's murder, and they need an outside opinion. Please, a half an hour to look at photos and discuss what the practitioners on site found. That's it," Aaron pleaded.

Goddamnit. Aaron knew exactly what buttons to press—just enough to reel me in and whet my curiosity. I had more than a few errands to run tomorrow, delivering the mirrors to Richan, my lesson with Gideon—and I'd hoped to visit Lee Ling as well. But now I was curious to find out exactly what Aaron thought he had. If I met him early enough and stuck to half an hour.

Why did I get the distinct feeling I was being had? "Fine. Where? And make it after 10 a.m.," I added when I saw the time. It was already 1 a.m. I was sleeping in.

He didn't miss a beat. "My place. I'll make breakfast—pancakes," he rushed.

I made a face. I would have much preferred a coffee shop, the police station, even the morgue. Going to Aaron's was . . . dangerous. Emotionally. Some patterns are hard to break, and going to Aaron's always put us at risk of falling back into them.

"And bacon."

God damn my pathological fondness for bacon. My mouth was already watering . . . Aaron knew to cook the pancakes in leftover bacon grease.

"Add hash browns and you have a deal."

"Done."

I still had the distinct impression Aaron was the one getting the better end of this bargain. "Aaron, one last thing," I said, hitting the bedside lamp and plunging my room back into the oh so wonderful darkness.

"Name it."

I snuggled under the covers and pulled the comforter up to my neck, touching the hot water bottle with my bare feet, willing the heat to warm the rest of me. "Don't you dare call me before 10 a.m."

I hung up and shoved the phone back under the pile of pillows beside me. As I drifted off, I couldn't help but think that if I could leave the dead to rest, the least they and their memories could do was leave me to sleep.

CHAPTER 3

LONELY HEARTS AND HUNGRY SOULS

I didn't wake up until ten, and it was the sunlight, not my alarm or phone, that did the deed. Wonder of wonders, and not just because Aaron took my early morning call ban seriously—sunlight in November along the northwest coast was a near miracle. It was the best morning I'd had in weeks.

After throwing on a concert T and track pants, I meandered into the kitchen and started the coffee. I left the bacon in the fridge— might as well eat Aaron's—but threw a bagel in the toaster to sop up the coffee.

I opened the kitchen curtains to let the rare sunlight in and went so far as to drag the Arborite table and chairs across the linoleum so I could sit in it. I filled my coffee cup, let the sun warm my back and checked e-mail on my laptop.

The usual awaited me: two new e-mails from Nathan Cade fans asking for seances, one of the two lawyers in the city I was still willing to do business with needed me for a will dispute, and, last but not least, there was an e-mail from the Youngs letting me know Astrid had yet to make an appearance. Well, that was good news at least.

While I finished my coffee, I fired off a handful of soft replies—
I always checked seances with Nate before agreeing to anything—
but I could fit the will dispute in. I closed my laptop and, coffee in
hand, tracked down the text with the ghost-binding chapters Gideon
had ordered me to read. I found it on my coffee table and slid it into
my backpack to study later.

No phone buzzing, no Nate—my morning was downright peaceful. As I stepped into the shower, I wondered if Nate had run into
his Edie Sedgwick ringer. I made a mental note to ask him about
it later. Despite all the tabloid gossip about celebrity ghosts wandering around haunting people and places, they were a lot rarer than
the stories would have you believe. Take Nate. Unless you were an
undead devotee of Damaged Goods, beyond scheduled performances Nate was literally a ghost.

As I showered, I found my curiosity drifting and wondered what
the hell Aaron had to show me.

I'll admit, I entertained the idea that the White Picket Fence
Killer was somehow acting from the grave. It wasn't impossible.
Ghosts, poltergeists to be exact, are known to exact vengeance on
the living. And unlike most ghosts, they *can* kill people, and Dane
was certainly a prime candidate for turning poltergeist, being an
unrepentant serial killer and all. And Katy Price's kidnapping and
the murder of her entire family did fit Dane's MO.

But that was part of the problem. Like most serial killers, Dane
had been a meticulous planner. He'd had a pattern, a method, one
he stuck to, every detail carried out to the letter. Each murder a new
vignette, the bodies carefully choreographed in 1950s or '60s dress.
The arrangement of the corpses, the musical chairs, were their very
own signature.

I saw two problems with Katy and her family's murders. The first
was that, no matter how meticulous Dane might have been in life,
poltergeists can't stick to a plan. No matter how hard they try, things
usually devolve into an undead temper tantrum. I didn't see him
sticking to his old methods. But new isn't really in a ghost's vocabulary
either—even a serial killer's. Killing Katy before Dane had found his

next family of victims also didn't make sense, not unless there was a whole new crop of murders and a new kidnapping to uncover.

The supernatural can wreak havoc from across the barrier—but most of the time the actual cause is less mysterious, even human.

Until last night, I'd held out hope Katy was still alive. Now, the only help I could offer was in interviewing the victim's ghost.

Then again, maybe Aaron would surprise me. Maybe there was new evidence that really did prove it was Dane.

God help us if that was the case.

I stepped out of the shower and dried off before fixing my wet hair with an elastic and throwing my jeans and T-shirt back on. Time to head to Aaron's.

I packed the mirrors for Richan—minus the wool blankets, as Gideon had suggested—and, after a moment, decided to wear my blazer. It wouldn't hurt to send a message to Aaron that I was there to work, not, well . . .

That had been the other thing since Cole. Aaron had made it clear he wanted to get back together.

I couldn't. Not while I was an apprentice to Gideon. There'd be too many questions I wasn't ready to answer. I'd managed to put the conversation off for now, but eventually . . .

Problem for another day, Kincaid.

I grabbed my phone.

On my way, I texted, and slid it into my pocket before he could message back, then grabbed my bike and headed for the door.

Despite our conversation last night, despite the fact that I'd agreed to go over, I couldn't forget that Aaron had been the one to tell Captain Marks that I could bind Dane.

My grip tightened around my bike handles.

Aaron knew better than that, and when I'd outright refused, Aaron had had the audacity to behave as if I were a teenager who had to be cajoled into doing chores, as though I were the irrational one.

I pushed my bike into the freight elevator. Not worth getting riled up over now, Kincaid, I told myself. You said no.

Still, as I rode the freight elevator down, Hawk in hand, I couldn't help but worry that Aaron was going to bring up the issue of binding Dane once more. He hadn't mentioned it on the phone, and I hoped my worry was misplaced, but when it came to Aaron, well, I'd been wrong a lot over the past four months.

The blazer, and the distance between us I hoped it would signal, was for the best.

I reached the lobby and was met by yet another new sculpture I had to negotiate my Hawk around. A trio of Smurfs turned prostitutes had been added to the Care Bear trash bin campfire.

I did my best not to make eye contact with soliciting Smurfs, stoned Care Bears or the overly excited My Little Pony centaur, which was difficult as they'd been placed in a ring around the elevator—for maximum impact, no doubt—and manoeuvred through the rest of the 1980s pop culture–themed graveyard of lost toys. Well, art is a form of communication. Maybe the point was to induce eighties flashback terror.

My phone buzzed before I reached the back door. I hesitated.

Maybe I should answer and make sure Aaron knew that ghost binding, even of Dane, was still off the table?

I let it go to voice mail and pushed my bike outside before getting on and gunning it.

Pushover? Possibly, but there had been the promise of food. It was only in the past month I'd finally felt organized enough to stock my fridge with real groceries . . . but the starvation mentality from living on oatmeal and rice was still very real in my head. And stomach. I made a face as it growled in agreement—or perhaps in protest that I wasn't yet at Aaron's.

I took off down the viaduct and headed for Aaron's in Fremont, wondering again what exactly it was he had to show me—or if I was wandering into another colossal argument.

∗

"Oh, *hell* no," I said as soon as I stepped into Aaron's apartment.

It wasn't Aaron standing in the entrance, guilt written all over his face, that inspired my disgust. It was the man sitting at his kitchen table with a shit-eating smirk. I spun around, only to find Aaron blocking my exit.

"Wait!" Aaron said, holding out his arms, in defence or conciliation, maybe both.

"Aaron," I managed, my face hot. "Is this your idea of a bad joke?" Because it sure as hell wasn't the breakfast he'd promised me.

"Detective Baal was acting under my orders, Ms. Strange," Captain Marks called out. I turned to face him and his thinly veiled contempt. "I asked him to invite you, nice and polite like, to the bargaining table, as it were, since we don't exactly have a good track record in that regard." He sneered at the last part.

"The polite part or the invitations?"

"Both." He gestured to the table. "And look—Baal has gone to such trouble to make us a nice spread. Would be a shame to let it all go to waste." He dug into a plate of syrup-drenched pancakes. All I could think about was wiping that grin off his face. Instead, I turned on Aaron.

"I swear to god, open that door right now or I'll—"

"You'll what?" the captain shouted. A bully tactic, meant to make you jump, which is exactly what I did. He laughed, and all I could do was bunch my fists.

The captain kicked out the chair directly across from him. It scraped loudly against the tile floor. "Have a seat, Strange. Listen to what I have to say—you're already here. Detective Baal over there will even pour you a cup of coffee." He held up his own in mock cheers, still visibly amused at my discomfort.

Unfortunately, I *was* already here, and clearly the captain wanted to talk. I had no illusions as to what would happen if I stormed out. He'd come up with another way to talk to me, probably involving a jail cell. He'd done so before. I shook my head and took a seat, shooting Aaron a look that I hoped communicated my fury.

Still grinning, the captain picked up the plate of bacon, passing it my way. "Here, Strange, try the bacon. Detective Baal's not a half-bad cook."

"What do you want?" I asked as Aaron slid a cup of coffee in front of me. The fact that Marks was so visibly enjoying himself really pissed me off.

"Can the attitude, Strange. There's been a new development in the Martin Dane kidnapping case. Katy Price has been found in Portland, Oregon. You've been following the case since we last spoke?"

"Hard not to, since the kidnapping has been all over the news." The media had jumped on the terror bandwagon, assuming it had to be Dane from beyond the grave. As I'd said, I had yet to be convinced.

"Go on, Strange." The captain winked at me, a mocking gesture, and slid a manila folder across the table towards me. "Indulge me and take a peek. You know you want to."

Against my better judgment, I gave in and flipped the folder open—if only to assuage my curiosity as to what it was about this murder that had catalyzed this ambush.

Jesus Christ . . .

Despite working with the dead day in, day out, it's never easy for me to look at bodies—especially those of murder victims. It's ten times worse when they're young.

I'd seen the Missing photos of Katy online and on TV. Katy had been a pretty girl—athletic, long-limbed, a tennis player and academic achiever. I'd like to think her photo went viral out of hope she'd be discovered alive—that maybe the constant iterations of her face and the gruesome specifics of Dane's string of murders would inspire people to listen for muffled cries or report suspicious behaviour in their neighbourhoods—and not for the ratings that a sensationalized serial killer murder spree and a pretty young face inspire, not for the morbid fascination the public has with disasters—brimstone and fire.

I like to think that even I can be an optimist sometimes.

No young woman deserves to be murdered, but with Katy, people just couldn't help but feel the injustice. She was that kind of girl, the definition of a good kid. She'd done well in school, respected her curfew, excelled at team sports, dressed modestly. Unlike how I'd been as a teen. She was also white. Most of Dane's victims had been white, meaning the public outcry had been threefold.

Regardless of race and affluence, Katy should never, in a million years, have found herself the target of a serial killer, in the hallway of her own school, no less.

But she had. Her entire family had somehow offended Dane's sensibilities. As I'd said to Astrid last night, there are some people for whom death really is unfair.

There were ten photos in total, which I spread across Aaron's tablecloth. I'd like to say I didn't flinch at what I saw, that I was immune to crime scene photos—the violence and death frozen in time. But that would be a lie. I pushed my own emotions aside and forced myself to look.

The first five images looked as if they'd been taken in a 1950s-style kitchen, except the walls were rough-sheared wood and the ground was dirt, as though this was a barn. Renovated for occupancy, though the occupancy seemed to be intended for the dead. There was a chrome and Arborite table not unlike the one Nate had found us, except this one was done in shades of light blue and orange.

I whistled as I examined a close-up of Katy. She'd been dressed in an outfit that clearly reflected Dane's fantasy, a bright-pink 1950s-style poodle skirt paired with a T-shirt-style white button-up blouse and black patent Mary Janes. The clothes looked vintage, and her dark, curly hair had been pulled tightly back into a short ponytail.

"Definitely his trademark," I said absently. The purpose of the imagery and what it meant to Dane was anyone's guess—but rumour had it he'd had an unnatural obsession with the "good old days" and had targeted families that might have offended 1950s sensibilities: same-sex couples, single parents and divorcees, outsider and intro-verted kids who dabbled in drugs, alcohol or the Otherside. What the hell had bothered him about Katy and her family was anyone's guess.

It definitely fit part of Dane's MO. But was it him? I ran through the possibilities in my head. Serial killers are a pain in the ass when they're dead—classic poltergeist fodder, since the hunger to kill people never dies. Still, abducting a person in broad daylight without an audience . . . In my experience, poltergeists don't do anything subtle or by half measures. They are all about chaos, on as large a scale as possible.

"It could be a copycat, or maybe Dane's found a fan," I said. "You'd be surprised how great serial killer ghosts are at homing in on the one person on the other side of the mirror who is just itching to dabble in a little mayhem and murder."

Marks shook his head, and for the first time since I sat down the amusement faltered. "The experts have ruled out a copycat. It's Dane all right."

"How?"

Marks shook his head. "Not your concern. The experts are sure. The photos?"

That only made me more dubious, but I turned my attention back to the series of photos. I frowned—there was something odd about her position.

"Shit." There were five of Katy sitting across from herself at the orange-and-blue kitchen table, arms folded, staring at her own body. It was her ghost. Her mirror image, wearing the same blue skirt and white top. The corpse must have been strapped to the chair, the way it sat up straight.

That alone wasn't so strange. Ghosts have no problem being photographed. Neither was her hanging around her own body. When a person is violently killed or suddenly dies, often their ghost doesn't cross the barrier—not immediately. I'd even come across ghosts who followed their corpses around, as if by this action they reclaimed a fraction of control over the event that had stolen their life. Sometimes they even tie themselves to a place—a home or a death site. This was one of two reasons I never stepped a damn foot inside a hospital if I could help it.

No, Katy hanging around her body waiting for it to be found wasn't outside the norm—but there were a lot of other things wrong.

"Ghosts don't appear in the clothes they died in." I tapped the photo. "She should be dressed in something familiar—her own clothes, track pants, T-shirts, sneakers, a hoodie, jeans."

"Could it be shock?" Aaron asked.

I frowned, considering the question as I went back to the photos, searching for the time stamps, momentarily letting my own curiosity take precedence over how uncomfortable this meeting was. "Possibly, but . . ." I stopped, realizing what else was needling me about the photos.

The five photos of Katy's ghost had been taken over twenty-four hours, at four- or five-hour intervals. The most recent had been taken yesterday afternoon.

Exact same posture, same position of the head . . .

Not wanting to talk to Marks more than absolutely necessary, I held a photo up to Aaron. "Does she ever move? In between shots?" I asked him.

He shook his head. "Not an inch—and she hasn't said a word, either. She was still there yesterday evening when I last spoke to my contact, Stephan," he added, anticipating my next question.

I looked for even the slightest alteration in her ghost's position between the different photographs.

"Okay. That is odd," I admitted, when I couldn't find one. Ghosts are anything but still. They move, interact with their surroundings and the people they come in contact with—that's the point. They don't say "the restless dead" for nothing. But by all accounts Katy was a statue.

I gave Aaron a sideways glance. "Is there any preliminary on the toxicology report? A chemical or drug found on the scene?"

Dane had strangled all his victims, but not before injecting them with a neurotoxin, one that immobilized them without killing them. He then posed them around the table, locked in, watching the horror unfold. Dane had been careful with the strangulation, using compression on both sides of his immobilized victims' necks to avoid breaking the hyoid bone and crushing the trachea. It was a coroner from California who first noticed it, the slight bruising on the side of the neck of a young victim, hemorrhaged eyes. On further inspection, he found the damage to the artery.

It was subtle—the kind of subtlety and effort people go to when they want to keep their methods hidden—or show off.

"None on the scene," Aaron said.

"Time of death?"

Marks answered this time. "Two days ago."

"Any sign of Dane?" I asked, searching Marks's face for anything behind the smirk that would tell me he was lying.

"Above my pay grade. And classified."

Bullshit. "I'll give it to you the photos are intriguing." I returned his smirk. "I've looked. What do you want?"

Captain Marks sneered at me, and Aaron cursed under his breath.

"Depends who you ask," Marks said, dropping his napkin over his plate of unfinished food. "The FBI want you to fly down and consult. See if you can figure out how Dane's still killing from six feet under, amongst other things. Me?" He stood and came around the table to hover over me. "I don't care if you figure out the how. I want you to find and bind the son of a bitch."

"Captain, that's not what we discussed," Aaron warned. "Kincaid already said—"

I cut him off. "No." It was simple, to the point. I wasn't binding a ghost—not even Dane. "Better yet, tell them to get Liam Sinclair."

The captain didn't seem too put off by my refusal. "Well," he grunted, heaving on his heavy jacket. "I'll let you take that up with the FBI, in Portland," he said.

"No. As in not until hell freezes over and pigs fly—"

The captain didn't let me finish. "Cut the crap, Strange. You and I both know you can't resist sticking your nose in a good murder. Doubly so when a ghost is involved. Baal, make the travel arrangements." To me, before he closed the door, he added, "Consider yourself shanghaied."

I kept silent for a grand total of ten seconds after the door shut behind the captain. I turned on Aaron. "How the hell could you?"

"I swear, Kincaid, I let him know we were meeting, but I didn't know he was going to show up here. If I had any idea . . ." He bowed his head. "I'm sorry. Really sorry. I should have known better."

I was still furious and would have liked nothing more than to scream at Aaron, but the sincerity on his face convinced me. He'd been bamboozled as well. Some breakfast . . .

With nothing to say and an empty stomach, I did what any self-respecting practitioner would do: I dug into the breakfast of bacon, hash browns and pancakes. Aaron had the good sense to let me eat in silence.

When I had finished, he cleared my plate and returned to the table carrying two refilled coffees, mine black, which he passed to me.

After taking a long moment to glare at Aaron and let him know just how pissed I was, I returned to the manila folder the captain had left behind.

Aaron kept quiet while I spread things out for a second time.

There were only two very brief FBI reports included with the photos—heavily redacted, which was odd for paranormal cases. The first was an account of the new murder scene, and the second was a coroner's report. Strangulation was the cause of Katy's death, but the toxicology wasn't back and wouldn't be for a month at least.

Well, it was consistent with Dane's MO at the very least.

Now, where was the report I really needed? I leafed through the folder but couldn't find it, only photographs of the grisly scene. I glanced up. "It says in the redacted report there was a practitioner on site."

"There was."

I frowned. "Then where is the paranormal analysis? They're standard at the federal level. All FBI paranormal investigations have them."

"They decided they wanted a cold read from you," Aaron said.

I sighed and resumed my perusal of the photos and two sheets of paper. A cold read was one thing—but redacting entire sections of reports or outright omitting them? I needed something beyond photos to go on. Otherside and bindings don't photograph.

"Aaron, I'm not sure what you and the captain expect here, but if *I* can't see the Otherside, and no practitioner has given me a report of what *they* saw . . ." I piled the photos and reports back in the folder. "On the surface, Dane looks good for it," I admitted. "But it still doesn't mean it's him, Aaron. It could be an accomplice, a *living* one, and despite the 1950s scenery, there's only one victim this time. *If* it's Dane, he's changed his pattern." Serial killers have predictable patterns, impulses that mete themselves out, more so once they are dead. If it was Dane somehow reaching from the grave . . . "And you're both ignoring the fact that no one has seen Dane's poltergeist!" Despite the kidnapping of Katy and the murder of her family, Dane's ghost hadn't been seen since Liam Sinclair's disastrous raising.

"Dane evaded the authorities for *years*. He could be doing the same thing now."

I sighed. "You're thinking like the living, not the dead. Poltergeists like a show, they want terror and mayhem as widespread as they can get it. Movie theatres, shopping malls, concerts, buses, *schools*—the bigger the audience, the better. I have a hard time believing Dane took Katy and killed her family without putting on some kind of show, no matter how good he looks for it." Aaron was frowning at me, still unconvinced, so I added, "Look, it's not a bad theory, but a poltergeist doesn't care about getting caught anymore, because it can't. They're undead, pent-up balls of rage with no restraint. The idea that Dane has somehow found a way around that is . . ."

Is what? Dubious? Still circumstantial? But the image of Katy's ghost frozen in the murder scene stopped me. I picked up my coffee and leaned back in the chair. A week she'd been missing, and kept alive where exactly? And by whom? What that must have done to her—waiting to die. "I will give you that the frozen ghost is intriguing, and despite Marks ambushing me, I want to help her. What does the on-site practitioner say?"

It was subtle, but Aaron flinched.

I zeroed in. "Who is it?" The FBI were involved, after all. If they suspected a paranormal element, they had a roster of the best practitioners in the USA to draw from . . . minus myself. I wasn't federally licensed, because I hate paperwork and paying extra for bureaucracy.

He hesitated, but just for a moment. "It doesn't matter who. A paranormal case like this comes around once a century, Kincaid. Stephan is a friend in the FBI who specializes in the paranormal. I told him about you, and he wants a second opinion. Yours. On site."

I made a face. "Considering their taste in practitioners, that's not as complimentary as you might think." I did not want to be thrown into the same professional camp as Sinclair, strangled by my own zombie.

And I couldn't help asking myself whether the FBI really did want my opinion or, like Marks, did they think I could bind a ghost? Considering it was the FBI, they should have plenty of both practitioners and binders on staff. I can't count how many murder victims I've helped the Seattle police interview, but I hadn't even made the FBI's top ten list. Granted, I didn't have a federal licence. And now they were asking for me?

I hid my grimace behind the coffee mug—a perfectly clean and unchipped, unstained white mug, so unlike my own mismatched kitchenware.

Damn it, what are you getting yourself involved in this time?

"There'd be ground rules, Aaron," I started. "First, I don't give a shit what the captain says, I'm not there to bind any ghosts—for anyone."

Aaron nodded. "Agreed. And what else? You said 'first.'"

I let out a breath. "My second is that your friend Stephan, or whoever is in charge, is paying me a flat consulting rate—just to fly down and look."

Aaron didn't even blink. "That can be arranged. And the third?"

I smiled. The next one was for the captain. "That this goes on record as a federal consultation, *not* through the Portland or Seattle PD."

This time Aaron hesitated. "I don't foresee Stephan having a problem with that, but it will piss Marks off."

I shook my head. "Tough. It'll help with my federal practitioning licence application to have a federal case under my belt." I said it casually, matter-of-factly, but Aaron's frown only deepened.

"A federal licence— Kincaid, that's—"

I arched my eyebrow, daring him to finish.

"Ambitious," he settled on. "The cost of the application alone— and then there's the insurance, professional organization fees—you have to maintain a standing with the Paranormal Law Enforcement Association to qualify for cases."

And it all cost ten times more than at the state level. Nate liked to blame video games for the invention of pay-to-play. He'd clearly never dealt with government-regulated licensing. And God knows why I'd need insurance—everyone they'd bring me in to talk to is dead.

"Believe me, my bank account will be hurting from that little racket over the next few months. But think about it, Aaron. I'm one of—what?—fifty practitioners in the US who've consulted for police departments? The only reason I don't work out of state is because I don't have a federal licence. I've never had the money or inclina- tion to try. Now?" It wasn't that I hadn't considered applying for a federal licence before; it had just always been outside my grasp. But since I was no longer working on retainer for the Seattle PD, and with the Youngs' retainer, maybe even this consult in Portland . . .

I'd started thinking bigger.

"Just think. With a federal licence, I could maybe even afford a place like this in a few years," I said, gesturing at Aaron's apart- ment—superior in both location and structural quality.

Aaron nodded, but his expression was far from convinced. "I don't argue with your reasoning, Kincaid. I think it's a fantastic idea. I ques- tion the timing. You've only just gotten back on your feet, and—"

I felt my cheeks heat up with embarrassment. Son of a bitch didn't think I could do it. Still, I said, "And what? It would open up an entire country's worth of work for me? You said it yourself: despite what Captain Marks says, I've got a decent reputation. How many paranormal units would be willing to call me up if I had the federal licence?"

"A lot," Aaron said. "I don't doubt it." The words were right, but there was tension in his shoulders, and that way he looked at his feet . . .

Finally, he glanced up, leaned across the table and folded his hands. "I think you should wait."

I stared into my coffee cup. There was still a quarter of a mug left, but I'd suddenly lost my appetite. Aaron didn't think I could do it.

"It's not that I don't think you're ready, Kincaid. I just think you should wait until you have a few more clients under your belt, and a safety net. And maybe wait until you can patch up your relationship with the Seattle PD."

My embarrassment quickly morphed into anger. "My *relationship*? You call that ambush with Captain Marks a relationship?"

"I'm not saying it's easy, and I'm not saying you're wrong." He ran his hand through his hair. "I'm saying that you're in a better position if you're a friend of the Seattle PD than an antagonist."

"Aaron! The reason I'm applying is that Captain Marks can't stand me. God knows it's the easiest way out for everyone involved. Captain Marks doesn't want a paranormal team, you've said as much. He reluctantly gave you and Sarah your positions back because not even he could cover up two paranormal murder sprees in the span of a month, and the city is pressuring him on poltergeist season. I'd think he'd be thrilled I'm applying for my federal licence. Hell, he ought to help me—I'd be out of his hair for good!"

"I still need you here. And I think the city would be worse off without you. I think you should fight for your place here—then get your federal licence. That's all I'm saying." Aaron didn't break eye contact with me.

He needed me.

I don't think he'd ever said that to me before—not the years we'd been working together, and certainly not the year we'd been dating . . .

Maybe Aaron was right. Maybe I wasn't ready yet. I mean, out of the two of us, look who had their life together? Aaron wasn't living in a just-shy-of-condemned warehouse alongside students and artists with an eighties cartoon fetish. He'd had a bank account for years longer than I had. He probably had things like investments, and a 401(k). Suddenly, all the accomplishments I'd been so proud of, the parts of my life that I had managed to get back on track these past few months, didn't seem so impressive anymore.

"I—ah . . ." I might have said more—I might have told him right then and there that he was right, I'd wait on my application—but I didn't get the chance, as my pocket heated up. My compact. Only one ghost I knew made the compact heat up.

"Ah—I have a call. I need to get this," I said, fumbling my phone out of my blazer pocket and heading for Aaron's balcony. I waited until I was outside and had the door closed behind me before flipping my compact open. I braced my arms around myself, warding off the chill—from the breeze outside and the Otherside—as I stared at the ghostly script making its way across the glass.

Have you delivered my mirrors yet?

Jesus, the ghost picked the worst times to nag.

"No," I said, knowing full well Gideon could hear me. "It's next on my list."

Apparently that was acceptable to Gideon because, wonders of wonders, he didn't complain.

I've had a change of heart for our lesson this evening. Instead of convening at your home, I want you to meet me in the archives at the university library at 5 p.m.

That was cutting it close. "We'll only have an hour before the library closes—"

I've arranged it already. Just be there at five with the remaining mirror and your dampening cloak.

I'd have to stop back home after Lee's and pick up the mirror, but it'd also allow me to cram something into my stomach besides coffee before our lesson.

"Fine, 5 p.m.," I said, shooting a glance at Aaron, watching me from the kitchen. "Anything else?"

Get inside or put on a coat. It's freezing and I can see you shivering.

I snorted at that, despite myself. But no more scrawl came, which meant Gideon was done. I pocketed the mirror and stepped back into the apartment. It was noon now and I needed to leave.

"Ah, work," I said to Aaron. "I need to go—wrap some things up."
Aaron didn't press, which I was glad for.

He walked me to the door and waited for me to slide my bike jacket on. "Please, Kincaid, will you go to Portland?"

I finished strapping my boot and stood up. Aaron was standing perfectly still by the door. I think it was the *please* that got me. And maybe my own ego.

"You've got me, Aaron," I relented as I eased my satchel over my shoulder, not wanting to jar the mirrors inside.

Aaron visibly relaxed. He hadn't been sure I'd say yes. Somehow that made me feel better about it. "Can you catch a flight down to Portland at six? Tomorrow? In the morning?"

I whistled. "Aaron, I thought you wanted me to help from the side of the living—not the dead."

He raised his eyebrows, giving me an imploring look—one he'd used to great effect many times before. It caught me off guard, as did the flutter in my stomach. It was always harder to think things through when he turned those pretty blue eyes on me.

"You're going to owe me one," I said, wondering how Gideon would take this. I mean, technically, my day job trumped our sessions, so travelling to Portland for a murder shouldn't raise any protest.

"Thank you, Kincaid." He grinned. "Do you need me to pick you up?"

"No," I said, perhaps a little too quickly. "I'll meet you there. You've got my details for booking?"

He nodded and there was another pause. "I'll see you at the gate at five-thirty? Ah—promise you won't—"

"I promise I'll make it to the airport in time. Just make sure I get the boarding pass tonight . . . *Really*," I insisted when the worried look didn't disappear.

An awkward silence stretched and I suspected the conversation was turning in a personal direction I didn't want it to go. Hoping to cut it off at the pass, I went for the door. "I'll keep an eye out for the boarding pass," I said.

"Kincaid . . ."

The ambush, strong-arming me into Portland, his disdain over my federal licence . . . My thin patience was at its end. I whirled on Aaron. "*What?*"

"We've barely talked since Max and Randall . . ." Aaron paused. "I just wish you'd tell me how you are doing."

But that wasn't what he was asking. He wanted an explanation—for all his calls that I'd let go to voice mail, my avoidance. Reluctantly, I could understand why.

"Look, Aaron, it's . . ." I hesitated. "I don't know what's wrong with me, Aaron. I'm not ready to talk—about any of it," I said, surprising myself with what I'd been avoiding telling him: the truth. I nodded at him and headed down the hallway.

I heard Aaron's front door shut behind him and winced.

"Kincaid, wait."

I stopped just shy of the elevator doors and braced myself.

"I'm trying, Kincaid," Aaron said as he reached me. "God knows I'm trying to understand—"

My temper flared. "What about my grieving isn't right for you, Aaron? Come on, I can see you're itching to tell me what I'm doing wrong with my life this time."

To his credit, he didn't take the bait. He shook his head and tried to make eye contact with me. "We don't talk anymore. At all."

"We just spent the last hour and a half—"

"Please just look at me."

Against my better judgment, I met his eyes.

"We used to talk about everything. Not just practitioner politics and the Seattle PD—the Otherside, Nathan Cade, hell, even the hypotheticals on long-lived zombies and the underground cities. But ever since—our—*my* problems," he corrected himself, "we've barely said a word unless there's a case involved."

He wasn't wrong. I stepped around him into the elevator. "I'm sorry, but we've grown apart. I'm not so sure that's a bad thing."

Aaron stopped the elevator door mid-slide. "I won't deny our relationship problems are my fault." He stared into my eyes, imploring me. "If that's really all there is to it—tell me and I'll stop giving you so much space. I thought that's what you needed, but . . ."

If only it were that simple . . . The part of me that craved the familiarity, stability and warmth he offered—what had been missing from my own family—wanted to say yes. But another part of me, albeit darker and colder, said that our troubles ran deeper than a change of scenery. As much as it pained me, that was the voice I listened to.

Part of me also wanted to tell him everything, about Gideon, Nate, Lee—but I didn't—couldn't—trust him like that anymore. And I felt guilty about it.

I stared at the polished elevator floor, anywhere but at Aaron's face.

"I'll see you at the airport tomorrow, Aaron," I said.

This time he let the doors close.

If only Aaron had said something weeks ago, after the debacle with Cole and Mindy—but that wouldn't have solved things either. Things had changed in my life, and Aaron was less and less a part of it. There was no sense dwelling on what might have been. As I rode down to the garage, the guilt morphed into something more sinister: hate for the weak part of me that still needed someone to trust and confide in.

Love stories always seem to be about a tempestuous affair that ends dramatically, or an unrequited love. But what about the loves that die a sick, slow death? Something that should have been cut off a long while ago but you've let its roots grow for so long that they're wound deep inside you, tightening by the minute. How do you extract something like that?

I couldn't love Aaron anymore, not with everything we'd been through. The mistrust and betrayal hadn't gone away—I still felt it keenly. And now that I was at Gideon's beck and call, well, that was an added complication, to say the least.

No, I was never going to tell Aaron about Gideon. I couldn't. Without a doubt, he'd never, ever, understand.

Aaron might be hurting, he might disagree with me, but he'd respect my space.

For now, a small voice inside my head said as I climbed on my bike and gunned it out of Aaron's underground parking. Why did he have to push, every single time? Or was there something wrong with me? I turned onto the road and shivered as a gust of wind hit me.

Maybe the Otherside had deadened me a little to the world of the living? Maybe it served me right.

I felt more alone than I had in months as I made my way back into Seattle to drop off the mirrors at Gallery 6.

As I headed for Richan's, the two mirrors tucked safely in my satchel, I pushed Aaron from my thoughts, replacing him with something useful, namely, the strangeness of the murders and Katy in her frozen state. As I rode, I set my mind to puzzling out just how the hell she'd got that way.

CHAPTER 4

TYING THE DEAD UP IN KNOTS

I reached Gallery 6 a little before 1 p.m., and even managed to find street parking near the front window. I checked the two mirrors first before lifting my satchel off the back, and was glad to see they hadn't chipped or cracked.

With a deep breath, I turned towards the gallery. Okay, Kincaid, let's get this over with.

Richan's space was right in the heart of downtown Seattle, near the convention centre, a tourist hot spot brimming with expensive hotels and a popular neighbourhood for wealthy Seattleites. It wasn't that I was intimidated—I was a guppy out of water. And I felt as if the people I passed on the sidewalk knew I didn't belong here as well.

Self-consciously, I slid off my leather jacket and tucked it into my bike satchel before pushing one of the tall glass doors open. I walked by two seaside paintings, one of a perfect day on a beach, the other the same beach but now with a storm brewing in the background. The contrast between the two was oddly soothing.

Richan might be a soothsayer, he might have made his fortune and business on the backs of ghosts, but goddamnit, I had to admit the man had taste.

I was relieved to see there were only three people in the gallery. A couple were speaking to Richan in front of an abstract painting in shades of yellow with splashes of black, orange and brown. I caught his eye, and though his silver eyebrows arched in recognition—not the pleasant kind—he didn't drop his salesman pitch for even a second.

I held up my open satchel and arched my own eyebrow, making sure to let a glint of the mirror's glass slip through, just enough grey to let him know what I was here for.

A brief flicker of surprise crossed his features. The smile didn't falter as he held up a hand with all five fingers, the universal sign for five minutes.

I nodded back and decided to peruse the art. Might as well. I had liked Cameron's art and hung the painting he'd given me above my couch. I'd refused to sell it when money was tight, even though it was easily the most valuable item in my apartment—no, make that the most valuable item I had ever owned. Still, I wouldn't part with it. Cameron had given it to me.

A nearby sculpture caught my eye. A life-sized kneeling man wearing a Venetian mask with a beaklike nose and brightly coloured robes. At first glance it looked as though he was prostrating himself to the heavens above, hands outstretched in prayer or pleading, a depiction of piety. And then I noticed the white finger bones reaching out of the ornate sleeves.

I leaned in closer. Sure enough, the glimpses of skin were mottled with a mixture of bone, tendons and muscles peeking through. Below the mask, the lower half of his face showed the same decay— half of his mouth was youthful, lifelike, pretty even, with full lips and a strong jawline, whereas the other half was bone, sinew and bared teeth. It was an incredibly realistic sculpture.

I peered through the eye slits of his Venetian mask. Two brown, lifelike eyes stared back at me. The artist had widened them into an expression of horror, not devotion.

Jesus Christ.

"It's a fantastic sleight of hand."

I jumped and swivelled.

Beside me, much closer than I would have liked, stood Samuel Richan, local soothsayer and self-made art expert, his presence every bit as cringe-inducing as I remembered.

He smiled, pleased with the discomfort he inspired. "The lifelike stare? More morbid than my tastes usually go, but the colours, the shape of the man—the inherent beauty in his build and bone structure, the clothes, the mask—it all distracts from the rot that's settled in. I had to have it."

Did he realize that the description suited him too? I opted not to point that out.

"Kincaid Strange. To what do I owe this pleasure?" he said. His mouth was fixed in a polite smile as he spoke, his voice was amicable, but his eyes conveyed a different sentiment entirely.

"Mr. Richan," I said, as politely as I could, trying my best to control the disgust I felt in his presence. I opened my bag to show him the mirrors, a smile plastered across my face, though I doubted it was anywhere near as convincing as Richan's. "I'm playing messenger today, I'm afraid. An acquaintance asked me to bring two art pieces in, of the mirror variety," I added, with emphasis.

Richan's eyes widened a fraction, but he only made a pleased sound, and held out his hands. "Ah, I was expecting these. Please, may I have a look?" He gestured towards the back of the gallery. I didn't want to go any farther into Richan's gallery than I had to but didn't see much choice.

"Lead the way."

I followed Richan to a white door that nearly blended in with the wall, and into a private work or storage room of sorts. There was a table, canvases, sculptures, most wrapped up but a few out and ready for display or inspection. Richan moved two canvases off his table, handling each carefully.

I placed my bag on the table and opened it, gingerly laying out each of the ornate silver- framed mirrors.

Richan clapped his hands and made another pleased sound as he picked up the first mirror. "You cast the bindings, I presume?"

Gideon didn't say anything about making pleasant chit-chat with Richan. "Don't you need to keep an eye on your customers?" I asked brusquely.

"My dear, what do you think I use ghosts for?" Richan said, rolling up his sleeves and exposing the scars that ran along his arms. He clapped his hands together once more.

Immediately, I sensed the change in the air, but only saw the shiver of Otherside that trails a ghost.

"Watch the shop," Richan ordered.

I felt the brush of Otherside as the invisible ghost headed for the storefront.

Richan turned his attention back to me. I tried not to stare at the latticework of scars on his arms. "Now, let us see what you've brought for me, shall we?"

In order to bind a ghost to the world of the living, it needs a tie and an anchor—preferably to something living. Oh, you can bind a ghost temporarily to an object or place, but it never lasts. That's where soothsayer scars come in—binding ghosts to the flesh of the living.

There were many symbols branded into Richan's arms that travelled up well past his sleeves. They were beautiful in design, if you could get past the red, burned flesh. Out of curiosity, I took a quick look with my Otherside sight. Thin, barely tangible whispers of Otherside lines drifted off his skin, like the delicately anchored threads of a spider's web, extending all the way back across the barrier. The tethers to his ghosts. There were dozens and dozens, and I noted with unease that some of the symbols near his wrists had gone dark. The ghosts who were already long used up.

If Richan knew I was looking at his brands, he decided not to comment—or look up from the mirrors. He made a show of turning them over, examining the edges and glass, as if looking for any imperfections. "As always, the frames are exquisite. Gideon knows my taste. Neither too ornate nor too plain." He turned the first over, examining the back. "Why, I rather believe these are antiques."

As Richan continued to examine the mirrors, I wondered how he could see the bindings. I didn't see any pooled Otherside that a practitioner might use to examine Otherside bindings. Did sooth-sayers like Richan have another way?

"Miranda," Richan called out, his voice carrying weight even though it was little more than a whisper. I watched as one of the Otherside threads tightened and began to vibrate, like a fishing line pulled taut.

I froze. That was the name of one of Richan's ghosts—the one he'd mentioned when I'd first met him in person at Club 9. A valu-able ghost to a soothsayer, one who could travel through time.

The ghost appeared, a young woman in a 1940s war ration–style dress, a dusty greyish yellow and red floral. Her hair was a dull brown, tinged with Otherside grey, of course, and her skin, ashen in death, looked as if it had once been a beautiful Mediterranean olive. Her face was youthful and retained some of the brightness she would have had while she was alive.

I shuddered. Miranda's eyes were hollowed and sunken, an unusually pale shade of grey.

A normal ghost except for her empty eyes—those carried decades of pain and sorrow. As I watched, she wrung her hands, her eyes darting around the room, reminding me of a fox my father had once caught in a trap in our backyard.

"Miranda," Richan snapped, "that's enough. Come here."

The ghost abruptly stopped her frantic movements and moved to Richan's side.

"I need you to look at the mirrors, Miranda— Ah, that's a good girl."

As I watched, Miranda stared at the mirrors, touching them with her fingers. As she did so, an Otherside glow settled over Richan.

"Beautiful work as always, wouldn't you say so, Miranda?"

The ghost nodded but kept her head down, eyes focused on the mirrors.

"The lines and symbols are exquisite," Richan continued. "Very stable. Yes, these will do marvellously. Send my compliments to

Lawrence. These mirrors most definitely meet my requirements."
He tuned his eyes on me. They were glowing, but not with the usual
gold. They had an Otherside ghost-grey cast.

He wasn't using Otherside, he was borrowing his ghost's eye-
sight. That was why Miranda's eyes were so sunken and tired-look-
ing, while Richan's were devoid of the symptoms of Otherside use
that should have plagued him, like they did me if I used too much.

I shivered and Richan smiled. "Ah, yes, I suppose you haven't
seen this particular method for seeing Otherside before. Consider
this a complimentary lesson—a tip, as it were, for delivering the
mirrors intact, and avoiding some of your more"—he looked me up
and down—"disagreeable tendencies. Your wardrobe has improved."

Taking a page from Gideon's book, I said nothing.

"Your new master's influence, I presume. So you're the new
apprentice?" he continued cheerfully.

I stayed silent. That only made Richan chuckle as he went back
to perusing the mirrors.

"She said it was you. My dear, sweet Miranda. I punished her for
telling falsehoods, though I suppose I owe her an apology. If I bothered with such things."

Don't engage, Kincaid. He's baiting you. I checked my temper,
stood up straight and slung my empty satchel over my arm. "Will
that be all, Mr. Richan?"

He peered at me with dark, narrowed eyes. Apparently a curt,
cool response was not what he'd been expecting. Or wanted. "What
exactly is it that Lawrence sees in you? I haven't a clue. You're brash,
undisciplined—Maximillian always said as much."

I drew in a sharp breath but remembered Gideon's warning
before I could answer. Under no circumstances was I to let on just
how deftly I could manipulate bindings and set mirrors—especially
freehand.

Richan misinterpreted the source of my discomfort. "Oh, yes,
we were professional acquaintances of a sort, your Maximillian
and I. Who do you think introduced him to Cameron? Though
if I'd had any idea what Cameron was really on about . . ." He

shook his head and *tsk*ed. "The folly of it. Here I was supposing Cameron was getting help from Max for his addiction. The financial loss in art sales alone . . ."

He watched me with keen interest, as if waiting to pounce on some shred, something I might do or say.

There was something more dangerous going on here than a discussion of Cameron's fate. Samuel Richan wanted something, and whatever it was couldn't be good for me. I swallowed back my anger. "That's quite a shame for you," I replied. Remember, Kincaid, the dead are tools to Richan, nothing more.

"I suppose Max never shared that we occasionally did business? Pity you'll have to take my word for it," Richan said carefully.

"Is that all?" I asked.

Silence stretched as he watched me, his lips pursed in displeasure.

"Yes," he finally said. "Go back to your tasks, errand girl, though I have to say I'm disappointed." He frowned. "I was expecting"—he made a waving gesture with his hands—"more."

He turned back to his mirrors and I took that as my dismissal. Fine with me. I was starting to think Gideon might be right—that there wasn't much behind Richan's growl.

I'd almost made it out of the workspace when a cold gust stopped me. Miranda floated between me and the workroom exit, peering at me with those sunken eyes.

"You," she whispered, her breath cold on my skin—which was odd for a ghost.

"Miranda," I whispered back, unnerved by the strange ghost's scrutiny. Miranda's expression was curious, critical even.

"They're waiting for you there," she said.

I shivered as the pale ghost-grey eyes bored into me, holding me in place with a sensation I didn't quite recognize. I tried to move but found I couldn't.

"Don't go," Miranda said. "It's better if you stay here. I can't see what will happen. They want you, to trap you, like all the others before." She shook her head. "Don't let them. Save yourself, Kincaid Strange."

I was caught off guard by both the strange warning and Miranda's odd, darting looks. Could she be talking about Portland? "Who is waiting for me? What do they want?" I whispered back, shooting my own furtive glance at Richan, who was preoccupied with the mirrors. "What should I be afraid of—is it Dane?"

Miranda only shook her head slowly. "Worse. What awaits you if you go—"

"Miranda!" Richan's voice was sharp and piercing, echoing off the ceiling and walls.

Miranda yelped and I felt her hold on me weaken. We both turned to see Richan walking our way.

"You wicked, wicked ghost," he scolded, his face twisted in rage, an expression that looked much more natural on him than the amicable smile. The evil shone through. "What did you tell her?"

Miranda, probably not the most stable of ghosts on a good day, crumbled. She cried out and twisted in upon herself, then in a burst of Otherside disappeared.

With his ghost gone, Richan turned on me. "What did you do to her?" he growled.

I shook my head. I still wasn't certain what had happened, or what she'd meant. "Nothing," I said. "She just stopped me. *Literally,* she stopped me—"

"You must have said or done something." I watched as another of Richan's brands flared gold. "And don't lie to me," he shouted, his voice carrying a menace that washed over me. He moved in close.

"I— Nothing," I said, unable to stop myself. "I did nothing."

Richan's eye narrowed. "My ghosts can't speak to anyone but me. People pay me great sums of money to speak to a ghost like Miranda." He reached out and grasped my arm at the elbow, pinching it.

Inwardly, I swore—I knew better than to let someone as dangerous as Richan get this close. Miranda had thrown me off completely.

He squeezed. "Tell me what she said."

"She—" I started, then stopped, as my head flared with a stabbing cold.

Richan swore and suddenly let go of me.

Light-headedness followed the painful chill. I reached out for the wall to balance myself. But with the light-headedness came a compulsion to speak. I stared at Richan. "What did you try to do to me?"

He grimaced, and I saw that he was clutching his hand as if it had been burned. Scratch that—it had been burned. I could see smoke tendrils, and the scent of seared skin hit me.

Gideon. That was the only explanation. But how? The bindings that gave me my Otherside sight—or the marks that spelled out the rule of our agreement—he must have hidden something else in them, a fail-safe or defence mechanism . . .

To stop someone like Richan from using Otherside on me. I realized what the soothsayer had tried to do, and it disgusted me. I glared at Richan and *tsk*ed. "Bad soothsayer." Jesus, binding ghosts and making the living do as he wished—no wonder Richan had made an absolute fortune.

"Tit for tat," Richan said, regaining his composure but still eyeing me warily. "A momentary and reflexive lapse."

I snorted, and Richan's mouth twisted. I'd somehow caught him off guard. No, Gideon had.

"Tell Lawrence it was a misunderstanding, and I won't pursue you stealing information from my Miranda."

"I already told you, I didn't steal anything from Miranda—she stopped me. There was little I could do but listen."

Richan bared his teeth at me. "She can't . . ." He trailed off, watching me once again with narrowed eyes.

I straightened my blazer. Damned, good-for-nothing soothsayer. I planned on asking Gideon what the hell Richan had tried to pull with the truth-telling compulsion. Was it borrowed sorcery like my Otherside sight, or something inherent to soothsayers?

"Go ahead and tell Gideon whatever you like," I said, and turned to go. Thankfully, the couple were gone when I stepped back into the gallery proper, and there were no wisps of Otherside to indicate the whereabouts of Richan's other ghost.

I strode as fast as I could across the floor, my motorbike heels clicking against the expensive, shiny tiles. It made me sick to my stomach to think how they'd been bought and paid for. On the backs of the dead.

I was near the entrance when Richan's clapping caught me off guard.

"Oh, I take it all back," he called out.

In spite of myself, I turned, my nerves still on edge.

"I see *perfectly* why Lawrence chose you as his apprentice. Bravo—and tell him I said that."

The words were harmless enough, but the threat was apparent. "Not interested, Richan. You might be able to hide what you are from the people who come in here, but I can see the kind of man you are just fine," I shot back. Those twisted scars running up his arms.

"Oh, and I almost forgot, the sculpture you were admiring—do you know why it's so special?"

I decided that my agreement with Gideon to be agreeable was more than satisfied. "It's as rotten on the outside as you are on the inside?"

Richan only smiled. "Why, he's dead, of course. Living Dead. More of an antique than art, but I like to think beauty transcends age."

I was close enough to the sculpture that it wouldn't take much effort to turn my Otherside sight on it. "You're bluffing. You said you had a distaste for the undead, remember?"

A slow smile spread over Richan's features. "Hmm, I suppose I did say that." His smile widened. "But that was before I found a use for one. I like my dead to be useful. Please," he said, gesturing at the man. "By all means, I'd be flattered if you'd give him a good look. Soothsayer to practitioner."

The smugness on Richan's face alone should have warned me off—but I looked anyway, and was soundly horror-struck by what I saw.

Sure enough, the trace of bindings—old, faded ones and newer, bright ones, layers upon layers of them—was there. It wasn't a sculpture made to look like a corpse. There was no doubt it was a zombie.

It had to be in agony, twisted into a beseeching position for how long? Was he even sane in there? Was there a person left?

I turned on Richan, fists clenched. "I ought to—"

"You ought to what, Kincaid Strange?" He waved at the zombie. "That is my property. A priceless piece of artwork I had specially imported from Italy—on loan, in fact, from Saint Mark's Basilica. Completely and totally my legal property."

I clenched my fists by my side, shaking in disbelief. But Richan continued, leaning in until I could smell his minty breath. "Do you really think you're the first practitioner who's tried to relieve me of my property? Take care, Kincaid Strange. I extend hospitality not to you but to your master. From the rumours I hear, you have difficulty leaving the property of others alone. Nothing more than a common *thief.*"

I just stood there, my throat dry. "You're a horrible, evil, small man."

His smile didn't falter. "You haven't a clue what real evil looks like, Strange. I hope for your sake the sorcerer breaks you of that arrogant streak. Ghosts, apprentices—they're like horses: only good after you've thoroughly whipped them."

I glanced away from Richan, back to the zombie, wishing I could free him.

"You disturb those bindings one bit, Kincaid Strange, and I will have the police down here in no time flat, arresting you for vandalism."

I would have liked nothing more than to destroy the bindings.

I didn't, though. Because Richan was right. And I didn't need to give the police any more bones to pick with me.

I headed for the door.

"Pleasure doing business with you, Kincaid Strange. You can be sure we'll be seeing a lot of each other. And send my sincere apologies to Gideon Lawrence for my earlier transgression. I'll pay whatever fine he deems fair for touching his property—"

I was out the door before I had to listen to another word.

Still shivering from the cold rage I felt for Richan, I climbed on my bike. I really needed to head to the underground city now—to tell Lee about the zombie and hopefully clear my head.

I'd managed to get out of Richan's with my backbone intact and my dignity only somewhat sullied.

Something else bothered me, though. Gideon. I had the sense I'd given away something about him to Richan—but I'd be damned if I knew what.

CHAPTER 5

COLD HEARTS ON THE GHOST TOWN TONIGHT

I picked up the whisky glass and held it to my forehead. The cool moisture felt nice—which was counterintuitive considering I hate the cold. I went with it. It was that kind of afternoon.

"Let's just say it could have gone a hell of a lot better, and leave it at that," I told Lee as she slid by with a tray of drinks for a group of zombies. Zombies that, unlike Richan's guest, were not frozen . . .

I'd made a beeline for Damaged Goods right after Richan's, and had spent the past twenty minutes filling Lee in. Rarely did I have a drink in the middle of the day or before a lesson with Gideon, but after my encounter with the soothsayer . . . Evil emanated off the man.

"Seriously, Lee, what is wrong with me? I had a simple set of instructions. How did I let myself get pulled into Richan's web?"

"A zombie, you say? Sane?"

I shook my head. Lee wasn't nearly as appalled about the zombie as I'd expected. "No idea—I couldn't speak to him—her." Or help them. I swirled the chilled stones in my glass and shuddered at the memory of Richan's final words to me.

I'll pay whatever fine he deems fair for touching his property.

I slugged back the remnant of my drink. "He was an *art* piece."

"Richan meant to scare you," Lee said, passing me a second whisky sour across the bar. "He is a master manipulator. He catches ghosts, after all. He would have to be."

"Well, he succeeded, with flying colours." On the ride over, and as I'd walked through the underground, I'd replayed the delivery of the mirrors again and again in my head. Several times I'd almost turned back around to see what could be done for the undead art piece. To hell with Richan and Gideon.

But in reality, I'd just been happy to get away from the soothsayer.

"If he went that far out of his way to intimidate you, there was a reason. What did you do?"

"Oh, for Christ— Lee, for once, can you stop it with the victim blaming? I swear to god, all I did was walk through the door and hand him the mirrors."

Lee *tsk*ed. "And in the process told him you are Gideon Lawrence's new apprentice. I imagine Richan hoped to earn that position himself."

I'd just taken a mouthful of whisky sour and did my best not to spit it over the bar, managing to keep it to a small dribble down my chin.

"Seriously, am I the last practitioner in Seattle to know anything?" I sputtered, wiping my face with my sleeve. Richan had known enough about Gideon to be gunning for my unwanted job? Oh, that did not bode well. Richan not liking me was one thing, but jealousy?

Lee sighed. "Richan is a long-standing member of the living paranormal community. A deplorable one for the methods he uses, but he is an expert on soothsayers and his art—both the paranormal and that which he sells," she clarified. "Rarely do the corrupt and evil-minded maintain good standing amongst the living unless they become adept with the politics and familiar with the players. Richan did just that. He is also the kind of man who covets power. It only makes sense that he would campaign to become Gideon's next apprentice, and, therefore, would want to determine for himself what qualities you possess that won out over his. I'm only surprised he didn't believe his ghost, Miranda, when she told him you were the apprentice. Miranda is very good at divining these things." Lee searched my face. "Tell me again what Miranda said to you."

That was another part of my encounter that had left me unnerved.

"She implied someone is hunting me." Or something. "And that I shouldn't go to Portland, I think. That they're waiting for me. I figured she meant Dane."

"Hmmm. Perhaps. Though even Dane's poltergeist should not be a threat to you. Or no more threat than you've dealt with recently."

I shook my head, took another sip and held up my glass. "With friends like you, Lee—"

Lee made a face. "Even if Dane's poltergeist is on a murderous rampage, you are an adept practitioner. He should be scared of you, not the other way around. No, I believe she meant someone else."

"It could be she was warning me away from Katy's ghost. She's paralyzed," I added, and quickly filled her in on the photographs, the ones Aaron had shown me of the murder scene and victim.

"Possibly," Lee said, though she didn't sound convinced. "Though that raises the question, why is she not a threat to anyone else?"

The bead curtain in front of Lee's saloon door rustled as more customers walked in, and Lee began lining up shot glasses on the counter. She added a spoonful of formaldehyde-preserved brains to the bottom of each glass before topping them off with absinthe. The nice thing about being a bartender for the deceased is that the dead tend to order the same things.

"No, I don't believe Miranda was warning you off the ghost, or even any one person. She speaks in riddles, not specifics. Remember, she may see the future, but the futures she sees are never set—only images, mirages, possibilities with their own mix of probabilities thrown in."

"So I have nothing to worry about?" Except a jealous Richan, an angry Gideon, a fresh Dane-style killing in Portland . . .

Lee pursed her lips as she reached for a bottle on the top shelf labelled *Whisky* with black marker. "I believe Miranda was warning you to be on the lookout. Miranda is an oracle. She is a very good diviner and reader of the future. If she says there is something waiting for you in Portland, I would caution you to be very careful. Or better yet, do not go. That is another wise course of action. Possibly the wisest." Her words hung in the air as she loaded the shot glasses on the tray and headed for the zombies' table.

I got the hint: that I rarely took the wise course of action as far as she was concerned.

I took another sip of my second whisky sour, and was mulling over Miranda's words when I felt a chill in the air.

"You're slipping, K," Nate said, appearing on the bar stool beside me. "Rumour has it you managed to piss off Richan in less than five words. Awesome. You know that conversation we had about you saving our collective skins?"

I shrugged. "I couldn't have pissed him off that much. You're not bound yet."

Nate narrowed his eyes at me. "You're a real asshole, you know that, K?"

I raised my glass to that. With Lee absent, he started to rummage behind the bar until he found a beer glass—which he began to fill.

Lee's problem.

Fresh glass of beer in hand, Nate glowered at the bar. Now that was odd. Nate usually perked up when he had beer. Come to think of it, it was also odd for Nate to be back this side already after a night out. "How was last night? You finally meet Edie Sedgwick?"

Nate sighed, looked up and gave me a sideways glance. "Okay, but you need to promise to be gentle with me."

I thought about it. "You know as well as I do it really depends on what you did."

He looked back down at the bar. "Here we were, having a couple drinks, talking music—she was totally into me. Then all of a sudden she gets up and says she has to go to the washroom, she'll be right back . . ." Nate looked over his shoulder, as if she might appear.

I stared at him. "Nate, she's a ghost, not a zombie, right? So she doesn't actually need to ever—"

"Habits are hard to break!?"

I glanced at Lee, who had returned to the bar. She took a look at Nate and shook her head.

"Nate, Edie is long gone, isn't she?" I said.

Nate sat up, slapping the bar with his hands, even managing to make a sound. "She ghosted me, all right?"

I raised my eyebrows at him. *Ghosted* had a number of connotations in this instance.

"Did she touch you somewhere she wasn't supposed to? It's okay, Nate, you can point to the spot on one of the zombies if it will make it easier."

He snorted at me. "Har de har har."

Nate might just have the worst taste in women—living or dead. I sipped on my whisky sour while he sulked. "She stuck you with the bar tab, didn't she?"

Nate shook his head. "I don't know what happened. Seriously, K, we were having an awesome time—ask Lee."

I glanced at Lee, but she was wisely staying the hell out of it.

"Then this zombie with really wild white hair wanders in and heads out the back, and the next thing I know, she's got to go to the bathroom and never comes back. I don't get it. What'd I do?"

I put my head between my hands. Jesus . . . "*Nate*, that was zombie Andy Warhol—she stood you up for Warhol." Might even have a racket going—the free bar-tab tour.

Nate's frown deepened. "The soup can artist? Do they know each other or something?"

"I—" I stopped. I was not getting into this with him right now. Remember, Kincaid, Nate was around before Wikipedia and Google. When you could still reasonably not know the obvious . . . "Google it, Nate." I returned his sideways glance. "You mean to tell me you've been here all night and all day?"

He gave me a sheepish shrug. "I mean, she said she was coming back, and then, you know, I was hoping . . ."

"You lost track of time, didn't you?"

Nate stared back down at the bar, looking more than a little embarrassed.

I decided to let him off easy. Nate had a blind spot left over from life. It was only a few weeks ago now that we'd found out Mindy, Nate's girlfriend while he was alive, had been the one to help orchestrate his death.

The fact that Nate had made an effort to meet someone else, after two decades of pining after Mindy Pine . . .

I took a sip of my drink—a small one. This was my second and I still had to ride to the library tonight. "You have a bar tab and I have a job for us, what do you say?"

Nate shook his head. "I don't know. Halloween kinda took it out of me. I mean, I know times have changed, but the campus concert where they had me dress up in fairy wings and all those kids had the rainbow horns on their heads—I mean, what was I supposed to be? A lumberjack fairy? Wouldn't that be the opposite of a fairy? Lumberjacks cut down trees."

"Unicorns, Nate. They were dressed as rainbow unicorns. And it's not another college concert. It's a murder case in Portland." I quickly filled him in on the new murder scene and the paralyzed Katy Price. "I just want you on call in case I need you to try and talk to her. It's a strange one, Nate. Ghosts don't normally stay still like that. I could use a ghost's perspective—and let's face it, you have an eye for things gone wrong with Otherside." It was true. Nate had an uncanny knack for spotting inconsistencies in Otherside, something not all the dead or practitioners have.

"You'll cover my newest outstanding bar tab with Lee?" Nate asked with a sigh. "Seriously, K, I had it paid off for—what? A month?"

Nate feeling bad about a bar tab . . . I gave him a surreptitious glance. "Who are you and what did you do with Nate?"

He sighed and gave me a crooked smile, a sadder one than I was used to. "I know, I know—ghosts don't change. That doesn't stop us all from trying occasionally, does it?"

My heart went out to him. Nate had been a reckless man-child obsessed with his music and living life to his version of the fullest. But that didn't mean he was shallow. Nate was aware of his faults, just as he had been while he was alive, and he wasn't blind to the consequences of his actions.

"This isn't me fronting your bar tab, Nate. It's work."

"Tomorrow?" he said, staring back at the bar, still melancholy.

I nodded. "Bright and early. Be listening in and ready to cross over and be my eyes and ears—invisible like."

He nodded. "I won't let you down, K." To Lee he said, "I'm out of here, Lee. K's"—he gestured at me—"you know."

Lee barely gave him a glance, looking to me instead for my nod. She knew I was good for it.

I waited until Nate vanished, and even checked to make sure he'd dispersed back to the Otherside, before waving Lee over again. It wasn't that I didn't trust Nate; he was easily one of the most loyal friends I'd ever had. He'd stuck by me during the past four months when I'd hit rock bottom. When Aaron hadn't.

But there were some things Nate really didn't need to know I was looking into. Especially since our conversation last night about not pushing Gideon.

"Any headway on what I asked you to look into?" I said, quietly, casually.

Lee glanced around the bar, but most of the patrons were well out of earshot. She leaned across, a wary look on her face. "I have. But I do not know if this is the path you wish to pursue."

"I'm not looking for a way out, Lee—I have no intention of breaking my bargains—not anymore. What I need is information."

Part of my new deal with Gideon, the one that made me his apprentice and assistant, was that I couldn't try to get out of the arrangement or do anything that might betray him.

But that didn't mean I couldn't arm myself with knowledge. Which was what I'd asked Lee to provide.

"I'm not pulling a fast one, I promise. I just need to know more about sorcerers and Gideon's history. Lee, I barely know what

I've gotten myself into. You said yourself I walked into this deal blindfolded."

Lee snorted, her green eyes narrowing. "I fail to see how your ignorance is my responsibility. Helping you arm yourself against Lawrence is not the act of a friend."

I made a face. Yeah, I'd thought she might have an issue with that part. "Try not to think of it as arming me. Think of it as helping me protect myself. From the unknown."

Her face hardened. "There is a fine line between survival and offence—take care to remember that, Kincaid." But she didn't walk away. "I made the inquiries on your behalf amongst my contacts. I didn't use your name, I simply said that Gideon had moved in and I wished to know as much as possible about the sorcerer."

"Lee—" Shit, I hadn't expected Lee to ask around so openly. The last thing I wanted was Gideon finding out and coming after her . . .

"Don't worry. The sources I used are very discreet. One, a historian, in fact, who specializes in the occult and less-known histories of the dead, turned up something promising. He knew of the sorcerer."

"Lee, can I stress how not good that is—"

She hushed me. "I said he knows of Gideon, but not for the reasons you think. He collects books—not spell books or anything that would attract Gideon or his ilk, but history books and diaries."

I sat back, mollified. If Lee said she knew what she was doing—well—she'd been the uncontested zombie queen of Underground Seattle for a century. Who was I to question her methods?

"What did they tell you?"

"Well, for starters, you mentioned Gideon was burned for witchcraft?"

I nodded. I'd found accounts in the university library—a reference to Gideon being tried for supernatural crimes. I'd also found out how long he'd been a ghost: a thousand years. I'd meant to go back to the text, had had the best intentions of retrieving it, but I hadn't done so, lest Gideon discover it. My relationship with the ghost was prickly enough as it was. Even if I wasn't trying to break our deal.

So I'd gone a different route. I'd turned to Lee.

"He gave me the impression the record of the event was muddled. That there was a woman involved and possibly a child that had precipitated a falling-out with his king or warlord, or whoever it was he served."

"What kind of falling-out?"

Lee shrugged. "Well, if a woman and child were involved, I suspect it was the sort of falling-out that's occurred all over the world throughout human history—one woman, two men."

"Gideon doesn't strike me as the kind of person to get in a bind over a woman."

"You'd be surprised what some men do for the attentions of a woman. Either way, my friend was under the impression that the falling-out had more to do with the child than the woman," Lee said, then disappeared into her office.

"Lee!" Leave it to her to wander off mid-conversation.

She returned a moment later, gliding gracefully towards me, her dress just barely brushing against the wood floors.

"Since you will be in Portland, there is a friend I would like you to call on—professionally speaking. In the Portland underground."

The Portland city of the dead—a sister to Seattle's underground. There were four underground cities of the dead along the west coast: Vancouver, Seattle, Portland and San Francisco. Seattle was arguably the largest and most important of the four. Though they all had access to the harbours and San Francisco had its fogs to cover the movements of the dead, Seattle still had the most robust underground trade economy and ease of travel. Forgotten railways, old tunnels, thick forests, a sea dotted with remote islands, and a dark sky at 3:30 p.m. in the dead of winter allowed even the more obvious dead to evade the eyes of the living. But Portland had its own charms. It was remote, and the locals seemed much less aware of the bustling city beneath their feet.

The four cities also had their own characters, personalities and varied populations. Portland was filled with frontier zombies and ghosts, and they had a reputation for shooting the living first, checking to see if you were a trespasser later. You did not want to find yourself alone in an underground Portland alleyway, especially not one with a zombie.

Even with my reputation as a practitioner and Lee as my contact, I'd hesitate to enter the Portland underground. The dead are protective of their secrets . . .

"Lee," I said carefully. "I don't know if I'm going to have time for the Portland underground. I have no idea how long I'll be staying—or how busy Aaron or the FBI will have me on site."

"My historian acquaintance resides in San Francisco and I asked him to send the journal that mentions Gideon to my friend in the Portland underground. It arrived this afternoon."

She pulled a white card from her pocket and passed it to me. It had been decorated on one side with Lee's red calligraphy-like handwriting: *Honoured representative of Lee Ling Xhao*. On the back was written a name in blue pen: *Celeste Bergenn*.

"I've told her to hold the journal for you." She lifted her eyebrows. "For a small favour."

Of course there was a favour. "I notice you're conveniently distancing yourself from the journal and me in case Gideon gets wind."

"And using the favour you now owe me for procuring the book to pay back one of my own. You are welcome," Lee said, with a perfectly straight face.

I was reminded once again why Lee was the undisputed queen of the zombies. I gazed at the card. The name didn't ring a bell, but I'd never made myself familiar with the Portland zombies. "What does she need?"

"A good practitioner, for starters. She needs some—help," Lee said after a moment. "I would go myself or send Mork, but since you will be there . . ."

Helping a zombie. That could mean a number of things, from reworking bindings to tissue preservation to running errands above ground. Still, it was in my wheelhouse, and in exchange for a book detailing Gideon's past . . . "Provided I can get away from the crime scene, and—much bigger if—they let me past the gate."

"They will."

I let out a breath. Lee couldn't be that confident without reason. "Where can I find this Celeste Bergenn?"

"She runs the Mandarin Boarding House."

"Chinese territory?"

Lee shook her head. "The interior. The city proper." She took the card back and added a phone number. "She will be expecting you. Call her if you run into problems—which you won't." She handed it to me, and I slid it into my jacket.

"No promises," I warned, lest Lee get the wrong idea that it was a done deal.

"I am confident your curiosity over the sorcerer's history will inspire you past any inconvenience." She glanced up. "You will do your best, though?"

I sighed. "Yes, I promise I'll do my best." And I would. I didn't promise Lee anything lightly. And she was right, I wanted to read whatever that journal had to say about Gideon for myself.

I'd probably be in Portland overnight and reasoned I could slink off for a couple of hours in the evening. Besides, the Portland underground might not be a half-bad place to ask some questions about murderous ghosts in the area.

Another underground city—with its own zombies, rules and arcane quirks. I felt a twinge of anxiety.

Lee caught the change in my mood. "Are you upset with my bargain? Is there a problem?" she asked, her eyes narrowing.

"No—of course not." I patted my jacket pocket where I'd tucked the card. "Thank you for this. I owe you. I just . . . I don't know, Lee. I used to think I knew about the Otherside and the dead, but lately—"

One of her black, perfectly drawn eyebrows arched. "You have been made aware of just how much you do not know?"

I nodded. "It's not just one thing, Lee. A wraith, a Jinn—those things I could overlook. But lately it's everything. The paralyzed ghost in Portland, Aaron and everyone else insisting Martin Dane is somehow involved, hell, take my job last night," I said, and filled her in on Astrid, my baby poltergeist ghost.

Lee listened, with great interest.

"She's still only a ghost, Lee. That much I'm certain of. I checked. There's no *real* danger." Provided the Youngs listened to my warnings about not hosting any dinner parties in the near future . . . "Or not yet."

Lee looked unconvinced. "I would tread carefully. Some ghosts seek out practitioners like you—"

I made an incredulous face. "They're *all* looking for practitioners like me, Lee."

She continued as if I hadn't said anything at all. "—*and* some don't always know their own machinations until it's too late. Ghosts are selfish by nature, but they can also be predatory. And sometimes the dead's selfishness allows them to circumvent the laws of Otherside. It would serve you well to remember that."

I'd learned over the years that Lee didn't caution against something unless there was a very good reason. "Astrid couldn't break past my pentagram—she had to play by the rules, just like any other ghost I've summoned," I said, though not as certain as I had been a moment before.

Lee was quiet for a moment as she rearranged the glasses in the well. "Think on this: if no one bothers to tell you that a door is closed to you, are you breaking a rule when you open it? Perspective is crucial. On occasion the dead find themselves with control over the Otherside they shouldn't have. I'm not saying that that is the case here, but there may be more than meets the eye. Like this Martin Dane," she said, stopping to fill a glass for a heavily bearded ghost in logger's red flannel that appeared at the bar a few seats down. "You are certain Martin Dane cannot be involved?"

"Well, Aaron and an entire team of FBI schooled in the paranormal are apparently convinced he is, though they're all playing their cards close. They want a cold read."

"I thought that was your preference," Lee said, whisking my empty glass off the bar. "Going in on a case blind. For objectivity's sake."

"I can't shake the feeling that Aaron and the captain are hiding something on purpose—something they really don't want me knowing before I'm on site. That worries me."

"Yet you won't know until you get there. No?"

No, I wouldn't. And that was the problem with Miranda's warning as well, wasn't it? I checked the time. It was 4 p.m. now. An hour until my lesson. I wanted to get to the library early and do my homework in peace. I settled up my bar tab, grabbed my satchel and headed for the saloon doors.

"One last thing, Kincaid," Lee called before I had slipped out the door. I waited as she set a tray down and glided around the bar and across the floor, more gracefully than I think most professional ballet dancers could.

My first warning should have been that Lee didn't shout what she wanted across the floor. She waited until she was within whispering distance.

"Be careful in the Portland underground, Kincaid. You will gain entry, but they aren't nearly as welcoming to practitioners as we are here. Tread carefully, and keep your eyes open."

I nodded, and pushed the saloon doors open once again. "Lee, don't take this the wrong way, but if that was your attempt to inspire confidence . . ."

"Safe travels," Lee said.

I braced myself for my lesson with Gideon as I walked away from Damaged Goods and through the Seattle city of the dead to collect my bike from the rain sewer.

I wondered how the sorcerer's ghost would take my Portland job . . .

Knowing Gideon, it wouldn't be good.

CHAPTER 6

CARROTS AND STICKS

I stopped at my apartment to retrieve the third mirror and hit traffic on the way to the library at Washington State University campus, then made a pit stop at a coffee shop to read the chapters on ghost binding, making sure to conceal the book behind my bag. You never know when someone with a bone to pick against practitioners might be lurking nearby—with phone camera ready to instantly post images to social media. I reached the library with only fifteen minutes to spare, locked my bike and ran up the front steps.

The paranormal archives desk was unoccupied by the ghostly librarian who haunted the floor, but an access card had been left out—something Gideon had arranged, I imagined. The librarian had died in a car accident a few months back but, oddly enough, the library had yet to replace her ghost with a living librarian. I wondered if that might be Gideon's doing as well. It was hard for the dead to keep inhabiting their old lives once the living world around them stopped pretending as well.

I headed into archives and quickly unpacked the remaining mirror, checking to make sure no damage had been done in my haste.

Since the paranormal floor of the library conveniently held a massive reference library and was neutral ground, as Gideon liked to say, we often used it for our frequent work sessions. Initially, I'd lugged practice mirrors I was working on between the apartment and here until an evening two weeks ago when I'd dropped one, cracking it and rendering the bindings useless. After that, Gideon had made a deal with the ghost librarian to guard a collection of mirrors we kept here from prying eyes. I retrieved them from their hiding spot, tucked behind the books on a shelf in the back corner.

Ten minutes and counting until Gideon arrived.

I unwrapped the practice mirrors and added the mirror from my bag to the pile. A ghost binding mirror of a sort—I was even more certain since I'd delivered two to Richan. I couldn't quite stifle the shiver as my fingers brushed against the primed Otherside. Maybe it was only my imagination, but unlike some of the other sorcery-related bindings Gideon had me doing, these ones felt wrong. Sick, even.

A cold breeze wafted up against my shoulder as I examined the mirror.

"Gideon?" I called out. The floor was deserted, and it wasn't like him to arrive early. Still, the Otherside chill didn't fade—and it wasn't coming from the mirrors.

I abandoned my mirror and searched the area. Maybe the librarian had returned. "Carol," I called, "is that you?"

Still no answer. That was odd. The chill in the air was definitely paranormal in origin. I slid my Otherside sight into place and checked the desk, then behind the shelves. Still nothing.

But the chill was intensifying. There was no trace of Otherside, except from the mirrors on the table where I'd left them.

There.

I spotted a halo of Otherside in the air beside me—not as intense as a binding or symbol, or even a ghost, but it was there, thicker than it should be.

As if it had slid across the barrier through a mirror or a weak point. But there was no weak point in the library.

So where was it coming from? Not the mirrors. I scanned the immediate area and caught my reflection in the window. It was clear against the darkening sky, but cast in Otherside grey. That must be where the halo of Otherside had come from—the window. I knew for certain there had been no weak point in the barrier there before. Well, Gideon was certainly capable of setting a window.

A test? That wasn't like the ghost—he preferred precision over surprises, and an apprentice with hands shaking from fear didn't make for precise bindings.

But if not Gideon, then who—or what?

"Sometimes the rules of the Otherside get broken," Lee had told me.

I couldn't stop myself. Quickly, before it dispersed, I walked over, my heart pounding. I reached the window, and sure enough, there was a thin fog of Otherside seeping out, pooling inside the glass. There was no set that I could see—no lines, no symbols, no bindings. The window reminded me of the weak points near the water, or the iron Pergola in Old Seattle when it rained. A natural weak point that leaked Otherside.

But that shouldn't be possible—there was no salt water here, no iron—and mirrors and windows had to be set. They didn't just *become* weak points.

Impulsively, I reached out and brushed my fingers against the greyish glass.

Ice ran through me, an inviting pull. Unstructured Otherside, wild, searching, like water through a canyon, and it had found what it wanted—or something close enough.

The sane voice at the back of my head piped up: *Otherside isn't wild, Kincaid. It's an element, like water or wind. It doesn't think, it doesn't seek out, it just is.*

Despite the chill, despite the raw Otherside burning my nerves, I wanted nothing more than to leave my hand where it was. My inner voice screamed at me not to touch Otherside I didn't understand.

I pulled my fingers back, albeit reluctantly. And that's when it struck.

A slick of Otherside snaked out of the window, and tendrils of gold crept up my arms.

Desperation, fear, longing overwhelmed me.

But there was a wrongness about it, an inky-black pit of despair and anger that was wound through, like rot through a tree, seeking me out, looking for somewhere inside me to dig in its hungry claws and drag me down. Something very dark.

It had found me. And it liked what I had to offer.

The pull of it, the way it coiled towards me . . .

An obsession.

I yanked my hand back and stumbled into the desk behind me, then braced myself and prepared to attack. To strip every trace of Otherside off the glass surface and send whatever was behind it back where it belonged . . .

I started to pool Otherside. And stopped. What had scared me? The window? I searched the glass, but there was nothing there. I rubbed my hands and wrists, which stung, despite there not being a mark on me.

A mark from what? I searched the library, but besides myself, nothing was here.

I worked my wrists, but try as I might, I couldn't shake the feeling that something had been stalking me, watching me, lying in wait. But my mind felt fuzzy—I couldn't land on a thought.

Gideon had stalked me for days, thinking I was a thief—but this . . . this felt more predatory, primal. It made me ill.

That was it. I shook my head as a flicker of my memory pierced the fog. Something had reached out for me, and whatever it was felt of rotting, decay. It felt infectious, *sick*.

The fog cleared as I held on to that sick feeling . . .

"Psst. What are you looking at?" a woman's voice whispered beside me, young and curious.

I swore and spun round, coming face to face with one Astrid Young. She was sitting on the desk beside me, cross-legged and dressed in a red-and-black plaid skirt, moto leather jacket and matching motorcycle-styled boots. Her hair was artfully braided and laid across her shoulder. She was close, her face mere inches from mine—appearing inquisitive as she looked from me to the window. Her rage from the evening before had apparently vanished like so much Otherside smoke.

I swore again. I'd been so engrossed in the damn— I frowned. What had I been engrossed in? It was on the tip of my tongue, a sensation.

I searched the desk. The mirrors? That didn't sound right—

"Well?" Astrid asked.

Well, whatever it was, it was gone now. I could look for it later.

I turned my full attention on Astrid. She sat calmly, expectantly, now waiting on the library desk.

A number of questions ran through my head. The most important one made its way to my mouth and vocal cords.

"What the hell are you doing here?"

Ghosts cross the barrier all the time—through mirrors left open, or more frequently through weak points in the barrier. They pop up all over Seattle—especially at this time of year, when the rains set in—and of course there are always ghosts hanging out by the water. But the mirrors I kept here for my lessons weren't portals. Nor was the soothsayer mirror.

Unless Astrid had come via another mirror and found her way to me . . . I remembered how Nate had been attracted to the soothsayer mirrors when I removed the wool blanket of obfuscation. The way it was removed now.

Confirming my theory, Astrid pursed her lips and gestured at the exposed mirror on the table. "Well, I went looking for you—I was hanging around your apartment, as a matter of fact—or, well, around your mirrors." She frowned. "You know how hard it is to get a glimpse of anything in your apartment?"

I sighed. "That's on purpose, Astrid," I said, not unkindly. After all, Astrid was a new ghost and I was a practitioner. It wasn't exactly going against her nature to seek me out. "You're not supposed to be able to walk in on any practitioner you want. It's called privacy."

Her lips stayed pursed, but her forehead crinkled. "That doesn't seem fair at all. Especially considering the retainer my parents have paid you. I would think I should be able to stop in any time I like."

I shook my head. "Not the way it works. How did you cross over?" I added, to get her back on topic.

"Well, it wasn't easy," Astrid said, pouting, as if pained by the memory. "I looked and looked for a spot, and none of the other ghosts were any use. They kept sending me on goose chases— All right, all right! I'm getting to the point," she rushed as I crossed my arms. "It took a while, but eventually I found my way across the downtown core—through the big wrought iron gates."

"The Pergola," I corrected her, closing my eyes.

"Yes, well, I crossed over and then was wandering all over Seattle looking for you. I was trying to find your home when this"—she wrinkled her nose—"beacon? like a lighthouse? or a big flashlight?— was over this way, so I came looking. And here I am." She smiled broadly. "And here you are!"

Well, at least part of that made sense. The Pergola, left over from the early twentieth-century world's fair in Seattle, is a large wrought iron gate. Iron conducts Otherside spectacularly well, an effect that is only helped by the rain. The gate is a well-known portal for ghosts. In theory, if Astrid had been focused entirely on finding me, she might have inadvertently attuned herself to my Otherside signature before she crossed over. And it was possible that the unwrapped mirror could have acted like a beacon, leading her right to me, confirming my theory that the mirror lured ghosts in.

Maybe that had been the Otherside strangeness I'd felt a moment before? Astrid's obsessive search for me turned sickly? When it came to Otherside, odder things had happened.

I chewed my lip as I thought about the best course to take with her. The amount of effort and energy Astrid had expended to cross over and find me was troubling. It was obsessive, more than I liked to see in a ghost, and though she wasn't angry or exhibiting any of the poltergeist tendencies I'd seen before, it was still grounds for worry. Not least because it seemed centred on me . . .

"So, now that that's out of the way, what are we doing?" Astrid said cheerfully, smiling and clapping her hands.

The best way to get across to a ghost that they do not have permission to monopolize your attention is not to give it to them in the first place. I was well past giving Astrid my attention, jumping at her appearance like a practitioner on their first summoning.

I turned my back on Astrid and focused on the mirrors and the book I was supposed to be reading, covering the slight shake in my hands.

Astrid, being a ghost—a demanding one—didn't take the hint. "Hey—I spent all that time trying to find you, come on now! I need your guidance. That's what my parents are paying you for, no? And what are you doing with the bright, pretty mirror? I can't see you with your back to me."

I felt the Otherside chill as she peeked around my shoulder. Nope, definitely not taking the hint. I caved. "I'm busy—and about to be busier. What do you really want?"

She opened her mouth, closed it and opened it again. "I'm bored. And lonely," she added, throwing an imploring look at me.

I stopped short of rolling my eyes. "Well, then, I suggest you try and make some friends." I focused on the chapter Gideon had wanted me to read: "Ghost Binding Basics for the Advanced Practitioner."

Still Astrid didn't let up. "I tried that! I did, really! But I'm as bad at making friends with ghosts as I was with people. What *is* that you're reading?"

Gideon would be here any minute. The chapter on ghost bindings showed a slightly different configuration from the one I'd used on the mirrors for Richan, a different anchoring symbol, but there was so much cross-linking on both my practice mirrors already . . . "My homework," I said to Astrid, and added, "I'm working on ghost traps. For my teacher." I turned to face her, leaning in despite the chill. "They're like catnip for ghosts," I said conspiratorially. "That's probably why you like it so much."

I worked hard not to smile as Astrid's face blanched, even for a ghost. I went back to the practice mirror, tweaking the bindings until I was satisfied they matched the ones in the textbook. I wouldn't dream of using a ghost binding mirror on Astrid—but she didn't know that, and it was good for her to learn that not all practitioners are benevolent. There were one or two practitioners, besides Richan, in Seattle who had bite and wouldn't think twice about having some fun with a newbie ghost like Astrid.

Ah—there was where my symbol went. I added it to the practice mirror and felt the brush of cold over my shoulder as I started the last adjustment. Astrid was over her fear. "That one doesn't look dangerous—are you sure you've done it right?"

With a bit of quick Otherside work, I linked the symbol and finished the mirror. There.

I stepped back to admire my work. The practice mirror almost perfectly matched the ghost trap now. To be honest, I had a hard time telling them apart . . .

I checked over my shoulder. Astrid was still there—paler as she stared at the mirrors, hands gripped around the edges of the table as if to hold herself in place. It was futile, a reflex from life, but she did it anyway.

I shook my head and checked the time. It was 5 p.m.

"Look, Astrid, I'm sorry if you're lonely and having trouble making friends, but you need to try. Start small. Find a ghost boy toy, or set up a drag race. You like fast cars, and this time you can't kill yourself." I cringed as soon as it left my mouth.

Astrid looked at the ground. "I get it. You don't want me here. I'll go."

The guilt really sunk in. Astrid was lonely—and her family had me on an expensive retainer. And in the last few minutes, despite the strange, obsessive Otherside I'd felt when she first appeared, there'd been no sign of poltergeist-like behaviour. I supposed that deserved some kind of reward.

Rarely did I ever get to help ghosts. Usually I was corralling them—or moderately managing them.

Before I could second-guess myself, I said, "Look, Astrid—I'm too busy to dea—talk to you right now. Seriously, though, there's a ghost about to show up who scares the shit out of me. He won't take kindly to an audience. But what about another day? What if I called you over to talk sometime later this week? Promise," I said, when she looked skeptical. "I don't lie to the dead," I added softly.

And that was true.

Astrid pursed her lips, mulling it over. Just when I thought I'd have to send her packing the hard way, she cheerfully said, "Deal! But you promise it will be this week?" She gave me a sideways glance. "This isn't another practitioner's trick?"

Just how many practitioners had Astrid's parents employed before me? Astrid had only been dead a few weeks, and there weren't that many of us in Seattle.

"Yes. This week. But no more spontaneous appearances or haunting your parents to get my attention. Deal?"

She nodded emphatically, then turned up her nose as there was a spike of Otherside in the air around us.

"What is that?" Astrid said, looking nervously for the source.

I smiled. "The ghost I mentioned," I said, and added, "One who can cross the barrier all on his own. Stick around and you can say hi."

Astrid sniffed at the air and all of a sudden her eyes widened. "Are you crazy? I want nothing to do with him!" She vanished just as Gideon materialized a few feet from where she'd been hovering.

Well now, that was interesting. Just the scent of Gideon scared ghosts besides Nate. I'd have to remember that when I did summon Astrid.

As he took form, Gideon's ghost-grey eyes zeroed in on the table and mirrors. He sniffed the air before narrowing his gaze on me. "Who was here? Not the librarian, and certainly not your thief of a ghost."

I sighed. Gideon had taken to calling Nate a thief since he'd accidentally stolen a body from Gideon.

"No, a ghost I'm being retained to manage. She was haunting her parents." Gideon gave me a strange look, so I added, "They're paying me a nice retainer to make her stop being—well, herself. She was on her way to becoming a poltergeist. I've talked her down from it—sort of. She's a little obsessive. She came looking for me and the mirror—this mirror," I said, pointing at the remaining ghost trap.

"Ah," he said, his expression finally relaxing as his eyes settled on the mirror and the modified practice one beside it. "Yes, she would have been drawn to the ghost trap. It also explains why she smelt so hungry. The ones that hunger for their lives are always the first to come calling. Best not to encourage too much familiarity with her. She'll get greedy for your attention quickly. Draw your boundaries clearly and be firm."

I ignored the fact that Gideon had in effect just ordered me around my own day job. "Hungry? Greedy? That describes every ghost I've ever met."

Gideon *tsk*ed and inclined his head. We'd discovered that if we kept our conversations to bindings and ghosts, Gideon's pettiness—no, that wasn't quite it—irritability?—whatever the issue, it was less apparent when we talked shop.

In all honesty, I was so interested in what Gideon had to say about practitioning, ghosts and Otherside that I sometimes forgot about our arrangement. Or my bargains. The broken one and the one I was attempting to keep.

"There are as many shades of ghosts as there are people. I'll find you some appropriate reading material. The task at hand, please?" He gestured towards the mirror. "Your analysis?"

I decided to keep the strange, sickly Otherside I'd felt while Astrid was there for a later discussion. "Well, it's a ghost binding mirror. So were the other two I handed off to Richan today—and, not that you care, but he was an ass."

Gideon raised his hand. His eyes closed as he listened to me. He often did that. It was a feint, he could still see me just fine. Ghosts don't need eyes to see. Like flies, they can be facing away and still be watching you—or not. Sometimes they aren't paying attention when they appear to be staring straight at you. Gideon, I'd determined, closed his eyes when he was concentrating.

"Richan is always an ass," he said, surprising me. I'd assumed Richan and he were amicable. "And I care a great deal what the specifics of his reaction were, but we'll get to that in a moment. The mirrors?"

"You mean you sent me in there knowing he would try and scare the shit out of me—"

Gideon's eyes opened and they were darkening. "*The mirrors.*"

I knew a warning when I heard one. "I already told you, the three of them were—are—ghost binding mirrors." I trailed off. The way he was frowning had me second-guessing myself. "They *are* ghost binding mirrors, aren't they?"

He *tsk*ed. "Of course they are. Let me be more precise. What are the differences between this one and the two I sold to Richan? Since the other two mirrors are no longer in your possession, you may use your notes," he said, gesturing towards my research binder.

"Ah—well . . ." I started as I flipped through the pages. I hadn't a fucking clue.

"While you search, you can tell me what Richan did."

I gave Gideon a rundown of our meeting, complete with Richan's bullying tactics. "And he even has a goddamned zombie statue in his lair of an art gallery. An art piece from Venice!"

Gideon didn't look surprised. "Richan always was what you now call a drama queen. If he went out of his way to resort to threatening you, it was because Miranda was unpredictable." He flipped the pages of my textbook ahead and tapped the page. "It's a problem all soothsayers have with their more talented ghosts— do you know why?"

I shook my head as I searched the detailed illustration of a ghost trap Gideon had indicated.

Typically, ghost traps have two independent rings—one for attracting ghosts and one for trapping them. The mirrors I'd given Richan functioned this way, but the one I'd kept had points of crossover . . .

"Because a ghost that can jump through time inevitably jumps to times and places where their masters do not exist yet or are already dead," Gideon said. "It means a soothsayer's hold over their ghosts, despite the leashes that transcend time and the barrier, are little more than tentative. Richan is an anchor for Miranda, but he's not as much her master as he'd like the world to believe. No soothsayer is. It's one of their weaknesses. Contrary to his bluster, he spends a great deal of time placating Miranda and a few of his other ghosts. Otherwise, one day he might send them off and they will simply decide not to return. It's happened to him a number of times before."

Hunh. I'd assumed the ghosts were tied and bound to soothsayers.

"*Most* of a soothsayer's ghosts are bound to them, but those ones don't have the ability to traverse time. They're nowhere near as valuable as a ghost like Miranda. A ghost like her cannot be truly bound and therefore is never truly controlled. Now, was that all he said?"

I opened my mouth to say yes, then remembered that that hadn't been the case. "After Miranda spoke to me, he changed his tune and said he knew exactly why you'd hired me—and wanted me to tell you that." It hadn't seemed all that strange at the time—not with Miranda's cryptic warning about Portland and Richan showing me his trapped zombie, but come to think of it . . .

"Hmmm," Gideon said, watching me. "And nothing else? You're sure?"

I racked my brain. "I don't think so." I started to count off on my fingers. "Richan opened with arrogance, tried to goad me into picking a fight and then got thrown off by Miranda. I tried to leave, he yelled some more, then tried to scare me with the zombie." I shrugged. "If there was some other meaning, I missed it."

Gideon shook his head thoughtfully. "No. Despite Richan's polished appearance and wealth, he's still a lowlife at heart. His behaviour is consistent with that of a well-spoken thug."

"Is he right?" At Gideon's quizzical look, I added, "About knowing why I got the job. Is there something I don't know that he does?"

"Oh, I imagine Richan believes he has deduced something useful to him." Gideon gave me a thoughtful look, one that was devoid of his usual irritation, then added, "We have a serious problem, Kincaid."

Shit, he knows about Lee looking into his past . . .

I held my breath, and after more beats than I would have liked, he said, "But it's not your fault and there's no point concerning yourself over it right at this moment." He picked up my notebook and started flipping through the pages. Checking my work. "What does have me very concerned are Miranda's words. She is a ghost who is rarely wrong." His forehead furrowed and he glanced back up at me. "And why the hell is it you're going to Portland in the first place? And why the hell am I the last to hear of it?"

Ah, there was the cold, accusing tone I was used to.

As quickly and succinctly as I could, I described the case, and the peculiar circumstances surrounding Katy Price.

"I agree with your assessments," Gideon said when I was finished. "It is unlikely the ghost of Dane is perpetrating the murders, as tidy as that would be for the authorities. It is much more likely a copycat, as you suggest. For a poltergeist to do anything without an audience . . . And I assume they've attempted multiple summonings . . ." He trailed off and glanced at me again.

And here's where he forbids you from going, Kincaid.

"*But* Miranda's warning, the paralyzed ghost and the intensity with which the police seem convinced some paranormal element of the Otherside is involved most definitely warrants your interest. I approve of the excursion. I'll make appropriate arrangements in Portland."

"Appropriate arrangements?" I said. "I— Lee already got me a pass into the Portland underground—"

Gideon stopped me with a dark look. "As much as I appreciate Lee Ling Xhao's influence and power, there are paranormal elements and individuals she will overlook. I will make the arrangements by this evening. You will not have to deal with any of them, but they should know that we'll be there."

"We?" It came out—oh, hell, it came out exactly as I meant it.

Gideon gave me a sharp look. "I have work I need you to complete—and besides, I'm rather interested in this murder scene myself now. There aren't many natural phenomena that can paralyze a ghost in time or place, and just as few paranormal manipulations that can accomplish it. You saw an example of one today at Richan's."

I sighed. "I don't— Look, it's not that I—"

And there was the warning look again and the glittering black eyes. "*Thank me*, Kincaid. Knowing your propensity for almost getting yourself killed as of late, it'd be the most prudent thing you could do." Another arched eyebrow from where he sat on the table. "See? I'm not always the villain of the story."

My jaw clenched involuntarily. We'd been doing so well.

I couldn't stop myself. "In what universe are you not the villain? Seriously, inquiring minds really want to know how you spin that one."

For all his bluster, for all his arrogance, the ghost actually looked taken aback. "I've just offered to help you on one of your cases. For *free*."

There was that flicker of gold to match the black.

"Gideon, we're sitting here making *ghost binding* mirrors—for someone like Richan to use. If that doesn't make us bad guys, I don't know what does. Wait—I'm not the bad guy, I work for you under duress." I aimed a finger at the ghost's chest. "*You're* the bad guy here."

Gideon's cool composure vanished, and his eyes turned that dark, glittering black. "All mirrors are tools," he said, his eyes lowered and predatory, his voice icy. "They're about as evil or good as—"

"As a frying pan," I said. "Yeah, I haven't forgotten."

"And I don't like repeating myself," he warned.

I chewed my lip. He didn't get it. I grasped for an analogy, *any* analogy that didn't have to do with the dead. "Okay," I said, refusing to give in to my fear of Gideon's temper. "Pretend we're not making ghost binding mirrors. Pretend we're—I don't know, gun suppliers to train bandits. That's it! Imagine we sat out on the tracks and sold guns to bandits on their way to rob trains."

Another frown from Gideon. "A hundred and fifty years ago that might not have been a half-bad idea. There certainly would have been a demand."

Oh, for god's . . . "Except that we'd be giving things to the train robbers that we *knew* they would use to shoot people. Innocent people. Like the innocent ghosts that soothsayers use ghost traps on. Oh, come on, Gideon. You can't be that dense!"

His eyes shifted to an even darker shade, and the glitter of gold Otherside vanished. "I'm not dense, Kincaid Strange," Gideon said, his voice calm and even, frighteningly so. "And we agreed two weeks ago to cease with the verbal barbs."

We had agreed to that.

Gideon rolled his eyes. "My point is that you assume the sale of a dangerous tool equals ill intent, and judge both my clients and the train robbers accordingly without considering circumstance. It's a prejudice people of your age bring all too frequently to negotiations."

"Okay, but we both know Richan—"

"And I sold him what I consider a pair of *appropriate* mirrors."

That stopped me. The way he emphasized *appropriate* . . . I was missing something.

I turned my attention back to the third mirror and thought back to the bindings. Gideon had meticulously specified them, laying out the exact patterns he'd wanted. He hadn't left much room for improvisation, which was unusual. Gideon appreciated my skill set for improvising bindings from scratch and my freehand work, my ability to "draw" Otherside directly to my medium without a need to tether it to a china marker before setting things in place. But Max had been a traditionalist. He preferred to check my work before letting me finish a set. And while he'd appreciated my talent for mixing and matching bindings from different schools to find the most efficient method, he'd considered it showing off. It was one of the things that had finally driven us apart.

Well, one of many.

All three mirrors had started out with a basic binding that was essentially a hypnotizing beacon of light for ghosts. Not exactly productive for a ghost binder and soothsayer. Yes, they need ghosts, but they need specific ghosts.

"What did you think the assignment was exactly, Kincaid? Three mirrors, with what appear to be only the most subtle of differences distinguishing them?"

"The permissions are the same," I said, thinking out loud as I compared the bindings I'd used to make the mirrors. "But the link between the outer and inner ring—the trap and the snare—is only in this mirror." I pointed at the one I'd brought with me. "In the two I delivered to Richan, they worked independently."

Gideon gave the tiniest of nods.

All right, Kincaid—right track, but what does it mean? On a hunch, I flooded the mirror with Otherside, just enough to flush the bindings out, see what was running under the hood. The linked symbols pulsed as they should, but there was a discord now to the Otherside coursing through the mirror, as if a different note or beat had been introduced into a piece of familiar music.

"This mirror calls to different ghosts, doesn't it?" I said.

"Very good," he said, nodding for me to continue.

I looked back to the mirror, now pulsing out an Otherside call in a set tempo, one that was most definitely different from the beat of the other two mirrors.

"It's like the area code has been changed." I figured Gideon was actively dead through the 1970s and '80s—he'd know how phones worked. "I mean, it's a mirror, so it's more of a beacon than a phone call going out—"

"More of a filter, less of an area code," Gideon said. "Unlike a phone, it can't be changed once set in place. But you aren't completely wrong in your analogy. The tone of the Otherside signal being sent out is significantly different from the mirrors you delivered to Richan. What does it do?"

A filter on a mirror alters the ghosts that will hear the call. I used them all the time. For example, I often added things like, *Chris Doe, but girl Chris, not boy Chris, and eighty years old when she died.* The point was so I didn't need to sift through fifty Chris Does—more like one or two.

But this filter was much subtler, set into the mirror's primary, permanent bindings rather than added as an afterthought.

I added more Otherside. Only the outer ring primed and flared gold; though the rest of the mirror siphoned Otherside, storing it, none reached the inner ring. "It's acting like a pressure valve."

"Take a closer look at the rest of the mirror."

I did. While the mirror stored more and more Otherside, the outer ring pulsed, releasing a small amount each time. "Jesus, it's mimicking a weak spot in the barrier."

Gideon nodded. "Very good. That pressure valve, as you call it, creates a ghost trap that in its early stage perfectly mimics a break in the barrier. Unlike the ones I had you give Richan, which are easily distinguished as mirrors by most ghosts."

My mouth went dry. If a ghost stumbled across this kind of signature . . . Even Nate, who was paranoid about ghost binders, would be drawn in.

I felt the chill as Gideon stepped beside me. "This mirror," he said, "is a real ghost trap. The name of the desired ghost still needs to be specified here." He indicated a blank spot in the outer ring. "The mirror attunes the manner of baiting ever so slightly—for all appearances, a harmless break in the barrier. That is, until the right ghost passes through." He lifted his hand and the Otherside bindings that surrounded him sparked. "Like this," he said, and passed his ghostly hand over the mirror. The inner ring finally flared to life, then snapped upwards, forming a column of gold around his wrist.

A cage.

A ghost wouldn't know what hit them.

"The real brilliance of a trap like this is all ghosts but the one being targeted pass through unharmed and none the wiser," Gideon continued. His fingers danced and the cage and tethers fell away. "I've seen mirrors like this left for a decade or more before the right ghost travels through."

I could well imagine. Leave the mirror lying in wait like a snare in the snow, hidden from view. More and more ghosts hear about the mirror and it becomes a well-travelled crossing point. Then, when the right ghost attempts it . . .

It was nothing like the mirrors I'd given Richan. Those were run-of-the-mill ghost traps any practitioner could use. You write the ghost's name in the centre, prime the mirror and send out the call. The ghost shows up, even to take a curious peek, and the trap slams shut. But those ones were obvious, and only fooled the newest and most desperate ghosts. They could be avoided.

But this? This was the tool of a true professional.

"Ghosts aren't stupid," Gideon said beside me. "And the ghosts a soothsayer is after are fragile, sensitive to the land of the dead in unique ways. In life, that sensitivity often manifests as mental illness—schizophrenia, manic depression, autism spectrum, dementia. This vulnerability makes their ghosts more powerful, more valuable, but they also tend to be much more cautious and paranoid. They keep to tried-and-true paths, ones they know are safe."

It all made perfect sense. And it sickened me. "Turn it off," I said.

Gideon regarded me, not unkindly. "It's cut off from the barrier. No ghost can sense it. Only the two of us."

I shook my head. "Just please turn it off." I took a small step back. It was all I could do not to wrap my arms around myself. "Just . . . I get it. I understand what it does." What I'd made. And it was horrible.

Gideon's brow furrowed, but he shut the mirror down. "This mirror is designed to catch a ghost who has more tricks, as you like to say, than the average dead. There are many reasons I would choose to sell this tool to a soothsayer." He turned his grey eyes on me once again. "But *not* one like Richan."

I felt Gideon's gaze on me, but all I could look at was the abominable mirror I'd built.

"This is a very expensive mirror," Gideon continued. "It is specialized, rare, powerful."

I turned towards him. Powerful I understood, but expensive, *rare*? "That makes no sense," I said. "It's almost identical to the mirrors I made for Richan, the kind you find in a spell book. Hell, it only took me a half-hour to work it out—"

"*Almost* identical, and that leads us to the serious problem I mentioned earlier," Gideon said, and sighed. "Your obliviousness betrays your own bias. The change you made is not *insignificant*. It's what Richan suspects you are capable of. I didn't have you deliver the mirrors so Richan could verbally abuse you, Kincaid. I needed to determine if a low-level thug of a soothsayer would discern your particular talent."

I frowned at Gideon. Talent? "If using Otherside until I make myself physically ill is a talent, I have news for you, everyone in Seattle with a tentative toehold in the paranormal community is already well aware."

Gideon gestured once again at the mirror, highlighting the link I'd built between the two rings. "The double intricacies require the binder to be able to set a mirror freehand. China marker gets too much in the way, ruining the entire binding. Even the simpler, less powerful mirrors I had you give Richan are difficult for even an advanced practitioner using wax." He turned to me. "I don't know if Maximillian did you a favour or a great disservice keeping from you just how rare a talent it is to be able to freehand-inscribe Otherside. I suppose it's both, considering . . ." He trailed off, still watching my face.

"Considering what?"

Gideon shook his head. "Considering the kind of people in the paranormal community it can attract—dead and undead. The only practitioners who can set this type of mirror are ones who have a natural aptitude for freehand bindings, such as yourself. The only other way—"

"Is sorcery," I finished for him.

"I imagine Max thought you not knowing meant you wouldn't unwittingly expose yourself. I suspect it was one of the reasons he insisted you use the more pedestrian bindings."

I'd spent years thinking Maximillian discouraged my freehand Otherside work because it was his way or the highway. All the nagging, all the arguments that followed. If Max had stopped for one minute to tell me *why* . . .

"The whys are inconsequential now. Suffice to say, it is an asset which will make sorcery easier for you to learn, and it's what I believe Richan suspects you can do, and I'd rather not have people like him knowing about it."

And I didn't imagine I would want to meet any of them. Not if they knew I could make a mirror like *this*.

"From now on, if anyone asks, you're good with china marker wax—also a highly valuable skill, and it explains any perceived free-hand. Make certain over the next few months your china markers are with you at all times. Understood?"

I nodded, my stomach roiling. Max hadn't been berating me—he'd been trying to protect me—he'd *cared*. But the revelation was bittersweet. He'd tried protecting me by holding me back, keeping me ignorant. That wasn't easy to forgive or forget.

"In the meantime, I'll deal with Samuel. I imagine a well-placed threat or two should suffice. He's a coward at heart and depends too heavily on my spells and mirrors."

Any other day I might have argued with Gideon against intimidation tactics, even with Richan, but I had another question on my mind, one that mattered more than the possibility of a soothsayer getting bullied. "What would they do to me?"

Gideon glanced up.

"The kind of people I don't want finding out about my talent."

"Oh." He looked thoughtful. "I suppose any number of things. A few of the living out there who know enough to consider themselves sorcerers would likely try and bind you. It's possible if you're still alive, though they would probably kill you first for simplicity's sake. The dead, though? They make me look like the tooth fairy."

I nodded, my mouth still dry. Was Gideon trying to scare me? Of course he was, but he also hadn't sold the powerful mirror to Richan. He had some boundaries . . .

And now he was bundling it up . . . in the blankets I'd designed.

"I thought you weren't selling that to Richan?"

"Oh, I'm not. I wouldn't dream of giving Richan a mirror this powerful, even if he could afford it. But I never once said I didn't have a buyer. And for these inventive cloaks of yours as well," he said, tapping my blanket. "I'll let you know if I require more. It may become a lucrative new business for me. Thank you, Kincaid."

Just when I began thinking Gideon might not be the devil . . .

"Oh, and before I forget, I need an introduction," Gideon continued, as if nothing more than a run-of-the-mill lesson had occurred. "The doctor of the dead? The one you speak with in the mortuary."

"Dr. Blanc? The coroner?"

"Yes. Or have you already forgotten that I am sorely in need of a body?"

I licked my lips. Yeah, Gideon hadn't mentioned that particular project of his in a while and I'd hoped it would stay on the back burner. Doing Gideon's bidding myself was one thing. I was used to dealing with ghosts, and despite Gideon's, well, *unique* attributes, he was still a ghost. Bitching about past mistakes and regrets, paranoia, megalomania—it was all par for the course.

But Dr. Blanc? He had no *real* experience with the paranormal, and worse, he was drawn to ghosts and zombies like a moth to a flame. He'd be at Gideon's mercy. He wouldn't know what hit him.

"What about Lee Ling's assistant, Mork—I mean James?" I corrected myself. "In Damaged Goods? He's creepy, but he has access." I crossed my fingers behind my back at the white lie. I *suspected* Mork was a mortician, morgue assistant or medical school dropout, but I didn't know for sure.

Gideon shook his head. "No. I need someone with better knowledge of modern science. James has a deft touch, but . . ." Gideon trailed off then nodded at me absently. "Your Dr. Blanc is a better choice."

"I . . . ah . . ." Shit.

Come on, Kincaid. A reason, any plausible reason not to introduce them . . .

Gideon glanced up, his eyes narrowing. "Make the introduction, Kincaid." He didn't sneer at me—he'd stopped doing that a while ago—but the warning note was there. "That's an order."

I swallowed. "Gideon, it's not that simple. Dr. Blanc is . . ." What? Naive? Uninitiated in the tempestuous nature of the dead? All of the above? I didn't get a chance to finish.

There was a hard set to Gideon's mouth as he closed the distance between us, chilling the air in front of me. He stopped shy of touching me, but barely. "Call Dr. Blanc. And remember, the next time you try to cast me as the villain, Kincaid, that I'm the only ghost this side of the barrier standing between you and the dead and undead you never want to meet."

And with that, Gideon disappeared. With the mirror. I stared up at the fluorescent lights of the library. I'd walked into that one. Gideon was sensitive to anything that even hinted at me not following his instructions to the letter. "Why, oh why can't I catch a break with that damn ghost?" I said to the ceiling.

But no one answered me. Not even the librarian. She knew when to keep quiet—so why the hell didn't I?

I headed for the stairs and outside to where my bike waited for me. And to think Richan had wanted the job of Gideon's assistant.

I reached my bike and secured my bag to the back.

Gideon played an insidious psychological game. He justified the verbal abuse and snide comments by deifying himself as the supreme authority of the paranormal. *You should feel honoured I deign to yell at you over your lacklustre bindings.* Gideon wasn't the first teacher I'd seen use those kinds of methods.

It sucked. And it was a lousy way to teach.

I manoeuvred my bike past a few buses dropping off and picking up students. I tried to pay attention to pedestrians and cyclists, but my thoughts didn't want to emerge from this particular rabbit hole. Memories of my own family fought and clawed their way to the surface.

My mother always said she loved my father's *passion*. They fought because they both ran hot.

It was a stupid excuse to be assholes. The truth is, they were both master manipulators.

Well, Richan might be the kind of man who invited that into his life, but I wasn't subscribing. I wasn't Gideon's apprentice because I wanted to be, I was here because I had to be. And I needed to remind myself of that—especially when Gideon had one of his kinder moments.

A red light I'd been caught behind flickered green. I kicked my Hawk into gear and headed for the viaduct and home. If I was to have any chance of making my flight tomorrow, I needed sleep.

And I had an introduction to make. It might kill my soul to do it, to give in, but my hands were tied.

I laughed, remembering something my mother had once told me. That I was no better than her and someday I'd end up just like her.

In a way, she'd been right. I'd gone and found a relationship that mirrored my parents' and felt just as inescapable.

A gust of wind hit me straight on as I turned onto Pike. I shivered and corrected my bike. My thoughts had me on autopilot. Something Aaron would thoroughly disapprove of.

Speak of the devil. After reaching my building, I checked my phone and saw that my boarding pass for tomorrow was there.

Now Aaron was far from perfect, but he, well . . .

What? Was interested? Wanted me again? I sighed and put the phone back into my pocket as I wedged the door to the lobby open. Maybe that was part of my problem too: I didn't know a good thing when I saw it. It was ingrained in my DNA—I didn't know how to have a relationship that wasn't a fight. I needed to win at something, to overcome—to do battle.

I wished I could go back to a simpler time when my biggest worry was whether Nate would show up to a seance on time. I was happy then.

Just because my arrangement with Gideon came with a handful of tolerable moments didn't excuse the bad ones. I'd learned from my mother that ignoring the ugly stuff is a great way to end up dead. And despite hanging out with ghosts, I had no intention of joining them any time soon.

As I rode the elevator up, my thoughts drifted once again, this time to the Portland crime scene and Aaron, who was normally reserved when making connections yet was convinced Dane's poltergeist was involved in the new murder.

If all my recent troubles with the dead in Seattle were any indication, whatever was waiting for me in Portland wouldn't be good.

CHAPTER 7

COLD ENOUGH TO WAKE THE DEAD

Aaron hadn't been wrong to worry about my ability to get up before the crack of dawn. I set five separate alarms at three-minute intervals. After the first one rang, I swore and managed to hit the Snooze button. The second time, I cursed Nate; it wouldn't be the first time he'd played a practical joke. It was the third one that finally got me up.

I brushed my teeth and left a quick message on the bathroom mirror for Nate and/or Gideon saying simply that I was on my way to Portland.

I had just enough time to shove the personal essentials into my backpack, then I turned to my practitioning equipment. I'd had the foresight to set aside a couple of compact mirrors, sage, china markers as per Gideon's instructions, and a good-sized mirror—the kind you might find in a locker, already set and tinged with a ghost-grey cast—in a large zip-lock bag on the kitchen table.

The Transportation Security Administration examined any and all practitioning goods—books, herbs, mirrors, china markers. An industrious individual had unleashed a ghost of the poltergeist variety on a plane about seven years ago, resulting in the most notorious emergency landing in the USA since 9/11. Since then, set mirrors had been banned.

I hoped I'd be cleared with Aaron by my side.

I wore my blazer underneath my leather jacket, a pair of dark-wash jeans and new, unscuffed bike boots. A little more casual than I'd like for airport security, but professional enough to get by.

The last thing I did was pull my rat's nest of hair into a tie, wrapping it into a low ponytail before sliding on my helmet. It was 4:45 a.m. and I didn't have a drop of coffee in me.

Still, I gave my apartment one last check to see if I'd missed anything. On a whim, just before ducking out the door, I grabbed a lipliner and an unset makeup compact and slid them into my pocket. Those *probably* wouldn't be confiscated, they were only makeup after all. If the TSA took my tools, at least I'd have something to conjure a ghost with.

I gave myself a once-over in the bathroom mirror. *Not bad.* I pushed my bike out the door and wrestled the door locked behind me. A few minutes later I was on a mercifully empty highway on my way to Sea–Tac Airport. I guess, if there was one silver lining to an early flight, it was that there was next to no one on the road.

Not a bad thing, as my mind was set on wandering . . .

Most of the time when I sleep, I dream. Vividly. Maybe it's my exposure to Otherside or maybe it's just me, but over the past few months my dreams had been more—restless. Cameron, Max, Randall, most recently Cole appeared in them with alarming frequency. The dreams were always silent, cold, airless—unwelcoming to the living. Sometimes it was only one, or two, or all of them. No one spoke, but, regardless of how foggy the details were, one thing always rang clear.

They were disappointed with me—even Max. *Especially* Max.

And right when I was on the cusp of discovering what it was they were so disappointed about, I woke up. None the wiser, but with a sense of foreboding, and a feeling that I had missed something, some commonality in their deaths, something slightly beyond my understanding.

Now, I'm a practitioner, but despite what the world thinks, we're not a superstitious or particularly spiritual bunch, not like the voodoo practitioners. Oh, I certainly used a substantial number of voodoo bindings in my repertoire, particularly for raising zombies, but I wasn't a believer, not the way Max had been. He'd been born and raised in the deep-rooted voodoo community in New Orleans. I didn't believe that some spirits were conduits of God, and that listening and meditating would make their messages clear.

Unlike Max, I didn't believe dreams carried some greater meaning from the Otherside. I suppose I was too jaded for that. Or I'd met too many ghosts. The dead like to convince you to waste time listening.

No message, no divine intervention. There was something deeply comforting in the thought that I was the master of my own destiny—I had agency over my happiness and misery.

But that didn't mean I thought dreams should be ignored.

I did believe that dreams brought to light truth that only your subconscious sees.

Which was why the recent restlessness disturbed me so much. Last night, along with the silent scene I'd grown accustomed to, I'd dreamt about a cold, dark place. Wet, dark, rotting, a buzz of discordant Otherside like a worm in my ear. As if the living and the dead had been melded together in a sickly, unnatural tableau.

An empty pit, hungry, desperate, starved for something to eat. And it had been calling to me.

It had revolted me, I thought with a shiver.

No, that wasn't right. I'd wanted to go to it.

Rarely did a dream have the power to shake me to the core like that, and I'd had a few unsettling ones.

Something at the library last night had made me feel ill, right before Astrid had appeared. Probably my subconscious, taking that quagmire of emptiness and running with it. Though what it meant . . .

I reached the airport parkade, locked and paid for my bike, and was heading for the skywalk when I felt the cold, telltale twinge beside me.

I kept walking. No charity cases before coffee . . .

"Excuse me? Miss?" came the thin, barely audible voice of a man—young if I was any judge, though I refused to look.

Keep walking, Kincaid, don't look, don't make any movements that tell the ghost you heard him . . .

I'd noticed that ever since Gideon had "gifted" me with Otherside sight and the permanent bindings over my face and on my wrist that marked me as his apprentice, ghosts had shown more interest in me. As if they could sense me, the way they had sensed my old mentor Max, who'd been a medium.

I felt the cold of the coalescing ghost strengthening, even as I hurried, my motorcycle boots clipping along the pavement.

"Miss?" came the desperate voice. "I'm sure you heard me—please, I just need a moment."

If I had a dime for every time a ghost said that . . .

I looked around for someone, but, it being just after 5 a.m., the parking lot was empty, not even a security guard. Shame, otherwise I would have had an idea as to whether the ghost had made himself visible. He might just be probing, seeing if I could see him, if it was worthwhile expending any more energy to get my attention. Ghosts around the water weren't too out of the ordinary, but a ghost at the airport?

I winced—I couldn't help it as the ghost went right through me to get in my line of sight. Sure enough, he was visible. Tweed suit, businessman, I'd wager, maybe in his late twenties, though I had trouble placing the time. He was either from the 1970s or a deceased member of the more recent hipster movement. I was leaning towards the latter . . . His face was earnest enough, even worried.

Damn it, Kincaid, not everyone is a lost soul, not realizing they're dead. He went right through you, he knows he's a ghost. Don't say anything, you'll only encourage him . . .

He got out of the way as I walked past him, and I hoped he'd given up. That was short-lived, however, as once again the ghost ghosted me.

"Miss? I know you hear me—please, I really just need a minute. I have an important message for you!"

I didn't stop, but I was curious. Could Gideon have sent a message for me through another ghost? He usually just appeared himself, but I'd only been working with him for a few weeks now. I was the first to admit I didn't know all Gideon's predilections. Maybe . . .

I frowned and tried to keep walking, but the ghost had seen me waver. It smelled blood.

I turned around before the ghost could ghost me again. "What? What is it you need? And make it quick, I have a flight to catch."

Suddenly the face, which had been so earnest and worried a moment ago, broke out into a wide smile, and the ghost even stood up straighter. It was like he'd won the lottery.

Shit . . . I'd been had.

The ghost didn't want anything except my attention. And like an idiot, I'd given it to him.

"Did you know you have a fantastic ass?"

Oh, for Christ's sake . . . a pervert ghost, who stalked unsuspecting women in a parking garage.

I resumed walking away. What the hell were you thinking, Kincaid?

No coffee paired with 5 a.m. and a potentially lost, worried ghost. That's what you were thinking . . .

His laughter followed me. And why wouldn't he follow? Having got my attention and succeeded in making me uncomfortable. My bright-red face told anyone that.

"I mean, like, a fantastic ass! I'll bet your tits are grade A too. Why don't you show me?"

He thought he was so damn funny. My face felt hot. God, I hoped Aaron had coffee for me on the other side of security . . .

I felt it then and froze—a cold, hard pinch right on my backside, followed by a peal of laughter. The rage burned up inside me as I turned around.

"Oh my god, the look on your face is priceless. Man, you are such a winner," the ghost managed between shrieks of laughter. "You know, I was sad for a while after that stripper clocked me over the head with a beer glass in Vegas—lousy way to go, but dead is so much better." He stopped laughing and looked hard at me then, his eyes turning an unsettling shade of red. "No one can stop me now!" he sang out, still cackling.

That was it. I pulled a compact mirror out of the zip-lock bag and flipped it open.

The ghost stopped laughing and his face fell at the sight of the ghost-grey mirror. Now whose look is priceless? I thought.

I tapped the barrier and loosed the Otherside into the mirror, activating the siphon. I didn't bother adding in the parameters— I just needed a siphon, any ghost, all ghosts in the vicinity.

The ghost looked worried, scared even. "Hey, wait a minute. You can't . . . I mean . . ." His voice trailed off as the mirror turned on. The smart thing would have been to run, fast and far, but he didn't move. That's the thing about ghosts and mirrors: resisting them takes a hell of a lot of willpower. Which this ghost didn't have. Moth, meet flame.

"Don't you, like, need my name or something? Look, I'm sorry, can't we just work something out?" He was paralyzed.

"Wrong day, wrong girl," I said, and let the siphon loose right at him.

He put up a respectable fight, but my mirror's siphon was powerful, and as soon as it sensed it had a ghost in its grasp, it latched on. The Otherside had its own claws, and it dug in.

The ghost didn't stand a chance. Seconds later, the catcalling poltergeist was sucked through the mirror, back to the Otherside where he belonged. Hopefully, not to return in the near future—if at all. I closed the mirror off before dropping the Otherside I'd held in my head. I mentally chided myself as silence once again descended on the parking lot. Dispensing with the ghost had taken me less than a minute, but here I was, 5 a.m., and already I was tapping Otherside.

I reached the skyway and noticed the sign, which had been put up hastily if the block marker letters were any indication.

BEWARE, POLTERGEIST IN THE VICINITY.

I snorted and pulled down the sign, tossing it in the garbage.

Would have been a real help to post it at the garage entry. Assholes.
And they called that a poltergeist?

My cell rang. It was Aaron. I answered as I stepped onto the
skybridge and headed into the airport proper.

"How goes, Kincaid?" he asked, not quite able to keep the tinge
of worry out of his voice that I might not yet be out of bed—or at
the airport. I wondered briefly what would happen to Aaron if
I missed the flight.

"Lousy start to my morning," I grumbled as I headed down the
escalators towards the departure gates. "Better now."

"Better? Kincaid, please say you're at the airport—"

There was panic laced in there, so I rephrased. "I've been up
since 4:40. I spent half an hour driving un-caffeinated to the airport
and ran into an asshole poltergeist in the parking garage. I'll explain
when I see you—speaking of which . . ." I spotted him at the bottom
of the escalator and waved. He waved back and I hung up the phone:
5:15 a.m. Fifteen minutes to spare. I was downright early.

"How was the ride over? And what's this about a poltergeist?"
Aaron asked, falling in step beside me as we headed towards
security.

"Didn't you see the sign? Never mind," I added, when it was clear
he hadn't. "Asshole pervert ghost who was hanging around the
parkade. Don't worry, I took care of him. You wouldn't believe . . ."
But I trailed off, deciding not to elaborate on the indignity I'd suffered. It was just a pinch on the ass, after all. And we were going to
have enough to deal with once we landed in Portland, without
Aaron worrying over paranormal sexual harassment . . . "Tell Sea–
Tac they owe me coffee."

I started for the security line, but Aaron lightly touched my elbow
and steered me towards a station with no line off to the side, manned
by a bored-looking TSA agent. He straightened up as we approached.

"The captain called ahead and said we'd be bringing sensitive
equipment through," Aaron said to me quietly.

I frowned as the agent scanned my boarding pass and went
through my bag. "Did you blackmail him?" I whispered. To say that

the captain was one of my critics would be putting it mildly. I had a hard time picturing him doing me any favours. Practitioners were all bad apples to him—charlatans, gypsies and thieves, peddling lies and parlour tricks, giving the ghosts a reason to leave the Otherside and make trouble.

Tell that to the ghost who just pinched my ass. Or, let me guess, it was my tight jeans and my motorcycle that earned me that bit of unwanted ghostly attention. If I had been a good little girl and wasn't travelling to the airport by myself at 5 a.m. . . .

I was practically shivering with pent-up anger as I took off my boots and jacket. It wouldn't matter if I went everywhere with a chaperone and dressed in shapeless slacks and shirts, there would always be *something* I was doing wrong.

"He wants you on this case," Aaron whispered.

Yeah, and he'd also made no secret of the fact that he didn't want me anywhere near the force—or the city. And now he was calling in favours, getting us through airport security.

What was it about this case that had compelled Captain Marks to overlook his usual contempt for practitioners?

"Why all the favours, Aaron?" I asked. Because, god help me, I couldn't think of any altruistic motives Captain Marks might have.

He tensed slightly, then said, "I think it's best if you see for yourself."

Aaron went through the metal detector and then it was my turn. I'd placed the bag with practitioner supplies in the tray last, leaving the compacts open. The security guard glanced at them then up at me, eyebrows raised.

Aaron cleared his throat. "Captain Marks and FBI agent Wolf spoke to your supervisor about this equipment, I believe. We take full responsibility for it. Ms. Strange is a well-known and licensed practitioner," Aaron added.

I almost snorted. *Infamous* might be more accurate.

The security guard gave me an evaluating look. "Just wait here," he said, and stepped aside to make a call. The seconds ticked by.

A different man emerged from behind a mirrored door and

stepped our way. My heart pounded, thinking maybe Aaron's confidence had been misplaced.

The new agent gave me a good long stare, meeting my eyes as I swallowed.

And then he turned to Aaron. "Detective Baal, give my regards to Marks," he said, and waved us through.

My heart was still pounding as I slid my boots and blazer back on, then tucked my things into my backpack, including the leather jacket. They hadn't even made me check my supplies. "That was the easiest time I've ever had going through airport security," I whispered to Aaron. What the hell was going on in Portland?

I caught Aaron giving me a quizzical look.

"What?" I asked, wondering for a moment if the Otherside I'd used this morning showed somehow on my face, darkening the circles under my eyes, paling my skin.

He glanced down at his shoes, his face reddening. "Nothing. This is just the second time I've seen you in a blazer in the last few days, is all." After another moment, Aaron added, "Ah—the ghost in the parking lot—I overheard one of the agents saying that, ah, well, he—"

Oh, for Christ's sake . . . it was too damn early in the morning for this. "Yes?"

Aaron cracked a smile. "I'll bet the look on his face was priceless when you sent him packing. Did you pinch him on the ass?"

I rolled my eyes. "And here I thought you were going to mansplain to me the right way to handle a sexual harassment poltergeist." I checked my boarding pass for the gate number and started sliding my backpack on, then, thinking better of it, handed it to Aaron. "Here, you wanted me to bring my supplies to the airport at 5 a.m.? You carry it. I'm getting coffee."

I didn't look back over my shoulder—though if I had, I imagine the look on Aaron's face would have been priceless.

My mood picked up as I made a beeline for the gate. Made it to the airport on time, got through security without a strip search and interrogation, and Seattle was already down one asshole pervert wannabe poltergeist, thanks to me. And was that my beloved green-and-white mermaid placard past the walkway? Off to a rocky start, but things were looking up.

Get to Portland, Kincaid. You won't know what's waiting for you until you take a look for yourself and talk to the on-site practitioner.

I pushed the unsettling memory of my dream aside as I ordered two coffees.

As I waited, I checked the weather in Portland on my phone. Overcast with a chance of rain. Great. I paid for the coffees and joined Aaron. My dream last night had proven prophetic about one thing at least: something dark and cold most definitely awaited me in Portland.

As we stood there waiting to board, I hoped dismal weather was all my subconscious had predicted.

CHAPTER 8

QUAGMIRE

Disembarking from the plane, fully caffeinated, I was dying to ask more questions about the catatonic ghost but held back. Aaron had been emphatic that the FBI wanted a cold read. I had mixed feelings about that—apprehension and, I'll admit, a little excitement. I'd done some quick searches the night before on PubDead, the online archives for paranormal research, and come up short on immobilized ghosts—at least as far as the respected journals were concerned.

I cleared my throat. "So is someone meeting us here, or . . . ?"

"Yes, Agent Stephan Wolf. Keep your eyes out for a tall guy, a few inches on me, dark-brown hair—was chin length the last time I saw him. We had a couple of college classes together. Paranormal criminology at WSU," Aaron added, scanning the arrivals area, frowning. "He should be here already."

I spotted Agent Wolf before Aaron did, walking through the glass doors at a quick pace. I have a unique name—it tends to stand out, as does Aaron's last name, Baal, both of which were written in neat black marker on a piece of white cardboard he was holding up. He was young and attractive, with long, dark hair, dressed in a nondescript but well-tailored suit and dress shoes. My reaction surprised me: I had a pathological attraction to blonds, and neither dark hair nor the man-bun set did much for me. My personal bias aside, Agent Wolf definitely had my attention.

"There he is," Aaron said, and raised a hand to wave him over. As Agent Wolf headed our way, we regarded each other with mutual curiosity.

When he reached us, I averted my gaze and found something terribly important inside my backpack. I found him unsettling in a way I couldn't put a finger on, and it wasn't just his piercing hazel eyes and the spark of attraction. I had no problem working with men I found attractive. I'd worked with Aaron for a year before we got together, but while it was never a problem, you could have cut the tension between us with a knife.

No, it was something in the calculating way Wolf had looked at me.

Aaron and Agent Wolf shook hands. "It's been a while, Aaron. Thanks for coming down at such short notice."

"Stephan. Happy to help." Aaron turned to me. "This is Kincaid Strange. She's our—consultant at the SPD," Aaron said, tripping over the words.

Once again the hazel eyes were on me, giving me the confident, measured look of someone whose job depends on judging first impressions.

Agent Wolf extended his hand. "Ms. Strange, Aaron's told me quite a bit about you."

This time I held eye contact.

"Nice to meet you. Ah, but I'm a free agent, actually. I don't work with the Seattle PD anymore. I'm here as a favour to Aaron. And for the money," I clarified.

Aaron visibly tensed. *That's right Aaron. I'm not a tool in your box, to be trotted along as a Seattle PD employee when it suits your interest. Get used to it.*

If my claim surprised Wolf or struck him as odd, he didn't let on. "All the same, thank you for coming. And please call me Stephan. Aaron does. We go a ways back."

I realized I didn't want to give yet another person an excuse to write me off. He didn't have to like me, but I wanted his respect.

"Stephan Wolf—there's a seventies rock music joke in there somewhere," I said, hoping to break the ice.

The corners of Stephan's mouth turned up in a half smile. And there was that flutter again . . .

Watch it, Kincaid. He is not thinking the same thing you are— and Aaron is standing right there.

"If I had a dime . . ." Stephan said. He glanced down at his watch. "Well, we can get to know each other better in the car." He nodded towards the exit and parkade beyond. "I'm just in the garage. Tried to get here earlier, but with traffic and navigating this place . . ." He shrugged and headed out the door. "Everyone on the scene will be standing around waiting."

Everyone?

Aaron and I followed, trailing a few steps behind.

Once Stephan had pulled far enough ahead, I elbowed Aaron. "You didn't say anything about a crowd," I hissed. It couldn't be reporters— though the kidnapping and murder of her family had garnered plenty of press coverage, there'd been no coverage of Katy's murder. I'd assumed the FBI had arranged some clandestine media blackout.

"No," Aaron whispered, "I said we needed to get in early to see the site *ahead* of the crowd, the forensics teams. I never said the FBI and local law enforcement."

My mouth turned acrid and I started to sweat. I hated using Otherside around law enforcement. Some police saw practitioners as essential, but most still viewed us as . . . well, undesirable would be putting it politely.

"And what the hell was that about you being a free agent?"

I sighed. Best to get this conversation over with as well. It had been a couple of weeks in the works.

Aaron was still talking. "Getting you your job back rides a hell of a lot on how this case goes. You think they don't talk to Captain Marks? If it gets out—"

I made a derisive noise. "The captain is never hiring me back full-time." He'd made that abundantly clear to me in private conversation. "This is me looking out for myself professionally. I already told you, I'm going for the federal licence."

Aaron fell silent, but he didn't look happy. "I think you're making a mistake," he finally said. "Or at the very least, you need to think it through more. Three months ago all you wanted was your job back, and now you want to expose yourself to law enforcement all over the US? You're not ready."

I wanted my old job back, but it didn't exist anymore. And I didn't want to play Captain Marks's games.

The dead don't move on. They obsess about the past. After encountering Cole and his decades-long grudge against Nate, I'd made a resolution to move on with my life.

It was a little disconcerting that Aaron didn't get that.

Then again, Aaron got the job done first. The last few times, I'd been . . . well, not the first thing on his mind.

He used to look out for you, a small voice whispered in the back of my mind as we reached the car, a dark-blue sedan that reminded me very much of Aaron and Sarah's and inspired some of the same anxiety.

Stephan had opened the trunk and Aaron threw his bag in.

Last chance, Kincaid.

I touched Aaron's arm while the trunk was open and we were still out of Stephan's sight. "We need to get a few things straight or this isn't going to work at all. I'm not a consultant with the Seattle PD. Not anymore. I'm a free agent, hired by the Seattle PD to help with this particular case."

"I'm going to pretend you didn't say that—"

"Why? Because it might get back to the captain?"

Aaron gave me a hard look and I expected him to argue, but instead he grabbed my bag, put it in the trunk. "All right, Kincaid. You're right. It's none of my business."

The ridiculousness of the statement caught me off guard. "Did you expect me to ask your permission?"

He made a face. "No, of course not, but for god's sake—" He ran his hand through his hair. "Come on. Stephan is waiting for us," he said, and walked around the car to climb into the front seat.

I stood there for a moment. Was it my imagination or had there been something off in Aaron?

But he was right, Stephan was waiting for us. I slid into the back seat. By myself.

After we set off, I cleared my throat. "So, Stephan, Aaron says your people are convinced the White Picket Fence Killer, Martin Dane, is behind Katy and her family's murders, but I have to admit I'm dubious. Usually I get brought in when evidence definitively points to the paranormal. From what I've seen, all we have is a catatonic victim's ghost. Unusual, but . . ."

I trailed off as Stephan glanced at me in the rear-view mirror.

"Aaron says you had a practitioner on site, but you've withheld their reports. Was there something wrong with them? Have they been fired?" I searched for the best way to phrase what I wanted to say next. "I guess I'm just not sure what it is you think I can do for you that they haven't."

Awkward silence descended, and Stephan and Aaron exchanged a look.

"The circumstances are unusual," Stephan finally said.

I waited, but neither Stephan nor Aaron was more forthcoming.

I sat back in my seat and let out a slow breath. When people speak in mysterious terms, it usually means they're making up for something—like their own hypothesis not panning out.

Was it too late to ask for a cash retainer?

"Well, how about you start by telling me why you've had Aaron bring me in? The FBI has a lot of qualified practitioners on retainer," I asked as we left the city proper and headed into rural stretches of land.

Stephan's shoulders tensed. "It's best for you to meet our practitioners in person," he said.

Practitioners? I frowned and leaned forward in my seat. "Aaron—I was under the impression there was only one—" I started.

"You're here for a second opinion," Aaron said, cutting me off.

I felt my temper rising. Aaron had *explicitly* told me . . .

No—I stopped myself. Aaron had said they'd asked for my opinion, that they wanted me on site. He'd led me to *believe* there was only one practitioner already working with the FBI, but he hadn't outright said it.

I sat back in the car seat. The son of a bitch had manipulated me. This was the FBI. Why the hell weren't they coughing up names?

Stephan cleared his throat. "Ah—well, your name came up early on when we were raising Martin Dane, before the Prices were murdered and Katy disappeared. You're talented with poltergeists and raising zombies—and please don't take this the wrong way, but my bosses decided at the time to go with someone a little more . . . media savvy. What with all the press coverage at the time." He said it almost apologetically. But my mind was already spinning.

Oh no.

Please, Lord, I know I often take your name in vain, never pray, think forgiveness is a one-way street for suckers, but please don't let it be him. Please say they had the brains to bring in someone else . . .

After the fiasco with Dane's zombie, I'd assumed they'd fired Sinclair. No one in their right mind would keep him employed, would they?

Stephan continued. "He—ah, has a very impressive resumé, though without your experience on paranormal crime scenes and cases." He nodded his head ever so slightly, not taking his eyes off the road. "Despite the—ah—setback with Dane's zombie, he's still confident, I'll give him that, and my bosses are still quite taken with him. He came highly recommended."

I'll bet. By a couple million weekly viewers and the relieved families of deceased wayward teens, estranged relatives and suicide victims everywhere . . .

At least Stephan's tone hinted at his opinion of the practitioner's confidence and glowing recommendations—namely, that they hadn't been warranted. It might not be a complete bust if he was willing to listen to me.

I shut my eyes. *Thank you, Lord up on high, for absolutely nothing.*

"Not that this is a media case." Stephan cleared his throat. "The Canadians can't speak highly enough about you, and we were all impressed with how well you handled recent"—he exchanged another glance with Aaron—"incidents in Seattle. We have no qualms about your discretion . . ." Stephan trailed off.

"But I'm no Liam Sinclair," I said, finishing the sentence for him, and closed my eyes. No matter how hard I tried, no matter what I did, no matter how *good* I was—hell, even if people respected me, I was *never, ever* going to be a Liam Sinclair. I didn't have the charisma for it.

They'd actually kept the man on retainer as their practitioner even after he proved *completely* incompetent—on national TV, no less, raising Dane as a zombie. Celebrity was more important to these people than whether he could do the job.

Which raised the question, how badly had he screwed up now for them to be bringing me in?

"They made the wrong call, Kincaid. So did Sinclair if he thought he was qualified to be here," Aaron said.

"After the new vignette was found featuring the Prices, we didn't have time to switch out our practitioner. Not with the girl missing," Stephan offered.

"Katy," I said simply, using her name to give her a shred of dignity. "Obviously, you found her."

His eyes darted to me in the mirror once again. "Sorry if I come across as insensitive. I've been working Dane's murders for a while. I've learned not to get your hopes up."

I didn't reply. What did one say to that? The downside of working serial killer cases: the perpetrator gets better at killing people and evading law enforcement, and you get more callous with the victims.

"I don't know what the hell your bosses thought they were going to get out of Sinclair after that zombie fiasco. He's a talk show host, for—" Aaron said.

"What did he do?" I said, interrupting Aaron. As Max had always said, one thing at a time. When dealing with practitioning and bindings gone awry, figure out what went wrong first before you try to fix it. Otherwise, you run the risk of continuing the mistake.

Stephan paused, then said, "Like I already told you, Aaron, it wasn't my call. And as to what he did? I really think you should see for yourself, Kincaid." We came to a red stoplight and Stephan turned to face me. "There's a reason you haven't seen Katy's murder in the news."

I was tempted to ask more, but Stephan's clenched jaw stopped me.

As we waited for the light to change, I turned my attention to the scenery outside the window, the open fields and fences. I had a deep-rooted inclination to push for answers, but I didn't want to alienate Stephan. Stephan was one of the more respectful law enforcement people I'd met—which meant he was likely very good at his job. Mediocre detectives and agents disparaged practitioners, laughing us off in favour of their own ego-fuelled theories. But the good ones? They know damn well how fast a skilled practitioner can crack a case—especially the cold ones.

The stoplight turned green and the car was once again moving. Stephan's eyes stayed fixed on the road and didn't drift to the mirror again.

That was probably a good thing.

All Dane's previous murders had specifically targeted the sub-urbs—upper middle class, large lots, white picket fences. But the only houses I could see now were old clapboard houses at a distance from the road, surrounded by fields and the odd pocket of trees. I could spot a few sheep and cows grazing in the morning light.

Definitely not Dane's usual hunting ground. For all his kills, he'd never targeted a rural family. Yet more evidence he wasn't behind this. And they still were mum on a poltergeist sighting.

The car slowed and took a sharp turn down a narrow dirt road— one that had been hidden by overgrown alders. It lurched along the gravel, and dust kicked up mud on either side, signifying it had rained recently. On either side was underbrush—mostly the deciduous, oily-green salal that flourishes along the west coast—along with birch trees and various shrubs and evergreens I didn't recognize or know by name. I caught the back of an old-fashioned red mailbox and realized we were on someone's driveway, not a road. This must be the farm from the photo.

The driveway wound its way through the brush until it reached a shallow depression that had never been properly drained and was now host to a significant puddle. There were potholes hidden underneath, each and every one apparent as we drove over it. So, not recently maintained.

There was a faded orange tie attached to an alder tree up ahead, and the dirt driveway made a sharp left turn. We exited the thick brush onto an overgrown field, the grass damp from the rain and flattened by all the feet as of late. The barn stood in the middle of the clearing—a faded red, the paint peeling away, exposing the grey, weathered wood underneath. It had a slanted tin roof decorated with patches of moss.

It was the kind of building you expect to see in a horror movie, one where a demonic clown or family of cannibals lives.

But it was what lay beyond the barn that really had my attention.

Oh, that was not good.

The morning activity had started. Police checked ID as people came and went, most of them forensics and FBI, all congregating in and around two large processing tents near the barn. Stephan slowed down to show his ID to a police officer blocking the driveway, before pulling into a makeshift parking lot where a small fleet of cars and vans—civilian, police, technical, maybe a dozen or so in total—were parked in a crescent-shaped row.

I was silent as the three of us got out of Stephan's car, ready for the bone-chilling cold that surrounded me as soon as my foot touched the flattened grass. It crunched with frost under my motorcycle boots. I didn't need to open my Otherside sight to know what was waiting for me. But I did, while the three of us stood there, Aaron and Stephan talking quietly about what had already been uncovered.

My eyes fixed on a shallow body of water barely visible behind the barn, dotted with moss-covered trees.

The sun had been trying to break through the clouds and it finally won out, lighting up the field and barn with a soft yellow glow.

The sunlight mixed with the gold Otherside that layered the ground as far as I could see, like a paranormal morning fog. The body of water behind the barn was shallow enough for bulrushes. It was impossible to say how large it was, or how far back it extended into the woodlands, thick with brush and trees.

"Stephan, Aaron?" I said. The two of them were still discussing technical points, evidence the forensic teams had dug up, mostly dead livestock, and the property ownership trail. They were too caught up in their own conversation to hear.

"Aaron," I said, raising my voice and reaching out to grasp his sleeve. I pointed at the swamp. "I *really* wish you'd told me this was here," I said.

Aaron frowned at me. "The marsh? I didn't think it was relevant."

"Do you see something?" Stephan asked.

The strongest concentration of Otherside was over the water. I headed for the tree-laden bank, not waiting to see if Aaron and Stephan would follow.

Sure enough, the Otherside got stronger, thicker, until it was almost impossible to see past the spongy shoreline. Aaron had called it a marsh, but, considering the trees and sheer amount of Otherside pooling over its surface, I considered it a swamp. The Otherside even went beyond the water, covering the trees, shrubs, barn, licking over the grass and extending out towards the forest.

My god, I might even be looking at a bog, considering how much organic material had to be decomposing to let off this much Otherside. And I couldn't see a damn thing, only the glittering gold of Otherside. I dropped my sight before claustrophobia sunk in. The Otherside faded away, if not the chill, and the clear morning sun once again illuminated the water's surface. A lesser practitioner could get lost in the Otherside—hell, *I* could get lost in that Otherside. Stories abounded of practitioners who wandered into a bog, swamp, marsh, take your pick, never to be seen again, so enamoured of the siren song of easy Otherside. The practitioners who wandered into the bogs of old were only ever found as mummified corpses. It wasn't a fun way to go. I could feel the pull now, drawing me in. I shivered, trying to break free.

Shit.

I froze for a moment, wondering what I could possibly do, how I could possibly see anything of value at a crime scene covered with this much Otherside without putting myself in danger. Was there even a precedent for processing a crime scene with this much Otherside? Hell, I might be *writing* the precedent.

I shook my head, turned on my heel and headed for the car. "All bets are off," I said.

I'd set the precedent once before. No one, absolutely no one, thanks the trailblazer. Too hard to do when they're trying to blame them. Sinclair was welcome to the fallout a case like this would cause, I thought as I strode towards the car. Well, at least now I knew why it was so much colder here than at the airport.

"Kincaid, what's wrong?" Aaron said, running to catch up to me.

I shook my head but didn't slow my pace. "If you're fast, maybe you can cancel our hotel, save the deposit." I didn't exactly savour the idea of sitting at an airport all day, but it'd beat freezing here. I shoved my hands into my pockets.

Stephan appeared at my side, glancing back at Aaron.

"I don't understand," Aaron hissed. "Did you see something? Kincaid! Hold on—tell us what's wrong."

I made a face but didn't look at him. He hadn't known. Why would he? It wasn't like there were a lot of marshes or swamps in downtown Seattle . . . This might set a record for my shortest contract ever.

I tried the car door, but it was locked. I shot Stephan a dirty look, but he didn't move to get his key. He'd known what I was getting into, and hadn't said a damn thing, not at the airport, not in the car.

I tried the door again, to no avail, and turned to Stephan. "You wanted a professional opinion? My professional opinion is it's a waste of time bringing *any* practitioner here because none of us can give you a definitive analysis of Otherside with this much background. This place is *covered* with it. You might as well send me home, because I can't tell you anything about this scene." Hell, I couldn't even help them with a ghost out here, let alone a poltergeist.

And if Liam Sinclair could, he was a hell of a lot better practitioner than I was.

CHAPTER 9

BLINDED BY THE LIGHT

Aaron shook his head. "All right, you're going to have to walk me by this again, Kincaid. What do you mean, there is Otherside everywhere? It always goes back across the barrier unless it's bound here." He looked confused. "Doesn't it?"

I closed my eyes and leaned against the car door. Stephan at least had managed to wrangle us some coffees, so my fingers were slightly insulated against the paranormal chill. Interestingly, Stephan hadn't launched into an argument to convince me to stay. He'd listened. Carefully. Still was.

I took a sip of the coffee—it wasn't bad, a little burnt. Either way, it settled the chill and consequently my nerves. I shook my head, still trying to wrap my head around the sheer volume of Otherside. If anything could induce claustrophobia in a practitioner, this would be it. Which was all sorts of irony considering that we were in an open field.

Even when I couldn't see it, I was aware of it, around my legs, touching my skin, *everywhere*.

I shoved my own discomfort back down, and when I was ready, I looked Aaron in the eye. "Normally the answer would be yes, but this place is—different. This is a swamp, or maybe a bog. It's . . ." I paused as I tried to figure out a way to explain what was remarkable about it to someone who couldn't see Otherside.

"The two most common ways for Otherside to appear on this side of the barrier are for something to die or, the harder way, when a practitioner taps the barrier and pulls it over. All living things release Otherside when they die, and unless a practitioner harnesses it quickly, it drifts back across the barrier. But it doesn't *all* leave. Organic matter gives off Otherside as it decays. There are microbes, bacteria, fungi, worms, insects, that are all involved in the further breakdown of organic material, and they live and die, shedding their own small amounts of Otherside." I paused as I tried to think of a good analogy. "It's not unlike the radiation archaeologists look for when dating bones and other organic objects. An ecosystem, by definition, is a continual mix of life and death. We only see a little of it in the city, like we only see a little starlight, but out here?" I held my hands out towards the farm and swamp.

"So all nature leaks Otherside," Aaron said.

"You're talking about background Otherside?" Stephan said. "I'm familiar with it, but that's all it's supposed to be—background. Practitioners work around it all the time—graveyards, forest trails."

"You've worked outside the city before and never had a problem," Aaron added.

"That's because different ecosystems leak different levels of Otherside. Sand is a very poor source of Otherside compared with soil, which is much more hospitable to microbes and small organisms. How rich an ecosystem is with life—"

"Plays into how much Otherside is released on a daily basis—life and death, that sort of thing," Stephan said.

I nodded. "Swamps, marshes, estuaries, fens and bogs are some of the most nutrient-dense ecosystems on the planet. Why do you think so much modern voodoo was developed in Louisiana? The

Everglades, the bayou?" And unlike me, those practitioners had experience working with a lot of background noise.

The two of them still didn't look convinced. I couldn't entirely blame them, they couldn't see what I did—they only felt the chill. I struggled to come up with an analogy that would resonate. "It's like when someone throws bleach over blood. Your luminescence test picks up the bleach but can't distinguish the two, yes?" They both nodded. "There is so much Otherside here, my normal tests won't work reliably. Sinclair must have mentioned something about it if you've got him on the case." Unless he was trained in Louisiana and just assumed every practitioner knew how to deal with it.

Aaron and Stephan exchanged a glance.

"So the barrier here is thin, then? Like the harbour and the iron gate downtown?" Aaron asked.

I thought about that. "Yes and no. This place is different. Those places in Seattle are small pockets—easy for ghosts to find. I'm not sure what a ghost would make of this place. Too much Otherside might disorient them, make them wander." I turned towards the swamp again. "But in theory, there should be some permeable spots—especially along the edges."

"Something that a ghost, say a poltergeist, might find easy to use, like their own personal doorway?" Stephan asked.

It was a shrewd question. I reconsidered the agent, his arms crossed, standing relaxed as he regarded me. It struck me that he wasn't particularly surprised by my reaction, or put off the way Aaron was. "Possibly," I allowed, and met his hazel eyes again.

I saw more than a little respect there, and not a bit of surprise. Sinclair had shared more about this place than Stephan was letting on.

Shrewd or not, I wasn't letting Agent Wolf lead a discussion on Otherside. "*Or*, it might act like a cage, and be the reason why Katy's ghost is still here and paralyzed, trapped. It might be that ghosts can't come here at all." Which would mean they were looking for a living perpetrator, not a poltergeist. I added, "If we're looking for a living killer who knows Otherside, that might be why this place was chosen."

That got Stephan's attention. "How so?"

"Someone familiar with Otherside who stumbled upon this place would know that the ghost of someone who dies here would be exponentially more likely to return," I said. Swamps, voodoo and zombies aren't coincidental associations. "If someone is murdered and can get back easily to their body—" I shrugged. "Some killers have a ghost fetish." They wanted to see their victim's traumatized ghost, a sick souvenir, proof of their deed. Considering the location, it was no wonder Katy returned. And considering the traumatic circumstances surrounding her death, well, no wonder she was sitting at the table in a catatonic state.

"Either way, I can't help you. There's too much Otherside for me to see in front of my face to do anything for Katy, let alone work bindings or find someone else's." I was useless here.

Neither man replied. Then, after a moment, Stephan said, "I would think more Otherside would be a good thing, not bad."

I pursed my lips. "But that's just it, I'm not qualified to make a predictable analysis." Neither was Sinclair, from what I knew of him—unless he spent the better part of his youth in the bayou. "Of course there's paranormal activity around here. How could there not be? You need a practitioner from Louisiana or Florida—Everglades or bayou trained would be best. Someone who specializes in background. They might even know what's happened to Katy. It could be shock from this much—" What, stimulation? "Everything."

As confident as I was in my decision, disappointment sunk my stomach. This was supposed to be my stepping stone to a federal licence . . . "As much as I would *really* like to help you, Agent Wolf, I am just not the right practitioner for the job."

I tried to open the car door again, but Stephan gripped my arm. I froze and we locked eyes. *Friendly* was not the word I'd use to describe his expression.

"Please. You're already here. At least take a look at the barn. I won't hold you to it. I just—" His face became desperate, but only for a moment. "I really need a second opinion. Please."

Let it be said I hate it when people beg.

I turned back around to face the marsh. There was something I recognized about its scent of decay and rot. It felt like the Otherside disturbance at the library, the one I had attributed to Astrid. I frowned. Why the hell would they be similar? I tried reaching back, to remember exactly what it had felt like, but try as I might, the scent of it, the signature, stayed foggy. Not enough coffee, I wagered.

I let out my breath. You're going to regret this, Kincaid . . .

"All right. Let me take a look at Katy and see if I can do something for her. But I want it on record that I raised serious concerns over doing *any* Otherside evaluation this close to a marsh, swamp, whatever this is."

Stephan held his hands up in acquiescence.

I nodded for Aaron to stay by the car. As I followed Stephan to the barn, that familiar sick feeling struck me once again—like the fever of a bad cold or flu setting in. I glanced back at the swamp. What the hell was going on?

For the briefest moment it felt as if something was watching me. I closed my eyes and pulled my Otherside sight up. But beyond the thick fog of Otherside billowing out of the water, there was nothing.

I shivered again. Just the heebie-jeebies, Kincaid. Get a grip.

✳

If not for the mailbox at the start of the long driveway, I would have written the place off as abandoned. But an abandoned place wouldn't have the brush cleared from the driveway, and though the small field around the barn was overgrown, it hadn't been that way for long.

Someone had definitely maintained the property within the last year.

The barn itself seemed in serviceable shape—weathered wood, but still sturdy-looking despite the wet climate, though I supposed there could easily be dry rot hidden underneath.

I scanned the roof, walls and ground, but there was no electricity, satellite dish or telephone lines that I could see above, and none coming from the ground.

A retreat of sorts, then—intentionally removed from civilization? Something else bothered me about this whole scene.

"You said Sinclair was still working the case, didn't you?" I asked Stephan.

"Yes."

I waited, but when no more information was forthcoming, I said, "Well, where is he?" In his shoes I'd be waiting, with bells on, to make sure my work wasn't misinterpreted.

"In due time, Kincaid," Stephan replied with a shake of his head.

I scanned the nondescript van I'd spotted tucked between the forensics vans. There was no sign of Sinclair anywhere.

Very odd.

The barn door opened and a pair of techs exited carrying a large plastic sifting crate between them. I didn't have a chance to get a good look as they passed by, but I thought I caught sight of small stones in the crate, unevenly shaped shards of mixed colours.

Stephan caught the door as they left, hinges squeaking with recent neglect. "After you," he said.

I obliged, my curiosity piqued despite my apprehension. The interior was spacious and lit with portable floodlights. It was bustling with people in white jumpsuits, their hair, hands and feet all covered, collecting dirt samples into plastic sifting trays and plastic bags. I counted five cordoned-off plots of soil that were being surveyed.

It was a full forensic workup. An awful lot of activity for one murder. Perhaps this barn was more than a stage for the macabre?

Inside the doorway, there was a closet-sized rectangular tent made of a clear plastic sheet tucked against the barn wall and filled with shoes, jackets and personal things.

"Clean suit only," Stephan said, and handed me a white suit, hair cap and booties. I took them and dressed, leaving my motorcycle boots in the tent.

I had a strange sensation, my senses tingling as I wrestled with the jumpsuit. I caught Stephan watching me with critical eyes.

"What?"

He smiled and removed his dress shoes. "Oh, just that it took you minutes to flag Spalt swamp as a problem."

"Seconds." I watched as he struggled to slip on white paper booties that were slightly too small for his feet. "You did know it'd be an issue—the swamp," I said, certain of my guess.

His expression stayed neutral. I shook my head and turned my attention to my own damnable booties. There was a serious lack of ergonomics in their design, and Stephan was as much of an asshole as Aaron.

"Was it a test?"

Stephan didn't answer.

"Well, it was a waste of your time. Aaron and anyone in Seattle could have told you I was a real practitioner."

A darker expression—and something else I couldn't quite interpret—clouded his face. "Oh, I've learned to take things people say about practitioners with a grain of salt of late. Ask anyone in the country and they'll tell you we've got the world's best practitioner on the case. I hate having my time wasted too, Kincaid Strange."

"How long did it take Sinclair to figure out the swamp was a problem?"

Stephan snorted as he stood. "Sinclair didn't tell me anything. His assistant did."

More and more interesting. If I was in Sinclair's shoes, I would have insisted on doing all the analysis myself. Even if his assistant was the one who made the mistake—and make no doubt about it, there was a mistake, that was the only reason they'd have me in— Sinclair's reputation would still take the hit.

Or maybe he was slippery enough to wager any mistakes would slide right off, like water off a duck . . . except that might be insulting to ducks everywhere.

"Hired Sinclair and got his assistant. Doesn't seem like a fair trade."

"Oh, no. We didn't hire him. Sinclair volunteered. I'll be back in a minute," he said, and headed off to talk to a nearby group of technicians sifting through dirt in a cordoned-off square.

I knew why the FBI had wanted Sinclair in the first place: his experience handling media and his charisma. But what was so interesting about this case that had inspired Sinclair—and the studio—to halt filming on his hit syndicated show? People like Sinclair didn't volunteer out of the kindness of their heart? Not when millions of dollars per episode were on the table.

Once I was sufficiently covered, I stood and took stock of the activity once more.

Now, where the hell was my ghost?

Stephan finished talking to the group of technicians and returned, his face unchanged, but the muscles in his neck were more tense than before.

I sighed. "All right, Agent Wolf. Where's Katy?"

He paused. "What do you see here? Paranormally speaking."

I gestured at the inside of the barn. "It helps if I have a general idea what you're looking for. This place is covered with Otherside—you already know that."

"Indulge me. A quick read. Then I'll take you to Katy."

I shook my head but closed my eyes, sliding my Otherside sight into place. I took a look at the barn.

The inside of the barn was covered in a thin layer of Otherside and I had to rein in my nerves as the glittering fog enveloped me. No surprises there, considering the swamp outside.

Deep breath, Kincaid.

I let it settle in. There was still too much—I could barely see in front of me, let alone around the room.

A thought struck me. What if I could slide back my Otherside sight a fraction? Eyes opened, I played with the filter, the bindings I'd bought from Gideon. Normally, they slid in place over my eyes, like a pair of sunglasses. I tried sliding them halfway. It took a moment, and I had to hold them in place, but it worked.

Time to give things a second look.

The Otherside was still there, but now I could see details of the barn seeping through the fog. Not perfect, but better. I focused on sections, hoping something would jump out at me.

Otherside gathered in the soil where one of the forensic teams was working. I concentrated on the dirt, and the more I looked, the more obvious the difference in the levels of Otherside became. Where the forensics team worked was the kind of Otherside increase I'd normally associate with a burial—a dead animal, heavy compost, manure. Or a dead body.

I gestured at the square and said, "There might be slightly stronger traces consistent with decomposing material in those areas, but I can't say for certain and I don't think you'll find anything fresh."

"Noted," Stephan replied.

I waited for more, but Stephan didn't offer. I continued my painstaking survey. It wasn't until I'd reached the far side of the barn, away from where everyone was working and collecting their samples, that I found what I was looking for: a smattering of Otherside that bled through the fog—brighter patches and ribbons like streams reaching through the air and across the ground from behind the wall. Or that's what it looked like at first glance. It was still fainter than I would have liked, which I attributed to the background Otherside from the swamp, but the thin streams were most definitely there.

The sign of a ghost.

I pointed to the wall. "There's another room back there." I dropped my Otherside sight and looked at Agent Wolf, who had been watching me. "That's where Katy is." And if there was any evidence of Dane's poltergeist, I'd wager I'd find it there as well.

Stephan gave me a wry grin and I dare say a look of admiration as he headed over to the wall and pushed. A large panel slid to the right. The wood had been deftly attached to a recessed sliding door. A secret room. I might have commented on it, but the inside, well, that had already caught the words in my throat.

The scene matched the kitchen in the photos, a 1950s- or '60s-style kitchen—rounded chrome fridge, Arborite and chrome table, stove and counters all done in bright colours and shined to perfection.

And there was Katy's ghost, still sitting in the chair at the kitchen table. I recognized her from the photos as well, the tight ponytail her curly brown hair had been forced into, the blue poodle skirt, white short-sleeved blouse, knee socks and Mary Jane shoes—all consistent with Dane's preferred time period.

She ignored me as I stepped into the room, Stephan silent behind me.

"Katy?" I tried, quietly, so as not to startle her. She sat motionless, unblinking, not acknowledging our presence.

All right, Kincaid—what's going on? One piece at a time.

Her dress alone was unnerving. A normal ghost, one who isn't too psychologically damaged when they die, will revert back to things they typically wore every day—familiar items, not what they died in. I'd done some light reading on the flight down, background information and photos of Katy I'd requested from Aaron. She'd been a typical sporty teenager. She'd liked track pants, hoodies, runners . . . And her expression. Even from here it was blank, staring but unseeing.

And she was still staring at her own body, propped up and tied to the chair. It left me speechless, frozen in my tracks. I drew in a sharp breath and held it as the pickled scent of formaldehyde hit me. It didn't cover the scent of death, it never does. I often think the formaldehyde makes it worse.

She'd been seventeen. Seventeen years old. And she'd been staring at her own dead body for, what, two, three days?

This was sadistic, even by ghost binding standards. Of course, I'd seen the photos, but I'd assumed they'd taken the body away afterwards.

"What the hell is going on here?" My voice was barely a whisper—that was all I could manage with the anger coursing through me. "How long has she been staring at herself?"

"She won't let us move her body," Stephan said.

I gave him a long, hard look. "I was under the impression this ghost was catatonic."

Agent Wolf made a face. "I'm embarrassed to say I told you a half-truth. Mostly she stays exactly as you see her—until we try to take her body away. Then she gets violent."

I narrowed my eyes at him. "Like a poltergeist?"

Agent Wolf shook his head. "No, not like that. She throws things, screams, flies around the room, that sort of thing, until we put the body back. Then she collapses back at the table, crying."

Well, that wasn't *unheard* of. Ghosts of the murdered are often reluctant to accept the fact that they are dead. Instead of trying to take things with them, they hold on to their fast- cooling bodies for, well, not dear life, but for the hope of it.

"Are you telling me that between Liam Sinclair and your FBI paranormal unit, no one can deal with a little haunting?"

"Oh, they can dismiss her," he said, the harder, more critical look back. "But they can't do it without getting me answers first. Aaron says you can get a traumatized ghost to talk."

I nodded. I'd seen more than one traumatized ghost prodded one too many times into madness. Still . . . "I'm not sure I would have gone ahead with the embalming—not in front of her." The idea of it made me a little sick.

But Stephan raised his eyebrows. "I agree. She was already like that when we arrived."

So the killer did it.

"How did you find her? Out here in the middle of nowhere?"

"Need to know, Kincaid. And right now, you don't."

I took in the scene once again, and sighed. I didn't think arguing with Stephan would get me anywhere. "You should have told me. About the embalming and her reaction to moving her body," I said, and, eyes on Katy's ghost, I slowly approached her body.

"If it makes you feel better, I didn't tell Aaron either."

"A little." Though I suspected there were other details about this case that Aaron was privy to and I was not.

Still keeping Katy in the corner of my eye, I crouched down to examine her body. It felt as though I was submerging myself in cold water, a side effect of the Otherside hovering close to the ground. Still no movement from the ghost.

I wasn't a forensic expert, but assuming otherwise normal conditions, I guessed she'd been dead for three days—maybe four, considering the cold. I kept my Otherside sight at bay while I examined her. Usually there are small differences between a ghost and its corpse—bruising on the body that's missing from the ghost, even a slight difference in hair or grooming. But in this case there was nothing. They were identical—both their expressions fearful, even the bruises around her neck that hinted at strangulation, just like the rest of Dane's victims.

I'm not squeamish around the dead, but even I had to look away from both Katys. The expressions also told me she'd been resigned to her fate when she died. She'd known there was no escape.

I stood and slid my Otherside sight halfway into place again. I searched the ground, the walls, even the vintage appliances, carefully and slowly walking around the room, trying not to disturb the scene any more than I had to. I was about to give up; if there was evidence of Otherside bindings beyond the marsh's background, I couldn't see it.

"There's no way I can talk to Katy now, not without talking to Sinclair, his assistant and whatever other practitioners you've had through here first, and seeing what they've tried. She could be shocked into some kind of behavioural loop . . ." I trailed off as I spotted something on the ground underneath the Arborite table. A flicker, a brighter thread of gold amongst the blanket of Otherside—faint, but there. And there was the glint of something else. Something metallic. "Has forensics already gone over this room?" I asked, crouching back down into the chilling fog.

Stephan nodded.

I brushed the ground with my boot, clearing away what turned out to be loosely packed dirt, uncovering a sheet of metal that lay underneath. A door? No, it was too thin for that, and too polished. "They either missed something or—" I glanced at Stephan and frowned at his carefully neutral expression. "You decided not to tell me. Got it," I whispered.

I brushed away more dirt until I'd uncovered the edge of the sheet. It was the same kind of polished metal I often used in lieu of a mirror, only this one was much larger.

And it was covered in bindings.

Even muddled with the fog, they were there, distinct.

I thought about trying to clear away the swamp fog. I might be able to siphon some out of the way . . . but more would just come in to take its place. Otherside isn't a physical object. It can move through walls as easily as air when it is dispersed.

The bindings on the metal sheet were complex and jumbled, and not symbols and configurations I recognized.

Well, Kincaid, when faced with something complicated, start with the one thing you are sure about. The body.

I went back to Katy's body and, this time, really searched for traces of Otherside. There they were, faint at first, a collar of Otherside bindings covering the skin around her neck, small, hard to see, drawn in a short, thin, tight hand. Precise and neat. "Do you have a writing sample from Dane?" I asked.

"I can get it."

I nodded. "I think it would be very useful." It is possible for a ghost, even a poltergeist, to set bindings, but if Dane's script was less refined, I could rule him out.

Could the bindings be for animation? No, not the right kind of arrangement, and not covering nearly enough of her body. A summoning, perhaps? That would explain the ghost, and there are cultures and rituals that use a body to summon a spirit.

The symbols didn't strike me as archaic. I recognized some of them as voodoo—consistent with Max's traditional style, but more elaborate.

Ghost binding, then? Not one I recognized, but bindings done in the fashion of a collar would fit symbolically.

I got Stephan's attention. It wasn't hard, he was *still* watching me intently. "Her body—her neck, to be precise—is decorated with bindings I don't recognize."

"Any idea what they do?"

"Haven't a damn clue," I said, then decided to hedge my answer. "Except that it's not the work of an amateur. They could have been intended to animate her as a zombie, summon her, bind her, or some other ritual I'm not familiar with. Without knowing more about them, I can't make an educated guess. I can't even tell you if they were added before or after her death."

I checked Katy's ghost to see if she'd manifested the bindings as well as the bruises. She hadn't. "The bindings on the body are absent from the ghost. As to what that means?" I shrugged and looked at him. "Were any of Dane's other victims wearing Otherside bindings on their neck?"

Stephan sighed. "I don't know if anyone ever thought to look before now."

"I thought you said you'd been working on the White Picket Fence murders for a while. You are in the paranormal unit."

"Initially, they only brought us in to contact the ghosts of his victims. We didn't take over until Katy was kidnapped."

Interviewing victims and potential witnesses for clues and hints—that explained why they wouldn't be looking for Otherside. I made a face and turned my attention back to Katy and the piece of sheet metal nearby. "Get a practitioner out to the old crime scenes to search for metal sheets or mirrors—and exhume what victims' bodies you can. Tell them they're looking for very fine, tightly scripted, collar-like bindings—around necks, wrists, ankles. They'll know what that means."

Links, loops, even some modification of more general symbols. The bindings here were as advanced as anything I could do. Whoever made these was good. Very good. Maybe sorcery good.

I banished that thought. Lately, I'd been seeing sorcery everywhere—it was my lessons with Gideon that did it.

I retrieved my notebook from inside my jumpsuit and began tracing the symbols onto the page, both the ones that decorated Katy's neck and the ones on the metal, making a note about the bindings being absent from her ghost's neck. I'd get Aaron and

Stephan to photograph them for their own records. What I really wanted was to show them to Gideon—maybe even Lee. Rarely are things new in the practitioning world.

When I finished copying and was satisfied with the reproduction of the symbols and patterns, if not the exact flourishes, I stood and rejoined Stephan by the entrance. The entire time I'd been working he hadn't taken his eyes off me, and whereas under normal circumstances that wouldn't have been an unwelcome thing . . .

As soon as I reached him, I knew the question before he asked. "Could Dane's poltergeist do this?"

I thought about it carefully before answering. "It is within the realm of possibility, but we should determine if Dane's previous victims showed Otherside bindings before we jump to any conclusions."

"Would the strangulation marks match? If his ghost was involved?"

I nodded. Though forensics wasn't my wheelhouse, any ghost, even poltergeist, was essentially a copy of its living self. "A poltergeist certainly." I gestured at the sheet metal and Katy's neck. "But I'm willing to stake my reputation that if Dane is involved, he had practitioner help."

"You don't think ghosts can use Otherside?"

The question was quick, with the kind of intonation that Aaron and Sarah used when they were trying to catch someone in a half-truth. Or an outright lie.

"If he's a ghost that can use Otherside like this," I replied, "and he's bent on killing people, you have way more problems than I or any practitioner I know could possibly help you with. I'd recommend leaving the state. Or moving inland—Salt Lake City and Nevada I hear are ghost free, though the Salt Lake City property bubble will kill you." Everyone wanted to pay a premium to live ghost free.

From the way Stephan's jaw tightened, I knew he didn't like my answer. He'd wanted a simpler, less glib solution. My cheeks flushed with embarrassment. I wanted to earn Stephan's respect and not scuttle my chance at a federal career before I even got a licence, but Stephan was hard to read, and despite wanting his approval,

I didn't appreciate how little information he was offering. My own attraction to him also didn't help.

"All right, Kincaid Strange. We'll exhume what bodies we can and I'll have a team survey any of the old vignette sites. Next question: do those bindings have anything to do with my catatonic ghost?"

"I can't tell you. Not without researching these bindings. I'm not familiar with over half of the symbols."

He looked up from his notes. "But you have a way to find out?"

I kept my face neutral. "*Maybe.*"

Stephan went silent for a moment, then seemed to make some kind of decision. "All right, what kind of help do you need to find out?"

Bingo. "Everything Sinclair and his assistant have given you, for starters. A forensics and coroner's preliminary report, more details about this place and how the victim was discovered—you know, all the stuff I normally get before stepping on a crime scene."

Stephan smiled politely, but despite what I considered a very reasonable request, I got the distinct impression he was working on a way to tell me no. I stopped him with a raised hand.

"Did you feel that?"

He gave me a quizzical look but then froze in place and began searching the room with his eyes.

There'd been an unmistakable twinge of ice in the air, colder than the room already was with Katy and the fog. It was subtle at first, then more insistent. Like a hesitant probe—a question being asked.

I turned around slowly to face the ghost. She'd moved her head, and now she was looking straight at me with wide eyes.

I held my breath, not moving. I hoped Stephan knew enough to do the same.

With the exception of poltergeists, ghosts are usually timid, wary. They're more vulnerable—emotionally and physically—than you might guess, especially when it comes to an unknown practitioner.

I waited for Katy's ghost to move again. She didn't, only kept her wide eyes fixed on me, as if she was waiting.

I relied on the other truth regarding ghosts—that most of them, even the most traumatized, are just looking for someone to talk to. "Katy?" I said quietly.

Another brush of cold, and the Otherside fog swirled around us. The ghost's lips parted, as if forming words, and her head turned back to face her body.

"Do you hear that?" Stephan asked.

I nodded, registering a faint sound coming from her. At first I thought she was gasping for breath—she'd been strangled, after all—but then I saw the droplets landing on the table.

She was weeping.

That is something else ghosts often do. Cry. And they produce real tears.

I picked up more movement—a flicker of her eyelids, muscles in her neck contracting, her eyes slowly tracking the Otherside swirling around her. My ghost wasn't catatonic anymore.

"What do you want me to do here?" I whispered to Stephan.

For the first time, his neutral expression faltered, betraying worry. "How fast can you set a containment pentagram?"

I frowned at the request. A containment pentagram is to keep a ghost restrained. "I thought the whole point was to get Katy moving?"

Katy jolted at the sound of my voice, like a scared rabbit. Stephan opened his mouth to answer, but I shushed him as loudly as I could without disturbing her more.

She relaxed, but her crying continued, her eyes fixed on me. There is no one best practice for starting a conversation with an upset ghost. They are still people, with their own individual tics. Even if someone had designed a manual for engaging distraught ghosts, Katy's situation wasn't exactly typical.

"Don't practitioners normally talk to ghosts?" Stephan said.

I shot him a look. "Aren't the FBI experts in dealing with murder victims? What do *you* suggest I say, Agent Wolf?" I whispered to Stephan.

"*Victims*—dead bodies and relatives. I leave the talking to practitioners."

He did have a point.

I turned my attention back to Katy. Well, Stephan had said she'd become frantic when anyone tried to move her body. Though she was crying, she wasn't doing anything like that now, which I took as a positive.

I sighed. First things first, Kincaid. Let's see if you can get her to talk.

"Stay by the door," I told Stephan. "I don't think she's dangerous, but—" I took two steps forward, until I was standing beside the table, hopefully blocking Stephan from her view so she was forced to focus on me.

Her crying worried me. Distraught ghosts expend more energy. It's the emotion, not the movement, that drains them.

"Katy, my name is Kincaid Strange. I'm here to help."

The sniffling stopped. Her lips moved, but no sound escaped.

"I can't hear you. Can you try a little louder?" New ghosts often misjudge the volume of their voice—erring on the side of too loud or too soft.

She paused and managed to find her voice. "I'm really dead, aren't I? Dead, dead, dead."

Well, at least she was coherent. I nodded. "I'm afraid so, Katy. I'm so sorry this happened to you. Is that why you're still here? Just in case you were wrong?"

She shook her head, slowly, deliberately. "Kincaid Strange? Strange, strange, strange," she said, as if caught in a trance, trying to remember something. And she was repeating things in threes. Ghosts are drawn to things in threes. Where do you think the Bloody Mary mirror game came from?

She was moving slowly, as if through molasses, but still she startled. "Oh, no. They've lured you here, haven't they?"

I felt a jolt, remembering Miranda's warning, but I didn't let on. It was possible that, despite Katy's catatonic state, she'd been listening to the forensic technicians and FBI, and heard my name in conversation.

"I promise I'm here to help you." I took a slow step closer.

Katy shook her head, her sad expression shifting to panic.

I held up my hands and stayed where I was. "I just want to talk."

"No, no, no—I can't hide. Don't you understand? He'll find me, anywhere I go."

"Do you mean Dane?"

Katy shook her head. "I'm not afraid of him anymore. I can't run, not like you." Her movements were still lethargic.

A ghost binder. I searched Katy, but for the life of me I couldn't find the threads—no trace of the Otherside collar that decorated her body either.

"He left me here for you to find," she said, shaking now. "He took all the rest."

"Who? Are there other victims?" The last thing we needed was another vignette. "Katy, did Dane murder you?"

She nodded three times. I took that as a yes.

"You said others. Did Dane take someone else? Are—were they here?" I asked, keeping my voice measured as I continued to scan the room. "There was nothing you could have done to help them—"

"Ask her why Dane targeted her and her family," Stephan called from the doorway, where he'd thankfully retreated to. I shot him a look, but Katy was the one who answered.

"You don't understand—Dane isn't the one to be afraid of—" Her face whitened—a feat for any ghost—and she shot furtive glances at the rafters. "He's coming for me—I can feel it in the air."

"Dane? Another practitioner?" But Katy was becoming frantic. I searched for the Otherside that would tell me another ghost's or practitioner's bindings were at work. I even checked the piece of exposed sheet metal, the rafters that now drew Katy's gaze, but for the life of me I couldn't find the threads. There were no bindings, no extra Otherside beyond the background, now faintly scattered everywhere. Maybe if I set a pentagram around her . . . I decided it was worth the risk of scaring her. "Katy, I'm going to set a penta-gram—no one will be able to take you anywhere—"

"Oh god, you don't know yet, do you?" More furtive glances around the room. "You have no idea." She fixed me with eyes that were more haunted than a seventeen-year-old's had any right to be. "I haven't got much time—he'll find me soon. He's coming,

I can feel it—and he's angry, so angry at me—I've said too much."
Her eyes drifted back to her body. "You shouldn't have come—you
shouldn't have come—you shouldn't have come. He'll want you
next, I can tell from looking at you. He won't be able to resist—"
She jerked forward like a rag doll, cut off mid-sentence, as she
fought against some invisible force. One that for the life of me
I couldn't see.

Still, I wasn't taking any chances. I pulled a globe, fast. Pulling
a globe had got easier for me these last few weeks, ever since I made
my deal with Gideon for my Otherside sight. Before, my stomach
had churned each and every time, followed by sweats and fever
when I channelled too much—but now? A little pull in the small
of my stomach and a slight chill was all I felt.

"Just hang on—"

"What's happening?" Stephan called, and I made a motion for
him to stay back and ignored the chill in my body. Explanations
could wait.

Katy's eyes darted around the room. "Oh no, he's here. He said
he would come, once you arrived." And then she leapt from her
chair in one smooth, rapid movement.

Shit. I abandoned my pentagram. Katy darted amongst the rafters like a frightened animal, her lethargy gone.

Stop, for Christ's sake, so I can set another pentagram.

"Kincaid—" Stephan said, now standing beside me.

I could pull a globe and tease her out, but it might send her
farther down the rabbit hole of terrified madness. "I *think* she's
replaying her death," I said. "Or a version of it. Like a modified,
continuous loop every time she gets upset." But the drop in temperature and the scent of ozone I picked up was awful real for a
ghost's imagination. "Katy, hold still!"

But she didn't answer me. She fled faster through the rafters.

"It's not a loop. It's got to be Dane," Stephan said.

I was reluctant to take my eyes off the ghost, but I shot him a
sideways glance as he searched the room as well. He'd moved so his
back was to mine, watching, guarding . . .

It hadn't been a guess. He was certain—he *knew*. "Stephan—" I started.

Katy screamed and I abandoned my question. It could wait until later.

Katy cowered in the corner of the rafters, hiding from something only she could see. She wrung her hands with an unnatural, frantic speed, each movement more terrified than the last.

"Go back to Seattle, Kincaid—before it's too late—before you get tied up in knots like the rest of—"

She never finished the sentence. Her translucent hands flew to her throat as she choked, gasping for breath. The breath strangled out of her, like when she'd died. But this was different—

She gasped and flickered, then grasped at her neck. She started to fade. I caught sight of thin gold threads flickering around her neck as her haunted eyes stayed fixed on mine.

The temperature dropped even lower. I could see my breath now, and a frost catching on the dirt ground. It wasn't the kind of cold that follows a ghost; it was the kind that follows a practitioner's set. A big, powerful set of Otherside bindings.

I thought I caught a glimpse of Otherside coalescing into bindings around her neck, as if fuelling a working that was wrapping around her ghostly limbs like vines. But I couldn't make out the details. If it wasn't for all the background clouding things . . .

"Stephan! There's a ghost binder."

On impulse, I threw the Otherside I had pooled at her—all of it, everything I could. If there was a weakness, a fault in the bindings that were manifesting around her, it was my best, my only chance at disrupting them. And the only chance Katy had left to get free.

As soon as I released the globe, I gasped. Something icy reached in, and it didn't just chill—it burned, like a hot poker shoved through the veins in my neck, creeping into my skull and obscuring my vision.

The room flared gold around me, and I screamed against the cold and blindness.

When my vision returned, I got one hell of an eyeful.

Thin gold threads of Otherside hung in the air, ones I hadn't seen before—and all of them led to Katy, like marionette strings.

"Kincaid?" I heard Stephan yell behind me. Was that the first or second time he'd called out? I felt his hand grip my shoulder. "You need to stop—you're turning grey."

There was worry in his voice, but I shook it off along with his hand.

Had the marionette lines been there before? Had I not been able to see them?

Dirty, dirty, dirty bindings, as a ghost might say. And two practitioners could play at that game. I might not bind ghosts, but I could summon them. I reached out with my Otherside and, working as quickly as I could, freehand wove it around her arms, torso, neck, legs. When they were finished, I whispered, "Katy, I summon you."

It was all the prompt my bindings needed. They flared and, like vines suffocating a plant, continued weaving around Katy's limbs, choking out the thinner threads and symbols. Her fading halted and the thin gold bindings loosened and retreated.

She looked at me with the briefest glimpse of hope. "I think it work—" Her voice was choked off once again as the other practitioner's bindings doubled down, this time attaching and strangling my own bindings. No—wait, that wasn't right . . . It wasn't strangling my bindings, it was sucking the Otherside right out of them.

My bindings faded and fell apart as the Otherside was drained from them.

Katy managed to loosen the ghost binder's grip enough to speak.

"It's a trap," she managed, her voice reedy and eyes wide as they bored into me. "Run now, Kincaid Strange, before it's too late."

The bindings around her neck flared once more and Katy let out one last, agonized scream. And then whatever had grabbed hold of her, whoever was pulling the threads that controlled the binding, dragged her under.

And right before our eyes, the ghost of the young woman who had been Katy vanished.

"Kincaid?" I was vaguely aware of Stephan standing beside me, hand on my shoulder, sounding short of breath and rattled. Couldn't say I blamed him. "What the hell just happened?" he asked.

I shook my head, staring at the spot in the rafters where Katy had been a moment before. There was no trace of the threads, no trace of the symbols I thought I'd caught amongst the fog. No trace of her in the Otherside fog. She was gone.

And I hadn't been able to help her.

I'd lied to her, with good intention, but it still made me sick to my stomach. Everyone lies to ghosts. I tried not to. "She was bound," I said.

"How?" Stephan said, his face grim as he spun me around to face him. "And where did she go?"

I'd have loved to know that myself, especially after I'd launched more Otherside than any practitioner, especially a ghost binder, should have been able to handle. "The Otherside, but in someone's collection, a holding cell . . ."

I trailed off. Stephan's reaction puzzled me. He was clearly troubled by what he'd just seen—intensely so—but not surprised.

Ghost binders, soothsayers, are lay-in-wait predators, they trick their prey, but they aren't nearly as adept at handling Otherside. They don't violently attack out in the open like this; they trap their prey and confine them to the Otherside in holding cells, which Stephan would know . . .

Son of a bitch. I turned on him, fists clenched, all my anger at my own ineffectiveness and unpreparedness channelled at him. And rightfully so.

"You *knew* this would happen, didn't you? You knew a ghost binder was involved in this case before you even sent for me. Unbelievable!" It wasn't a question. They had a practitioner on site—Sinclair must have figured it out. Why the hell they'd decided to keep it from *me* . . .

Stephan's eyes hardened and his nostrils flared as he tried, with only partial success, to rein in his own frustration. "*Where* did she go? You saw the bindings, you saw it coming before it happened. So *where* did she go?"

I was taken aback by the strain in his voice and the aggression as he raked his hand through his hair. Worlds different from Aaron, who hid his emotions, covering them with logic.

"I don't know," I said, not backing down under Stephan's stare. "It was as if my bindings were consumed. I've never seen anything like it—"

"Make an educated guess."

I shook my head. "I can't. You haven't given me enough to even do that." This was getting ridiculous. Caution was one thing— I could understand that, I was an outsider after all—but we were well into stupid territory now. "Give me something, Stephan. How did you find the body? And why Katy? What's so special about her that a ghost binder would go to this kind of trouble?"

A shadow passed over Stephan's features.

"Hey, *you* invited *me*," I said. "If you didn't want me asking questions—"

"It had to be you."

I waited, and when he didn't elaborate, I gestured for him to continue.

He sighed, his body finally releasing the tension. "Ingrid, Sinclair's assistant, spotted something . . ."

"What? What the hell did she spot that could have possibly justified any of this?"

He made a pained expression. "I'm sorry," he said, and I got the distinct impression it was only partly heartfelt. "We couldn't get in just any practitioner. We needed you—"

I didn't let him finish. I started counting off on my hand. "I could have prepared: set a ring in place to protect her, found another practitioner to run interference, sent in another ghost to confuse the binder—" Hell, if I'd known the details, I could have consulted Gideon. God knows the ghost found this sort of thing interesting.

First a poltergeist, now a ghost binder, of all the things . . . I *hated* ghost binders. I'd worked a case in Canada where a ghost binder had been hired by a crime gang to silence the murdered victims' ghosts permanently before I could talk to them. Ghost binders aren't easy to catch, and they are downright dangerous, but there are *ways*.

I pointed at the rafters. "That didn't need to happen—"

"But it would have." The statement, so certain and final, came from a new, high-pitched voice—a woman's. I turned to see who was behind a voice that was overly exuberant for this early hour—for *any time* of the morning.

At the entrance stood a young woman my age, maybe a year or two on either side, and tall—or much taller than my five-foot-three frame. She'd forgone the forensic jumpsuit but hovered at the doorway. She was fashionably dressed in a delicate white blouse and tailored tan pants, wearing the kind of shoes that should never be exposed to a swamp. *Pretty* wasn't the word I'd use to describe her. She *was* pretty, but *striking* would be more accurate. Bright redorange hair and fair skin that complemented it perfectly, the mix of colouring that only natural redheads ever seem to have in tandem, as every teen who ever tried to dye their hair red in high school can tell you—including myself.

Her hair had been woven into fishtail braids and wrapped around her head . . . an expensive and time-consuming luxury, though I caught a few misplaced strands of frizz.

I frowned. The braids hadn't been undone in days. Practical, then, not vanity. And, I noted, her face was clean of makeup, her naturally red eyelashes and eyebrows plenty enough colour to frame her cornflower-blue eyes and other features.

This woman might not waste time in grooming luxuries, but she didn't have to. Unlike me, she'd won the genetic lottery.

She smiled shyly and held out a hand towards me. "Ingrid Sinclair. I work with Liam on the show. I'm his assistant—and his cousin," she rushed to clarify. "And you must be Kincaid Strange. I've so been looking forward to meeting you."

Normally, pretty women—especially ones like Ingrid—intimidate me. I go in expecting the worst. It's not a good trait; it's judgmental and not something I'm proud of. But Ingrid had an infectious personality—cheerful, open and candid, the kind that conveyed a rare warmth and friendliness.

My initial hesitation faded away, replaced by embarrassment at my knee-jerk reaction. I shook the offered hand. "Kincaid Strange, nice to meet you," I said.

She glanced sadly at Katy's body as she shook my hand. "There really was nothing you could have done. Agent Wolf said you'd be coming today, and it looks like you've unfortunately confirmed my own findings. Like Liam, I'm also a practitioner. Oh, dear," Ingrid said, faltering with concern as she glanced between the two of us. "She did find the fog, didn't she?"

Stephan nodded, but I detected frustration once again, and this time not directed at me. Well, at least I wasn't the only one who elicited that response from him. Somehow that made me feel better.

"Kincaid found the swamp fog, and she figured out Katy was being bound. I—ah—wasn't expecting you until later, Ingrid," he added gently. "I still have things to go over with Kincaid. If you could—"

Ingrid was undeterred. "I told him you'd find the swamp fog in record time, didn't I?" I caught the admiring glance Ingrid directed Stephan's way, and noted that Agent Wolf seemed to return it—for a moment. Then, as if remembering I was still there, he glanced back at me, though I detected a note of embarrassment.

Well, Kincaid, that crush was short-lived. Practically took care of itself.

"The fog is quite amazing, isn't it?" she said to me. "If it wasn't for—"

"Murder, ghost binding and torture of the dead? Yeah, I'd say those were pretty terrible circumstances." I glared at Stephan. "The ones everyone here knew about except me?"

Ingrid shook her head, blue eyes downcast. "I'm sorry, but we had no choice. I found something in the bindings holding Katy." She looked back up. "Your name."

The trigger that had set off whatever—whoever—had bound her. I felt my temper surge and clenched my fists. They'd hidden everything from me because *I* had been the trigger. They'd wanted to see if I would set it off.

Son of a bitch.

I turned my anger on Stephan and Ingrid in equal parts, all thoughts of earning respect gone. "Your plan was to get me to step in the barn and see if that poor girl's ghost would be bound? What the hell kind of circus are you idiots running?"

"I tried to undo them, but we were on a timeline. I'd hoped— well, I'd hoped I was wrong, and bringing you here might prevent her binding . . ." She trailed off. "Brett said if you knew, you wouldn't come."

Brett?

I turned to Stephan. "Just how many other practitioners do you have on site for this sick joke?"

Ingrid's expression turned uncertain and she glanced again at Stephan. "You—told her about me, didn't you?" she said, looking worried.

Stephan sighed. "We—were getting to that. Kincaid Strange, meet Ingrid Sinclair—Liam Sinclair's show assistant, licensed practitioner and world-class ghost binding expert."

Ghost binding expert? I looked Ingrid over once again. Surely there was no way this woman, all smiles and sunshine . . .

She shot Stephan an impatient look. "I asked Agent Wolf to speak to you before you arrived. We've hidden enough from you. Stephan should have told you—all my ghosts have told me the horrible experiences you've had with my kind before," Ingrid said, and started rolling up her delicate sleeves, exposing the telltale pinkish scars that ran from her wrists all the way up her arms. Ingrid's expression turned earnest. "I'm not just a ghost binding expert, Kincaid. I'm a soothsayer."

For a moment, I just stood there. Stephan and Ingrid watched me expectantly. I'll admit it, all I could do for a few long seconds was stare at the bindings on her arms, all of them bright with Otherside, the threads emanating off them extensive . . . *Jesus*, there were more of them than even Richan had, and he'd had years, *decades*, to bind ghosts.

There was a part of my brain—the professional, intelligent part—that desperately wanted me to suck it up and stay for the explanation of what had just happened.

But the other, more volatile, angry part of my mind, which knew what ghost binders can do, what they *enjoy* doing . . . it told me to call this complete and utter shit show what it was. It won.

"Fuck this." I turned on my heel and headed for the entrance, retrieving my boots and stripping the clean suit off in record time. I left Ingrid and Stephan scrambling to catch up as I left the barn.

I might be a practitioner without a lot of professional options and not much of a safety net to fall back on, but no way in hell was I going to work a crime scene with a ghost binder, especially after I'd just seen a ghost tortured by one. Not now, not ever.

There were some lines that hurt too much to cross.

CHAPTER 10

RUNAWAYS

"Kincaid, wait. Please, you don't understand. I—I mean me, Stephan and Katy need your help!"

I sighed as Ingrid chased after me. The frosted ground, now softened by the sun, squished under my motorcycle boots. I could only imagine what it was doing to her cream-coloured heels.

Don't add an assault charge to this disaster, Kincaid.

"I'm very sorry, but this is beyond my capabilities," I said through clenched teeth.

To her credit, Ingrid caught up and kept pace with me.

"Please just let me explain!"

"What, someone else managed to bind a ghost before you did? Not interested." I headed for the car. Eventually someone would agree to drive me back to the airport. Speaking of which, where was Aaron hiding? I owed him a piece of my mind. If he'd had *any* idea . . .

Anger flooded my senses and I could barely see straight. I planned to end the conversation with the slam of a car door, but Ingrid, tall and athletic, leapt ahead of me. She swivelled to face me, blocking the sedan.

"If you'd just give me a minute to explain," she pleaded.

She looked so sincere.

If it was Richan, I'd probably have thrown a punch already. But I couldn't bring myself to do it, and my hesitation had nothing to do with her wide eyes and disarming nature.

The inky blackness I'd seen in other soothsayers just didn't emanate off her. She didn't *feel* like soothsayers did. It threw me off.

Unfortunately, nothing short of violence was going to get the woman out of my way.

I relaxed my hands, letting them hang loose by my sides, and breathed, willing the anger away. As much as I deplored soothsayers, I wasn't going to resort to violence just yet, especially not with this many cops as witnesses. Memories of my fists pummelling Mindy were still too fresh in my mind.

"Look, I'm certain you are a perfectly nice, lovely young ghost binder," I managed. "You might even treat your flock of enslaved ghosts real well. But we have a serious, deep-rooted ethical conflict, one we're definitely not going to resolve in a half-hour, so if you don't mind?" I gestured for her to move away from the car door.

Ingrid's face fell, but she didn't offer any more resistance. She stepped aside. I grasped the handle. It was locked. Damn it.

I turned to see Stephan approaching. "Would you mind?" I said, gesturing at the locked door.

Stephan didn't argue with me outright, but his expression had lost its earlier friendliness. His regarded me coldly and placed a light hand on Ingrid's shoulder, a supportive gesture. It made me doubt their relationship was entirely professional.

I felt a twinge of disappointment, but the rational part of my brain reminded me I had enough male distractions in my life . . .

"How about you go get Liam from his trailer," Stephan said softly to Ingrid. "While I chat with Kincaid?"

Oh no. He was not going to guilt me into any kind of apology. I hadn't been given any of the information I needed, and as a result something horrible had happened. That was on him, not me. And Aaron.

My anger surged—Aaron *knew* better.

I glared right back at Stephan.

Ingrid bit her lip and, with one last, hopeful glance my way, turned to go. "I really do hope we can work together to help Katy."

Anyone can sound sincere with enough practice, Kincaid. Randall, Richan with art clients and artists like Cameron, even Max. Just because she's a beautiful, earnest young woman doesn't mean she's genuine. Inside, she could be as cruel and dark as Richan. Even worse, since she pretends to care about the ghosts bound to her. And if the scars I glimpsed under her sleeves were any indication, there were a *lot* of ghosts bound to her.

Damn it, I needed out of here.

I waited until Ingrid was out of earshot before I turned on Stephan. "So what was the plan? Ask me onto a crime scene completely blind, then hope I didn't notice the ghost binder on staff?"

He grimaced. "Yes and no. I didn't have a choice about omitting details—we needed to be sure about . . ." He trailed off, then finished, "Whether you could assess the crime scene first. But I'd hoped you'd get to know Ingrid a bit before she told you." He glanced at Ingrid's retreating form, as if looking for something else to say to convince me. He settled on, "She's not a bad person."

And Aaron *must* have known. Son of a— I scanned the grounds for him and crossed my arms. "Where is he? Detective Baal?"

"I asked him to go over the forensic data we've collected. We need fresh eyes on more than the paranormal aspects, and I was hoping it'd give you and me some time to talk."

Oh, for . . . I tapped the roof of the sedan, none too gently. "Car. Airport," I said. "You can tell Aaron what happened." I'd be certain to update him via text, likely laced with more than one expletive.

Stephan's mouth made a hard line. He seemed to be wrestling with a decision. "I'll take you wherever you'd like to go—airport, hotel, back here to yell at Aaron—but give me half an hour to explain everything. I'll throw in lunch—my treat."

I snorted. "Lunch is the absolute last thing on my mind." When Stephan didn't move, I softened my voice. "Look, Stephan, I'm not intimidated by tough cases, and you might very well have a fantastic reason for this shit show, but I don't do well with secrets and lies, not when it comes to work. And this . . . ?" I gestured at the barn.

"A professional lunch, and if I don't change your mind . . ." He trailed off, looking at me more earnestly than Ingrid had.

I was not immune to Stephan's charms. Damn it, Kincaid. I arched an eyebrow. "Wherever I want to go?"

He nodded.

There were enough warning signs here to scare away any sane consultant. But if I left now, I wouldn't get any answers about how a ghost had just been bound right in front of me—and why no one had taken steps to stop it.

My curiosity won out.

I grabbed the car handle. "Talk fast, Agent Wolf—I'd like to make it out on an afternoon flight."

Stephan grinned at me, possibly the first time I'd actually seen him smile since we'd met. He reached into his pocket, the lock unclicked, and I opened the passenger door.

"And they better have coffee," I added, sliding into the front seat.

As Stefan backed down the driveway, a silence settled between us and I searched for something to focus on. I settled on the drawings I'd made of the bindings on the buried metal sheet and those that had been drawn around Katy's neck.

As I sat back and perused them, I kept my thoughts to myself. Stephan and Aaron weren't the only ones who could subscribe to the school of not giving too much away.

✳

Fifteen minutes later, we reached a worn wooden road sign painted with the words *Welcome to the Town of Spalt.*

Well, *town* might be a generous label for Spalt. Fruit stands, a grocery store, a gas station and a few small shops stood like dandelions along the less than pristinely maintained single-lane highway.

Stephan pulled up to a shop with another hand-painted wooden sign above the door. This one read *Subs and Sandwiches.*

"Hope you aren't a diet nut." He gave me a tentative smile. He'd relaxed since we'd got away from the barn. The crinkles around his eyes and the lines on his forehead had smoothed out. He'd even whistled softly to himself during the latter half of the drive.

"As long as they have bacon on the menu and a decent cup of coffee, I'll be just fine," I told him, hopping out of the car, less upset about the detour now that my stomach was grumbling.

"Apple wood smoked, maple smoked—I think there's even smoked boar bacon on the menu."

That earned him a grin. So few people my age appreciate the different kinds of bacon. "I notice you didn't say anything about the coffee," I said.

"That's because it's better than good. It would be sacrilegious to sing its praises to the uninitiated."

He held the door open for me and a bell loudly announced our entry. "Practitioners first," he said, and I obliged. There was another hand-carved wooden sign just inside the door that directed patrons to seat themselves and order at the counter. I took the initiative and grabbed the only free table left by the window. No one native to the Northwest wastes sunshine in winter.

I gave Stephan my order—the double-smoked boar BLT and a large coffee—and while he headed to the deli counter, I took the opportunity to do something I loved to do in a new place: people-watch. What kind of people lived in a small town like this?

For the size of the town, the restaurant was surprisingly packed. Most tables were filled with groups of three or more; only the smaller two-seaters were left empty. Most looked over the age of forty, but not old enough yet to be retirees. Farmers? Cottagers? It was awful late in the year to be up at the cottage—and despite the large swamp, I'd seen no signs of lakes or rivers of the sort vacationers flock to.

"It's a farming community," Stephan said, sliding into the seat across from me while balancing two white mugs brimming over with steam.

I took one, wrapped my hands around it and sipped the hot liquid, still not completely recovered from the swamp's Otherside chill. As promised, it was good—better than the white-and-green mermaid's offerings since it was decidedly on the lighter, less burnt side.

"I won't lie, Stephan. It's not a religious experience, but it'll do." I gestured towards the door. "And on the ride over, this didn't strike me as farming land." There'd been no patchwork fields in shades of green and yellow on the way in.

"Livestock, marsh plants—cranberries, blueberries, wineries." He took a sip of his coffee. "This area was settled in the 1800s by German and Austrian immigrants, and if the hipsters who run the craft brewery are to be believed, the original barley, wheat and hop strains the settlers planted are still here—heirloom crops."

Interesting—and nothing to do with the murder. "I'm curious what an old German town has to do with this case." I sipped my coffee. "Oh, yeah, and while you're at it, you can explain why no one told me about the ghost binder on staff."

Stephan chuckled. "Aaron warned me you prefer to get to the point. All right. There are two reasons for the secrecy, and both are classified." He paused long enough to let that statement settle as he stared at me over his coffee. "It goes no further than this table. Aaron doesn't even know the full extent, though for what it's worth, he says you're trustworthy." He paused again. "Katy and her family aren't Dane's only new victims. There are dozens, maybe hundreds."

I tried to wrap my head around that statement, while Stephan waited patiently. Aaron had first contacted me about Dane a week ago, when Katy had gone missing . . . and since then, more victims? Potentially hundreds?

"Why hasn't there been anything in the news? Not even the undead branch of the CIA can hide *hundreds* of paranormal deaths . . ." I trailed off as the significance of his phrasing sunk in. He hadn't said *murders*. "Ghosts. His other victims are ghosts," I said quietly.

Stephan nodded. "Every last one of Dane's victims' ghosts has gone missing. The first report came in from the Lindstrom family, one of Dane's earliest victims. Bill Lindstrom's mother bought a mirror after her son and grandkids were killed so she could still visit them. She said it wasn't like them to miss a Sunday dinner. Initially, our office ignored her missing ghost report, figured they'd moved on." He shrugged. "They're ghosts. But over a matter of days, it escalated. More of the original victims were gone. And then the local Portland practitioners started calling in, and then the sooth-sayers, all reporting their own missing ghosts . . ." He paused to sip his coffee and stared down at the table.

"And then?"

"And then we saw one of Dane's previous victims being taken, while we were interviewing him. Just like Katy—immobilized in place one moment, then dragged off screaming silently." Stephan tried to conceal his shudder, but not well enough. He turned his hazel eyes back on me. "The missing ghosts are classified information."

Which on the surface seemed ridiculous, but when you dove a little deeper it made perfect sense.

If it got out that a serial killer was rounding up or, worse, some-how harming the ghosts of his victims—that it was even possible . . .

Smaller things have triggered mass hysteria.

"Exactly like Katy?"

Stephan nodded. "Minus the body. They were unmoving, unspeaking, exactly like you found her."

"Bindings?"

"You can see our practitioners' notes yourself. As soon as you agree to stay."

I ignored that and instead asked, "How does Dane fit into all this?" Dane had been many things—a monster, a sadist, a torturer—but he hadn't been a practitioner. How would he know how to manipulate Otherside? Because, sure enough, Otherside was involved.

Stephan inclined his head. "Sinclair initially ruled Dane out, despite the fact that the first missing ghosts were all his victims. He thought it was more likely some practitioner was fooling around with soothsaying, playing a sick joke then taking it a few leaps too far. But then Ingrid had the bright idea to see if she could get one of the paralyzed ghosts to talk—practitioner-style. She thought if she could get through for one moment, just one, they could tell her who was behind it. She broke through"—he snapped his fingers— "and as soon as she did, they were dragged away, just like Katy."

Unfortunately, that was a fairly common strategy for keeping a ghost quiet. I'd seen it in the organized crime case I'd worked in Vancouver. What's the best way for a gang leader to make certain the ghost of a victim doesn't talk and tell the police where all the skeletons are kept? Keep a talented practitioner or ghost binder on retainer to make certain they can't. But a dead serial killer binding ghosts? That was new.

"The first disappearance we wrote off as a fluke, lack of preparation. We tried to contact another of his victims, this time with a pentagram, and Ingrid and Liam both on deck to run interference. Having them there did nothing. The third time, Ingrid tried binding the ghost beforehand, but to no effect, and that's when we decided the ghost disappearances were outside the usual realm of paranormal activity.

"When Katy was found here, Ingrid recognized the binding symbology. It was the same one we'd seen with the other missing victims' ghosts. The metal sheet, markings on the table—all similar."

"Katy was expecting me—or whoever put her there was." I said it offhand, but at the look he gave me, I added, "There's no way she would have known my name. If I were in your shoes, I'd say that would make me a . . ." I trailed off before I said *suspect*. Shit.

Stephan shook his head. "A suspect? I considered you briefly, but the motive isn't there and you haven't left Seattle in over a year. You don't associate with poltergeists, or any other ghosts that can pull that kind of damage—Nathan Cade isn't the type—and Ingrid's ghosts swear up and down you aren't involved, so there's that."

I inclined my head, then took a long sip of coffee before saying, "I was pissed off that I wasn't even on your FBI's list of practitioners to consult on Dane in the first place," I said. "Aaron knows that."

"Yeah," Stephan said, nodding slowly, his hazel eyes evaluating me. It's not every day someone offers up a motive after they've been cleared. Supposedly cleared. "But you're not the revenge type." He paused for a moment, then added, "And you're not the fame type either. We did you a favour not calling."

"A favour?"

Stephan must have seen his misstep. "Clearly some assumptions were made that shouldn't have been. If we're being completely frank, I wasn't certain until today you weren't behind this. But you were caught as flat-footed as the rest of us. Unless you're a fantastic actor," he added, the corners of his mouth turning up in a slight smile. "Though if you were, I think you'd be doing something a lot more lucrative with your talents than helping seedy lawyers contest wills."

The personal analysis wasn't exactly comforting. Neither was the fact that the FBI paranormal division had obviously researched me. But at least I wasn't a paranormal serial killer suspect. This time. Learn to accept the pulled punches when you can, Kincaid.

Besides, I had a much bigger problem: Katy had asked for me by name.

"You didn't need a consult at all. You brought me down here to see what would happen, what Katy would say if I actually showed up." And to finish clearing me as a potential suspect.

"If it makes you feel better, we didn't think you'd be in any danger. Liam was on hand and Ingrid monitored things closely from outside the barn. For what it's worth, I'm sorry for the runaround. I'd rather have you think I was clandestine and incompetent, and rule your involvement out, than . . ." He trailed off.

I filled it in myself: than invite a killer or an accomplice to waltz in armed with everything the FBI knew about the crime scene.

"I decided it was worth the risk," he said.

I also wasn't particularly crazy about the findings. Whoever was behind these new murders had a vested interest in me.

"And we weren't lying about the consult. Which brings us to the second reason for the secrecy and why we brought you in."

He paused and stared at his now-empty mug. "Liam Sinclair isn't an incompetent practitioner. He's dying. He's in the late stage of Ram's Inn syndrome."

"Jesus . . ." I managed to cover my mouth before I spewed coffee and glanced at the neighbouring tables to see if anyone else had caught a sliver of our conversation. They hadn't. In fact, most of the lunch crowd had cleared out or were about to leave. Still, I lowered my voice. "Ah—god, that's . . ." What? Horrible? Ram's Inn was the last thing I'd expected Stephan to say. "How far along is he?"

"Far enough it's a problem," Stephan said solemnly.

Well, it explained why I hadn't seen Liam anywhere on the crime scene.

It goes by different names: Ram's Inn and Norfolk syndrome in the English-speaking Western world, Wolfsegg in Austria and Germany, Polveglia in Italy, Bhangarh in India—an uncannily similar nomenclature, derived from famous haunted places. Ram's Inn syndrome is a rare curiosity in the medical community, a disease that only strikes practitioners and their ilk. As long as people have used Otherside and contacted ghosts, there have been cases of Ram's Inn syndrome.

It starts harmlessly enough: headaches, lethargy, a cold that chills the bones and never seems to go away. If I had hypochondriac tendencies, I'd probably be convinced I had it every other day of the week. Most practitioners imagine they have it at some point. But unlike the normal aches and pains that come with practitioning and using Otherside, the symptoms never go away. They pile on top of each other. Cold becomes a case of permanent chills, lethargy morphs into an inability to leave the bed, and the headaches become a permanent fixture.

So, you stop using Otherside for a week or so, take a break.

And that's when things get much worse. That's when the pain starts. Cramping muscles, painful chest spasms, shivering, feverish sweating, and insomnia. And it only abates once the practitioner contacts the Otherside. And the cycle starts again, the symptoms getting worse and worse each time.

Doctors describe it as an autoimmune disease, the body attacking parts of itself most affected by Otherside. But when the practitioner finally clues in and stops using Otherside, the body overcompensates, and a whole new round of attacks begin.

Damned if you use Otherside, damned if you don't. Ram's Inn is rare, completely unpredictable and always fatal. You can't catch it or pass it on, but there is no way to determine if a practitioner is vulnerable to the syndrome until it's too late.

I'd taken a page from Nate's philosophy on worrying regarding Ram's Inn; namely, I tried never to think about it. It affects men almost four times more than women, so I reasoned I was at more risk of developing ulcers from worry than of acquiring Ram's Inn.

Still, shitty luck for Liam Sinclair. Was that why he'd lost control of Dane's zombie? And how the hell had Liam been hiding his symptoms on national TV and keeping them out of the tabloids?

"Ah—Ram's Inn is fast-acting . . . How is he?"

Stephan shrugged. "The autoimmune medications give him some symptom-free breathing room between cycles, but they're getting shorter and the symptoms aren't abating as much as they did even two weeks ago. He spends most of his time sleeping, keeping away from people. Ingrid handles the day-to-day."

If he was still somewhat functional, then he couldn't have had Ram's Inn for more than a year, maybe as little as six months.

"How much longer does he have?" The question just kind of came out.

Stephan shrugged. "Hard to say. A few weeks, a few months. He's bad, Kincaid. He can use all the help he can get. We're lucky to have Ingrid. We'd be lucky to have you. If you're worried about Dane, we're prepared to offer what protection we can if—" He stopped short. "If something happens. We're in a better position to offer protection than the Seattle PD." He arched his dark eyebrows. "Might even be better protection than some of your other, more *eccentric* friends."

There was no doubt in my mind he meant Lee. And that was debatable. Still, I kept quiet. Things were never quite what they seemed in this world, were they? I couldn't offer an answer. I wasn't ready to.

I had two questions I needed to ask first. "I get why you wanted me down here, and I get the secrecy." It was common sense: if Dane was involved, and all roads pointed in that direction, then he had to have a living accomplice, one who knew their Otherside. "But you still haven't told me how you found Katy in the first place. If her ghost couldn't leave, and none of the other victims steered you this way . . ."

"Stephan is leaving out the most important part."

I froze in my chair, then slowly turned around. Standing directly behind me was a tall, broad-shouldered woman who I guessed was in her seventies but seemed remarkably sturdy. Her thick grey-blond hair was pulled back into a tight bun. She wore a heavy apron over a flannel work shirt and carried two sandwich-laden plates.

"So you're the new practitioner?" she said to me, friendly enough with a terse smile that mostly reached her eyes.

"Yes, and I'm a good one," I shot back. "I've worked a lot of murder cases. I know my ghosts. And my zombies." I smiled at her.

"Gran," Stephan said, "your timing is impeccable. Allow me to introduce Kincaid Strange. Kincaid Strange, this is Bergen Wolf, my grandmother."

Stephan wasn't kidding when he said he'd grown up in the area. And that explained the similarity in features—nose, jawline—and, now that I was looking for it, they had the same hazel-coloured eyes. Even their height and muscular body type, the kind common in people whose families have spent generations on farms. Minus his grandmother's fairer colouring, the familial resemblance was definitely there.

She slid the plates in front of us and, to my surprise, pulled up a chair. I realized that the restaurant was empty now except for the three of us. That unnerved me even more than her sudden presence. I started to rise, but Stephan stopped me with a hand. "Remember? You wanted answers."

"Let's get a look at you, then," Bergen said, and turned a warm but piercing gaze on me. "I expected you to have more signs of Otherside use, but I can see there's barely a hint of it on you. Not like the other poor fellow," she whistled, and exchanged a look with her grandson. Then pointed at my plate. "Go on, you don't want it to get cold. I'll talk while you eat. You're a slip of a thing, you look like you need a good meal."

When people tell me I ought or ought not to do something, I usually do the exact opposite, out of principle. But in this instance, well, my stomach won out. Besides, Stephan was inhaling his food.

"I suppose Stephan hasn't told you about our ghosts? No, I can tell he hasn't got to that yet," she said as I took an enormous bite of my smoked boar bacon BLT.

"More ghosts?" I shot Stephan a look.

"Oh yes," she said, her eyes widening. "Small town with a history of old families—over two hundred years' worth. Then you add that swamp."

Ghosts are drawn to a few things—water, the trappings of their dearly departed lives, set mirrors and anything else that gives off a hint of Otherside. A place where generations of your family lived and died feels more like a home than a rented apartment lived in for a couple of years. Not that you couldn't get attached to a new place, but it is less ingrained. History is a powerful attractant for a ghost. It pulls them, draws them in like nectar draws in bees. Eventually, an old town or even an old homestead begins to make its own Otherside, drawing more ghosts in. Add in a watershed or a lake or river . . . Eventually, with enough ghosts trying to stay, the place itself starts to take on an afterlife of its own.

It isn't good or bad—or avoidable. It just is. Families tend to adapt.

It clicked. The proximity of Spalt to the farm where Katy's body had been found, a history of ghosts, even Stephan's position with the paranormal leg of the FBI . . .

"Your family ghosts live here, don't they?"

"More than even a practitioner like yourself can imagine," Bergen said, leaning in. "My parents, grandparents, cousins, even a brother." She lowered her voice and added, "My daughter, Stephan's parents."

I glanced at Stephan. He nodded, though made a face at the personal revelation. "A car accident five years ago."

"They told you about Katy," I said, looking between the two of them. "What else did they tell you?"

Bergen made a face. I stared at them both.

"Oh, come on. Ghosts gossip more than a pack of high schoolers."

Finally, Stephan gave his grandmother a small nod.

"That Dane's hiding in the swamp," she said.

My gut reaction was to say it was impossible—there was no way he could be hiding, it wasn't in a poltergeist's nature, not with this many people milling around. But the way she said it, the certainty . . . "You're a practitioner, aren't you?"

Her face was impossible to read. "Not exactly."

I shook my head. I decided if she was another ghost binder, I didn't want to know. "Okay. I believe you." I took another bite of my sandwich. "Now introduce me to one of these ghosts."

Stephan and Bergen exchanged a look.

"That's the tricky part," Bergen said.

People can get funny with the family ghosts, overprotective. But I'd need to speak with the ghosts directly. "I'm not—it's not that I don't believe them," I started, though it wouldn't be the first ghost to lie with something juicy to get a practitioner's attention. "But if they're right, then there are details that can help me track Dane." And whoever was behind the bindings. "Look, it's hard to explain, but trust me, my methods work—"

Bergen didn't let me finish. "I don't mean that I won't let you talk to our ghosts, I mean I can't. And it's why I asked Stephan here to bring you to me." She leaned across the table. "You find ghosts people have made disappear. All those ones up in Canada, that was you?"

I swallowed. "Yeah. Those were all me." Like I said, there was an awful lot of organized crime in Vancouver. I had a knack for tracking down ghosts no one wanted found.

Bergen studied my face. She and Stephan had the same intense stare. She made a *tsk*ing sound after a moment. "Right after they told us about the poor girl, our ghosts vanished as well. All of them, every last one."

A few ghosts here and there was one thing, but an entire swamp full? "How haunted was the bog?"

"Very," Stephan said. "And they vanished almost down to the minute I stepped on the plane with Ingrid and Liam to investigate Katy."

"They were terrified of something," Bergen added. "Behaving just like that poor girl, and it wasn't only that ghost Dane they were afraid of, though they didn't ask for you like Katy did," Bergen offered. Stephan frowned, and she added, "Oh, don't mind me. I can't help but hear you on the phone in the living room. Your voice echoes. I'll stay out of the way of your murder cases." Her eyes hardened. "But I want my family's ghosts back."

"Gran," Stephan warned, "I brought Kincaid here to talk. Not to find your ghosts."

"Hmmm. Yet I'm thinking if she's after Dane and looking for the others, she might as well look for mine. Seems to me, if someone's out there stealing ghosts, they're probably keeping them in the same place." She swept up our mugs. "Refill your coffee, Kincaid? It'll only take a sec."

Stephan sighed as soon as his grandmother was out of earshot. "Gran doesn't mean any harm. She's telling the truth about the ghosts—that they saw Dane and that they're missing," he said earnestly.

"And that they're all connected? Your family's swamp ghosts, Katy, and Dane's old victims?"

"Probably," he admitted. "Though I don't know why. It's complicated for me to be using FBI time and resources looking for my grandmother's ghosts, especially my parents' ghosts, when I already have their statements," he admitted. He then leaned across the table, the suddenness and intensity of the gesture sending the butterflies rustling in my stomach once again. "Kincaid, do you know what the paranormal unit does at the FBI?"

"Investigate federal cases where a paranormal element is involved and enlist practitioners to provide assistance contacting victims."

"We solve *crimes*," he said. "Katy's murder is a crime, possibly involving a poltergeist of a known killer and possibly a psychotic soothsayer. The disappearances of her ghost and the ghosts of Dane's earlier victims are relevant to the case, but the ghosts in the swamp?" He shook his head. "It's not a crime to bind ghosts. Not even a whole swamp full. Not even when they're family."

"But—they're witnesses. Your grandmother just said they saw Dane's ghost in the swamp. That's proof he's still active. They might know where he is. And what if they saw the murder, or the events leading up to it? At the very least, it's removing evidence, possibly tampering with it."

Stephan inclined his head. "We don't get as much leeway as they do in Canada to go looking for potential witnesses. Not unless they're tied to an actual crime, like fraud and murder. And considering the ones in question are my own family ghosts? I'm already treading a grey area working a murder in my own backyard. *I* have to pool *my* resources into finding the ghosts of the people who were murdered."

I picked up on the not-so-subtle hint. "I'm going to take a wild guess that as a consultant, one who is also under some kind of FBI protection as relevant to the case and a potential target, I have more leeway?"

He grinned. "I suppose you would," he said, and then his smile fell. "But I don't think you're necessarily the target, Kincaid."

"Why else would the ghosts be asking after me? Katy said—"

Stephan shook his head. "That he wouldn't be able to resist you. But I think Dane or whoever is pulling the strings now wants you here because of what my gran just said. I know serial killers, and one thing they all have in common? They all want their genius discovered eventually. They all want to be famous."

"And I'm the practitioner who used to find missing ghosts."

Bergen returned with three mugs of coffee and sat back down. "So, practitioner. What will it take for you to find my ghosts?"

I shot a surreptitious glance at Stephan, but he was concentrating on his mug. Ghost binders, serial killers, missing ghosts. That was the kicker, though: it was stacking up to one hell of a mystery. That, and this woman wanted me to find her ghosts, not get rid of them.

I sighed. Nate would say I'm a sucker. It's a wonder I don't have an apartment filled with stray cats and dogs.

Instead, I collect wayward ghosts.

"Why don't you tell me more about these swamp ghosts," I asked her.

"We're an old town, Ms. Strange. My great-grandparents and most other people who settled Spalt were from the same small region in northern Germany that bordered a large bog. My grandparents didn't care one lick about religion, but they knew ghosts. When they came over, the first thing they looked for was a bog or swamp. You never appreciate the dead until some illness sweeps through the town, and a dearly departed great-grandparent remembers what caused it or how to stop it. The living are bad at remembering things more than a generation, but the dead?" She shook her head. "Until two weeks ago, that swamp was filled with our dead—it always has been. Grand-parents, children who didn't make it through bad harvests and win-ters, boys who went to all the wars and returned as ghosts, victims of the 1918 flu, tuberculosis. I remember hearing babies in the marsh crying out for their mothers when I was a little girl—though that's not so common now as babies don't die like they did in their first year." She sighed. "Never lasted long, which is a good thing. I like to think the other ghosts took care of them, or some power that be came and whisked them away. It seems a cruel fate for a baby not old enough to understand they were alive to linger in death. Oh, yes, that swamp has a history with this town. We respect our dead here. We talk to our ghosts, we aren't afraid of them. We visit them twice a year and whenever else the fancy takes us—or did until a few weeks ago."

"Is it possible they were scared off? That they fled somewhere else they thought was safe? Like to the Otherside?"

"How do I say this . . . the swamp *changes* things. The ghosts have rules. They'd never abandon us—not over something as simple as a poltergeist. Knock on wood, we've only had one of those before. A poor young fellow who went off to war and found his way back violent and vengeful. No, they wouldn't leave over the trouble that's in the barn across the swamp. Something pushed them out."

Bergen's hazel eyes bored into me as she spoke. The way she talked about the dead, visiting them in a swamp—I don't care how isolated their small town might be, Spalt's relationship with their dead was unusual, and reckless.

There were no overt signs of Otherside—no unnatural chill, no sign of Otherside use on her face or Stephan's, but . . . it couldn't hurt to check. I blinked, ever so slightly, and slid my Otherside sight into place. I looked at Bergen's face, though if she noticed anything unusual, she didn't let on. Then I caught it, a glimmer of Otherside over the counter—*engraved* into the counter—and the door, and the tables, even carved subtly with the grain into the old wood floor. Small symbols and runes, some of which I recognized to mean welcome, home and hearth. Our food had been engraved with symbols for health and nurture. Even the bacon had been decorated with the smallest etchings—forgiveness and thanks for this animal we've sacrificed to eat.

No wonder the food and coffee had tasted so damn good. I looked up at Bergen with a little awe. There was only one group of people who used Otherside like this. "Jesus, you're a witch—a *real* one."

Bergen let out a low whistle, sat back in her chair and clapped. "That might just be the most entertaining thing anyone's said to me in years. Will you look at that, Stephan? Right out of the blue. Not even Sinclair caught on so quick. And it takes this little slip of a thing a lunch to figure it out." She laughed again and gave me a shrewd, appraising look. "Oh, you impress me. Now care to tell me how you figured it out without tapping the barrier? You are a practitioner, after all? Unless you fibbed a bit about that, and you have a bound ghost hiding?" Her eyes darted around the room.

"Ah—no," I said, trying to recover. Jesus Christ, I was sitting in front of an honest-to-god witch. One whose family had survived how many centuries of purging, betrayal and witch hunters? "I, ah, have another method," I said, not wanting to disclose more than I had to regarding the unique source of my Otherside sight.

"Oh, there's a whole town of us. A lot of towns like us, next to bogs, swamps and marshes. All of us have our tricks, passed down

over centuries. We've learned to keep to ourselves. And our ghosts."
Her eyes took on a steely look, not unlike one I recognized from
Gideon. "Now, how did you figure it out?"

I swallowed, wondering how much she knew of sorcery. "I— It's
a long story," I said. Voodoo priests and some ghosts can tell if you're
lying; I had no idea if witches could too.

That perked her interest. "Some voodoo trick I haven't heard of?
I know you were the apprentice of a powerful voodoo priest."

I wondered if Bergen could see my own Otherside bindings. She
could certainly use Otherside if the bindings around the deli were
any indication. Or perhaps it was more like soothsaying, where the
ghosts do the work. I changed the topic. "I'm a practitioner. You
probably know more about ghosts than I do, and I don't know any
witchcraft." I shook my head. "I'm just not sure how much I can
help you."

Bergen *tsk*ed. "If we could find them ourselves, we would have
already. Insanity is repeating the same action over and over hoping
for a different result—or is that stupidity? Or both? Either way, it's
time to approach the problem differently, I think. I need someone
like you. One who can find missing and stolen ghosts. Keep whatever secrets you like." She nodded at her grandson. "He needs you
to help him catch a killer. Me? I'm more simple. I want to hire you,
Kincaid Strange—we, the witch coven of Spalt, want to hire you to
bring back our ghosts. *Every last one of them.*"

There was power in her words—I felt it course through me.
Kindling the air. Sure enough, the air was tingling with Otherside
that wove itself into patterns to the rhythm of her voice. It wasn't
just the inscriptions on the furniture, food and building. Her very
words carried Otherside. *Find, help, favour.* They were hard to
ignore. Not just because of the witch magic, but because she was
begging me.

There was a chill in the diner and the door chimes rang of their
own accord.

Oh, hell, if I was looking for one ghost, I might as well look for
a village . . .

I stood and held out my hand to Bergen. "No promises, but I'll see what I can do. Consider me on the case."

We shook, and her strange Otherside tingled up my arm, different from Gideon's bargains, but a bargain all the same.

I turned to Stephan. "You want me to help you with your murders and finding Martin Dane's poltergeist? I think it's high time I got a better look at the swamp and talked to Liam Sinclair."

CHAPTER 11

FOXES IN THE HENHOUSE

We headed back to the barn, but this time I had Stephan stop his car halfway down the driveway, away from prying eyes and the ghost binder. I needed to get a better feel for the swamp, and it gave me a chance to probe—my way. I hadn't forgotten Gideon's warning against using my own particular talents in front of other practitioners.

It also gave me a chance to question Stephan.

As we exited the car and I picked my way through the salal bushes and mud, I asked, "So who owns this place?"

"A holding company. We contacted them and they didn't even know about the barn. It was being rented out as agricultural land—cranberries. When we chased the tenants, it proved a dead end. The only thing real about them were the rent cheques, always delivered on time for the past five years."

Hunh. An awful lot of trouble to hide this place, and well before Dane's murder spree. Considering the sheer volume of Otherside, it'd be very attractive to a practitioner up to no good. "And the original owners?"

Stephan shook his head, picking his way behind me, more careful on account of his dress shoes. "Parcelled-off lot of land. Happened fifty years ago."

I saw a pool of water up ahead, knee-deep maybe. This ought to be far enough in, and far enough away from prying eyes. I braced myself and readied for the claustrophobic fog of Otherside. *You can stop any time*, I reminded myself.

"Do Ingrid and Liam know about the missing swamp ghosts?" I asked Stephan.

"Gran doesn't feel comfortable telling them—she doesn't trust Ingrid because of the ghost binding. Liam and Ingrid suspect something is up with the swamp, though, on account of there being no ghosts at all."

That wasn't surprising. This much Otherside always attracts ghosts . . . I shrugged off the last bit of reluctance and slid my Otherside sight halfway in place. "Can't say I blame your grandmother." I opened my eyes. Fog, fog, fog, as far as the eye could see.

"Do you like people judging you on your profession?"

Even through the thick Otherside, I could see Stephan's face, unimpressed, cast in ghost grey. "No, I suppose not. But ghost binding poses an ethical dilemma. It's not personal." Or no more personal than not letting a convicted criminal into your house for Thanksgiving dinner. I'm forgiving—but not that forgiving.

He was silent while I felt out the swamp's Otherside. Then, "I know about the ghost binder the Vancouver police used, the one who was dirty. I know why you won't work in Canada anymore." His eyes narrowed. "I'm sorry I wasn't completely forthcoming with you, and that's on me, but Ingrid really isn't the same situation, is it?"

I felt the anger inside me start to build at his defence of Ingrid. Stephan had a point. That made it worse . . .

I sighed, forcing my professional hat back on with great effort. "I'm not a complete asshole. I appreciate the situation. I'll even work with your soothsayer. That doesn't mean I'm happy about it."

"You might not agree with her, you might not even like her.

I'm not asking you, I am begging you to work with her—just briefly. To compare notes," he rushed.

I motioned for Stephan to step back and faced the swamp. Time to get a proper read.

I settled in and looked at the water, the moss, the fog, even the rustling of the trees. The Otherside fog touched all of it, rising from pools of water and saturating even the air. It was my second time pulling a globe today—I'd have to be careful. I tensed, ready for the nausea, but just like at the barn, the swamp somehow dampened the effects. Probably on account of so much Otherside being available.

All right, swamp. Let's see how you behave, shall we?

I let out my pooled Otherside in waves. The fog dispersed and swirled around in response.

Now, that was odd. Some sections of the fog hadn't budged an inch. I pooled more.

"Your grandmother is quite confident the swamp's resident ghosts don't cause mischief."

"She knows them better than I do."

"Hmmm." This time I pushed more Otherside over the water, concentrating on the patches that hadn't moved. Sure enough, as the lighter Otherside fog cleared, thick, branchlike limbs of it remained, traversing the swamp as far as I could see.

"So," I ventured, still working out how to word the question, "your grandmother is a witch, your hometown is full of them . . . Is it genetic?" I asked hesitantly. "I mean, are you a witch, warlock, wiz—"

"No," he said, cutting me off. He was emphatic, and abrupt enough in his denial, but when no explanation was forthcoming I couldn't help myself asking, "Is it a choice then? Training? Considering your line of work, I'd think—"

"I don't have the talent for it, all right? Whatever Gran looked for . . ." he trailed off. "I'm not a witch, and can we please leave it at that?" Stephan said, his demeanor making it clear that that avenue of conversation was personal. And closed. Despite my curiosity, I desisted with my questions. Mostly because I'd made him so visibly uncomfortable. I sent more waves of Otherside the swamp's way, but the branches stayed unmoving, despite the lighter gold dust fog swirling around them. The more fog cleared, the more I realized the Otherside branches were everywhere, winding around the trees, through the air, dipping into the water.

And they stayed steady in the wake of the disturbance like a solid, stable mirror binding would. But it was all too big. I couldn't be looking at a binding set, could I?

I sent out more Otherside, blowing away the fog in rippling waves, uncovering more and more of the mass. It was as if a living, breathing tree of Otherside had rooted itself in the swamp. A massive set. Feeding in and feeding off.

I turned around and took the opportunity to take a good look at Stephan with my Otherside. Nothing. Not a trace of bindings. But then again, Bergen had had none either. I crossed my arms. "What about you, Stephan? What do you think of the ghosts that are supposed to live here?"

He frowned, my question clearly catching him off guard. "I've seen and spoken to ghosts since I was a kid—everyone in this town has, as long as anyone can remember. They're like family. Many of them are."

Including his parents. I narrowed my eyes. The Otherside fog was drifting, licking at Stephan as if recognizing him. I looked down. Otherside collected around my feet, but all it did was settle back to the ground.

"And you can't recall any of them having ever caused trouble?" On the ride back, that detail had bothered me. Bergen trusted the ghosts too much. The majority of ghosts don't mean harm, and a few can even be inspired to care for the odd living—like Nate, albeit for selfish reasons initially. And that was my problem. Ghosts by their very nature are not altruistic. They are selfish.

A few of the ghosts should have naturally leaned towards mischief. It didn't matter that the town inhabitants were their own descendants—children, grandchildren and all. A few years dead and ghosts start to forget what it was like to be a member of the living.

It always starts harmlessly enough. Waking family members in the middle of the night to discuss a book, or some piece of gossip glimpsed in the mirror or overheard from another ghost. Or wanting to play with great-grandchildren. No one pays it any mind, some even encourage it. A few nights of lost sleep isn't the end of the world. And it's understandable—people get lonely, the dead aren't any different.

But over the decades an innocent midnight visit turns into a treasure hunt, where some long-lost ancestor might lead their very own grandchildren into a forest, a construction site, a lake. Forgetting the little things, like the fact that children can't swim, or don't always watch for traffic, or can't find their way home alone after dark. They forget about the things the living learn to fear. The ghost might even realize their mistake, too late, and try to save the child. They might succeed, but by then the damage is done. They are no longer a loved relative watching over their descendants, but a dangerous apparition.

I arched an eyebrow at Stephan, who was looking defensive now, or maybe just uncomfortable with my personal questions. I continued to prod. "There was never a great-great-grandfather children were warned to stay away from, the one who tries to get the kids to search the swamp at night for—I don't know, a lost whisky flask, a pot of gold—"

"Those are leprechauns. What's your point?"

"My point is, a ghost isn't the most reliable witness. Which, if you've interviewed as many ghosts as I think you have, you know. They lie better than the living, and some of them can weave a hell of a story, all the better to keep their living audience riveted." I shook my head.

He gave me a terse smile. "You make ghosts sound like those Nigerian princes who keep asking me to help them sneak money out of their country."

I smiled back and, letting my Otherside sight go, uncrossed my arms and gestured around me. "How does your grandmother get the ghosts to behave? Are they bound to the swamp?"

Stephan's face darkened. "Just because I don't have a problem working with a ghost binder doesn't mean I believe in binding them."

"Witches don't bind ghosts?"

"My grandmother and the rest of Spalt forbids it. We'll leave it at that."

There was a warning in there not to go further. I ignored it.

"Compulsion, then?" I gestured at the swamp. "Those giant bindings I'm assuming are your grandmother's work? To keep the ghosts in check?"

Stephan swore and closed his eyes. "She didn't think you'd find those. Liam and Ingrid didn't. Yes, they're witchcraft. And they aren't compulsion—they're harmless. They're rules."

Tomato, tomahto. I closed my eyes and felt for the Otherside before opening them again. Find the ghosts, not our secrets—wasn't that the way it always was?

I felt the witchcraft now—foreign, and softer than practitioning, less tangible, melded into the swamp.

And powerful. If the ghosts hadn't been bound to the swamp, it meant that, regardless of what Bergen claimed, nothing was here to prevent the ghosts from leaving. The rules were an agreement that let them *stay.*

Compulsion is how practitioners of all stripes make a ghost who is either reluctant or misbehaving, well, behave. But there are boundaries. It is voluntary—not usually a problem, as ghosts like an audience. And the part I didn't like to mention to lawyers who hired me was that compulsion doesn't involve forcing a ghost to, say, answer a question. Otherwise, the answer really wouldn't have any legal standing, would it?

No, the trick with compulsion is that though the ghost is agreeing to the rules of my bindings that brought them over—don't kill anyone, don't set the house on fire, tell the truth, don't empty my bank account to bet on the ponies—they don't have to stay. Or speak.

"Your grandmother has turned the swamp into a giant conduit. Like a massive set mirror." Though it was more . . . natural—or melded with the swamp itself, for lack of a better word. I'd never considered trying to etch something as large as a swamp, bog or lake. My practitioning toolbox didn't work like that—I needed to see the whole thing.

And Bergen hadn't quite been telling the truth. If the ghosts were frightened enough, they could have taken off, amongst other things, I imagined.

"The swamp ghosts warned your grandmother about Dane, yes?" Stephan frowned, but nodded.

"I wonder where Katy was being held for the two weeks she was missing. I mean, I imagine she was kept in that barn on the edge of your family swamp for a few days at least, alive."

Another cautious nod.

"Funny the ghosts didn't bother to mention that. Not until it was much too late." I shrugged. "That sounds like an awful lot of mischief to me, and complicity. Not fetching someone to help a young girl in trouble, especially if they knew. It was only Dane and whatever else frightened them that spurred them to action." I turned to face Stephan. "Like I said—selfish."

Bergen and the rest of the witches had mistaken the ghosts' adherence to their rules and a desire for attention from the living for good-naturedness. So did a lot of people, including experienced practitioners.

They wanted me to find their ghosts? It meant I got to be an asshole. "Do the rules work on any ghost, or only ones who live here?"

Stephan frowned. "Any ghost. Or that's how it's supposed to work."

I rocked on my heels in the damp soil and whistled. I assumed Dane had been using the barn for a while, but had he killed there before Katy, while he was still alive? If he had, it painted the swamp ghosts in a much more sinister shade. "If Dane killed Katy in this swamp, then your grandmother's rules either failed or someone found a hell of a loophole. Let's see if it's the former, shall we?"

I pulled out my compact and lipliner. *Nate, you there?* I wrote.

I counted to ten, then twenty. If Nate shirked his duty, so help me . . .

"Nate?" I said into the glass.

A moment later, the ghost's characteristic capital letters appeared. *WOAH, K—WHERE THE HELL? CAN BARELY HEAR YOU.*

The swamp was probably running interference. "Hold on, I'm going to bring you through," I said, and flooded the mirror with the remaining Otherside I'd held on to.

Within moments, Nate had coalesced in front of me.

His brow furrowed and he turned in a circle, twice. "Woah, what the fuck, K?"

"It's a swamp."

He stopped his turn and gave me a sideways glance. "Like, seriously horror movie creepy, K."

Yeah, and you're about to find out just how creepy. "Look, I'm running an experiment." I searched the ground until I found a small stick, not too sharp. I picked it up and held it out to him. "Do me a favour. Throw this at him," I said, pointing at Stephan.

"*What?*"

I'm not sure which one said it first.

"Both of you trust me and take one for Otherside science. Now throw it," I said to Nate.

He took the stick and frowned at Stephan. "K, I might hurt him."

I shook my head. "Just make it a chest shot. Come on. It won't hurt. Stephan's a big, brawny, farm-bred boy. He'll barely notice it." Though from the look Stephan gave me, it was abundantly clear he wasn't pleased.

Nate looked at the stick and then at Stephan, then back at the stick. "I don't know, I—" Nate paused and made a pained face. "I just really don't want to, okay?"

So the witch's rules were still working. But how well? I slid my Otherside sight back into place. "Come on, Nate. Just do it."

He turned to face me. "No!"

The Otherside from the swamp was brighter around us—and, interestingly, pooling around Stephan. Not the tree root–sized bindings, which stayed immobile, but the fog, which was pulsing like a heartbeat. Little Otherside fireflies flickering around him.

"Nate, stop being a sissy ghost and throw the stick." And this time I pushed Nate, my best friend, with my own Otherside compulsion.

The swamp Otherside flared in response to my own, and Nate looked increasingly uncomfortable. "I already told you, K, I don't want to!"

I crossed my arms and pushed harder. "Nate, you throw things all the time—at cops, the cat that kept yowling on the fire escape—"

"Jesus! Fine, K! You want me to throw the stick? I'll throw the goddamn stick."

With that, Nate launched the stick. At me. It hit my chest with a weak thwack before dropping to the ground, leaving a streak of mud on my jacket.

"Oops," Nate said. He had the sense to look somewhat contrite.

I tried to brush the mud off. "Well, that answers my next question," I said to Stephan, who had covered his mouth with his hand.

Oh, yeah, that's it, yuk it up.

"Well, the good news is the swamp's rules are still intact. You can tell your grandmother that next time you see her. The bad news is the swamp doesn't enforce rules for ghosts to do no harm. They make sure ghosts can't do something to *you*."

"Me?" He looked so genuinely startled that I was inclined to believe him. Though, he could also be a great actor. Stephan interviewed criminals for a living. I gave him the benefit of the doubt.

"The rules protect the witches, families and I imagine other people who live here—the ones she wants to keep around," I explained. "It means Dane's poltergeist would have had no trouble killing a girl, or anyone come to think of it, provided they weren't one of *you*."

Stephan appeared deeply troubled by my revelation. He turned to face the swamp, searching it for something.

I sighed, deciding to voice my reservations. "I want to believe you, Stephan, but I'm having a real hard time with the you not being a witch, and considering just how much you've hidden from me—"

"Will you please stop with the witchcraft?" Stephan turned back to face me, flustered. "Yes, witchcraft is familial and it's passed through the maternal line, but men usually don't inherit it. Damn it, I cannot believe I'm telling you this. I'm not a witch. For the last time, I'm telling you the truth."

There was something in his voice, in his expression, something I couldn't quite put my finger on that told me I should believe him. And if Stephan wasn't a witch, it would explain why he was in the dark on how his grandmother's swamp worked exactly.

"Nate, want to do me a favour and take a quick look around the swamp for any other ghosts?"

"Any one in particular?"

I shrugged. "Run-of-the-mill. Oh, keep your eye out for a serial killer."

"Jesus fucking—serves me right for agreeing to this," he said, and started to fade. "If I'm not back in half an hour, send out a search party." And with that, he disappeared.

I stood there awkwardly with Stephan, who was still staring at the swamp in a much less affectionate light, as if only just now seeing the mysterious and powerful entity capable of malevolence that I saw, not his grandmother's harmless construct.

Part of me felt a little sorry for him. The other, shrewder part crossed her arms. "Anything else about the swamp I should know?"

Stephan let out a breath. "No. I imagine you have a better grasp of things than I had. Or thought I had."

I had to admit he was in a tough spot. I'd just uncovered one hell of a family secret, and unintentionally found its darker side. Hell, it wasn't every day a practitioner found real witches, or a swamp fuelled with this much Otherside. And Stephan hadn't treated me like an undesirable, like a freak. He'd been nice to me. The innate spark of attraction I had for Stephan stirred. I opened my mouth to say something reassuring,

I didn't get the chance. Stephan had turned to face me, and all the vulnerability and discomfiture had vanished, replaced with the stern FBI agent. He didn't look happy.

Shit.

"Tell me, Kincaid Strange, why are you so interesting to Dane and Katy? Because you being good at finding ghosts can't be all of it."

I stayed silent. I'd burned the one friendly bridge I had on this case.

He snorted. "That's what I thought. No, Kincaid, I think you have everything you need about this swamp," he said, the corner of his mouth twisting almost into a snarl. "You're a consultant, and my grandmother has hired you to find our ghosts. So get back to the consulting and I'll decide what information is necessary. Are we clear?"

I stared him down. "Yeah. We're clear," I said.

His phone buzzed, and we broke eye contact. He turned around so I couldn't see the screen. "Aaron's back in Portland. He's helping us account for the rest of Dane's victims, see if a handful of the ghosts managed to lay low. He'll try to make it back here, but if not, I'm to take you to the hotel." The phone buzzed once more, this time with a call. "I need to get this," he said, and headed back to the car.

I kicked myself as I watched him go. What the hell are you doing, Kincaid? You need friends, not enemies, in the FBI. I should have been more careful questioning him about the swamp. Stephan's family, his parents, were missing. And Stephan wasn't wrong to question why Katy had been asking for me. I figured I was being drawn into this case because of my knack for finding missing ghosts and a serial killer's desire to have his genius unveiled. There was also my talent for working freehand with Otherside—but only Gideon knew about that. And there was the remote possibility that this had to do with Gideon himself. If Gideon didn't have enemies out there, I was one of the My Little Pony/Smurf centaurs littering my apartment lobby.

The killer's interest was most likely due to my strong track record uncovering ghosts. A serial killer's desire to match wits with a practitioner, prove how much of a genius he really was, to himself and others . . . That had to be it.

I'd seen crazier things. While I waited for Stephan to return, my mind worked. I could just make out the barn and the still-busy crime scene up the road. There were things about the bindings in the barn that bothered me. Their strength and permanence for one.

I shivered against the cold, keenly aware of the thick Otherside fog that surrounded me. The November afternoon sun had done just about all it could with regards to warming me up. I considered going back to the car for the Thermos of coffee Bergen had given us, but didn't want to interrupt Stephan.

And where had Nate got to? It did not take this long to search for ghosts in a swamp, did it?

I started to worry, and was opening my compact to find him when I caught sight of his translucent red flannel shirt and yellow T-shirt through the trees. He was barrelling towards me.

There was a change in the air: it filled with the sweet, clean, pungent scent of ozone, the kind that heralds the beginning and end of thunderstorms.

What the hell was Nate running from? I realized he was shouting at me.

"K? That serial killer? He's wearing a fucking hideous twin-set— and he's pissed!"

Shit. The chill in the air deepened, but this time it wasn't the November climate. I scanned the ground, the trees beside me. They were all covered in a thin layer of frost.

"Definitely a 'get off my porch' kind of asshole, K!"

Why the hell was Nate still here? "Nate! What are you waiting for, head back to the Otherside!" I shouted while I pulled a globe. Third one of the day and counting. This time I felt the nausea pooling in my stomach.

He was less than ten feet away now, and he stopped suddenly, hovering over one of the shallow pools. He spun in a circle, searching the air around him. Nate was scared. As scared as I'd ever seen him. "I can't!" he shouted.

Oh, hell.

And then Dane shot out of the swamp, heading straight for Nate.

In life, Dane had been the ultimate suburban soccer dad, the friendliest neighbour, the favourite coach, the unassuming colleague. The portrait of a serial killer: the least likely suspect to a casual observer. But his sporty American appearance in life took on a particularly ghoulish quality in poltergeist form.

And here he was—in all his pastel matching-twin-set glory.

Singing . . . and charging at my terrified ghost of a roommate brandishing—I squinted to make sure I wasn't seeing things through the swamp fog—a cheerleading baton? Well, Dane had coached a cheerleading squad . . .

"Here's a story, of a ghost named Daney, who was chasing all the beatniks off his lawn!"

I cringed at the disturbingly gleeful rendition of a popular seventies theme song. Despite the musical and clothing choices, I wasn't about to underestimate Dane the way the detectives had for so long.

"Nate! Bug out!" I shouted. He'd warned me, he'd done his job— there was no foul now for removing himself from the fight. Once he was on the other side of the barrier, Dane wouldn't be able to find him.

"I told you, K—I can't! I'm stuck!"

Dane stopped, turned and looked straight at me. He whistled. "Well, now—and here I thought I was chasing rabble out of my backyard. What a delightful surprise you are, young lady." His eyes glowing a solid red as he looked me over. "I see we've got a uniform penalty." He *tsk*ed, licked his finger and made a sizzling sound. "Those jeans are tooooo tight. And is that a flannel I do detect?" His grin widened and he slapped the baton in his hand. "Bricka bracka firecracka sis boom bah, burn that grungy flannel, Daney, rah, rah, rah." He twirled the baton overhead as he sidestepped like a rocketeer. Then he vanished.

There was no time to react before a chill seized my left shoulder. I spun and came face to face with Dane. He pulled down the brim of his red baseball cap, then raised his finger to his lips. "Shhhh— be vewy, vewy quiet," he grinned, and sighted Nate down the baton as if it were a rifle, his eyes glowing redder. "I'm hunting gwunge wabbits."

Oh, when the poltergeists start quoting Elmer Fudd and Bugs Bunny, it's not a good sign. Where was a pentagram when I needed one?

"Now, just stay right there, son," Dane said. He vanished and reappeared behind Nate, wrapping an arm around his throat.

"K! A little help?"

Dane shushed him, going so far as to stroke Nate's messy shag. "Hold still, and Daney will have the malcontent youth beat out of you in no time. Starting with this mop," he said, and viciously tore out a clump of Nate's hair.

Nate was a lot of things—he was resourceful, quick, intelligent, and less of a coward than he let on, sometimes even brave—but he was no match for a poltergeist like Dane. He screamed like a girl.

Freehand pentagram it was. I searched the swamp floor. There were enough dead leaves and pine needles from the autumn fall. I started scratching out a pentagram with the heel of my boot. "Hold on, Nate," I shouted, as I tapped the barrier and flooded the ground with Otherside—praying, willing, that it would stick despite the Otherside fog that filled the place.

"K, like, sooner is way better than later here," Nate shouted, as Dane ripped out another patch of hair and snatched at his flannel shirt.

"Stay still, grunge boy. I'll have you looking like a respectable young man if it kills you! Again."

My pentagram was small and rough, but it would hold. I hopped into the centre of it. "Now, Nate!" I shouted.

Nate shot towards me like a frightened rabbit.

"Grab on," I shouted, and readied to set the pentagram.

"To what?"

"To me, you idiot!"

I waited until I felt Nate's ghostly arms wrap around my shoulders. Dane whistled. "Now, I don't think we've ever met, young lady. I'd remember a head of unruly curls like that. Is this," he said, gesturing to my pentagram, "about the jeans critique?" He sucked in a breath and floated around us. "They *are* a smidge too tight, and not the most flattering on your short frame. But don't think me a total prude. I did let the girls do a racy cheer to Tiffany a few years back. *I think we're alone now, there doesn't seem to be any ghosts around*," he sang, then stopped, his eyes flaring red. "Oh, no, wait—here's one! And it's trespassing on my lawn!"

Just as Dane lunged forward, I pushed Otherside into the symbols, activating the perimeter of my pentagram. Gold flared up around us, putting a barrier of Otherside between. He slammed up against it, his face contorting in rage.

"Yeah, yeah—big bad serial killer poltergeist." I was confident Dane couldn't penetrate my wall of Otherside. Now, how to stop and hold him. Though I hated to admit it, what I wouldn't have given for the ghost trap mirror—not to bind him, mind you, but to stop Dane and any future show-tune renditions in their tracks. I fished out my compact instead, and with the tip of my nail started to inscribe symbols that would turn it into a siphon. It had worked once before.

"Kincaid!"

I swore as I spotted Stephan rushing through the brush towards us. In the panic, I'd forgotten he was still here. I waved him back, hoping Dane wouldn't see him. I couldn't be certain Dane was bound to Bergen's swamp rules.

Thankfully, he took the hint and retreated back into the car, phone to his ear, just as Dane launched the baton at me. It, unlike Dane, sailed right through my pentagram, narrowly missing my head.

"K, I've got a bad feeling about this—we should get out of here," Nate said, recoiling as Dane pressed his face against the Otherside that was shielding us.

"Let me in, let me in, let me in!" Dane squeaked in a high falsetto.

"How the hell did this guy end up a serial killer?"

"He got fed up with families who didn't subscribe to his values. Dress code violations, swearing on the field, failure to volunteer for team barbecues . . ." I shook my head. The list went on and on. "You name it, if it offended his Norman Rockwell sensibilities, he killed them."

"You forgot the yoga pants," Dane hissed through my barrier. "I did the world a favour—yoga pants are not casual soccer parent apparel!" He screamed the last part and banged on the barrier harder.

Nate cringed. "There's something seriously wrong with the swamp, K—with *him*."

"I'll say. Chasing the American dream to death."

Nate gripped my arms. "Naw—it's more than that. Please, K, ditch me and *run*. I'll—keep ahead of him. I'll, like, I don't know, wave my flannel like a matador?"

Dane slammed both fists into the barrier. For the first time, it wavered. "I'm getting tired of this, you two grunge monkeys. Get out of the penalty box and play fair, will you!"

"You could play a few Dead Men CDs for him. That might get him going." I finished the last symbol and turned the compact mirror on the poltergeist. "Nate, the only one here about to run is Dane."

The mirror siphoned the Otherside off him. I smiled to myself as Dane struggled, bracing against the tiny mirror's pull. "Why, you—you're a dirty practitioner, aren't you? Ohhh." For the first time since appearing, Dane actually seemed angry—furious. "Black hair, grunge ghost—I know who you are: Kincaid Strange, here in my swamp." His eyes flared blood red. "Didn't your mother ever tell you it's not nice to talk to the dead?" He snarled.

"Don't worry, Dane. Taking care of it."

"I call foul!" Dane shouted. "Practitioner on the field!"

I frowned. What was that around his neck? Glittering . . .

Ghost bindings! Dane was bound. But by whom?

"K! Watch out!" Nate screamed in my ear, but it was too late. The bindings had flared.

"Gotcha!" Dane's hands were through my pentagram, around my neck. "It's murder time. I'm thinking I'll add some slit wrists this time—a change for me, I know, but in the spirit of nineties angst and disillusionment."

Shit. I struggled and kicked as he lifted me off the ground, clawing at the ghostly fists that held me while Dane laughed.

A sickly, evil feeling seeped into me—the same one I'd felt earlier today, and last night at the library. Jesus, it was in the swamp, or using it. I tried to shout, "Stephan!" to warn him to run, but I was choking, strangled by the darkly tinged, sickly Otherside and Dane's manicured hands.

"K, what do I do?" Nate's voice was frantic.

Reflexively, I kept grasping at Dane's hands, but my fingers slipped through them, chilled and useless.

"Get Gid—" I croaked, but Dane cut me off with a shake.

"You know what the problem is with girls like you? You act like it'd kill you to fit in, go with the flow. The world would be a better place if girls like you still idolized the cheerleader, pined after the high school quarterback—tried to be nice," he spat.

"Girls like me never looked up to the cheerlead—" He choked off my words. Why do poltergeists always go for the neck?

"And don't get me started on your slacker grunge star. Never amounted to anything, I'll bet."

Nate snorted. "Shows what you know—"

"Nate! Run," I managed, hoping Nate heard me and for once did as I said. I had more ways to stop a poltergeist. Without waiting to make sure Nate had gone, I reached for Dane's wrists, my fingers chilling to the bone as they passed through.

Dane grinned. "Give up, kiddo. It's a lost cause. But take heart— I'll make sure I dress your corpse up in something pretty. Appropriate. I'm thinking crinoline, maybe a poodle skirt?" He launched into another theme song, one I recognized from a kids' cartoon. *"How dead can you get? You'll never ever know till you've met. This polter-geist, Martin Dane is his name, that's right! Murder time!"*

Two months ago, a poltergeist strangling me through a penta-gram while singing show tunes off key would have had me panick-ing. But I'd met a lot of monsters as of late. They barely fazed me anymore, despite my instinctual fear. As Gideon said, the only things behind the barrier are ghosts. There are no demons, no devils, no gods. Only the dead.

And a poltergeist, even one as warped as Dane, I knew how to deal with.

"You know, I was told I'd get a girl practitioner," Dane whispered, his expression turned wistful as the oxygen was choked out of me with one hand and he stroked my face with the other. "A *naughty* one. They promised I could have fun with you. If I behaved."

"Who? Who said you could have fun with me?" I whispered. For a murder ghost, Dane was taking his sweet time with the killing and torture. Why?

Because someone else was pulling the strings, and *they* wouldn't let him.

Dane's smile faltered. "Not what you should be worrying about. Shhhh—just a little longer and we'll go make you into a *proper* young lady. Won't that be nice?"

If one more man told me what I was supposed to do today . . .

"Now, how about a little role play? I squeeze and you scream. It'd make me *oh* so happy."

Rule one of dealing with a serial killer? Keep them talking. Dane, for all his blustering, couldn't kill me. Yet. I needed more information on who had promised Dane a practitioner. I forced myself to laugh. "Go fuck yourself, you pervert."

The first crack in Martin Dane's facade showed. His smile faltered and his eyes glowed red. "Language, young lady."

I blew a raspberry at him. "Blow me, eat shit—"

Dane shook me, hard. "I told you to watch it—I don't tolerate that kind of language. You're supposed to try and act 'nice' so I won't kill you—that's what the rest did." Dane was losing it. He wanted screaming, crying, pleading. I was going off script by staying calm. Like all poltergeists, he wanted hysterics.

"Let me guess," I said. I tapped the barrier, hoping he wouldn't notice in his anger. I started to pool as much as I could, not too much at once, but slowly and surely. Bindings around his neck, stalking instead of eviscerating his prey, killing outside his pattern— all signs of a bound ghost. I took a gamble. "I'm going to make a wild guess you made a deal with a ghost binder, Dane. What did they offer you? Please don't say it was just little old me. A spree of killing and torture? Broadway tickets at the very least?" I forced myself to grin back at him. "Tell me. How fun is it really, having to do someone else's bidding? Fuckhead."

Bull's eye. Dane threw back his head and roared. His face changed: his eyes blackened, the sockets reddened, and his teeth morphed into bloodstained metal points. He squeezed my neck once more and grimaced at me.

"Two days, Kincaid Strange. Forty-eight hours my jailer promised I could play with you. Do you have any idea how much fun I can have?" He made a show of looking me up and down, and sneered. "Shame you're not my type, but I'll make do. First thing on my list is to kill that unruly curl with industrial-strength relaxer."

I kept my eyes wide and stayed silent. I waited until his smile returned. Then I reached up and pushed my own hands into his translucent ones still wrapped around my neck.

"Any last words, song requests, before we start the transformation process?"

"Yeah. Eat Otherside." I bared my teeth, and pushed every ounce I'd pooled at him.

Raw Otherside flooded the poltergeist, and his eyes widened. Ghosts love Otherside; they feed off it, need it. But too much Otherside, concentrated, all at once? It disorients them. Which is why he let go of my throat. "Owww! Mother, that hurt!"

And that's when I really hit him. From where I sat in the mud, I threw as much Otherside as I could at the poltergeist, until I had him in a cage of it—a giant golden net.

Dane screamed, slamming his fists against the Otherside mesh. "No fair! I'm claustrophobic."

"Time to send you back." Where was my compact? I scanned the ground wildly and found it lying in a pile of leaves. I lunged for it, but before I reached it, something wrapped around my ankle and pulled me back.

Dane was standing over me, free of my Otherside net. *Grinning.* "Well, well. Looks like the tables have turned. And I've changed my mind. You *are* my type, Kincaid Strange. The kind that doesn't know when to quit."

I could hear voices shouting from the roadway—Nate and Stephan must have gone for help. I didn't dare take my eyes off Dane's striped sweater set.

Rule number one, Kincaid. "How?" I asked him.

"That's for me to know and you to find out in two— Oomph!"
Dane reeled back as something leapt onto his back and wrapped
around his neck.

"That's for calling me a no-good slacker! I'm a fucking rock
star and you're singing off-key in a golf sweater. There is no fucking competition . . . Run, K!" Nate shouted as he clung to Dane's
back, pummelling the poltergeist's head over and over. "And we
were depressed and disenfranchised because of dickish assholes
like you! And—K? Seriously, move the fucking boots—one in
front of the other!" Nate shouted, clinging to Dane as the stronger
ghost tried to dislodge him. Nate couldn't actually hurt him; he
was no more than a distraction.

"K, for the love of—will you just run!"

I couldn't just leave him. A glint from the bushes caught my eye,
something metallic. A mirror, larger than my compact. It slid across
the leaves until it was directly under Dane.

"Out of the way, Nate!" I shouted.

He looked at me as if I was out of my mind, and then caught
sight of the mirror. He let go of Dane and stumbled back into the
swamp, until he was submerged in the Otherside fog.

Dane straightened his sweater and cap and turned his red eyes
back on me. "No one, I mean *no one*, musses my sweater. You'll pay
for that, you and your little ghost dog. I don't care who wants you
alive— What the *hey*?"

Dane looked down as the mirror underneath him activated in a
flash of gold Otherside—but it didn't just flare, threads of Otherside
lashed out towards the poltergeist, paralyzing him.

Dane stared down at his feet. He tried lifting one then the other,
but they were tethered to the glass. He looked straight at me, radiat-
ing hate. "Oh, you've got to be fudging kidding me. This is so not
what I signed up for."

Dane's voice was strangled off as the Otherside threads crept up
his ghostly limbs, tying themselves up in knots as they went, and
pulling him into the mirror.

It was a ghost binding mirror. Gideon. He'd come to save me, son of a bitch. Nate had got through. I could almost kiss him. Hell, I could kiss Gideon—

"Gid—" I started, then stopped.

There was a man standing in the brush just outside what was left of my pentagram with his hand outstretched. He was no taller than Nate, with the same mouse brown–coloured hair. He was pale, paler than was healthy in the sunlight, and dressed in a tweed jacket, which gave him a hipster charm. He was leaning against a tree, watching me.

Even though I couldn't make out his green eyes from this distance, I'd seen the man enough times on television to identify him. Liam Sinclair was the one who had saved me. Not me, not my mentor, Gideon. The TV celebrity.

It shouldn't have pissed me off as much as it did, especially considering the last few minutes, but goddamnit . . .

"Kincaid!" I heard Stephan shout. I turned around, and spotted him standing with three other FBI agents at the edge of the road. Stephan, a man with no Otherside talent, hadn't abandoned me. I'd seen other grown men run for the hills, but Stephan had stayed and called for help.

He jumped a few pegs higher in my esteem.

"Don't think this is over, Kincaid Strange!" I turned my attention back to Dane, who was gnashing his bloody, sharpened teeth. Only his head remained above the mirror. "You and I have some promised business. Two days." He spat the words. "I always keep my word."

And then, before Dane could sputter any more threats, the mirror pulled him through.

I was sitting in a swamp full of mud and who knew what else, but after that, I needed to lie down. For once, I ignored the wet and cold as I took stock of my mortality.

Nothing had worked—the net, my compact, my pentagram, not even calling Gideon. One malfunction I could understand, but all four?

"Stephan, I uncovered a few problems with your poltergeist," I called out, if just to stop them from calling an ambulance.

I reached for my throat and it was tender to the touch. Why oh why do the poltergeists always go for the neck?

"My god, are you all right?" I opened my eyes to find Liam Sinclair standing over me looking concerned, his green eyes bright in his white face.

Oh yeah, and to top things off, the celebrity practitioner had saved my life.

It'd take a while before I could look at myself in the mirror with anything resembling respect.

He held out a hand. "Please allow me."

I took it but considered how pale he was, his eyes rimmed red. I started to ease myself out of the mud.

To my surprise, he gripped my hand and pulled me up.

I shook my head, trying to clear it. Dane and the Otherside had done a number on me. I was weaker and more light-headed than I should have been. And once again, there it was, that dark sensation, foreign, touched with Otherside, just on my periphery, trying to get in.

"Kincaid?" Stephan looked panicked as he made his way over to us. I needed to tell him about the darkness. It was important, I knew it was. Twice now I'd sensed it here . . .

Liam put a tentative hand on my back. "Are you all right?"

I looked up directly into his green-blue eyes, made famous by the frequent close-ups on his show. In person they were dazzling—almost otherworldly.

His expression was concerned and sincere as he eased an arm under my shoulder and started to help me towards the others. To my surprise, I let him.

"You must be Kincaid Strange. I'm Liam. My strength might be greatly diminished, but the immunotherapy drugs do wonders these days."

"Ah—thank you," I said, still trying to clear the fog in my head, surprised that Liam admitted to his syndrome so openly. And that he was as functional as he was. I'd certainly never heard of any treatment for Ram's Inn that worked as it appeared to for Liam.

Then again, he probably had access to medical treatment well outside the reach of a normal practitioner. I looked around for Nate—and found Stephan had almost reached us. I really did need to tell them about the dark sickness I'd sensed. It was too much of a coincidence . . .

"I'm glad I was able to help, though I fear I'm not the conduit of the dead that I used to be, if I ever was a particular talent," Liam said, making a pained face as he helped me to the road.

Other FBI agents made their way towards us, and my resolve to bring up the darkness I'd briefly touched faltered. What was I going to say—that the swamp felt *wrong*? I was trying to build credibility, not ruin it. Which was more likely: that there was something inherently sickly about the swamp or that my imagination, fuelled by too much Otherside, was once again acting out paranoid tendencies?

"I can't even chase off a poltergeist in decent time anymore. I'm sorry it took me so long. I had trouble setting the mirror in this fog," he said, and from the sincerity in his face and voice, I believed it.

I was at a loss for how to respond, and more than a little shocked. I'd expected Liam to be more stuck-up, full of himself, smarmy. No, that was a lie. I wasn't just expecting, I'd been *hoping*.

He didn't strike me as any of those things. He seemed humble, *nice* even. And whatever he thought he'd lacked in speed while banishing Dane, he made up for in fantastic timing. "What were you doing out here?"

"Complete chance. I've been trying to get better reads off the swamp—when I'm able. It's about all I can do to help Ingrid. I heard the commotion and saw two ghosts fly by." He frowned at me. "Was that Nathan Cade, the *rock star*?"

"Yeah. Long story."

Liam looked around, steadying me up the hill, which was comical considering his frail state. The others met us and Stephan took me from Liam. I was glad, if only to gain some distance from the odd practitioner and my conflicting impressions of him. On top of that, Stephan was warm. And smelled nice. I couldn't say the same for myself, after lying down in the swamp mud.

"Are you all right?" Stephan asked.

"A little the worse for wear . . ." I wavered again as to whether I should tell Stephan about the unsettling sensation I'd read from the swamp. He'd grown up in a family of witches. Nothing I could say about the swamp would be that strange, would it?

"There's something—" I started.

"It's really quite a beautiful place. Minus the murders, poltergeist, bound ghosts," Liam interrupted, keeping pace by my side even as Stephan practically carried me back to the car. "Did you happen to see the markings on Dane's neck?" he asked.

"Liam," Stephan warned, "she's half-dead. It can wait."

No, it couldn't. I'd almost forgotten. "Hard to miss—just like the ones on Katy."

Liam nodded. "I'm certain it's a ghost binding. Someone is controlling him—they have to be." He regarded me. "You arrived this morning?"

I inclined my head. "More or less."

He gave me a half smile. "Welcome to the swamp."

"If you two are set on talking it over, you'd better fill me in," Stephan said, though there was exasperation in his voice.

"Nate found Dane in the swamp. I tried to banish him back across the barrier." I shook my head. "Nothing worked until Liam's ghost binding mirror." It irked me to have to say it, but it was true.

Again I considered sharing what else I'd sensed, but Liam jumped in. "Dane was bound. He has the same markings around his neck as Katy. He was resistant—to everything. Almost." He looked back at me. "Ghost traps still work."

If Liam hadn't sensed what I had, and he was by all accounts a better practitioner, who's to say I had?

Stephan nodded, but there was a slight frown on his face. He looked at me for confirmation. I nodded.

"He won't be back today," Liam offered. "Not unless whoever bound him calls him back. I suppose then we have a problem."

Stephan gazed around the swamp, unconvinced.

"Agent Wolf, I assure you, the ghost is gone," Liam said.

Stephan sighed. "I'm sure you're right, Mr. Sinclair. It's just Dane has"—he paused as he tried to find the right words—"been making a habit of proving you wrong."

Instead of arguing or defending himself, Liam simply nodded. "Quite right."

We'd almost reached the car when I stopped.

"Oh no! Nate—he headed back into the swamp. He was having trouble crossing back over."

Liam held up a hand. "I saw him cross as soon as Dane was gone. Whatever interference was there went with Dane. It's a good point, though, to the investigation," he continued, turning to Stephan. "Kincaid's ghost couldn't cross back while Dane was here. It might explain how his other victims' ghosts were so easily trapped."

For a second it looked as though Stephan might say something about the swamp, or maybe even his family's ghosts. He stopped himself, and only nodded. He then let out a breath and looked me over once again. His face softened.

"Let's get you into the car before you catch pneumonia," he said to me. "You, Liam and Ingrid can trade notes tomorrow."

I agreed wholeheartedly. I let him open the door for me and climbed in, reaching for the Thermos.

There was a tap at the window while Stephan headed around to the other side. It was Liam. I rolled the window down. "Please," he said, "when you've recovered, will you give me a call?" He passed me his business card. "I'd feel much better knowing you'd fully recovered. Dinner maybe? To talk about those bindings on Dane," he rushed to add.

The only thing I wanted this evening was to crawl into a warm shower and then a warm bed. But the way he searched my face, with genuine concern . . .

"I'll try," I said, surprising myself and pocketing the card. "If not tonight—"

"Then tomorrow." He smiled and headed to another black sedan that pulled up. I rolled the window back up, poured myself a hot cup of coffee in the lid and leaned back while Stephan started the car.

Stephan was quiet as he began driving slowly towards the barn.

"Well, we got one question answered," I told him. "Dane's definitely after me as a next victim. I'm next on his list. A *mark*."

Stephan didn't argue with me. Or say anything.

"*Two days*," I added.

"Two days to find out how to stop a dead killer." He took his eyes off the gravel driveway for a moment. "Sure you don't want to rethink heading back to Seattle yet?"

I rolled my eyes. Two days to find a dead serial killer who planned on doing unspeakable things to me? Seattle was sounding pretty good. If I was smart, I'd be back on a plane tonight. Good thing people rarely accused me of being smart.

I sipped my coffee and willed it to warm me up. I didn't have time to be cold and hungover. I had a serial killer to catch.

CHAPTER 12

PORTLAND AFTER DARK

An hour later, after I'd been cleared by a first aid attendant, Stephan drove me to my hotel in Portland. The attendant had hemmed and hawed about discharging me, but with little more than bruises and a bad case of the shivers, there was really nothing she could do but order me to get rest and stay warm. I hid my relief. I had an ulterior motive for getting away from everyone, Aaron and Stephan included—one I didn't care to share . . . I had somewhere else to be tonight.

If Dane attacked again, well, Liam and Ingrid were at the swamp. I tried not to think of that eventuality.

"We need to account for Dane's original victims. All of them," I said. "Once we've got a complete list, I suggest you send any other practitioners you have on contract to the places their ghosts were last seen—or, if they haven't been seen, then where they were murdered. Tell them to look for Otherside, even the slightest amount. Let them know the symbols might be buried or hidden—on furniture, floorboards, even old possessions, like clothing."

Stephan kept his eyes on the road, but his brow furrowed as,

I imagined, he worked out the logistical nightmare of accomplishing this task. There weren't a lot of licensed practitioners who had the necessary skills to assay the sites. That's the problem when your profession is considered a social taboo: there's never enough talent around when you really need it.

"I'll work on it. See if Liam knows any practitioners who can do it on short notice." We reached a stoplight and he looked over at me. "Anything else? Information I should pass on?" he added, more than a little coldly.

I bit my lip and swallowed. "They'll be looking for soothsayer-style bindings—commands, holds, traps—any- and everything a soothsayer would use to hold a ghost in place or bind them." I cringed inwardly at the thought. Even I didn't understand how the symbols worked. I really would need Ingrid's help deciphering them, and it irked my sensitivities and conscience in all the wrong ways. Yet another damned deal with the devils . . . "Ingrid and Liam are the experts," I said, not quite hiding my resentment over the fact that I needed them. "They can fill everyone in on the details."

If Stephan sensed my discomfort, or even cared, he gave no indication. "I'll get their input." The car was moving once again, and his eyes were fixed on the road.

I took a deep breath and considered for about the fifth time whether I should try to smooth things over. Instead, I covered the shaking of my hands by gripping the now-empty coffee Thermos tightly. Now that I was away from the fog and the adrenalin from my meeting with Dane had dissipated, my nerves were jittering. It was too soon, too soon after the death of my friend, Cameron, and Randall's betrayal, too soon after the wraith, to be facing my own mortality once again. Even though I'd taken every measure to protect myself, I could have—would have—died without Liam's help. No matter how much I turned the events over in my head, I couldn't pinpoint what I'd done *wrong*. I'd gone in prepared, or thought I had. I'd set a pentagram—it should have *worked*.

Dying from my own ineptitude and stupidity was one thing—but dying due to bad luck? That was a bit harder to wrap my head around.

"Aaron is on his way to the hotel. I told him what happened. With Dane. He was looking into the information we have on Dane's old victims. He has a knack for finding things I miss."

Probably a good thing Aaron hadn't been there. I'm not sure I'd have been able to keep my anger in check under the circumstances. "Did Detective Baal know about Ingrid?"

Stephan hesitated, but only for a moment. "He knew. He thought you should see the case first-hand before making a decision." He glanced at me in the mirror.

My temper flared once more. Aaron had purposefully not told me a soothsayer might be involved, when he *knew* how I felt about them.

Still trying to make my decisions for me.

I clenched my teeth and pushed my feelings down. I'd deal with Aaron's judgment later.

Stephan pulled up to a small boutique hotel. It looked charming, with an older building facade, marble columns and angel-like gargoyles overhead. It had personality and was the sort of place I preferred over the conglomerate brands. Yes, this would do just fine.

I got out of the car, backpack over my shoulder, conscious of my mud-soiled clothes. Hopefully, the hotel had laundry. At least my leather jacket had saved my blazer.

Stephan rolled down the passenger window. "We'll see you tomorrow a.m., and if you find anything in the meantime . . ."

"You'll be the first to know," I said. He hesitated and I added, "Dane won't catch me off guard again. If he shows up . . ." I trailed off. What the hell exactly would I do if Dane showed up? Have Nate distract him while I hid under the bed? "Even poltergeists have to recharge."

He nodded and started to roll up the window.

"Listen—" I started.

He paused but didn't look particularly happy about it.

"Look, I'm sorry if I was callous about your family's swamp earlier. It wasn't personal—"

"Save it," he said, cutting me off and looking equal parts incredulous and exasperated. "I'll say one thing for you, Kincaid, you live up to your reputation. A people person you are not." He shook his head. "Not exactly sure what I was expecting. Don't worry. It'll only catch me off guard the once. See you bright and early tomorrow."

And with that, Stephan rolled up the window and drove away.

I felt like an asshole. Relieved to finally be on my own for the first time all day, but an asshole all the same. Still, my shoulders sagged as some of the tension drained away.

The hotel was called the Berlin, and just inside the door was the placard explaining its historical origins in frontier Portland. It had been built by a German couple who migrated for the gold rushes and decided to open a boarding house and saloon.

Frontier code for whorehouse with a side of rooms and booze.

Despite the likely sordid origins, it was definitely the kind of place I preferred. Either serendipity or Aaron had done his homework. In any case, it had worked in my favour. These places always had old silver-backed mirrors in the bathroom.

Following a swift check-in, keys in hand, I headed past a decent-looking lobby restaurant and upstairs to my room on the fifth floor. There was indeed a sizable mirror in the bathroom that suited my needs.

I dropped my bag on the chair, checked for bedbugs and, when I was satisfied I wouldn't end up with unwelcome stowaways, unpacked a change of clothes and freshened up.

Then I set the mirror in the bathroom and messaged Nate.

Adventure time.

Nate was much faster getting back to me this time.

NO FUKING WAY, K.

Tough, I wrote back. *I need you. Be here in twenty. We're heading into the city.*

Nate didn't write back. But an obscene gesture did doodle itself in Otherside fog.

He'd show. If for no other reason than to berate me. And to

assuage his own curiosity. Despite being dead almost twenty years, he'd never been to the Portland underground.

Aaron was across town. In rush hour traffic, he'd be more than an hour. I could be out and back before he or anyone else was any the wiser.

I braced myself and wrote my next message.

Gideon? I held my breath, waiting for the ghost to appear.

One thing I had to hand to Gideon—he didn't disappoint. I'd just released my breath when the ghost coalesced in front of me.

"I expected you to contact me earlier than this, little practitioner." I heard him before I felt the telltale chill.

"Well, it took me a little longer because I found something interesting for you."

Gideon snorted. "I doubt that. I've seen my share of serial killers."

"Gideon, far be it from me to argue with you, but I'd almost be willing to bet you a year of servitude that you haven't seen a serial killer like this."

"I've seen my fair share of ghosts on a killing spree as well. They're called poltergeists." He paused and frowned at me, his eyes narrowing. "What happened to you? Where did those bruises on your neck come from? You're covered in Otherside!" His nose crinkled. "And something else."

On the drive to the hotel, I'd wavered on just how much to tell Gideon about the swamp. The ghost was condescending and irritable at the best of times. But I quickly dismissed hiding things. I needed his help.

I held out my arms. "A murder, the ghost of a serial killer whom I can't banish, witchcraft, and an Otherside-filled swamp. You're welcome," I added, and filled him in on the more pertinent details, including the discovery that Dane or whatever practitioner was helping him had a vested interest in me. "I mean, there has to be a practitioner involved, yes? Unless you think Dane could do any of that alone?"

Gideon shook his head. "No. *I* could, but . . ." He trailed off. "A swamp with that much Otherside—I haven't seen something like than in ages . . . And witches, you say?"

I nodded.

Gideon inclined his head. "Even longer since I've seen any of them. And that explains the scent on you—Otherside tinged with compost."

"The way Bergen talked about the swamp, I got the impression it was rare but not unusual."

Gideon appeared to lean back as he considered my question. "Well, not unusual to them. But witches are masters at hiding themselves and their watersheds. If they don't wish you to see them, you won't. Point to you, then, little practitioner, though I'm not taking a year off your apprenticeship. This counts as interesting. You're excused for not calling me earlier. Let me see the bindings you say you found at the scene."

I retrieved the sheets I'd copied at the barn and spread them out on the table. In the excitement, I'd forgotten to hand them over to Stephan. "This one I found on the girl's neck, and this was on the metal plate. Buried under the dirt."

He touched the paper with his translucent hand. "Oh, and congratulations for not ending up almost dead this time," he said offhandedly. "Though I suppose I have the other practitioner to thank for that?" Gideon examined them, but rather than interest, I saw a dark expression cross his features. His eyes shifted to a glittering black. "Are you certain you copied these exactly?" he said.

"I think so. I can show you where the barn is on a map and you can go take a look for yourself." Gideon didn't seem to have any difficulty appearing and disappearing whenever and wherever he liked, so there was no reason to think he couldn't go directly to the scene.

But Gideon shook his head. "Not yet. If a coven of witches have an entire swamp to control their ghosts, they'll certainly have an alarm system in place for someone like me. This will suffice for now." He brushed his fingers along the diagram I'd made of the metal sheet.

"Do you know what it is?"

"Yes, unfortunately. It's a very special ghost trap." I waited for him to elaborate. Gideon looked increasingly uneasy. "I know what it is because I designed this. It's one of mine—with some alterations to the workings and purpose, but it's unmistakable." He placed the sheet back on the desk, still staring at it. "It's a trap meant to cage a ghost—but this one has been modified. Instead of a cage, it puts the ghost in a stasis."

I stared at him. "Ah—how?"

"I don't know!" he shouted as he turned to face me, his eyes flashing pure black, his lip turning up in a snarl.

I froze, uncertain what I'd said wrong as Gideon glowered at me.

He turned back to the desk and the drawings. "I'm sorry," he said tersely. "That wasn't deserved. Whoever did this is very good. I don't know how they did it. Or why."

I swallowed, hoping Gideon's anger had passed. "What was it supposed to do?"

"It's a type of cage. Most often used for catching and controlling poltergeists. I've sold a number of them over the centuries, they aren't a secret . . ." He made an irritated *tsk*ing sound, then added, "Like the ghost trap mirror we worked on yesterday, I am selective with whom I sell these to—I haven't sold one in years. They're dangerous." He said it as if it were a bad taste in his mouth.

"Why is it dangerous?" My voice was small.

He glanced up at me and for a moment the dark fury was back. Just when I thought he wouldn't answer, he said, "Because this kind of trap can be used on the living. This *has* been used on the living"—he gestured at the sheet in disgust—"to kill and bind their ghost. That's what this new design is for. It is *not* my original intent." The air around him crackled with Otherside.

Jesus Christ. One of Max's rules had always been never to use bindings for the dead on the living. I'd seen what had happened to Cole. He'd accidentally turned himself into a living-dead wraith, using bindings on himself meant for the dead in a misguided attempt to steal Nate's talent. Twenty years later, it had drained him into a living husk. A powerful and vengeful monster.

And here I was talking to one. A monster.

I forgot my fear at the implications.

"Who did you sell it to? You said you kept track of everything." We could find them, track down who might have got it, narrow down the list of practitioners . . .

Gideon shook his head, still examining the image. "I don't know, Kincaid."

"What do you mean, you don't know? I thought you were selective—"

He turned on me, eyes glittering. "Yes, all right? I am selective, but this isn't an original. It's been modified. They've taken my design and stripped out all of my identifying features—every last one." I watched as Gideon's eyes turned pitch-black again. "Someone went to a great deal of trouble to hide where this came from. I need to find out who, and how many practitioners it's been shared with."

"Why? So you can make sure they pay you?" I knew that wasn't the reason, but for the love of God, I couldn't stop myself.

"No!" The chill in the air around me deepened. He wasn't angry, he was furious. More furious than I'd ever seen him. "Because one of my bindings has been used on the living!"

I waited until the chill subsided, then asked, "Would you have sold it if you had known it *could* be used on the living?"

Gideon was silent.

"It's not that hard a question." Just say no, Gideon. If he said no, I could maybe stomach this apprenticeship. If said no then he wasn't that black-hearted and evil. A trap for poltergeists was one thing . . . "Gideon?"

"I don't know, all right?!" There was exasperation, anger and something else—regret, maybe—written on his face.

It was my turn to be silent. Slowly, Gideon's eyes faded back to the familiar ghost grey.

"I never would have sold it for *this* purpose. You can be certain of that. There would have been conditions to the sale. Was it bought with this purpose in mind? Possibly. I'm not a mind reader. Or it could have been gifted to someone, passed through generations of a practitioning family without my knowledge, then lost, even stolen. I don't ask those questions."

I kept silent.

Rather than changing the subject as I expected, Gideon became more animated. "Why do you have to look at me like that? Why do you have to twist and confuse everything with your—"

"What? Morals?"

We stood there, staring. I realized the temperature had dropped once again.

But, for possibly the first time ever, Gideon was the one who backed down.

"I would ask that you stay— I know there is great personal risk to you, but—"

With some relief, I noted that the darkness had abated. I let go of the breath I'd been holding.

"I need to know who got a hold of these bindings and what their end goal is. If only—to rule a possibility out. I'll stay close by. And I wish to see this swamp tomorrow."

Unleash Gideon in this state on a paranormal FBI team? Even I could see he wasn't himself. And his usual self was terrifying enough.

"What do you plan to do? I mean—if you tell me what you're looking for—"

"I didn't ask for your opinion, *apprentice*." The bite in his words made me wince. "You can be certain, if I ever require it, I'll ask." He shook his head and turned once more to the diagrams.

God help me, I tried again. "Gideon, if I'm putting myself in danger, I should have a say—"

"*Fine.* You want a say? Here is your say, Kincaid. Stay, go. I don't care. But if you don't stay, you can consider our apprenticeship over. You can be my messenger for the next five years to pay off your debt."

Oh, for Christ's sake. I stayed silent. I hadn't meant to threaten to leave. I hadn't even considered it—not just because of the unexpected complication of Gideon's tangential involvement, but because I wouldn't feel right leaving a trap that dangerous in the hands of a serial killer. I would have helped Gideon despite our agreement. It was a matter of my own ethical code.

It hurt, it actually hurt, that he didn't think even that well of me. Just when I thought I might be able to stomach the sorcerer . . .

I tried to keep my face neutral, but something gave me away.

Gideon made another disparaging, irritated sound. "I *hate* it when you look at me like that, Kincaid Strange. The disappointment, the judgment, your code of ethics . . ." He turned back to the bindings that had drawn him down a darker well than usual.

We stood in awkward silence for I don't know how long, Gideon all the while staring at the binding.

It was Gideon who spoke first. "Tell your thief to keep an eye out for the poltergeist. I doubt he's contained in the swamp, not if he's collecting his old victims. It won't be the last you see of him. I'll set my own alarm. Hopefully, that will dissuade him until the morning. If you're still in Portland tomorrow, I expect to hear from you at the scene when you have a moment away. Look for other traps and warn the two soothsayers if you feel it necessary, but omit any mention of me."

And with that, the ghost vanished. I sat down, not knowing what the hell to think—or how the hell I should feel.

After collecting myself, I helped Nate cross over the mirror. Despite my freshly rattled nerves, I still had one task left tonight.

"Please say you had a chance to ask the Portland ghosts the best way into the Portland underground." I'd told Nate to nose around after Lee Ling had given me her own instructions.

"Ah, yeah. FYI, K, this place is a serious ghost town. It's got *me* spooked just how many ghosts there aren't—"

"*Nate.*"

"Fine. The few ghosts I did manage to find all say there are two ways in. Well, two for the living and zombies, and a third for ghosts, but I'm guessing we're not using that one."

I gestured for him to hurry it up as I unpacked my backpack.

"The first entrance is through the sewers. Not recommended, but it's still definitely in use, and goes straight to the docks."

The waterfront gang led by the undead Captain Derrick ran the Underground Portland docks. He'd been one of the most profitable

Portland shanghaiers of his lifetime and now had a thriving trade in "exotic" zombie delicacies. Meaning fresh brains and human flesh—making that entry point a definite no.

"And the second is through Old Portland, down an alleyway by one of the light rail stations. Apparently the door is Otherside marked—you can't miss it."

I sighed. Lee Ling had told me to use the entrance in historic Portland, but I'd been hoping to avoid it. I'd be walking straight through Celeste's courtesan territory, and though Lee swore her friend had given me safe passage, well . . . Lee had odd ideas about what constituted "safe." I doubted Celeste would do me any harm, but her zombies? I trusted they wouldn't kill me and eat my brains, but a little "friendly" roughing up might be in the cards. Some good old-fashioned intimidation and light torture?

It wasn't out of the question.

Which is why I'd planned ahead. There were a few rumours floating around regarding the Portland underground city and the dead who ran it. Seems they weren't nearly as friendly with the local practitioners. Fewer of the living travelling underground meant there were fewer surface goods reaching them.

I checked the time on my phone: 5 p.m. A bit early, but it'd be plenty dark by the time we reached the train station and I got a look at the entry point.

Was it possible Dane might be out looking for me already? If that was the case, I'd be little safer here than in the underground. Besides, I wanted to exit the hotel early to avoid the chance of running into Ingrid or Liam—or Aaron, for that matter. I was still angry over—well, everything. I didn't want to listen to his reasons.

See no evil . . .

My bag now contained my hotel key, a small set mirror and a bag full of china markers. I tucked the cash I'd brought for just this occasion into a side pocket. My compact mirror and phone I tucked into the inside pocket of my leather jacket.

Satisfied I was equipped only with the necessities, I tied up my hair in a bun and pulled on a hat. My mass of black, frizzy curls was too distinctive, too easily recognizable, both in the hotel and in the underground. "Come on," I said to Nate, tossing my backpack over my shoulder. "We've got a grocery run to make first."

We headed downstairs, and I was glad for the cap. Two uniformed police were stationed in the lobby, right smack in front of the main door.

Aaron. Stationing them there to send a message to me not to leave. Of all the . . . I stuffed my temper.

"Come on," I said to Nate, and ducked back into the elevator. "There's a laundry downstairs." I'd seen it on the amenities list and wagered the local cops weren't paid well enough to guard the exit down there.

As the elevator door closed on us, I shook my head. If Aaron didn't want me to leave, he could damn well tell me himself.

✳

"Kincaid, far be it from me to tell you what to do and how to do it," Nate said as I examined the brick wall, painted in graffiti.

"Uh-huh," I said absently as I brushed my fingers against one of the bricks. Lee's directions weren't exactly precise: "about ten steps to the left of the red door and five from the rusted metal one." Well, here I was, looking for two alley doorways in a not so hospitable-looking alley, in a strange city.

"But, you know, a serial killer like Dane hunting a girl like you, in an alley alone, with a ghost who, you know—can't do a damn thing?" He leaned against the brick wall. "K, this does not bode well."

Yeah, this was the spot. Only one problem: no Otherside markers. "Just give me a second to think. Did the ghosts give you any other instructions? On how to open the door?"

Nate floated beside me and stared at the wall. His eyebrows knit together. "No, I mean, they just said the entrance was around here."

"Lee basically told me the same thing. What about you?" I turned, arms crossed. "Anything?"

Nate shook his head. "Not from here, K—there isn't a trace of Otherside I can see." He shrugged. "Maybe throw something at it?"

Damn it. And here I'd been hoping I wouldn't have to pull another globe today. Well, the Seattle underground didn't exactly make entrance easy; no reason to think the Portland underground would be different.

And no turning back now.

"Keep an eye out, Nate," I said, and after glancing around to make sure there were no onlookers, I tapped the barrier. The cool Otherside flooded my head and the world around me took on a ghost-grey cast. This time, away from the swamp, I felt the nausea more intensely as the chill passed over me. Though it was a relief to see my fingers in front of my face, I found myself missing the swamp, and the ease with which I'd channelled Otherside.

I searched the wall once more. Still no Otherside markings that I could see, but there was more than one way to hide a door with Otherside. I sent three quick pulses of Otherside at the wall in short gold waves.

"K, did you see that, or . . . ?"

I nodded. It had been subtle, barely a flicker of gold in the air—but the Otherside had uncovered a spot on the wall that was obscured, or "glamoured," for lack of a better term. A thin sliver of the brick wall, no more than a foot across and jagged.

Nate waved his translucent hand through the glamour.

Ghosts can travel through walls. It's neither surprising nor particularly interesting when Nate sticks his hand through one. But it is interesting when the wall reacts—as this one did to Nate's Otherside, by wavering and flickering gold.

I felt the opening myself. It was small, a narrow gap in the brick wall just wide enough to slip through.

Otherside had been used, likely from the other side of the wall, to obscure the opening. Not the most functional solution—there was always the chance someone might accidentally lean on the opening and stumble through or witness a cat slinking through—but it was a clever means of concealing the entry point.

"Want to tell me what's behind the veil?" I asked Nate. He vanished and reappeared ten seconds later.

"Narrow passage. Keeps going a ways. No lights, but didn't see any zombies hiding in wait or, you know, ancient booby traps."

"It's an underground city for the dead, not an Indiana Jones movie."

Nate shrugged. "It could be two things."

"Less adventure movies, more looking for Otherside. Any alarms?"

"No, like I said, no—"

"Booby traps, got it already." I let out a breath and grabbed my phone from my pocket, turning on the flashlight. I did another quick search of the alleyway.

"Coast is clear, Indy," Nate whispered.

I held my breath and, feeling the edges of the bricks, slid through sideways, holding my breath as I felt my way through the mirage, the chill of Otherside snapping at my skin the entire way, the scent of ozone heavy in the air.

And just as Nate had said, I was standing in a very narrow passage, as if the building had been split down the middle.

I surveyed the dirt floor and brick ceiling. A tunnel more than an alley. There was no risk of me hitting my head—and with the exception of a few puddles near the entrance, the ground was packed solid. The locals and animals might be fooled by the false Otherside wall that hid the passage, but the rain couldn't care less.

With the help of my flashlight, we made our way down the strange tunnel. It reminded me of the Seattle underground, though these walls had cleaner lines, the red-and-brown bricks more uniform in size than the natural stonework I was familiar with.

The air was surprisingly fresh. We were both silent—despite Nate's jokes and certainty that there were no traps or zombies lying in wait. Every city has its own lifeblood, a feel to it, like a living, breathing thing. The cities of the dead are no different, and as a newcomer, you are never quite certain what personality runs under the surface, formed and moulded by the long-time inhabitants.

The Seattle and Portland undergrounds were like sisters. At first glance, they obviously had the same genetics and external influences shaping them: the west coast frontier, the North Pacific Ocean, a lot of rain, economies moulded by criminal creativity . . . They were as similar as fraternal twins, which meant their differences could be all the more shocking, and dangerous.

Whereas Lee Ling kept the Seattle underground running as a "relatively harmonious" tight ship, saying that Celeste "ran" the Portland underground would be generous at best. In reality, the Portland underground hadn't changed much since its inception sometime during the 1800s. It was still run by three gangs: the waterfront gang, the warrens and the courtesans. If the gossip was any indication, they'd been fighting ever since—a cyclical, never-ending, undead bar brawl.

The waterfront gang was filled with the undead sailors who manned the ships that sailed from Portland to Asia, as well as the lowlife undead who stocked said ships with unwilling sailors—both dead and alive. They were led by an equally morally repugnant zombie by the name of Captain Derrick. Derrick controlled waterfront access and many of the underground passages. Lee despised him, which is why I had steered clear of the storm drain.

Next were the warrens, the Chinese gang led by King You. Their territory comprised the masses of brick tunnels built by the Portland Chinese during the late 1800s and expanded on heavily by the undead. According to Lee, it was quite the engineering feat, stretching all over Portland and bridging the two other undead territories. Lee didn't despise You the way she did Derrick, but she didn't like him either. According to Lee, You couldn't be more uptight if he walked around with a railroad spike from his track-laying days stuck up his ass. Whereas Lee had dragged the frontier dead kicking and screaming into something resembling the twenty-first century, You had kept the tunnels firmly entrenched in the past. He also didn't approve of prostitution and refused to condone it in his territory.

Which left the courtesan-held territory, or, as Lee Ling liked to call them, the seamstresses, and I use the word very loosely. The courtesans had manned the brothels in frontier Portland when they'd been alive, and when they'd died and been raised as zombies, they saw no reason to change the status quo. Hotels and saloons still lined the main roads of the courtesan territory. Interestingly, it was the only territory with a town, so all of the gangs converged there. Lee had warned me that bar and sidewalk brawls were frequent occurrences, and if I didn't see a gunfight, I should count myself lucky, and if I did—I should run. The dead quickly forget that guns still kill the living.

If the Portland underground had a peaceful, law-abiding place, it was the world's best-kept secret. But Lee knew Celeste, the woman who ran the courtesan-held territory, and the two had a rapport, a friendship of sorts. According to Lee, Celeste was the most inclined to hold up her end of a deal.

What inspired an animosity that stretched across a century? Though the Chinese, the sailors and the courtesans weren't at war, they didn't like each other, and though they needed each other to perpetuate their undead survival, their individual interests were often directly opposed. Take the courtesans, who depended on the undead men and women who spent their money at the brothels and watering holes, or King You, who depended on his bricklayers to extend the massive warrens and the sailors for supplies. Captain Derrick also needed undead men and women to man his zombie ships. But, as in life, none of the undead were crazy enough to want to crew them—up to three years spent on a ship with only formal- dehyde-cured and dried brain preserves. There was a term living sailors used to throw around ships, *long pork*, referring to white human leg meat. The undead had their own version, pickled brains, and the origin was just as gruesome.

Captain Derrick was left with two options: kidnapping and coer- cion. He wasn't above either. Shanghaiing people had been a long- standing tradition during the Portland frontier times, so why not keep it alive?

Every six months or so, Captain Derrick and his sailors and the outright pirates would hold a shanghai raid of Celeste's courtesan district, and King You let him do it through his tunnels, with the understanding that the Chinese were to be left alone—and paid— for their trouble.

The last shanghai raid, according to Nate via the local ghosts, had been a month ago, so in theory I should be safe.

"How does knowing Lee get us in here exactly?" Nate asked.

"Lee knows Celeste—I'm picking up a package. She knows we're coming, so she should have someone on the lookout for us. In theory." I would reserve my judgment on Lee's contact until we met her in the flesh.

"Shoulda, woulda, coulda," Nate intoned.

I shot him a glare. "Quiet." I'd rather avoid any zombie attention—if we hadn't attracted some hidden eyes already.

"Oh, I'm musing what I'm going to say when we run into a pirate raiding party."

"We shouldn't run into any of Derrick's zombies here."

"I repeat, if and when I end up manning a ghost ship, I'm blaming you."

"Nate, how many times do I need to tell you, they don't use ghosts on ghost ships—"

"Pssst!" Nate stopped walking and poked me in the side, sending a chill through me.

I halted my steps. There was a shuffling sound ahead in the shadows of the tunnel.

"Welcoming committee," Nate whispered.

Finally. I lowered my flashlight, polite-like, so as not to blind some hapless zombie. I didn't turn it off, though, just in case it wasn't one of Celeste's. Bright LED lights are almost as good as jukeboxes and pinball machines for distracting a century-or-so-old zombie, especially one restricted to underground caverns.

"Hello?" I said. "Anyone there?"

The shuffling stopped. We waited as they sussed us out.

"Come out, come out, wherever you are," Nate chimed, loud enough that whoever was ahead would hear just fine.

If looks could kill, the one I shot him . . .

I heard the sharp strike of a match and yellow lantern light bled around the corner of a wall up ahead, though I couldn't see who held it. My nose crinkled at the scent of kerosene and sulphur matches. The light illuminated the narrow brick-lined passage ahead of us.

A zombie stepped out from around a corner, lantern in hand. He held it up to his face, illuminating a blackened grin—and not the friendly kind.

I got a decent-enough look at him in the kerosene-lamp light. Heavy, worn-leather spiked boots, dusty flannel shirt and wide-brimmed hat, soiled work jeans and his general size told me he was a logger, not one of Derrick's sailors. Had to be one of Celeste's folk—or, more accurately, one of her folk's patrons. That was promising.

I cleared my throat. "Guard duty, I presume?"

I watched his nostrils flare, picking up my scent. His skin and the whites of his eyes had taken on the telltale yellow gleam of a body maintained more by formaldehyde than good binding work. "You could say that," he said, licking cracked lips as two more zombies stepped into view behind him. One wore work jeans over his red flannel long johns, but his companion had only got as far as the long johns. When they forget to finish dressing, they're halfway to feral . . .

Almost respectable, if you didn't count the way all three zombies grinned and sniffed the air.

I removed my backpack slowly and held it out so they could see the weight, courtesy of my trip to the grocer's before heading down. "I have passage through to Celeste's territory, by way of Lee Ling Xhao," I said. "I even have a paper with me, if you want to see it." It was tucked inside a jacket pocket, and I reached for it.

Nate stopped me. "K, I really don't think these guys ever did much reading—in their previous life or this one," he whispered.

Point made. I held my hand back up.

The three of them exchanged a glance but didn't move out of the way. That wasn't good.

They began to murmur in voices too low for me to make out. A quick nod from me and Nate vanished, reappearing a moment later looking more perturbed.

"K, not to press the point here, but two of them are wondering what's in the bag and the guy at the back just wondered out loud what your brain tastes like and if Celeste would notice."

"Well, shit," I whispered. So much for safe passage.

I cleared my throat again and their whispering stopped. Maybe I could turn this before it descended into violence.

"Ah—guys, hate to burst your brainstorm here, but Celeste is expecting me. You can call her if you want. You can even use my phone." I held it up, waving.

The zombie holding the lantern, the one I assumed was in charge, stepped towards me. His two undead companions remained where they were but tensed, like bulls ready to charge. Oh, I did not like those smiles.

I slid my Otherside sight into place and got a good look at all their bindings. Decent work, not the best—there were a couple of stability flaws I could exploit fast. Cripple them, at the very least. I readied my finger on my phone flashlight. "Nate, get ready to grab the lantern," I whispered. I'd be able to see their Otherside bindings in the dark, as would Nate, but they'd have a harder time seeing us . . .

The zombie paused for a moment. "Celeste said you were some kind of big shot practitioner."

I let a little bit of the Otherside I'd held since the entrance bleed through. Maybe they'd have a sensible change of mind about trying to eat my brains.

"From where I'm standing, you don't look so tough." He licked his dry yellow lips. "And Danny thinks that pretty coconut you're carrying around smells awful tasty."

The three of them laughed.

Welp, so much for common sense.

I let more Otherside bleed out and got ready to pool more. "Just remember, you pulled the trigger," I said as the two muscle zombies charged.

I reached for their bindings, pulling the lines that controlled their lower halves, sending them both stumbling to their knees. At the same time, I turned my flashlight on. The zombie holding the lantern yelped and shielded his eyes, and the lantern dropped to the ground. A moment later Nate got a hold of it and blew the light out.

I went for the heart lines next, while they were down. With any luck, I'd have all three dismantled before one got to his feet.

"All right, that's enough, you dumb oxen!" A low, gravelly voice cut through the shouts of the other two zombies. Another lantern lit up the tunnel and a woman dressed in jeans, a heavy leather duster and a grey Western hat stepped out from the shadows. She was pretty, died in her forties, I imagined, and had had some exquisite work done to her face—it looked as good as Lee's. Next to no formaldehyde had been used to preserve her. Intricate work—and expensive to maintain. Her hair—a thick chestnut brown—was piled underneath the cowboy hat, but strands of it had escaped.

Her face wasn't just attractive, it was expressive, a feat for a zombie as old as Lee. And she was pissed. She stepped between me and the zombies, hands on hips, glowering at everyone. "Everyone hold your stupid-as-mud horses. That means you too, practitioner. I see that Otherside you're packing, even if these three numbskulls are too dumb to figure it out." She nodded at two of the zombies still on the ground, kicking one in the gut to make her point and grabbing the other by his ear. "What did I tell you two about not harming the Seattle practitioner? How did you get the message 'eat her brains'?"

The zombie groaned and tried to roll over, but Celeste pinched his ear again.

"Celeste, I presume?" I nodded at the three incapacitated zombies. "Fabulous welcoming party," I said.

Celeste nodded. "Aye, that's me. And don't take offence at these three idiots, dearie, I wouldn't have let you come to any harm." She looked me over, her smile widening. "Though considering how you took control, I imagine you don't get pushed around none too easy." She nodded back at the zombies. "They were supposed to meet you and bring you by my saloon, but they got it into their heads to be curious about just what Lee Ling sent my way." She turned to them. "Didn't think I'd hear you talking about jumping her, did you?"

She gave the zombie in the red long johns a smack over the head. "And this one, Danny, he's about three empty picnic baskets on his way to being a feral, aren't you, Danny? Eating girl's brains, what the hell's gotten into you?"

The zombie mumbled something that might have been, "Sorry, ma'am."

Celeste nodded at me. "You can put that Otherside away, Lee Ling's practitioner. These boys will be playing nice from now on. Or *else*," she said, pushing the tip of her boot into Danny's neck. She'd yet to let him up.

"Won't happen again, Celeste," he muttered.

"You're damn right it won't." She jerked her head at the other two. "Now get yourselves to the doc and tell him to patch up your bindings—and see if he can make Danny stop thinking about eating people's brains while they're still walking."

The three zombies finished picking themselves off the tunnel floor and shuffled away. Once they were out of earshot, Celeste said, "They mean well and do a decent-enough job guarding the entrance here, though Danny, bless his heart, never had the strongest mental constitution when it came to resisting temptation, even when he was alive. *Laudanum*." She whispered the last word. "I'm afraid I don't expect him to last much longer, poor thing. It'll be like when I had to put down my favourite bloodhound, Baxter, a few years back." She clucked and made the sign of the cross. "Damn thing wouldn't stop bringing home those tiny dogs the living young 'uns are so fond of now. Though can't say I blame him. I ask you, what the hell is the point of a dog that the rats beat up?"

She nodded down the passage through which the zombies had gone. "Come on. I've got your book behind the bar and I'm serving beer and whisky since I've got a live one—and a ghost, of all things. We can chat and you can fill me in on what the hell is going on that's got the Portland PD spooked enough to truck no fewer than three of you practitioners into town."

Celeste headed down the tunnel at a quick pace, lamp bouncing with her step.

"Well, you heard the lady," I said.

Nate swallowed, floating beside me. "Ah, did I miss something, or did Celeste say she has a dog?" Nate whispered.

"Had, past tense. A zombie dog. Lee Ling said she kept them as pets," I whispered back.

Nate just shook his head. "Zombie dogs. And I thought I'd heard of everything."

I inclined mine. "I have a feeling we're about to hear an awful lot more."

*

Underground Seattle looked similar to how it would have in frontier times—boardwalks, old building fronts, open market stalls. It was well-maintained and subtly updated as needed. Not modernized, but Lee made certain the infrastructure wasn't falling down. Though Underground Portland wasn't a crumbling ruin, it showed its wear. There were any number of shuttered and damaged buildings, though the brickwork was in surprisingly good shape. Another reason why Celeste and King You weren't at all-out war over Captain Derrick's trespasses, I imagined. King You kept the place from falling apart.

Celeste went out of her way to avoid the piles of foul-smelling mud dotting our path, and I followed suit. I realized what they were when we passed one of the many rambunctious saloons. A horse was tied to a wooden post, feeding out of a trough filled with hay and something wet . . . It sniffed the air as we passed by and fixed me with its large, formaldehyde-yellowed eyes, flicking its sparse tail and whinnying, baring its stained and incomplete set of teeth. I gave it a wide berth.

"Zombie horses," Celeste said. "Tried to get rid of them back in 1920 on account of a few going feral. Whole town threw a fuss—how could I expect them to go home without their horses?" She snorted. "A lot of bunk that was. Half of them live at these establishments, playing cards and drinking, with no farther to go than a flight of stairs or a short crawl to the dorms out back, but there's only so far I'm willing to push."

Celeste hadn't brought in electricity to her territory as Lee had, and only half of the street lanterns that lined the stone road were lit. The gas-burning lamps filled the air with an acrid scent. There were a lot of smells filling the air down here—not the least of which was formaldehyde. Where Lee went out of her way to try to cover the scent of death that permeated the very structure of her city, no effort had been made here.

They'd embraced it.

"Here we are," Celeste said, climbing the steps to a massive saloon-style building, easily the largest and best maintained we'd seen. It was three storeys, with ornately carved balconies wrapping each floor. The building itself was painted a soft maroon, set off by the whites and yellows of the windowsills and balconies. There was dust, but nowhere near as much as everywhere else.

The painted wooden sign at the entrance read *Celeste's Seamstresses*. Below, in smaller letters, was written *Accoutrements mended while you wait*, and *Inquire inside for reputable boarding*. Though I try not to make snap judgments, the two zombie women on the second-floor balcony in cleavage-accentuating corsets, waving and catcalling to the pedestrians below, greatly disputed the sign's claim. The general ruckus coming from inside, including a piano and occasional shrieks, also begged to differ.

Vice doesn't disappear with death, but the inhibitions do.

I couldn't decide if the building was ironically named or a carry-over from another time, a ridiculous attempt to circumvent the authorities when everyone had still been alive.

"Mind the drunks and watch your step," Celeste called, pushing the black saloon doors open.

The place was packed wall to wall with zombies in varying states of inebriation, arguing and engaged with . . . various companions, of the professional kind or otherwise.

It was one giant bar brawl waiting to happen.

Celeste pushed one zombie lying across the entrance under the swinging doors with the heel of her boot. She wove her way through the crowd and Nate and I followed close behind, acutely aware of the heads turning our way.

Our guide headed to a table in the corner, one of the larger ones with spacious, comfy seats. A zombie had passed out in one of the chairs. Celeste none too gently tipped the chair back and deposited the zombie on the floor.

She laughed. "Have a seat, Ms. Strange." I took one of the chairs with my back to the corner. She took a seat and waved to a woman behind the bar. A tray of glasses was delivered to our table along with a brown paper–wrapped package. "Welcome to my humble abode," Celeste said over a glass of whisky on the rocks—real rocks. She caught me looking and gave it a swirl. "Had to cut back on refrigeration last year. Some developer finally tore down an abandoned restaurant basement I was using for storage. If only they knew. Never thought I'd go back to salted ice blocks and cellars, but here we are. So tell me, Ms. Strange, what the hell has the Portland PD so riled up?"

I picked up one of the glasses and sniffed at it, while Nate slid into the chair beside me and happily gulped one, and then another, down. Not a whiff of formaldehyde. I didn't think there would be, but you can never be too careful. The safety standards for booze on the frontier had never been particularly stringent, and it had got worse during Prohibition, when a lot of these zombies were last alive. I took a slow sip. I'd thought about how to approach Celeste on my way down and had decided I needed information more than discretion. Considering what Bergen had omitted about the swamp, she was set on keeping secrets. And Stephan? I didn't have a hope Stephan would offer me any more insight either. Both of them wanted me to solve their problems, but like so many in the practitioning community, they didn't trust me.

I would try my best to earn their trust, but I needed a back door. I took a deep breath. "A poltergeist serial killer is hiding in the Spalt swamp. Goes by the name of Martin Dane, the White Picket Fence Killer," I said.

Celeste arched her brown eyebrows. "Is that a fact? That's the witches' swamp, if I'm not mistaken. They'll be none too happy about that. He's up to his old-dog tricks, I take it? Of course he is, otherwise they wouldn't need you and those Hollywood practitioners out here. Nothing those witches hate more than attention. A serial killer would bring that hailing down around them." She leaned across the large table, looking contemplative. "I imagine this has to do with that girl who was kidnapped?"

There was no point in denying it, so I nodded.

So, Celeste did know about the witches and their swamp. What about the ghosts?

"He's proving hard to find and harder to get rid of," I said, and sipped my whisky. Offhandedly, I added, "Oh, and he's stealing ghosts . . ."

Celeste's face turned guarded. "What ghosts?"

Bingo. She knew something. I shrugged. "Well, the ghosts of all his victims, including the most recent. Dozens. Oh, and the witches' ghosts. Those went mis—"

Celeste cut me off with a slap to the table. "Ha! I *knew* that old ox of a biddy was hiding something. Her eye always twitches when she's lying." Celeste rocked back in her chair, howling loud enough with laughter it earned us more than a few looks. "Those damned crones up by the old Spalt cranberry marshes lost their ghosts, did they?"

She snorted and made a derisive gesture, shooting the remainder of her whisky and taking another glass, while Nate, who was sitting quietly in his own chair, kept a wary eye on our surroundings while he nursed his own glass.

"Can't say I'm sorry to hear it. The selfish whole lot of them deserve it." She swore again. "Can't be bothered to lift a finger until it's their own problem, till one of their *own* goes missing." She snorted. "I'll bet they have you running errands for them now, don't they?"

I frowned and exchanged a glance with Nate. Until one of their *own* goes missing? "Wait a minute, just back up. Am I to understand there are more ghosts missing? Bergen didn't say anything about any others," I said.

Celeste gave a disdainful laugh. "Oh, of course they wouldn't mention any others. They weren't their carefully curated, well-behaved dead. They were Portland underground ghosts. 'Probably left or upset some practitioner, you know how those ne'er-do-wells are, coming and going as they please,'" Celeste said in a mocking voice. She levelled a finger at me. "That witch Bergen and the rest of her coven aren't welcome here anymore. I'd have half a mind to throw *you* out if it wasn't that Lee asked me personal to take care of you."

I frowned. "I—didn't know, I'm sorry. And I'm not working for them—not exactly. I was hired to stop a serial killer—sort of." And possibly as bait. I got the distinct impression Celeste had an inside line—and was more willing to share than the witches or Stephan. Why the hell hadn't either of them mentioned the other missing ghosts? "How many ghosts are missing from the Portland underground, exactly?"

"Oh, it's been going on for the better part of a year now," Celeste started. "Slowly at first, barely noticeable. A woman or man here or there, people who were drifting through and didn't stay as long as they meant to." Celeste gave me a pointed look. "Mostly the working women. That's what really got me thinking something was off."

"What do you mean?"

"Well, people upstairs get murdered all the time, most of them from the more notorious walks of life. Gypsies, whores and thieves. We've got a worse reputation than most, courtesy of Derrick, his crews and those damned boats." Celeste shrugged. "I have a soft spot for ghosts who met their end while in a profession of ill repute. Word got around and . . ." She shrugged. "I've always kept a seat for them here. They come through, have a drink on the house, and a place to haunt for a while if they need it before moving on, to the Otherside or wherever else they fancy. Been that way for over a hundred years. Consider it my charity work." She nodded at the tables of zombie loggers and the odd zombie hipster. "In return for bilking these louts out of their money. But a year ago, I started noticing ghosts disappearing."

I took stock of the bar. With the exception of Nate, there were no ghosts amid the zombies. Come to think of it, there'd been none outside either, and Nate had mentioned a sparsity of local apparitions.

I exchanged a glance with Nate, who was looking more and more uncomfortable by the minute. "Wait, are *all* the ghosts in the Portland underground missing?" he asked.

Celeste nodded. "Though most of them buggered off of their own accord—scaredy-cats, the lot of you," she said, directing the adage at Nate. "But a larger number than I'm comfortable with are missing. Like I told that damned witch, we're not talking one or two, we're talking around twenty women, and then the men, ones who were sitting here for twenty years and then one day weren't. And then there's been the last six months."

I frowned. "The last six months?"

She held up a finger. "Not one ghost, Kincaid Strange, not a single new ghost in all the past six months. I've checked the papers. People still die up there. So where are they going?"

I gaped at her. "Not a single ghost, that's—"

"Impossible?"

Our voices were drowned out by an escalating bar fight, and Celeste turned to shout them down. Thankfully, most of the zombies had lost interest in me. I sat back in the chair and processed what Celeste had told me. Dane's murder victims, a swamp emptied of ghosts and now a city. Were the disappearances related to the murders, or was something much bigger going on?

"You believe in coincidence about as much as you believe I'm good for rent," Nate whispered. He was visibly unnerved. I didn't blame him. Missing ghosts were a sore point for Nate, as his old record company had hired a ghost binder on more than one occasion to try to rope Nate into a Dead Men comeback tour. Slavery was perfectly legal provided the person—or rock star—in question was dead . . .

I really needed to talk to Stephan—or Aaron.

"Look, I'm not one to tell you how to do your business, but I'd certainly appreciate it if you looked into my ghosts—find out if they ended up on the market." She shuddered. "I almost don't want to know."

"The market?"

Celeste played with her glass, avoiding eye contact. "So Lee's never told you about that. But then, I suppose you aren't the type, so why would she?" She glanced back up, her face serious. "I imagine you've heard rumours about Derrick's business, stocking the ships with unwilling undead? Capturing them alone or on the odd raid?"

I nodded. I'd heard many stories about Portland's long tradition of frontier shanghaiing, from Lee and others.

She sighed. "Well, there's another trade that used to happen, before I put a stop to it. Bound ghosts. Portland has a history of disappearing people that I'm terribly fond of. There aren't too many of us left who remember the frontier days."

Ghosts for sale . . . "Jesus, you mean soothsayers are capturing ghosts to sell on a black market? To who?"

Celeste laughed. "You've got the right idea of it, but the soothsayers are the buyers, not the purveyors. Most soothsayers don't have time for catching ghosts, and not all of them are particularly talented at it." She inclined her head. "But there are a lot of ways to catch and bind a ghost, and for those practitioners with the knack, there's a lucrative black market for them. They just have to catch the rare ghosts with special talents, like being able to move through time or detect lies, and the obedient ones. But the ghosts who hung out in this city?" Celeste shook her head. "Temperamental, stuck in their ways, given to lives of vice and often crime. They would have been useless, which leaves me wondering why anyone would want them. Excepting the working girls and boys—I suppose they hold some value."

"Why the working girls?"

Celeste made a grimace. "And boys. Because an awful lot of them are broken—they're used to following orders. They're *obedient*." She said it like a dirty word. "Easier for the beginners to control. It's not a nice business." She glanced back up, looking at both of us.

"And it's not coming from here—from any of our territories, as much as I'd love to pin this on Derrick or King You. King You's own ghosts have gone missing, and Derrick has no use for ghosts. If someone caught our ghosts to sell, it's coming from the outside."

She picked up her third glass and sat back. "I'd consider it a favour Lee owes me paid in full if you'd look into it—though sounds like you might already be." She winked and picked up the paper package from the table and shook it at me, narrowing her eyes. "And of course, I'd consider us square for me holding this little gem," she said, waving the wrapped book.

Nate jabbed me with a cold elbow as Celeste waited. I fully planned on looking into the missing ghosts, but it paid to be very careful when bargaining with a zombie queen. "If the disappearances are due to the same source, I will let you know."

Celeste held up her hands. "That's all I ask, Kincaid Strange," she said, and passed me the package, leaning back and crossing her legs. It struck me that Celeste shared more mannerisms with a frontier pioneer than with a courtesan. Beautiful for sure, but rough spoken, and I dare say kinder than I had expected. More school-marm for wayward, misbehaving zombies than a jaded prostitute. I'd expected a woman more like Lee, refined and aloof. Celeste was a different breed, and I found myself liking her—not trusting, but as close as I dared in this place.

I picked up the journal Lee had acquired for me, the one that would hopefully shed light on Gideon's past.

"Don't suppose you'll tell me what Lee wants to know about that bastard?" Celeste asked. "I read it, of course."

Of course she did. And Lee hadn't ratted me out. I shrugged. "Just the messenger," I said.

Celeste smiled. "Well then, tell Lee from me that if that cursed bastard is hanging around, he's more trouble than he's worth. She should send him packing."

"Cursed?"

Celeste shook her head. "Never you mind, Kincaid Strange. A whole world of things you don't want anything to do with. Ghosts, poltergeists and Lee—you're deep enough into the dead as you want to be." She winked, and gave me a warning look. "Free advice? Just deliver the message with the book, and look into my ghosts—"

She was cut off mid-sentence as four zombies, men and women in various stages of undress, piled down the wooden stairs. "Celeste," one of them shouted. "It's Derrick and his men, they're coming back around!"

"Shit," Celeste swore, and stood fast enough to send her chair flying backwards. So did most of the other patrons who were sitting. All of them reached for firearms—six-shooters, shotguns, even a musket came out. An awful lot of guns in the hands of people who couldn't be hurt by them.

The zombie behind the bar threw Celeste a shotgun, which she caught easily. "Get to the windows! Fire as soon as you see the whites of their eyes—five thousand dollars to anyone who gets me Derrick's head!"

"K!" Nate's eyes darted around the room as the women in corsets and the men, many only in their long johns, raced to the windows. "Are we about to be in a gunfight?"

"I am, Nate—you're dead, remember?"

Celeste shot me a glance over her shoulder as tables were upended and piled against the windows and saloon door as makeshift barricades. Her brown hair had fallen from its updo and lay wild over her shoulders. "Raiding party for the boats," Celeste shouted at me. "If you planned on leaving, now's the time, and I'd make it quick."

The first round of gunfire rattled the building, a few lucky bullets sending shattered glass and booze to the floor. I dropped to my hands and knees. "What she said!" I shouted to Nate, and started crawling towards the saloon doors. Then I remembered the book.
Shit.

I searched the floor as more gunfire shook the building and Celeste's zombies returned fire. There were so many feet, overturned pieces of furniture and broken glasses. "Nate! The book!"

"Leave the damn book, K!" Nate shouted. He was floating in front of a window and a round of bullets shot through him harmlessly. Still,

Nate took offence—having projectiles hurled through you isn't pleasant for a ghost, and it's the thought that counts. He stuck his upper half through a broken window and the furniture barricading it, shaking his fists. "Hey, assholes! Dead already here, do you fucking mind?"

In answer, the zombies fired another round at him.

"Nate, stop playing with the zombies and grab my book."

He swore but quickly scanned the bar. "There's no time—now will you please leave?!"

Not without what I'd come for. I swore and crawled back to the table, one of the few too large to upend. I reached up to feel for it along the edge. It wasn't within reach.

One, two, *three*—

As fast as I could, I stuck my head up over the edge and grabbed it.

There was a lull in the gunfire. "There she is!" I heard one of the zombies shout from outside.

"Told you there was a live one!"

Oh, you have got to be kidding me . . .

"Hear that, Celeste?" The voice was deep and gravelly, like a smoker's—or someone who'd spent his life shouting over wind and waves at sea . . . "Five hundred dollars to any of your men or women who bring me the live one—but she's got to be alive."

The gunfire ceased and the zombies turned to face me. I clutched my book with both hands.

"Oh, go to hell, Derrick!" Celeste shouted back before giving her own men and women a dark look. "And a bullet in the back to anyone who takes him up on that offer."

Most backed down, though no one took their eyes off me.

To me, Celeste added, "I'd make yourself scarce, practitioner." She nodded to the rest of her people. "None of these folks were any good at avoiding temptation when they were alive, and now that they're dead?" She shrugged and turned her attention back to the window.

I ran for the exit as the gunfire resumed and crawled under the saloon doors onto the porch before anyone could stop me. Nate had vanished. I hoped to hell he was finding a safe route out.

"There she is!" I heard someone shout.

I dove behind the horse trough, hitting the ground hard. The zombie horse, who apparently wasn't much bothered by the gunfight on account of his face being buried in the trough, perked up. Then lunged at me.

I scrambled back against the porch as the yellow teeth grazed my jacket.

"Hold the gunfire! I said alive, you idiots, or none of us get paid!" the same deep, gravelly voice shouted. Captain Derrick, I assumed. He was a tall man, wearing a dark sailor's peacoat and a navy blue wool cap. Good enough to pass for living if he needed to, not decrepit-looking, but there was a meanness in his expression.

We made eye contact and he smiled, removing a cigar that was dangling from his mouth. "Use the poles," he said. Five zombie men stepped out of the shadows, all of them carrying poles with wire nooses on the ends. Oh, hell no.

There was a chill at my shoulder. "You know, K, 'told you so' just so doesn't cut it," Nate said, reappearing beside me.

"Please say you found a way out," I pleaded.

He inclined his head. "Sure, once you get past a couple dozen pirates and heavily armed sailors."

Zombie horse it was. I grabbed the reins and climbed on, all the while dodging the horse's nips.

"How the hell do you plan on making it run?" Nate hissed.

"You're helping," I shouted, staying low in the seat as more gunfire erupted, this time from the saloon at the men carrying the poles. I threw Nate the backpack, which I'd had the good sense not to take off. It still carried the brown parcels I'd picked up at the grocery store before heading into the city, just in case I found myself needing to barter with zombies.

I supposed the horse counted.

Here's hoping it liked pig and cow brains as much as it seemed to crave human ones.

"What the hell am I supposed to do with this?"

I swore as the zombified livestock tried bucking me off. At least the pirates weren't shooting at me—and Celeste's men and women had avoided me thus far. "Carrot on a stick—hold it out and keep it there. Just do it!"

"Fine!" Nate mumbled something about bad ideas going to fucking worse as he wrestled with the bag. "Here horsey, nice dead horsey," Nate cajoled the zombified horse, adding kissing sounds as he waved the two now-dripping brown butcher's packages at its face.

The horse stopped, stretched out its neck and sniffed at Nate.

"Shit! Asshole!" Nate shouted as the horse lunged for the paper. Nate took off down the street towards the tunnels and the horse followed, with me clinging to its back. And none too soon—Derrick's zombies were closing in.

"Shoot the horse," Derrick called out, and once again the gunfire resumed on all sides.

"K! watch out," Nate called out. The horse bucked as one of Derrick's zombies got too close with a pole, aiming the noose at my neck.

Nate dumped a bag of brains on the offending zombie's head.

My zombie mount's reaction was swift. It bit down on the zombie's shoulder, eliciting a piglike squeal.

"Yeah, you like that, assholes? That's what you get for shooting a ghost. You want more, zombie horse? Come and get it!" Nate shouted, and waved the remaining bag of brains at our attackers as the horse trampled the zombie who'd tried to rope me, holding the screaming man down with a hoof.

Derrick and his men slowly backed away from Nate.

As soon as we had enough room, I kicked the horse and pointed its head towards Nate and the remaining brains.

Its nostrils flared and it leapt after my ghost roommate, leaving the zombies and their poles in our wake. As we headed for the city exit, Derrick's words came back to me: *She's got to be alive.*

Somehow, I doubted very much Dane's poltergeist was behind the request.

There was someone else holding the reins to all this. And it was high time I found out who.

CHAPTER 13

LOST LOVES AND THINGS LEFT UNDEAD

I don't know if it was luck or a consequence of the general chaos, but none of Derrick's men managed to follow us. Nate went back to the hotel ahead of me to make sure the coast was clear of poltergeists and bounty-hunting zombies.

As I waited outside a nearby coffee shop—no money, so no coffee—I hoped no one noticed the stench from the undead horse, heavy on my clothes.

I didn't think I'd ever forget the smell.

I'd had to dismantle the horse. I felt a little bad about that, but though Nate had tried leading it back through the tunnels, each time, nostrils flaring, it had come right back. It was either dismantle it or risk it wandering into the streets.

After one too many glances from inside the coffee shop, I decided that, word from Nate or no, it was time to head back to the hotel.

On the brisk walk back, I checked my phone for messages and found a brief one from Stephan. As promised, he'd searched for any of Dane's remaining victims— or, more accurately, their ghosts.

He hadn't found any. He ended by saying he'd see me bright and early at the barn with Ingrid.

So if I assumed all of Dane's victims' ghosts were missing, and added in the Portland underground ghosts, plus the witches' swamp ghosts . . . As Celeste had said, it all had to be connected, but it didn't make sense for Dane to be behind it. Capturing ghosts takes finesse and a talent for Otherside, not fear and torture.

So did the bindings that had covered Katy's murder scene, and her ghost—and, for that matter, Dane's ghost as well. Someone else was pulling the strings, and employing some very advanced Otherside tricks to do it. Complicated, advanced Otherside tricks. Sorcerer's magic . . .

Stop seeing sorcerers lurking in every shadow, Kincaid. It's a ghost binding trick, nothing more.

Speaking of shadows, so involved was I with my phone that I didn't see the man standing just beyond the hotel entrance lights until it was too late.

Shit . . .

Aaron, dressed in track pants and a sweatshirt with the hood pulled up over his head, hands in his pockets, stepped into the light of the entrance. He gave a nod to the two Portland police officers whom I'd avoided on my way out of the hotel earlier in the evening. They headed inside, leaving the two of us alone.

I should have told Nate to be more worried about the hotel entrance.

Aaron wasn't smiling. "We need to talk."

No rest for the wicked. Add in no sympathy for the dead and there was my life motto wrapped up in one neat little package.

But instead of arguing, all I did was nod. I was too tired for a fight. A poltergeist I couldn't banish had made an attempt on my life and trigger-happy zombies had shot at me. And now I smelled like dead horse. God, I hoped that washed out.

And Aaron was right. Now that my own fury at him had subsided, we did need to talk. About the manipulation and liberties he'd taken to lure me down to Portland in the first place. And all the missing ghosts.

Aaron held the hotel lobby door open for me and we headed inside.

"I told Stephan he'd have to do better than a pair of beat cops," he muttered on our way to the elevators.

"Convenience store run," I lied.

"I didn't know the convenience stores in Portland had taken to serving shots of whisky." He said it in his offhanded way, but the furrow in his brow deepened.

"Those crazy hipsters," I said, and jabbed the elevator button.

Aaron didn't argue or probe. But there was resignation, and maybe even a little resentment.

The elevator finally opened and we rode to our floor in tense silence.

"I owe you an apology for Ingrid," Aaron finally said. "I'd be lying if I said I didn't know it would be a sore point."

"Just forget about it." At the look he gave me, I added, "I was upset about it earlier, but I'm over it—well, not over it, but we have bigger things to worry about."

The elevator door opened and I headed for my room, Aaron in tow. My stomach grumbled and I realized I hadn't eaten anything in hours. I was starving. I found the room service menu on the desk and picked out the BLT before offering it to Aaron. He passed.

I called down my order and added in a pot of tea—decaf. I was going to need my sleep.

"We have a problem," I said after hanging up. I turned around and looked out the window, crossing my arms. Despite the room's generous size, with Aaron here it felt cramped. Smaller. "How well do you really know Stephan?" I asked.

Aaron shrugged. "I knew him better six years ago, in college. We've kept in touch, but . . ." He shrugged. "It's never the same when you aren't sharing a dorm room. Why?"

"Because Stephan either doesn't know a number of things about this case or he's holding back." I filled him in about the missing swamp ghosts, without mentioning the broomstick part, and about all the missing Portland ghosts Stephan and his grandmother had failed to mention—though I glossed over the underground city part. Aaron looked increasingly worried as I laid out everything I'd found. "Even Nate commented on the sparseness of ghosts, and for Nate to notice—"

"I knew Stephan was from Portland, but I had no idea . . ." He didn't add that Stephan shouldn't be on this case—he didn't have to, we both knew it. Stephan's family had a stake in the investigation, he *couldn't* be objective . . . "You're sure the missing ghosts are connected to Katy's murder?" he asked.

I nodded. "I think a ghost binder is pulling Dane's strings and stealing the ghosts. I just don't know how. Or why."

The local ghosts had vanished slowly over a year, and Dane's involvement was apparently recent. Could Dane be a victim of the ghost binder as well? The collars pointed in that direction . . . But why on earth would anyone in their right mind go to the trouble of binding a poltergeist? They are nasty, unruly, dangerous just to banish on a good day.

I took a deep breath. "I'm starting to think all the Portland ghosts were practice."

"Practice? For what?"

"For Dane. Even a talented ghost binder would have a hard time wrangling a poltergeist, and Dane is a nasty one at that. They'd need practice. First the ghosts roaming Portland, and then the Spalt swamp ghosts—harder because of—" I stopped myself before I could say *the witches.* "Because of all the Otherside background."

Aaron didn't notice. "But to what end? To send him on a murder spree?"

Well, that was the one thing Dane was good at, if the number of missing victims' ghosts was any indication, and from the list Stephan had sent me, there were dozens of them . . .

"Son of a bitch." Not five ghosts, not ten, but *dozens.* "How many people did Dane kill?" I asked Aaron.

He furrowed his brow in concentration. "Ah, twenty-three—Katy makes twenty-four."

"And how many of them became ghosts, Aaron?"

He shook his head at me.

"*Twenty-four*," I said. The same number Stephan had confirmed with me by text less than half an hour ago. "Aaron, that's a hundred percent. There hasn't been a serial killer with that kind of ghost coefficient since Jack the Ripper." Most serial killers have a high ghost coefficient, since they traumatize their victims. Fear and terror always make it more likely the victim will become a ghost. "They were waiting for someone like Dane, someone who could guarantee them ghosts." And do the killing for them.

Aaron pulled out his phone and started texting—Stephan or the FBI, I imagined. "I still don't understand why anyone would go to all the trouble of binding a poltergeist to make them ghosts. There are ghosts everywhere, Kincaid."

I shook my head. "I don't know all the whys, Aaron, but for whatever reason, the ghosts of Portland weren't enough." Sold on a practitioners' black market, kept for a rainy day, used as target practice . . . "They need more."

"So head to another city, hit up the local graveyards on the way."

"*Or* find a poltergeist who can make ghosts on demand. One hundred percent, Aaron, that's his ghost coefficient. Everyone Dane has ever killed or *will* kill becomes a ghost. Katy, her family, *everyone*."

Aaron finished with his messages and slid his phone back in his pocket. "Everyone on this case has been looking at Katy as the victim of a serial killer. We need to look at her—all of them—like people. I just requested the case files from Stephan. They should be in my inbox by tomorrow. You don't know what the ghosts are for? I'm hoping Dane left some clues." He paused, then added, "Is it true? About Dane being after you? And that neither you nor Sinclair could banish him?"

I nodded. There was no point in denying it. "I'd be willing to write it off as a scare tactic, but . . . I got confirmation from elsewhere," I said. Captain Derrick had said he needed me alive, and Dane had hinted as much as well. "But I still have no idea why. Neither do Stephan or Liam. It might only be to scare me off—"

"Lure you down here only to scare you off?" Aaron gave me a skeptical look.

I made a face. "As to banishing Dane? He's already bound. It'd make exorcising a normal ghost difficult, but a poltergeist?" I shook my head. "Next time we meet him, we'll have to come up with something else." I needed to change topics. "What are you looking for in the case files, Aaron? You and I both know you don't go in blind."

"Closeted practitioners. I'm running on a hunch, and let's leave it at that until I find out more."

Well, if anyone could uncover paranormal secrets . . . Aaron knew the lengths—and methods—people use to scrub themselves clean—criminal intent or not.

Aaron ran his hand through his short hair. "I'm sorry, Kincaid. I was the one who pushed you into coming here. This is my fault—"

I stopped him. "Yeah, it is your fault," I said, letting out some of my pent-up anger. "You know better than to lie and manipulate me—about a soothsayer? Jesus, Aaron, what the hell has gotten into you? Six months ago, if someone told me you'd have pulled that stunt, I wouldn't have believed them, but lately it's as if I don't even know you—"

"I know. I'm trying to apologize. I said I was sorry . . ."

A knock at the door offered me the reprieve I needed. I retrieved the food and tipped the server a few dollars I had crumpled in my jeans pocket.

I poured myself a tea and held out the fries to Aaron. He almost refused, but there's only so much willpower people have when it comes to hotel french fries.

While munching, Aaron asked, "Is it possible for someone else to bind Dane?"

I thought about it while I chewed my sandwich. "I mean, I suppose it's possible. A stronger binder might be able to disrupt the original bindings tying Dane to the practitioner. Maybe even shift them over to someone new." I shrugged, biting off another generous mouthful and washing it down with hot tea. "But I don't bind ghosts. I've never tried something like that—I wouldn't want to. I'd be more inclined to break the bind, but then you'd have a loose poltergeist on your hands, and to be honest, I'm not sure I could do that. Whoever is behind this is good, Aaron. Despite what you see, not just any ghost binder could pull off a poltergeist."

"But it might be possible?" he asked, not hopeful exactly, but something close. Aaron rushed on before I could answer. "Dane's poltergeist strangled Katy. A practitioner might be pulling the strings, but Dane is still the one doing the killing."

I shook my head. "Aaron, stopping Dane would only be a Band-Aid solution—and it might not even be that. He could leave the city, find more ghosts—"

"Binding ghosts isn't a crime, Kincaid," Aaron said carefully. "Not unless it falls into witness tampering, and that's almost impossible to prove in court. I'm not saying you're wrong, I'm saying it would be hard to justify the resources prioritizing the binder—not if Dane could be stopped."

We were back to this. "For all we know, the practitioner behind all this has ten more poltergeists waiting in the wings. Perhaps not with Dane's particular ghost coefficient, but Dane is . . ." I searched for words that might sway Aaron's more practical sensibilities. "A lot of effort for minimum gains."

Aaron didn't let up. "Kincaid, I'm only telling you what Stephan and his bosses will say," he insisted. "It's horrible that ghosts are going missing. But they're already dead—including Katy."

I shuddered. That was a morbid way to think about it. Aaron could be stubborn, but he generally wasn't immune to reason. It was late and my patience was wearing thin.

"You'd be better off asking Ingrid. She's a ghost binder. Maybe she or Liam know a way to bind him," I acquiesced, and added, "But it's not the wise choice."

But my response didn't assuage Aaron. He took a seat in the chair opposite me and looked down at his hands, clasped in his lap. "I'm going to tell you something, Kincaid." He looked up, his face grim. "You're not going to like it."

My stomach dropped.

"The next time Dane comes after you, Captain Marks and Stephan's boss want you, Ingrid and Liam to bind him."

My ears filled with the sound of rushing blood and I gripped the arms of my chair. "No," I said.

Aaron watched me carefully. "I know you don't like binding ghosts—"

"No," I said, with more force.

Aaron sighed. "Captain Marks wants Dane bound—"

"No, you misunderstand me. I don't 'dislike' binding ghosts. I don't do it. Period. There's a pretty substantial difference there. Even if I were willing to consider it—which I'm not—it's not even in my wheelhouse."

"It's an order," Aaron said, simply.

My heart began to pound. I was glad I'd had the foresight to sit. "Tell Marks where he can stuff his request. Better yet, I'll do it. He shouldn't even be involved—this is a federal case!" I said, fumbling for my phone in my jacket pocket, hoping Aaron didn't see my hands shaking. The tips of my fingers were numb.

I felt Aaron's hand on my shoulder as he turned me round to face him. He'd got out of the chair and closed the distance between us. "Kincaid—stop, you don't understand."

"Yes, I do, Aaron. I understand exactly," I said, my anger rising. "Marks, you and maybe even the FBI wanted me to help solve a paranormal murder. I have helped. I won't bind ghosts. Ergo, Marks has probably told you to pressure me." I glared at him. "What you and Marks fail to grasp is that I don't care anymore. Marks won't let me work in Seattle, so I'll work everywhere else. I've already applied for my federal licence, so he can screw—"

"You're not getting the federal licence!" Aaron shouted.

I stared at him. He released me and sat back in the chair, looking up at the ceiling.

"God, Kincaid. I've been trying to protect you, but you just won't *listen*." He covered his eyes with his hands. "Captain Marks isn't letting you get a federal licence. *Ever*, Kincaid."

I stared at Aaron. "What are you talking about?" I said, my voice barely audible.

"It's so simple in its stupidity, Kincaid . . ." He looked exhausted. "The FBI have a dangerous ghost they can't bind. You think this is about the victims, a dangerous killer. It's *not*. It's political now, a security concern." He paused, letting the weight of what he was saying sink in. "Captain Marks, in his political manoeuvring, promised the FBI you'd bind Dane. He's a lot more powerful than you give him credit for, Kincaid. He's blocked your federal licence—insurance you'll follow his orders on this case."

Jesus.

"He made me rope you into this."

"And you agreed to bring me down here? Knowing how I feel about ghost binding?" I managed through clenched teeth.

Aaron lowered his gaze. "Yes, but I'm telling you the truth now. That has to count for something."

I breathed and waited for my anger to subside, to avoid saying something I would regret later. I took a deep breath and asked, "What did he threaten you with?"

Aaron grimaced. "The usual. My job, promotions that will never materialize even if I do what I'm told." He shook his head. "Nothing I haven't heard before. He can't fire me. He has no one else qualified or experienced enough to run the paranormal unit besides Sarah." And there were those serious eyes again, levelled on me. "It's you I'm worried about."

My federal licence. My escape route. "How?"

Aaron smiled. A wry, jaded expression that didn't sit well in my stomach. "Captain Marks is more politically connected than either of us realized. He has contacts, favours owed and family everywhere. Kincaid, it's personal."

A calm settled over me. "Tell him to hire another practitioner,"

I said. I'd head back to Vancouver. I could work there for a while
and be free of this complete and utter *bullshit*.

"You still don't get it!" Aaron snapped, the professional facade
he worked so hard to maintain crumbling. "The captain doesn't
care one whit whether he has a practitioner on staff. He cares about
power. Every time you've butted heads with Marks in the past, you
didn't just tell him no, you spat it in his face. *No one* tells him no.
He won't let you go, not until he proves he can make you do as
you're told. You think you understand men like Marks, Kincaid, but
you don't. He's dangerous."

Oh, Aaron couldn't be more wrong. I knew exactly the kind of
man Marks was, all too well.

"I can't believe I'm saying this," Aaron muttered. "But I'm begging you to do it, just this once. He has to prove he can control
problematic ghosts—because they're the ones who bring the paranormal into the public eye, and he doesn't want that."

This again. Marks couldn't deny the existence of the paranormal, but he blamed practitioners for its prevalence, the idea being
that if everyone just ignored them, the ghosts would go away. It was
verging on religious nonsense. And Marks's entire family were as
orthodox as they came.

"He says he'll leave you alone after you get rid of Dane."

I couldn't stop myself. I sat back in the hotel chair and laughed,
outright. Aaron was the one who didn't understand a man like Marks.
It wasn't his fault. He was the unwitting recipient of a Y chromo-
some, an upper middle-class existence, a colouring, demeanour
and way of dressing that had always, *always* bought him the benefit
of the doubt. Aaron had never had a man tell him he was worthless,
that he would amount to nothing. He'd never had someone pinch
his ass, laugh, then tell him he'd had it coming—for his tight jeans,
for his hair, for his smile, for his sex, for the audacity of *being*. When
he found himself on the receiving end of a slight, his first question
wasn't what he'd done to deserve it, or was there something *else* he
could have done?

I doubted that Aaron had ever been asked if he could have, should have, been *nicer*. No, he'd never experienced Marks's brand of bullying before, the kind designed to make you feel small, power-less, insignificant. Me? I'm a pro. I'd spent more than half my life under my father's thumb. A man who, just like Marks, thought the women in his life were pieces of property. A man who beat his daughter's mother in front of her and told me it was *her* fault, for not doing what she was told, for pushing him when he was in a bad mood, for fighting back, for not knowing her *place*.

A man who told his daughter that her mother had got what was coming to her, and if I didn't smarten up . . .

It was I, not Aaron, who had the full picture of exactly what was going on here.

First it would be Dane. Then there'd be another ghost, a zombie, a practitioner. Despite Marks's promises, they were hollow. It would *never* stop.

Aaron was right about one thing, though: this had absolutely nothing to do with binding a ghost.

The numbness in my fingers was gone. I stood and picked up my phone. "I'll handle it, Aaron. Leave it with me. I'll see you tomorrow."

Now Aaron was becoming frantic. "Kincaid, I'm begging you. I'll help you get your licence, I promise, I'll work something out with the captain as soon as this is over—"

"I'm still on the case, Aaron, but you need to leave this with me," I told him as I searched for the captain's number in my contacts.

There was Aaron's hand on my arm, stopping me. I looked up into his face. "How?"

One of the oldest tricks of manipulation. Convince them they no longer have the ability to say no. I saw through it, even if Aaron couldn't. "If push comes to shove, after this case, I'll go back to Vancouver—" I started, my voice even, calm.

"I don't want you to leave!"

I frowned at him and shook his hand loose. "Aaron—"

"Give up the apartment by the water and move in with me, Kincaid. I'll handle Marks for the both of us."

But he wouldn't. Marks would handle Aaron, exactly as he had these last few months. While I'd been feeling sorry for myself and angry at the world, Marks had been deftly manipulating Aaron right under my nose. Sowing a weeping, sickly rot through him, eroding his belief in me.

I'd been too wrapped up in my own problems to notice. And now Aaron was convinced *this* was the way to protect me.

And there was only one way to fix it, though it made me sick to my stomach, more than any Otherside hangover ever had.

I needed to take away Marks's bargaining chip.

"Aaron," I started, searching the hotel room carpet. "I'm—I'm so sorry if I wasn't clear before," I said, and almost faltered. "But we're done. We have been for months. You were wrong. We didn't just need a break . . ." I trailed off. "It's over," I said, simply, clearly, willing my voice to betray none of the uncertainty I felt. This was the kindest thing I could do for him, watching how Marks had used me to chip him down.

Aaron looked stunned. "What about a little over a month ago?" he said after a moment, his voice strained.

A month ago . . .

I'd been vulnerable—lonely, feeling sorry for myself. In a moment of recklessness, *need*, I'd gone home with Aaron. I hadn't thought anything of it. It hadn't meant anything to me except the comfort of familiarity. I'd assumed it hadn't meant anything for Aaron either.

"I'm sorry about that," I said, crossing my arms. And I was.

Aaron's face was unnervingly calm, but his fists, clenched tight at his side, betrayed his anger. "Who else are you seeing? Is it another practitioner?"

I needed to end it with Aaron for good. Whatever we'd had, Marks had sickened it.

Cut the arm off before the gangrene really sets in.

Fists still clenched, I levelled all the contempt and anger right at Aaron. "I don't want to be your girlfriend anymore." I didn't yell, but there was no room left for argument. Not even a little.

"You're not serious, Kincaid—I don't care how much Otherside you use, you're not that cold."

I didn't answer. That made Aaron angrier.

"What happens the next time you overuse? Who is going to pick your unconscious, freezing body off the ground, Kincaid, if it's not me?"

"Nathan watches out for me just fine—"

"He's dead, Kincaid! All your friends are dead!"

I didn't reply.

Aaron held my gaze as the seconds ticked by. Finally, he nodded. "I'm sorry, Kincaid. For everything."

And without another word, Aaron left my hotel room.

My stomach churned. I hated myself for hurting Aaron. That I hadn't seen just how entangled I'd become with his work.

But I hated Marks more.

It took five rings for him to answer.

"Kincaid Strange," Captain Marks drawled in a bored, mocking tone. Didn't ask why I was calling.

Fantastic, I much preferred it when assholes like him skipped the bullshit.

I got right to the point. "You don't have any intention of keeping *any* deal you've made with me. I'm not that gullible and I'm not that stupid."

He laughed. "No, I didn't think you were. Though it took you long enough."

"Let me get a few things straight. I'm working for the FBI to track down a killer." And find the missing ghosts, and hopefully stop a dangerous practitioner . . . "Not to bind Dane, for you or anyone. Ever."

He cut me off. "Only sick people like you talk to the dead. You're the reason we have problems with ghosts. You're a degenerate, and I don't pay degenerates."

My blood boiled, but before I could get a word out, he continued.

"Unfortunately, good, socially upstanding people like me are in the position of cleaning up your ghost mess. As far as I see it, you owe it to the rest of society to clean it up."

I found my voice. "You don't really believe any of that . . ." I said. He couldn't. Marks was a mean-spirited bigot, but he wasn't stupid.

"Here's the deal, Kincaid Strange. You find Dane and bind him. Or else. And don't even think of freelance. You work for me now. Consider it a penance for past transgressions and encouraging the dead."

Words formed in my mouth, but no sound made its way out. Aaron was right: the captain had never wanted me gone. He'd wanted me broken, under his foot, locked in a cage.

I was gripping something tightly. I looked down to find a glass in my hand. I didn't even remember picking it up. As my gaze shifted to the mirror and I stared at my pale, still-bedraggled appearance, I came close to throwing it. Hands shaking, I forced myself to put it down on the table but held on.

I shut my eyes. I was angry, livid, as much as I'd ever been in my life. But I didn't want to be like *them*. I never wanted to become my parents.

I squeezed the glass and breathed deeply.

Marks laughed at my silence. As if I was the dog my dad used to kick before my mother gave it away, the one that crawled back on its belly begging for forgiveness.

But I wasn't the dog that crawled back. I was the one who bit.

"You know," I said, my voice even, "the problem with you, Marks, is that you think you're a strategist, but really all you are is a gambler with a problem."

He snorted, but there was an uncertainty this time. I could hear it. I opened my eyes and allowed myself a thin smile.

"The very first time you dragged me into an interrogation room, you couldn't wait to make it clear you knew all about my father. You know he pushed my mother down a flight of stairs, not that you care about a bit of domestic violence gone wrong when there's a practitioner in the room. What you might not know is how lucky Dad was with the ponies. Used to spend weekends at racetracks when I was a little girl." In much happier times. "Made himself half a fortune. He had the strangest knack for picking winners. He said he knew which horse would win by their shape, the legs, the proportions. It was bullshit, of course. He got lucky—a lot. So lucky he mistook luck for knowing what he was talking about."

There was silence this time.

I half-snorted, half-laughed. "You know, before tonight, I was scared of you. I thought you might *actually* have something on me—but now?" A chill slipped into my voice. "You have *no idea* what it is that motivates me, Captain Marks. You know *nothing* about me, not a damn thing, just like my father didn't know a damn thing about horses. Congratulations, Captain. You just lost your first big bet. I'm not following your orders. If you have a problem with that, you have my lawyer's number. Any and all professional relationships that may have existed in the past are over. I have no interest in ever working with you again."

"I'll fire him," he growled, smart enough not to use Aaron's name over the phone, even if he was stupid enough to utter the threat. "I'll ruin his career. He'll never work again—"

"Aaron is no longer in my life," I shot back. "Do your worst. But if you do fire him, have fun with no paranormal unit this holiday season. And lose my number." I hung up the phone and tossed it on the bed, adrenalin coursing through me.

Marks had made a common mistake. He saw me as isolated, vulnerable, and assumed I'd eventually weaken and succumb to pressure. The thing they always forget, and Marks certainly had, is that most of us outsiders are used to bullies. We know what happens if you let them chip away at you. We know what happens if you don't fight back. We know, however dirty the fight gets, leaving it alone makes it worse.

There's a power in no. A freedom. A release, a relief. One I had learned the hard way to use. Was there a price? Absolutely, but the cost of staying quiet was always worse in the long run.

Despite my conviction, I was still clutching the glass on the table. I couldn't let it go. The anger was still there.

I breathed, deep. It didn't help, not like it should. This time, no matter how I willed it, I just couldn't let the glass go as I stared at myself in the mirror.

"K?" I felt Nate's cold hands on my shoulder, manifesting just enough to touch me.

Still I didn't let go. *I couldn't.*

Ice seeped into my shoulder. "K," Nate warned. "If you throw that, there's no coming back. *Please.*" I felt the chill from his fingers as they tried to pry the glass from my hand. "Trust me, you lose your shit this once . . . Beating Mindy to a pulp was one thing—she tried to kill you, it was self-defence, I get that, but this?" Nate appeared in front of me, between me and my reflection. "There's no one here, K, your life isn't in danger. You need to let go of the anger."

My fingers clutched the glass tighter. The only thing that held me back from launching it was Nate's calm, rational voice. If I gave in, even once, I'd be one step closer to becoming my mother and father.

I let go.

The chill of Nate's ghostly hand on my shoulder didn't falter. "You okay?" he asked.

I nodded, though my throat was dry.

Nate nodded. "Okay, I'm going to go do some reconnaissance with Aaron . . . Seriously, I wasn't eavesdropping. Much . . . Okay, I totally was, but I'm thinking, after that call with Marks, Aaron'll be getting his own. Two heads, eh?" He looked at me, his ghost-brown eyes meeting mine.

I exhaled slowly.

"You sure you're okay, K?"

I nodded, still staring at the glass I was no longer holding, keenly aware of how close I'd come to giving in to my temper, to the violence I tried so hard to avoid.

I felt Nate's cold, ghostly fingers under my chin as he lifted it back up. "Sit tight, K—I owe you, like, ten or something now. I've got your back."

He started to disappear, but I stopped him. "Nate? You heard everything with Aaron?"

He nodded.

"Do you think I made a mistake?" I said. "Breaking it off for good?"

"Naw. You did the right thing," he said, but then looked up, his translucent eyes meeting mine. "But that doesn't mean everything about it doesn't suck. It's not all your fault, K," he rushed. "Trust me on that one. From someone who knows."

And with that, Nate disappeared, back to the Otherside, to stalk Aaron—or Aaron's phone. I wasn't sure I cared anymore.

Alone again, I shivered. I needed to warm up. The carafe room service had brought up was empty, so I grabbed the coffee pot that doubled for tea. There were some passable tea bags tucked underneath. Any cup I made would have a residual coffee taste, but I was desperate for the warmth. From my Otherside use today, from Nate's chill . . .

Who is going to pick your unconscious, freezing body off the ground if it's not me?

I filled the pot with water then headed for the shower, trying not to think about Aaron's words. I turned the hot water on high, undressed and pulled on a bathrobe while I waited for the shower to steam up.

I stepped in, willing myself to soak in the heat, breathing in the steam.

It came on slowly this time—the sickly-sweet taste, like rotting fruit, finding a way in through the very steam I craved.

I went for the shower door, but a syrupy thickness stopped me, slowing my thoughts.

Help me. Release me.

It was back, a smell of desperation around the thought, a sadness—and fear. It pleaded for me to help it with frightened pulses— fear of heat, fear of darkness, and fear of something starving it, eating it alive. The compulsion to help it was overwhelming. I pushed and pulled for Otherside, but the sweet scent drowned it out, extinguishing all but the smallest spark.

Feed me.

Dark and cloying. I gripped my head and tried to push the presence out as the taste of dirt filled my mouth.

Obey me.

The pleading turned demanding, filled with a dark, sickly hunger. *Find me.*

The compulsion washed over me. Fight it, Kincaid—you have to fight it this time.

I held on to that spark of Otherside and wielded it against the darkness battering my mind.

Somewhere, glass crashed. Adrenalin coursed through me, breaking the hungry hold.

I shut the tap, threw open the door and grabbed a towel.

"Nate?" I called. There was no answer. I reached for the bathrobe. It was gone.

I swore under my breath. I'd left it on the hook—I was certain of it. I'd hung it there, right before the sickly presence returned. I was certain it wasn't my imagination—but what had triggered it? The water? My thoughts? Reminiscing about my fight with Aaron?

Another crash of glass in the hotel room.

Carefully, I peeked through the bathroom door. It couldn't be Dane's poltergeist—he wouldn't waste time breaking glass.

The crinkle of glass on tile reached me, as if someone was trying to sweep things up. Definitely not a poltergeist—they don't bother with dustpans.

"Nate?" I whispered.

The noise stopped.

No answer, but also no screaming or thrown objects. Now was as good a time as any. Slowly, surely, holding my towel in place, I stepped around the corner.

"Oh, you've got to be kidding me," I groaned, my relief at not finding Dane or some other malevolent dead tempered by the presence of my newest paranormal fan.

"Oh, there you are!"

None other than the ghost of Astrid Young was crouched in my entranceway, trying with mixed results to brush broken glass into a dustpan.

"You wouldn't believe how hard it is to pick up glass. It's so slippery! And here I was trying to get a hot toddy ready for you— Oh!

I suppose you need this," she said, holding up my bathrobe, which had been discarded amongst the broken glass. "The sound of the shower reminded me how much I loved wearing hotel bathrobes. I only meant to try it on, though it didn't work out quite as planned—"

"Jesus, Astrid. How the hell did you find me?" I grabbed the robe and turned my back to her before swapping it out with the towel. This was the second time the sickly, hungry presence had preceded Astrid's arrival. Could it be her? Possibly, though that wouldn't explain the swamp earlier today.

Astrid *tsk*ed. "No need to be a prude, Strange, we're all girls here. It's nothing I haven't seen before."

Then again, perhaps Astrid had been there, hiding. She did seem to have an uncanny knack for tracking me down.

"Not the point," I said, tying the belt tight. "And answer my question."

"Well," Astrid said, glancing at the floor and brushing it with the toe of a boot, the same ones she'd worn at the seance. They were paired with a skirt and she was carrying the blue bag she'd wanted—or a manifestation of it. "It's quite a simple, little thing really." Her face brightened and she flashed me a wide smile. "I thought about finding you, and here I am! You really are very bright. It's like you're a lighthouse beacon, but Otherside. It's quite pretty, did you know that?"

Well, that answered the how. Apparently, it wasn't just Gideon's mirror that had attracted Astrid to me at the library, though neither Nate nor any other ghost had ever mentioned me burning bright with Otherside before. "Why?"

"I thought about waiting for you to call, really I did, but then I thought wouldn't it be nice if I checked in to let you know how I was doing—behaving, that is," she rushed to add, and arched an eyebrow. "Like you were an accountability buddy." She glanced around the room. "Any sign of that ghost? Not the has-been rock star, but the dangerous, scary one," she said, not quite able to hide her curiosity.

I so did not have the time or patience for this . . .

"Depends which scary ghost you mean—there are a lot of them. Go back to the Otherside," I told her. Hadn't Gideon told me he was going to set an alarm for trespassing ghosts in my hotel room?

"Yes, but—"

I ignored her as I pulled out my bag of supplies. The fact that Astrid had made her way in here was worrying. Even Nate needed help crossing over—and my mirrors were as attuned to him as they got. But the possibility that Gideon had bailed on the alarm troubled me. What did I have? I rummaged through the bag and pulled out sage and an ash mixture Lee had sold me a while back to keep powerful ghosts at bay. I glanced up at the smoke detectors. Now, those did pose a serious problem.

Well, there was always salt; in strong concentrations, it repels the dead. I could set up some kind of pentagram around the room and then around my bed. It might not stop Dane if he made an appearance, but it would slow him down. It should also send Astrid packing.

Astrid didn't take the hint. She followed me across the room as I outlined a pentagram with the salt, close enough I could feel the chill through the bathrobe. And right after I'd warmed up in a hot shower . . .

"Now, I know what you're thinking, but I promise you I'm not up to no good. I have important things to talk to you about. Not the usual run-of-the-mill trifles that most ghosts probably bring you."

Said every ghost ever. My eyes fell on my clothes, which I'd left neatly folded on the counter and were now heaped in a pile on the floor. "Clothes, bathrobes. There's something called privacy, Astrid."

Astrid pouted. "I started off waiting, but then I got bored. I started wondering what kinds of things people without money travel with." She perked up. "You need more shoes and accessories, by the way, though I suppose the blazer and motorcycle boots are serviceable."

"Unbelievable." I sighed, stepped inside the larger pentagram of salt that covered the room and started a second, smaller pentagram around my bed. I'd do the doorways next. I wondered what the housekeepers would think . . .

Astrid was halted at the edge of the larger pentagram. A moment later she appeared in front of me, blinking her dark, ghost-grey eyes. Jesus, she really was attuned to me.

"It really didn't take me very long," she said, genuinely misinterpreting my frustration. "You don't have many things."

I tried not to roll my eyes and went out of my way not to meet her gaze. "Astrid," I said carefully. "What do you want? Besides to rifle through my paltry possessions."

She made a show of sinking into the deep cushioned chair, crossing her translucent hands on her lap. "I thought about going back to the Otherside like you told me to do. But it's awful boring over there, don't you think?"

"I wouldn't know, Astrid. I'm not dead."

"And then you weren't at your apartment—"

"*Astrid*," I warned.

She made another face, avoiding the salt and giving it a wary glance. "You know, I could have gone back to haunting my parents—"

I faced her, arms crossed—not an easy feat in the bathrobe.

"All right, fine. I just have a tie to you, like a thread. You burn very bright, more so than other people." She placed her chin in her hands. "Did you know that?"

Threads like that are common with family members and loved ones, but with a complete stranger? Maybe it was an artifact of the ghost trap mirror I'd been using at the library? I'd have to ask Gideon when he recovered from the latest snit.

I was starting to think the most likely explanation for the hungry, unnatural presence following me really was Astrid.

"Astrid, you need to go home. I'm here on a murder case. A young woman died horribly—"

"*Ah*, but that's what I want to tell you. I have information you need," she said, conspiratorially.

I turned on her. "What kind of information? And how did you come by it?"

Another pout, though this one was more smug. "Well, for that, I'm going to need something from you— No! I really do know something you need!" she said as I went for my compact mirror.

Hangover tomorrow or not, I was not going to let Astrid toy with me, not over a murder investigation.

"Dane," Astrid said quickly, sensing my ebbing patience. "You can't trap or banish him, can you? He breaks through your barriers and Otherside nets, no?"

I stared at Astrid. "You have one minute to convince me not to send you back."

Careful of the salt, she sat on the edge of the bed, looking very pleased with herself. "That's all you get for free, Kincaid," she said, and made a zippering gesture over her mouth.

I know ghosts. They lie, cheat, have next to no impulse control, and will do anything—*anything*—to garner the attention of the living—

But they also know how to throw a good hook.

It was a sucker's move, but I kept listening. "What's your price?"

She gave me a slow smile. "Like I said, Kincaid Strange, I want us to be friends."

I shook my head. No one, especially the dead, just wants to be friends. "Not worth it."

Astrid's eyes widened and darted around the room as I reached for my compact.

"Go meet some ghosts, make some friends and don't bother me again until I'm back in Seattle."

Her eyes landed on something behind me. "Wait! What if I can tell you more about him?"

"Who?" I looked behind me. On the dresser was the wrapped brown paper package I'd fetched from Celeste. The diary, the one that mentioned Gideon.

I whirled back on Astrid. "And what would you know about that?"

"Curses," Astrid said, baring her teeth as she spoke the word. "And that's *really* all you'll get until you bargain with me."

I knew that Astrid was grasping, trying to keep my attention. But I hesitated. What *if*?

I sighed. I was going to regret this . . . "Start with Dane."

"I want your promise first, written in Otherside."

"Uh-uh," I said. Astrid was not getting carte blanche. "That's not how this works. If you have information you think I need, then you have to tell me. I promise, if it's as useful as you think, I'll barter fairly."

"How do I know you'll keep up your end of the bargain?"

"Easy. Because I always do."

Astrid pursed her lips, but decided it wasn't worth quibbling. She threw her ghostly head of hair over her shoulder, a reflex. "Fine," she said, finding something interesting in her manifested manicure. "Dane's not as powerful as you think. It has something to do with that horrible swamp."

Now—that was awful interesting. "How do you know about the swamp, Astrid?"

"Easy. I followed you there," she said, not bothering to glance up from her manicure. "It's a horrible place. Even with all the free Otherside."

Nate had been to the swamp, but he'd described it as an interfering annoyance, not an Otherside amplifier—which it would have to be if the swamp was behind Dane's uncanny power.

"And what makes you think it's the swamp giving Dane the power boost?"

"If you *must* know, I ran into the psycho ghost. I ran, he chased, and stopped at the edge of the swamp."

"What do you mean stopped?" So Astrid had had no problem leaving the swamp in Dane's presence, when Nate had . . .

Astrid made an exasperated sigh. "That he stopped. He wouldn't leave the swamp."

I shook my head. "That doesn't mean he can't leave the swamp—"

"I didn't say he *couldn't*, I said he *didn't*. At first, I just thought he was being territorial, guarding the big pile of Otherside all for himself. But I ran into another ghost—"

"*What* ghost? And where?" Nate had looked and there were next to none to be found this side of the barrier.

Astrid shrugged. "I met her in the alley behind the hotel. Just another junkie who OD'd, a no one. And she was leaving like everyone else, a scared little thing."

Well, the leaving part rang true. I would have to check with Aaron and Stephan to see if there'd been a recent death. Maybe Astrid was somehow less threatening than Nate . . . "Astrid, this is important. Tell me exactly what she said about Dane."

Astrid lowered her head. "That I wasn't out of the woods yet, that Dane still might hunt me—but, and this is the important thing, that provided I stayed away from the swamp, he was just another poltergeist." She shrugged and tossed her hair once more. "And a run-of-the-mill poltergeist I can handle."

I had a very hard time believing that Astrid could handle a poltergeist, despite the fact that she was on the verge of becoming one. Still, there was part of her story that rang true. Could Dane's power, his ability to break my pentagram and resistance to binding, be linked to the swamp?

It would explain why Dane hadn't come after me, Ingrid or Liam yet—or why the practitioner holding the strings hadn't sent him. He'd be at a disadvantage, any one of us could stop a poltergeist in their tracks. And it meant he'd be much less likely or able to come after me here . . .

"So, do we have a deal?" Astrid said, interrupting my thoughts. There was a hungry look in her eyes, one that hadn't been there before. "Well?"

I shook my head. A sluggishness had settled over my mind. I must be desperate for sleep, because I was half-inclined to agree with Astrid. I was opening my mouth to say as much when we both felt the chill in the air.

Astrid's eyes widened. "I'll find you later," she said, and vanished.

Terrified once more of running into Gideon. Well, that wasn't a bad thing. God help me, I'd been about to ask what she knew about the sorcerer.

It wasn't Gideon who appeared, though. It was Nate.

"Hey, K, you wouldn't believe—" He trailed off and sniffed at the air as if trying to identify a lingering cologne or perfume. "Who the hell was here?" he asked, frowning.

I shook my head and grabbed my pyjamas, sliding them on behind the bathroom door before any more ghosts could show up. "My retainer showed up. Don't worry—she's gone."

"Uh-huh," Nate said, still sniffing the room and not looking convinced. He gingerly avoided the salt I'd set out.

"What was it you were about to tell me?" I asked, hoping it would distract him from Astrid. I'd fill Nate in on what she'd told me about Dane later—after sleep, which I sorely needed. I'd been tired before, but Astrid's visit had taken the last of my second—or was that third?—wind out of me.

"Ah, yeah. Aaron yelled at the captain—that was fun. Then he called Stephan and told him he's taking tomorrow to research Dane's original victims. Oh, and Katy—in the panic over Dane, he figures he might find something everyone else missed."

"Good," I said, and crawled into the bed, tucking myself under the covers. "Nate, I need to pack it in, otherwise I'm not going to be any use to anyone tomorrow. You mind?"

"Keeping watch? Naw," he said, and seemed to settle into one of the chairs. "I'll shout if Dane shows up, though Gideon better have something up his sleeve."

"It might be tied to the swamp. His power. Never mind, I'll fill you in tomorrow." God, did I ever need sleep. I never yawned like this . . . "Tomorrow. I don't think he'll be by tonight." I shut out the light.

Moments later, Nate cleared his throat. "Those, ah, all Dane's original victims. Their ghosts. They're really all gone?"

"Yeah." There was no sense lying. Not while I was this tired.

Another moment passed, then, "You're—ah, not—I mean, you're not going to end up like that, are you? Not dead, just—I mean, that would be bad, but—disappeared?"

I shut my eyes tighter. Nate wasn't asking for himself; he was concerned for me. "Nate, I'm not going to end up like that. I . . ." I sighed and ran my hand through my hair. "A while ago there was a chance, but Gideon, for all his assholery, actually seems to be looking out for me. I'll be fine. I won't end up dead or disappeared. I promise."

In the dark, I couldn't see if Nate bought it, if he believed my words. That might be a good thing, I thought, as I finally drifted off into a deep sleep.

CHAPTER 14

TALKING DEAD

A night under a thick, warm quilt with the heat cranked—on someone else's dime—still didn't chase all the chill away. I crept out of bed and hit the coffee machine, having found one last pack of filter coffee hidden in the cupboard. The clock read 7 a.m. I slipped into the shower while the coffee brewed. While I warmed up, I pieced together everything I'd learned—about the murder, missing ghosts, Dane, the Portland underground, the swamp and its strange Otherside.

And then there were my unanswered questions about Bergen and Spalt. How many witches lived there? Celeste and Bergen had both suggested a coven . . . And was Stephan a witch? He'd said no, and I was inclined to believe him. He didn't seem any more adept with Otherside than Aaron. But I didn't know very much about witches, did I?

It was a mess. Both the dead and the witches were holding on to their secrets tighter than was good for them, and it was making my job harder.

There were two things I knew now that I hadn't known yesterday.

Ghosts had been going missing around Portland for a while, and Dane's uncanny power and ability to crash through my bindings appeared to be tied to the swamp. Yet I had no idea why. With the exception of Dane, the missing ghosts had no obvious use, and Dane's value was dubious—hinged on his ability to kill people in a way that guaranteed them becoming ghosts. The only thing I was certain of was that someone had to be pulling the strings.

What I needed was the end goal. What did they need the ghosts for—and why Katy? Was the practitioner controlling Dane catering to Dane's inclinations, or was there something about Katy and her family I had missed? Look where the herd isn't, that was how I'd found the missing victims up in Canada.

Maybe Aaron would turn something up in the old case files. If a clue was there, I had no doubt he'd find it. In the meantime, I needed a game plan for Dane. I was going to need Gideon's help for that. Hopefully, the ghost was over his snit.

It was seven-thirty by the time I'd collected myself. I downed my coffee while I dressed in clothes that didn't smell like dead horse, shooting a wistful glance at my blazer, now dappled with mud from the swamp and in need of laundering. My leather jacket still needed a good airing, so a layer of flannel from my sparse wardrobe selection it was. Laptop and bag in hand, I headed downstairs to the hotel restaurant in hopes of finding breakfast.

The restaurant, a trendy adjunct that seemed as filled with locals as hotel guests, was busy. Luckily, I snagged a free corner booth as a family was leaving. What I planned to browse wasn't exactly suitable for over-the-shoulder curious viewing . . .

I ordered a pot of coffee, bacon, eggs and hash browns, and opened my laptop. A moment later I was searching "witches," "Otherside," "bogs," "swamps" and every other permutation of wetlands I knew. The most popular hits were tied to mythology, tinged with the odd pop culture and urban legend reference.

My coffee arrived somewhere between the history of the Salem witch trials and gossip that a famous up-and-coming InstaShot celebrity just *had* to be a witch.

One might wonder why it is that an experienced practitioner would start with broad web searches when PubDead was sitting right there, with its university-vetted and reliably researched resources. That would be my second stop, but the problem was that witches in general are a bit of an anomaly in the paranormal community. Everyone knows about them, can cite stories about them, most people can even name a few famous reputed witches, but no one, not even the so-called experts of the paranormal research communities, has any concrete facts about them. Part of that is historical: the Inquisition and consequent religious persecution over the centuries had made witches scarce. Those that hadn't been wiped out by overzealous witch hunters had gone deep into hiding. They'd hidden so effectively that researchers debated whether any witch communities had survived into the twentieth and twenty-first centuries.

But with Stephan and his family, I was faced with the genuine article. A real, distinct class of practitioner.

Gideon seemed to agree. Shame he wasn't in a better mood. I didn't feel up to testing the mercurial ghost quite yet, though my thoughts drifted to the journal, the one I hadn't had a chance to open.

I forced my attention back to the screen. By the time breakfast arrived, I had three possible leads.

The first was a hobby website from the UK on the paranormal nature of bogs and World War Two. According to the author, he'd purchased the bog property as a retirement plan—away from the city, a place to start a hobby farm. Almost immediately after taking possession, he'd begun running into ghosts on his daily walks, World War Two sailors and nurses, to be exact—German, French, English, Scottish, Irish—all sorts wandering through his bog, some looking for their family, others wandering aimlessly. Turns out a number of ships had sunk off the coast, mostly bombed but some from shipwrecks. There was a ring of authenticity to the account. He'd started the website as a historical record but also so people might find out what had happened to long-lost relatives. Those kinds of details, unlike witches of Hollywood, rang true.

I bookmarked it for later reading and moved on to the next lead:

a university lab in Denmark that was investigating the paranormal affinity of bogs. Their research was more scientifically arranged than the hobbyist's, and suggested that bogs, marshes and swamps are easier to set Otherside in, and that the resulting bindings are more stable and longer-lasting.

Well, that would certainly explain how the witches wove such extensive bindings through the swamp that lasted centuries.

The third and last lead was a historical account of a supposed coven of Danish witches who'd secretly transported Jewish Danes to a town in Sweden during World War Two. It was unusual for the simple fact that most Danish stories of witches feature spells and curse casting, or the historical autumn witch burnings—originally involving a suspected witch, substituted in the present day with a flammable straw crone. The traditional narrative rarely features witches as saviours.

The town was reported to be situated on a bog, but despite the best efforts of the Nazis, neither the witches, the Jewish Danes nor the town could be located. Pilots who flew over the area swore there was only an empty field. It was as if they'd disappeared. Or had never been.

The fabled town remained an enigma for much of the war. That is, until a bomber crashed in what had looked like a field but in fact was a town beside a bog, which was reduced to a smouldering, smoking ruin. Everyone, including all the witches, was dead—their camouflage adept at tricking the living but not so good at protecting them from an explosion. Otherside can be used to obscure small things—stairways, texts and Otherside supplies, a trap door—but a town and bog?

Together, it all confirmed Bergen's claim that the swamp could be a powerful tool for setting Otherside bindings, like a giant amplifying mirror. The same thing I had felt when I'd first tapped the barrier.

The other interesting tidbit was that though watersheds attract Otherside and ghosts, it seemed to take a coven, not an individual witch, to really harness this power. And the bog in Scandinavia had been much smaller, less than a quarter of the size of the Spalt swamp, give or take, from the blast area and what I could glean from maps. To be controlling *this* swamp, Bergen and her coven had to be powerful. Also considering Bergen hadn't thought twice about blowing off the Portland underground zombie queen, if Celeste was to be believed. Most practitioners with an ounce of common sense, myself included, steer well clear of insulting the under-grounds. Bergen was more powerful than she'd let on.

Despite the warm bacon and topped coffee, I couldn't help stifling a shiver. Whatever siphoned Bergen's ghosts away from the marsh had to be more powerful than the coven. I might just need to have another in-person chat with Bergen—*without* Stephan. I couldn't shake the feeling Bergen knew more about the practitioner who'd hijacked her coven's swamp—at the very least, how powerful he or she was.

I closed the laptop with a new sense of purpose and turned to the journal, the one for which I'd almost been shot by zombie pirates. I flipped it open, breaking the Schrödinger-like impasse I'd been keeping with it—delaying the question as to whether it really would help me understand my undead mentor and boss.

Popping the last piece of bacon in my mouth and draining the dregs of my coffee, I started to read the account that might just hold the key to one Gideon Lawrence.

The first entry, written in a flourishing script, was dated Wednesday, June 8, 1852.

This is the journal of Johnathan Christianson, a clerk of the East India Trading Company. Rest assured I am of sound mind and body, but some of what I record in this journal will test the faith of whoever might come to read these pages. For this story is not mine alone, but also that of Gideon Lawrence, a powerful sorcerer's ghost, and my mentor, teacher, and I dare say friend these past two years. A cursed soul who carries the anger of a poltergeist wherever he goes, the result of a failed, and in my opinion misguided, attempt to save someone long ago.

But that is where his story begins, not mine, nor the story of how our two paths came to cross. My own foray into the occult began six years ago, while I was working in the Dutch West Indies as a clerk for a trading house that had fallen into financial turmoil. It was there, set upon by yellow fever, that I met my first true person of the occult, a Voodoo Priestess by the name of Marie Sul. With the help of her spirits, her loa, her mystères, she nursed me back to health, and my passion for the occult and all things that reside behind the veil began.

The veil—another name for the barrier. It had fallen out of use in the early nineteenth century. And the trading companies that had been active in the East and West Indies had functioned as a cover for practitioners . . . On the surface, the account was believable enough.

I flipped through the pages. They were all marked in the top-left corner with a date, and each was filled with the same flourishing script and occasional diagram—but the final quarter of the book was empty.

Why had he abandoned the journal? A waste of paper at the time, especially considering how careful he'd been filling each and every earlier page. He wouldn't have lost it—not considering the contents and the hostility towards practitioners at the time. Perhaps he'd left the Company—or Gideon and he had gone their separate ways. Or something more sinister, perhaps? The pages weren't waterlogged, so I doubted a shipwreck. A murder, illness?

I was skimming through the final entries when a shadow passed over the pages.

Without thinking, I shut the book, the old sheets sending up dust and a musty smell. I looked up, expecting to see the waitress once again offering me a coffee refill.

Liam Sinclair was standing outside my booth, looking somewhat uncomfortable. His hands were firmly shoved in his blazer pockets, and his light-brown hair was tousled as if he'd just got out of bed and not paid much mind to his appearance beyond the obligatory showering and dressing.

He cleared his throat. "May I join you . . ." he started, then trailed off as he looked between the closed book and laptop, and my less than welcoming expression.

I thought I caught a slight flush of embarrassment—easy to detect on account of Liam's pallor, another consequence of Ram's Inn syndrome.

"I, ah, only wanted to see how you were doing after yesterday's run-in with Dane. I don't mean to interrupt your work. I never could stand interruptions—I'm embarrassed to find myself on the giving end."

I thought about letting Liam continue to excuse himself. He was doing such an admirable job talking himself out of taking a seat, it seemed a shame to waste his effort.

But I was here to work on a murder case. With him and his cousin. He'd saved my ass yesterday from Dane, and my snap judgments over his fame had proven unfounded. A pang of guilt swung my mind in the other direction. Besides, I couldn't talk about the missing swamp ghosts, but I could get his opinion on the missing Portland ghosts. He worked with a ghost binder, after all.

"Please," I said, clearing my material off the table and sliding it carefully into my bag. Liam looked undecided, as if not convinced of my sincerity, so I added, "Believe me, I'm probably the last person in this restaurant given to bouts of misplaced politeness. I spend too much time with the dead. I really was finished." I nodded to my empty coffee cup and cleaned breakfast plate. "I figured I'd try to grab another refill before heading to the barn." Where I'd have to face Stephan again and see if I could smooth things over. "Please—I mean it, join me."

And I found, with more than a little surprise, that I did mean it.

Liam slid into the booth across from me and waved at the waitress, who came by with a fresh cup for him and a refill for me. As he reached for his coffee, wrapping both hands around the piping hot cup, I noted the fingerless gloves and extra layers of shirts under his jacket—adding bulk along with warmth. Only a glimpse of his wrist peeked through, but even so, I couldn't help but note its thinness, the way the skin hung loosely from the bone. I searched his face for the telltale hollowness, noting only a slight sunkenness around the eyes.

No, I decided, the wasting was there, in his eyes, no matter how hard he might have tried to conceal it. I spent enough time with the recently dead to recognize when the living were heading that way.

I kept my observations to myself and sipped my coffee, taking my own warmth from it like every practitioner I'd ever met always did when given half a chance. *No, not long now at all.*

"I take it you slept well," Liam said, covering a cough with his hand.

"Ah—Dane didn't try to kill me again, if that's what you mean," I said. I couldn't help looking at his bone-thin finger peeking through the gloves.

He must have caught my look, because he added, "This damned syndrome steals the warmth right out of my bones, along with what wakeful moments I have left." He smiled. "Ingrid told me from the start I shouldn't have taken this case. She was right, mind you, though please don't let on that I said that. My ego couldn't take it then, and despite my own imminent demise, it won't now. Maybe because of it." He held up his cup. "To a practitioner's ego. The only reason I think any of us bother stomaching the dead."

Despite the macabre tone, his face remained animated and his eyebrow arched. "So, Kincaid Strange. Dane didn't visit you last night. And you look like you had a good-enough sleep—for a practitioner, that is," he added with a wink. "Either you think you are exceptionally gifted with wards to repel a powerful poltergeist or you figured out what Ingrid and I have suspected since we first caught sight of Dane a week ago," Liam said, and sat back in his seat.

"Dane can't leave the swamp," I said.

"Oh, he can leave—the missing victims' ghosts and sightings prove that well enough—but he doesn't have the power to resist a practitioner, not like he did yesterday. He's got surprising restraint for a poltergeist. Despite wanting all three of us very dead, he won't venture out of the swamp. Yesterday's events prove that in my mind."

I didn't think Dane could control himself enough to resist the chase after he'd smelled blood. I didn't think any poltergeist could. But instead of voicing that thought, I said, "Or someone has figured out a way to control a poltergeist reliably."

Liam nodded and sipped his coffee. "There is that. A theory you and Ingrid have in common."

"And you don't share your cousin's theory?" It was out before I could self-filter.

Liam gave me a terse smile. "I don't dispute the logic, Kincaid. I'm just not certain it matters."

I frowned at him. "What is that supposed to mean?" Of course it mattered—the whys and hows always matter when it comes to the dead and Otherside. Especially a poltergeist. As pessimists and perfectionists like to say, the devil is in the details.

Liam looked uncomfortable for a moment. "Well—" he started, then stopped as the waitress reappeared with the bill, a not so subtle hint. It was then I noted that the hotel breakfast crowd had thinned out. I glanced at my phone and saw it was nine-thirty.

Jesus, I'd lost track of time. Stephan might not have given me a start time—or any updates since yesterday's brief message—but the phrase "bright and early" had been used.

I reached for the bill, but Liam beat me to it. "Allow me," he said, and then, without waiting for my reply, signed the receipt with his hotel details. At my sound of protest, he glanced up and said softly, "Really—it's the least I can do for interrupting your work this morning—and for the chat. I confess, I was hoping to run into you and . . ." He gave me a sad smile. "I haven't had much opportunity to talk with our own kind since this occurred." He glanced down at the bill, tucking it back into the black folder, another flush of embarrassment on his face. "I find talking to the living keeps me lucid and the worst of Ram's Inn syndrome at bay. Besides," he said, sliding the bill towards the waitress and standing, "I'm willing to wager you think I'll owe you more than a breakfast if my suspicions are right about what is to unfold

today." He reached into his pocket to check his phone. "Ingrid is waiting outside for me. We're happy to give you a ride to the barn. Solidarity
in numbers, since none of us will be there in time to please Stephan."

I might have accepted working with a ghost binder, but that
didn't mean I wanted to be carpool buddies. "I've actually got—"
I paused as Liam's still-beautiful green-blue eyes implored me.
Besides, there had been something in Liam's cryptic revelation
about what he expected from Dane today . . . "Sure thing, I'd love a
ride," I finished, sliding on my heavy flannel, frowning as I made
sure everything was safely tucked into my bag.

I fell in step with Liam as he headed through the lobby.

"What is it exactly we're looking for today? We searched the site
pretty extensively yesterday—even before Dane showed up," I said.
When Liam's expression turned guarded, I held up my hands and
added, "Hey, not criticizing—I'm just trying to understand what
we're looking for—especially if Dane might rear his pastel twin-set
and flannel-hating head. Stephan was foggy on the details, and to
be perfectly blunt, so are you. No pun intended."

That at least earned me a smile. Liam swung open the door for
me, belying his own weakness. "Suffice to say they managed to
remove the body yesterday. I think it's prudent to take another look
at the murder scene, to see if there were any bindings we missed,
or may have . . ." He trailed off, distracted as a new-looking Audi
pulled up. I caught sight of Ingrid in the driver's seat. The car was
easily worth more than I made in a year. Maybe two.

I couldn't stop myself giving a low whistle. "So that's what celebrity practitioning buys these days," I muttered.

If Liam heard me, he decided—wisely, I might add—to pretend
he hadn't.

Ingrid smiled and waved as the sole hotel bellboy opened the
car doors for us. Liam slid into the front seat and I got into the back,
exchanging a quick hello with Ingrid. Maybe if I just pictured her
as the Shirley Temple of ghost binders . . .

It wasn't until the car had pulled away from the hotel and was
heading for the freeway that Liam turned to face me over the seat.

"Having a syndicated self-help TV show of any sort comes with its perks. And as to what will happen on site, forgive me if I worried you. Sometimes the dreams and nightmares . . ." He trailed off. " . . . seep into my waking hours." He made a good attempt at a reassuring smile, though I wasn't buying it. "We've seen the worst—and that's Dane." He turned back to face the road.

And now I really wasn't buying it. Liam was afraid of something besides Dane.

I sat back in the heated leather seat as Ingrid pulled onto the highway. Well, they certainly knew how to make a practitioner comfortable. My curiosity, however, wasn't the least bit sated. If anything, I was even more curious—and apprehensive—about what the day and crime scene held, and what exactly Liam thought he knew that I didn't.

TOO MUCH OF A GOOD THING

We reached the barn by ten, Liam offering no more hints as to what he thought we might find there. Ingrid made polite small talk while she drove, and I aimed for cordial if not friendly chatter. Liam's exhaustion proved a welcome excuse for silence most of the way.

The agents on the scene offered us polite nods as we got out of the Audi. I turned to Liam, who looked a little unsteady on his feet—and then proceeded to faint. I caught him, barely, before he sank to the ground. I knelt down beside him and his eyes fluttered. I held him up, surprised by how little he weighed; it had to be less than me, and he was taller.

"Liam!" Ingrid rushed to his side and knelt beside him, her hand over her mouth.

To my relief, his eyes opened.

"Are you all right?" I asked.

Liam managed to stand on his own, his face even paler than usual. "Fine—I—ah, I'm embarrassed to say I overestimated myself. After yesterday I thought . . . I'll be fine—really. I just need some rest—an hour or so. Ingrid, please—I can walk." But Ingrid insisted, taking him under the arm.

"Stephan should be here. He'll want to start. Tell him I'll catch up soon," she called over her shoulder as I watched her half-carry Liam towards the sole trailer.

"Strange!" I heard Stephan shout.

It took me a moment to spot him, huddled with three technicians over a box full of earth—from the barn, I imagined. There was no sign of Aaron—for which I was glad. I'd hoped on the ride over that he'd make a point of working off-site today after our fight last night. Knowing Aaron, he would have started early, so if he wasn't here . . .

But I still had Stephan to deal with.

Dust off the people skills and let's see what you can do to smooth things over, Kincaid.

He gave me an impatient look as I approached. I cleared my throat.

"Ah, you did say bright and early, and it's overcast, so technically . . ." I trailed off.

Contrite and apologetic, Kincaid. That was snarky and stupid . . .

Stephan shook his head and dismissed the forensic team. When they were out of sight, he crossed his arms and leaned against the truck.

"I'm sorry I'm late," I said simply. "There were extenuating circumstances." Which I needed to discuss with Bergen, if not Stephan.

The tension in his posture eased, albeit reluctantly. "You used a lot of Otherside yesterday. I know practitioning . . ." He trailed off. "Early morning was ambitious. Ingrid and Liam?"

"They're here. In their trailer. Liam fainted and Ingrid is helping him. She shouldn't be long."

Stephan nodded, taking it in stride. "Come on. I want you to have another look in the barn now that the body's been removed. Ingrid can join us later. I have a theory I want to run past you." He gestured for me to follow him and we headed towards the barn, grass crunching underfoot. "I'm sorry for snapping at you yesterday. You were trying to do your job and in retrospect I put you under a lot of stress."

What was this? An apology? I didn't get those often, reluctantly or not.

"Thanks, Stephan. And I should have been more sensitive about your family's connection to the swamp—considering the circumstances."

Stephan nodded, though his shoulders tensed once again. "Consider us even. I'll try to be more objective about Gran and the family swamp, and you can try not being an asshole."

"An asshole?"

"Your words, not mine."

He sat down to switch out his shoes. I did the same, and glanced over at him. Clearly, we were not even.

"Oh, and there are *way* more ghosts missing than your family's and Dane's victims. Try almost every ghost in Portland starting last year, which your grandmother knew about."

It took him a moment to catch up with what I'd just said. "Every goddamn ghost in Portland?"

I nodded. "Starting last year if . . ." I paused, not entirely sure how much Stephan knew about the Portland underground. Best to err on the side of caution. "According to my source."

Stephan nodded, a look equal parts disgust and resignation on his face. "Figures. Why they'd go straight for the swamp ghosts never added up to me. Gran should have told me that part, though I'm sure if I ask her, she'll say she had her reasons."

I really did need to have a little chat with Bergen—to see what else she was hiding and why. "Does your grandmother keep things from you often?"

Stephan took a deep breath and closed his eyes. I counted to five before he opened them again, looking calmer, though far from relaxed and still tired.

He glanced around the inside of the barn. No one was in earshot. His eyes softened as he turned to me. "I have a love-hate relationship with the Otherside," he said. "I love my family and appreciate everything they've taught me about their world, everything that's gotten me here." His eyes hardened. "But I hate the way they cut me out, the way they keep secrets just because . . ." He shook his head and focused back on his shoes.

"You can't see Otherside, can you?"

He made a face. "Oh, I imagine if I tried hard enough, I could, but witchcraft doesn't work like that. It's more—inherited. Witches live like they're already one of the dead, though, just like practitioners. But you're right. Whenever my gran showed me and my sister the swamp when we were kids, I felt like I was missing something. I didn't have it—still don't. My parents . . ." He shook his head, the tension and anger back, but this time I had the sense it wasn't directed at me. "Forget it. It's my hang-up. It just hurts having a complete stranger walk in and know more about my home from looking at it than I do. I'll get over it."

More technicians and agents filtered in, and we finished pulling on the clean overalls in silence.

Well, I had an answer for one lingering question. It was clear Stephan wasn't a witch—or was it warlock? Somehow it didn't feel right to press Stephan on nomenclature.

The silence stretched uncomfortably while I decided what to say. I couldn't help but think of my own tendency to keep things from Aaron. I'd been hiding, well, let's be honest, everything from him lately. The underground cities, Gideon, my reluctant and partially coerced foray into sorcery. Oh, I told Aaron things—but only when I absolutely had to. And now I'd ejected him from my life.

"You're right," I finally said. "We keep a lot of secrets. But there are really good reasons for that. And maybe I'll realize I'm wrong someday, but the only thing any of us, your gran included, can do is follow their gut." I looked at him and waited for him to meet my eyes. "And my gut says, even though you don't see Otherside, you're not planning on sharing half of what you know with the FBI either."

Stephan went very still, his dark hair hanging like a curtain over his face, hiding his expression.

I wasn't backing down.

He finished slipping on the sterile boots and glanced up, those pretty eyes meeting mine. "It was easier thinking you were an asshole."

"Assholes don't inspire introspection. Or apologies."

"Let's leave it at that for now, shall we?" He headed into the smaller side room, and I was left with butterflies in my stomach and wondering exactly what was in the undercurrent between us. And what I wanted there to be.

I composed myself and followed him back into the room where Katy had been murdered and her ghost imprisoned.

"What do you want me to look for?" I asked Stephan, as I stepped inside and surveyed the kitchenette. Just as Stephan had said, Katy's body was gone, though the chair remained and the rest of the room was otherwise the same.

"I got to thinking last night on something Gran always said about ghost binders. That they were plenty smart, but couldn't set a mirror worth a damn." At my quizzical expression, Stephan sighed and added, "Honestly, I don't know what I'm looking for, Kincaid. I can't get out of my head that Liam and Ingrid missed something. Please, indulge me and take a look at the Otherside. Focus on the ghost trap—and any other bindings you can find in the room."

If that's what he wanted . . . "I'll give you this, Agent Wolf," I said as I closed my eyes and slid my Otherside sight into place. "What you didn't get from your family in Otherside talent, you make up for in cryptic behaviour. You'd make a cutthroat voodoo family proud."

I was submerged into the suffocating fog before I could see his reaction. Careful of where I stepped, I peered into the Otherside.

After a moment of cringe-inducing claustrophobia, I spotted the bindings still decorating the metal sheet. "Have you analyzed the embalming fluid used?" Embalming fluids come in various compositions—the amount of formaldehyde used, *if* formaldehyde is used. The chemical composition can tell you a lot.

"Waiting on it. What do you see?"

"Well, a lot of Otherside fog—and the sheet metal is still here . . ." I stopped, frowning at the bindings on the metal, glittering gold. Now, that was odd. Where had those symbols come from? They hadn't been there yesterday, had they?

"Kincaid?"

"Ah—yeah. I may have found something. Can you grab my sketchbook from my bag—I need to see my notes from yesterday." I held my hand behind me and waited until I felt the book, unwilling to take my eyes off the metal sheet.

Once the notes were in my hands, I checked them against the bindings etched into the sheet metal. Sure enough, they were different. There were extra symbols added in the same tight scrawl as before. Shit . . .

"Stephan, someone reset the ghost trap," I said.

"For Katy?"

"No—for a different ghost—or person." I shivered at the thought that the trap might be tuned to someone still alive. "You have a security detail posted, don't you?"

"Throughout the night. No one was here, I guarantee it. Why?"

Then how the hell had they reset the trap? A ghost? Possibly, though considering how much trouble Nate had navigating this place . . .

"Who is the trap targeting?"

I shook my head. "It doesn't work like that—or this one doesn't." I finished copying the changes and checked to make sure they were accurate. I could be staring at a code for Dane's next victim, with no way of identifying them—or warning them. I glanced back at Stephan. "It's not the same as a mirror—where the name of the ghost you want to call is clearly written in the centre. Ghost traps need to be sneakier. They need to call a particular ghost but not give themselves away—or the good ones won't, at least."

"A lure, you mean?"

"Exactly like a lure." I sensed Stephan approaching me from behind and held out my hand. "Please, don't come any closer. In my experience, where there's one trap laid . . ." I glanced over my shoulder at him. "For all we know, it could be tuned to the swamp and your family . . . Ingrid should know more."

Stephan stayed where he was.

"Does Ingrid know? About your family?"

He didn't answer. I shook my head and went back to surveying the room. As I said, if one trap had been reset, there could be more—and if Gideon was right about the alterations the practitioner had made, they might not discern between the living and the dead. What the hell game was the soothsayer playing at?

"You two seemed close is all. It might be something to consider—she's the ghost binding expert."

"And Gran's about as comfortable with the soothsaying as you are. She only wanted to talk to you. Ask her, not me." He nodded back at the trap. "How did they do it? Reset the trap without anyone seeing them?"

"Great questions. Well, normally a soothsayer would send a ghost in, but considering how much trouble Nate had just appearing in the swamp, I don't see it. As to the why? There's a mirror in my bag—a large plastic makeup compact—and a china marker. Would you mind?"

Stephan fetched them for me. A moment later, I tapped the barrier and cold Otherside flooded my senses.

I crouched down and carefully wrote out the bindings for a new set with the china marker. Here goes, I thought, and flooded them with Otherside.

It set—sort of. The Otherside licked at the marker and tried to grab it as I flooded the mirror, but the binding it made was less precise, gripping the glass outside the lines.

I tried again, but with the same effect. The Otherside from the bog didn't just interfere with ghosts, it prevented practitioner bindings. But was it the swamp or the witches' workings? I wiped off the china marker quickly and undid my set.

"Okay, here's what I think," I said, getting up off the ground and heading back to where Stephan waited. "I think the residual Otherside from the swamp wreaks havoc with practitioner bindings."

"Which means a ghost can't set bindings here either."

I hedged my answer. "It means I couldn't have done it, and I don't think a normal ghost could either. I don't know about a soothsayer, or their ghosts." I glanced back at the ghost trap and the lines etched into the metal surface, and then at Stephan. "But like you said, a soothsayer can't set a mirror worth a damn. Why keep having to beat yourself up buying or designing a ghost trap, or sending a ghost through this fog, when you could make a trap that resets." Though how the hell you reset it without showing up yourself or sending in a ghost was the million-dollar question. "Ingrid might know something I don't, but we could be looking at a practitioning genius. I'm out of my depth."

Stephan gave me a wry smile. "A genius finds a way to change the world. A clever thug finds a better way to commit a crime. And that's all we have here, Kincaid. A clever soothsaying thug."

I thought about that. "Well, we agree they're smart. And we have a ghost trap that resets. It still doesn't bring us any closer to this soothsayer's endgame."

"Where's Aaron today, Kincaid?" Stephan asked.

The question caught me off guard. I'd assumed Aaron would have contacted Stephan himself . . . "Ah—he's looking for practitioning links in Dane's victims."

I couldn't quite interpret the expression on Stephan's face, but it was as if I'd confirmed something for him, though I didn't think it was Aaron's whereabouts.

"He's good at finding things in people's past they want hidden—" I stopped. Was my back pocket heating up? "Shit." I retrieved the compact, which was getting hotter by the second. Only one ghost did that.

Sure enough, when I opened it, there was Gideon's tight script scrawled across the glass.

We need to talk.

I glanced at Stephan, who was watching me, and held up the mirror. "Ah—a ghost—a contact. This will only take a moment," I said, and ducked under the tape that cordoned off the small room and went back out into the larger barn, where there were more people, more noise and less chance of being overheard.

"I'm at work—can it wait?" I said into the compact, once the coast was clear.

More time than usual passed before Gideon replied.

Where are you?

Yup, no question that the Otherside fog interfered with bindings . . . "The swamp. I'm testing theories and looking at the ghost trap. I'm not alone, either." I looked up to see if any of the FBI or technicians milling around had taken note of me, but they were buried in their own work.

Our usual routine when others were in listening range was to reconvene at another time. But, much to my surprise, Gideon's tight script scrawled across the mirror again.

Use any excuse and get away. Wait for me down at the swamp's edge. We need to talk. Now.

"What about Dane?"

He isn't here—NOW, practitioner. It can't wait.

The scrawl vanished just as Stephan stuck his head out to find me.

"Everything okay?"

I closed the compact. "Ah—yeah. It's nothing, but I . . ." I what? I needed to go talk to a ghost? I had an expert witness on strange occult occurrences? "I, ah . . ." I stumbled, acutely aware I was about to do the exact thing Stephan had just confided in me he hated about the practitioning community, the same one he'd grown up with.

Stephan sighed and rolled his eyes. "Just go do what it is you have to do. Keep your eyes out for Dane."

"I'll only be ten minutes—fifteen tops, promise. Really, it can't wait," I said as I ditched the overalls and switched out my slippers for boots. Almost forgot to broach his grandmother. I stopped at the barn door. "Stephan, I need to see Bergen again. Today, if possible."

He nodded, though he didn't look as though he relished another meeting with his grandmother. Or maybe he didn't like the idea of me, a complete stranger, on more familiar ground with Bergen than he was.

"And, Strange?"

I started towards the edge of the swamp and glanced back at Stephan, who was standing by the barn door.

"You're a terrible liar."

I ignored him and broke into a jog. Stephan had that all wrong. I lied just fine when I needed to. It was the not-wanting-to that tripped me up.

But secrets didn't always need to be smothered. Sometimes all they needed was a little space to breathe.

✳

I reached the edge of the swamp and picked a path where I thought I'd be far enough away from the activity that no one would see me but close enough that they'd hear me scream if Dane showed up. Hopefully.

I waited, staring at the water for a few moments. The air here was colder, chilling my throat. The pleasant, clean scent of late fall air mixed with the smell of rotting vegetation. A few small islands of varying sizes, patches of dirt really, dotted the marsh. Some even sported thickets of trees and bushes.

I could feel the Otherside here, even more than I had at the barn. I closed my eyes as it chilled my fingers and coursed through my bones, but unlike normal Otherside, this had an almost pleasant feel to it—seductive, caressing my throat, my lips, my skin.

As if it wanted me, had been waiting for me . . .

I shivered and opened my eyes back up. Gold Otherside hung in the air around me—glittering, beautiful and impenetrable. I held up my hand. I barely saw the tips of my own fingers through all that gold.

I slid my Otherside sight away. Sunlight broke through the trees once more, warming my skin even as the invisible Otherside still chilled it.

I tried to shake off the sensation that the swamp was calling to me . . .

"Like a moth to a flame, Kincaid."

I swore and spun around, finding none other than Gideon standing—or coalescing—behind me.

"Many a practitioner has been lured into a place like this, never to leave," he continued.

"Jesus Christ—a warning next time?" There was so much Otherside, I hadn't even felt him. "Poltergeist serial killer, remember?"

"The poltergeist is gone for now. You were already here, and warning you through the mirror would take more effort than I cared to exert." A moment passed and he added, "I owe you an apology for my temper last night. I wasn't myself."

A marked improvement from his usual greeting, and the second apology from him in a very short time. Gideon really wasn't himself. And I really hoped he hadn't ordered me down here just to apologize. "Sorry doesn't—" I started. Sorry didn't what? Didn't cut it? Wasn't good enough? "Thank you," I managed. I had to take what I could get with Gideon. I switched topics back to the swamp. "There are plenty of marshes and estuaries in Vancouver and Washington state, I've walked through them, and I've never encountered anything like this before."

"Most practitioners never do," Gideon replied, staring out at the black water. "Ghosts, zombies, practitioners—everyone touched by Otherside feels the pull. It's one of the reasons Louisiana and parts of northern Europe attract so many practitioners of varying stripes—in recent and ancient history." He paused for a moment. "But the pull here is exceptional." He turned to me. "How do these places produce Otherside?" Gideon asked.

I shrugged. "Life and death, the changing seasons. Animals die, plants shed leaves, bacteria breaks them down and the cycle begins again. It goes on everywhere, just there's a lot more here in one spot. It's really not that different from me burning needles or sage, or even sacrificing a sea urchin for an Otherside hit."

Gideon nodded. "I forget your century has a much better understanding of the science behind Otherside—or what creates it. You are correct. It's a by-product of the life cycle. But this place . . ." He looked out at the water. "Do you remember the mirror I had you working on the other night? How the mirror naturally amplified itself?"

I nodded. It had been cyclic—one ring feeding the other.

"Nature is the ultimate design master. Often, our solutions to problems mimic it. I've seen a place like this only once before, when

I was alive. A fen in the north, where Sweden is now. Not as strong, but still, on a night at the start of winter, when the fog descended, it wasn't uncommon for someone who'd been Otherside-touched to wade in and never return. The superstitious said the bog was feeding itself, drawing its prey into its clutches, though a few learned to survive inside it. The Otherside changed them, warped them. I spent a year trying to learn the bog's secret." There was a faraway edge to his voice—as if the swamp was calling to him as well. And then it was gone, his lip curling into a sneer. "It was filled with witches too."

I waited for him to say more, but if Gideon had anything to add about the witches, he decided to drop it. For now.

"Like the mirror, there was a natural amplifier in that swamp's centre—a peat bog, to be precise."

Now that was interesting. Bogs are one of the watersheds that can produce Otherside, but they are weaker than the other ones because they don't support enough life. They are acidic, and host only a few kinds of bacteria. It is where the bog people come from—both the bodies displayed in museums and the walking zombie variety, who are preserved in the peat waters, its own kind of mummification.

"Think about it, Kincaid. A peat bog is limited in the amount of Otherside it can produce because it doesn't support life."

"And the swamp supplies it. Its own amplification loop."

Gideon nodded. "One ring inside the other." He glanced at me. "A place like this is very valuable. Which is why I needed to speak with you." The ghost did something I'd never seen him do before: he hesitated. "I've been unable to track down the origin of the ghost trap. Neither have I determined who bound the poltergeist. It vexes me no end. Since the poltergeist is after you, though, I'll know when it next appears. I hope to track the binder down from there." His eyes darkened. "The recent events surrounding this place—the disappearing ghosts, the murder, the bound poltergeist, *my* ghost trap—all worry me."

"Yeah, well, if you loved the ghost trap, you're going to love this: it reset, and the target is different," I said, and filled him in on what

I'd discovered this morning. "How could someone reset it, Gideon, without being inside the room?"

Gideon frowned. "You're right. It couldn't have been a ghost—the swamp would negate their ability to wield Otherside. It's far more likely the culprit snuck back in—unless . . ." He turned to me. "Did you or the soothsayer check for blood?"

"Blood?"

"On the metal sheet, or elsewhere in the room? Soothsayers mostly use their ghosts to set their bindings for them—or the more adept purchase them from someone like me. They have the least affinity for the Otherside compared with other practitioners, such as yourself or a medium, like Max. When they do find themselves needing to set their own work, they require blood in addition to wax."

"Ingrid did mention soothsayers carve the bindings into whatever surface they're setting—"

He tore his eyes off the swamp and glanced at me. "If there is blood mixed with Otherside to be found, it means whoever is behind this is a powerful soothsayer. They're rarer. It narrows down our options and gets me one step closer to capturing the poltergeist." His eyes grew dark. "And once I have him, he *will* take me to his master."

"Poltergeists aren't known for their co-operation."

Gideon's eyes darkened even more. "He'll see it my way."

Knowing Gideon, I supposed Dane would. "This isn't only about your ghost trap, Gideon."

"Yes, your murder and missing ghosts. I haven't forgotten," Gideon sneered.

I let it go. "Speaking of murders and ghosts gone missing—I have no idea the motive behind the ghost disappearances, but I think I *do* know why they picked Dane for their dirty work," I said, and filled him in on Dane's ghost coefficient and Celeste's theory that ghosts were being sold on the black market. "I mean, is there a way to determine who might become a valuable ghost? Before they die? Like Miranda."

Gideon cut me off with a shake of his head. "It's not a bad idea, but they're not being sold. I checked. Every soothsayer market I remember— Oh, for the love of—"

I caught the waver in Gideon's body—a flicker, and then he started to fade before flickering back into existence.

"It's the swamp. I'm having difficulty staying here for very long. It changes its frequency—one moment it allows me here, another it wants me gone." He swore again. "I need to leave. I don't know when it will let me re-enter. Make your question quick."

Shit. "What the hell else could they possibly want with that many ghosts?"

He glanced up at me. "I'd love to know the answer to that myself. I have a few suspicions, but I'd rather . . ." He trailed off and glanced in the direction of the road. "There's someone coming." For a moment it looked as if Gideon was sniffing at the air. "Guard yourself around this place, Kincaid. It has a fouler, darker feel than I like. This much Otherside gives a place a personality of its own." His lip curled. "And be wary of the witches. Find out what else they know."

And with that, he disappeared.

A branch cracked behind me and I spun, readying to pool Otherside.

It was a raccoon—and it growled at me, before darting up a tree.

Of course it was a raccoon. I was seeing poltergeists everywhere . . .

A breeze from across the water rustled the leaves, sending strands of my hair into my eyes.

I wiped them away. A thick cloud of Otherside drifted towards me, so I slid my sight away before it engulfed me.

Despite the sunlight and cleared sky, I still felt it, chilling me to the bone.

Hunger, desperation, hatred.

I closed my eyes. Shit—I was so caught up with Dane and the trap, it had completely slipped my mind to mention the presence to Gideon.

Come to me, Kincaid Strange.

This time the thoughts were more formed—and they had a masculine edge. It was still a whisper in my mind, pleading, but also there was something else. A bargain.

Look what I can offer.

The Otherside slammed into me—unwelcome, unwanted. I tried to scream, but the cold caught my voice. White breath and a soft gasp were all that escaped my mouth.

Stop—too much!

But the Otherside came, along with a strange gleefulness.

I pushed it back, but the unwanted sensation still hit me. I gasped, this time from the cold pleasure. So much Otherside, and so easy.

All yours, everything yours, it cooed in my head.

And then it changed, replaced by the hunger, the anger.

If you leave him be.

I choked in pain as the Otherside tore from me. My head throbbed and nausea overwhelmed me. I had no resistance to it, none, until I was drained.

And when the pain subsided, I wanted it—I wanted all of it, every drop of that raw, beautiful Otherside back.

"Who?" I managed, licking my dry lips, my voice barely a whisper. "Who do you need me to stay away from?"

It exuded satisfaction this time—and disdain for me, for my pitifulness.

I didn't care—provided it gave me that Otherside back.

"Who?" I said again, louder this time, the cold scratching my throat. If only it would tell me . . .

It was gone. Vanished, back into the swamp.

I opened my eyes. *No!* I tapped the barrier. I didn't want that Otherside back—I *needed* it.

"Kincaid?" Ingrid's voice cut through the Otherside. "Kincaid? Is that you?"

I blinked—once, twice—

The hunger and the voice were gone. Just like that. And what the hell had I been thinking, tapping into the barrier like that? That was stupid, Kincaid. You need to use today—

"Kincaid? Are you all right?"

"Ah—yeah. Fine," I said, rubbing my throbbing forehead. I was drained and bewildered all at the same time. Gideon said swamps this powerful took on their own personalities. Is that what I'd just felt? My imagination conjuring a voice for the swamp's strange, dark pull?

I shivered as a breeze rustled the water and dead leaves. Get lost in the swamp indeed. I needed to be much more careful here . . .

"Stephan said you'd stepped away—I thought I might find you here," Ingrid called as she made her way down the shallow bank, watching where she placed her light-coloured shoes. She held two paper cups and handed one to me. "There was coffee in one of the tents. My ghost Brett says . . ." Ingrid trailed off, her cheeks flushing. "I'm told you like coffee very much."

I took it and sighed, grateful for the warmth. Stephan was right—it was easier when people were assholes. This was one time I would have preferred my own confirmation bias.

"Are you certain you're all right?" Ingrid frowned at me. "You look a little—pale."

I shook my head. "Fine. I was just . . ." It was my turn to trail off. I had no idea how to explain to Ingrid what had just happened without sounding a basket shy of a picnic or revealing more secrets than I was comfortable sharing.

Focus on what you do know, Kincaid, not what you don't understand.

"Really, I'm fine." Gideon had said to ask about blood. If there was blood, we really were looking at a soothsayer. "Tell me, Ingrid, what do you know about setting bindings with blood?"

Her face perked up with that. "Funny you should ask. I think I found something that we both need to see."

"Lead the way," I said. The chill pooled around my feet, frosting the grass around me, as if the swamp sensed I was leaving and wanted to draw me back.

But that was ridiculous. Wasn't it?

Places like this took on a personality of their own, that's what Gideon had said. Figment of my imagination or paranormal sentience, it clearly wanted something from me, but I'd be damned if I knew what.

CHAPTER 16

BAIT AND SWITCH

"Come look at this," Ingrid called from underneath the kitchen table. I made my way over, still nursing a headache, and groaned as I lay down beside her.

"See there? In the corner? It's easy to miss," Ingrid said, pointing to the plywood seat of the chair.

It took me a moment to find with my Otherside sight, but there it was—a small, finely drawn symbol. At first glance the style resembled the metal sheet bindings, though there were distinctive features I couldn't recognize. Ingrid grabbed her notebook and began to draw.

I had never seen anything quite like it. The Otherside was faint—more silver than gold, easy to miss, the lines were so fine. "I don't even know what it is." I turned to Ingrid. "What does it do?"

"It's an old ghost binding carnival trick—for performances by gypsies and fortune tellers—to keep ghosts sitting in the chair for their clients," she said, and showed me what she'd drawn. The loops reminded me of a handful of infinity signs overlapped on each other. "It's a fallback to Victorian and pre–Civil War times, when people were still terrified of ghosts possessing them. If the ghosts moved, the clients might run away without paying . . ."

"Like a ghost pause button."

She shrugged. "It doesn't actually hold a ghost in place—it changes the resonance of the Otherside around them, making it impossible for them to navigate, slowing them down substantially."

Now *that* was interesting.

"It's fallen out of fashion now but is still considered a classic sleight of hand. Often placed on a chair or wherever they wanted the ghost to stay. But that isn't what worries me—it's the method used to inscribe it." Ingrid nodded at the chair. "We soothsayers do things a little differently than the rest of you practitioner types. Usually, when we set a binding, we carve it into a piece of metal or wood, sometimes glass, then have a ghost prime it with Otherside. It's nowhere near as strong as a practitioner's set." She glanced up, red-blond eyebrows arched. "But there is a way for a soothsayer to set a powerful binding without a practitioner or ghost's help."

"Blood," I said.

She nodded. "But not on a mirror—it won't stick. But wood or cloth? Pass me that, will you?" she said, and gestured towards a box by the door. "It's drawn so fine and thin, I imagine only a blood kit would pick up any traces."

She took the moistened swab and carefully rubbed an edge of the silvery symbol that was only visible with my Otherside sight.

"I thought you needed a ghost to see Otherside?"

Ingrid grinned. "I'm afraid that's not entirely true. We can borrow it . . ."

She trailed off as she finished with the swab, and popped it into a sealed vial. She peered up at me. I couldn't help it—my eyes drifted to the carved bindings on her wrists.

"My point is, Kincaid, this is how Katy was frozen, not through the ghost trap." She gestured at the symbol on the chair. "And the blood may offer us a way to identify the soothsayer behind it."

"Why? Why go out of their way to hide the symbol?"

Ingrid sighed. "That I haven't figured out yet. Perhaps they were simply showing off? A sense of the dramatic?"

An awful lot of trouble . . .

Ingrid frowned and her eyes narrowed. "My ghosts are my friends. They can leave whenever they like, though none of them ever has."

Why can't she just drop it? "They're bound to you."

"Mmmm." She made a noise of agreement as she pulled another piece of paper out of her notebook. She set it on the ground and started drawing. "I hear you have a ghost."

"Not the same thing."

"No?" She glanced up from her notes, the drawing not quite visible to me yet. "Tell me, Kincaid, how do you make the rock star show up at university pub crawls, hmmm? What's your trick?"

"I don't *make* him do anything. He decides."

She rolled up her shirt sleeves so her binding scars were even more visible. The Otherside was so bright I had to look away.

She set down her pencil and folded her hands neatly in her lap as she considered me. "No, you charge him rent and enable him to continue a laundry list of lifelong vices into his afterlife. Like a pimp. And what about the will disputes? The victim interviews?"

"They *all* have a choice," I said, cutting her off. "Nate never has to perform. He also doesn't have to run up a beer tab. And no one ever has to speak at a will dispute. They can make faces at their relatives for all I care."

From the smile that broke out across her face, I'd said exactly what she wanted. "Exactly! Because you're the one who makes sure they have a choice, just like I make sure my ghosts have a choice." Her braids gleamed copper under the LED lights the FBI had brought in, and I felt that pang of jealousy again, over how she turned heads. I recalled how Stephan had looked at her when I first arrived. I'd been so sure there was something between them. Now? I didn't know what to think.

Ingrid smiled as she spread out the diagrams. "I'm not giving up on winning you over to my side of the argument," she said cheerfully, as she resumed drawing.

"Which would be?"

"That not all soothsayers are evil, of course."

Ingrid knew some things about me and my history, but clearly not enough.

Wanting to steer the conversation back towards the case, I retrieved my own notes and said, "They want us to bind Dane. The higher-ups in the FBI." I left out mention of Captain Marks. "To prove they can do it," I added.

She paused in her drawing, as if holding her breath. She nodded, not bothering to look up. "What did you say?"

"That it wasn't happening," I told her. "I catch ghosts when they're dangerous, not as part of a carnival show. And I'm not their employee." Or the Seattle PD's. "I'll help banish Dane, nothing more. You?"

"You were more eloquent than I was. I just told them to fuck off. Not even the insane soothsayers bind poltergeists." She glanced back down at her papers, but I didn't miss the grin. "At least we agree on one thing."

I wasn't sure I liked having common ground with a soothsayer. "Tell me about Liam," I said.

Ingrid stood, holding the diagram of the chair symbol out to me. "He's my cousin. What about him?"

"You're his assistant, right? You thought taking this case with him having Ram's Inn syndrome would be just fine?" I gestured at the diagram with my phone, asking permission to take a photo. She nodded and I snapped a few shots. She did the same with mine, brushing her fingers over the additions that had been made to the metal sheet trap, frowning.

"Assistant is the operative word. I'm not my cousin's keeper. And, rightly or wrongly, he thought he could do some good here, before his condition became too advanced."

I'd show the photos of the symbols Ingrid had found to Gideon later. Hopefully, he hadn't inadvertently sold the soothsayer that as well . . . "I would have thought that fiasco with raising Dane's zombie and almost getting himself strangled proved otherwise," I said.

"He did save you."

I glanced back at Ingrid. Her lips were pursed, her eyes focused on me.

"He made a mistake. I know I've made plenty, and I'm sure you've got yours. And luckily, it did no damage to his career. Though I imagine you, along with every other practitioner out there, jumped for joy at the idea my cousin was a hack. Don't deny it, I'm not mad, everyone did."

"And the teeth come out."

"No teeth," Ingrid said, without an ounce of hostility. She turned her back on me, her attention on the metal trap now as she checked my notes. "Just that you are not immune to wrong impressions."

I caught myself before I replied with something snarky.

I could have ended up like Liam. Still could. And I'm not sure I would do half so well under the same circumstances.

I shook my head and tried to focus on the case.

"Ingrid, if they could hide the symbol on the chair, why didn't they do the same thing with the ghost trap? You said it yourself, the trap is the big kahuna. Hell, they managed to reset it right under our noses."

Ingrid ran her hand along the back of her neck and did a slow circle, taking in the room once more. She frowned. "My gut tells me we're missing something important."

I remembered the collars both Katy's and Dane's ghosts had worn. "How common is it for a soothsayer to use a collar to bind a ghost?"

Ingrid shook her head. "Not at all. The signature was absent in Katy at first." She looked at me. "The bindings around her neck didn't appear until you arrived."

That gave me pause. "So, somehow either my presence or something I did was the trigger." I nodded at the chair. "Probably the same one that had to release her when I arrived."

"Perhaps." Ingrid frowned as she considered it. "Possibly, but . . . Do you know why soothsayers don't bind poltergeists, Kincaid?"

I suppressed a snide remark and shook my head.

"It's not only because they're unpredictable. They're powerfully disobedient. You might be able to bind one for a short period of time—a few hours, a day—but eventually they break the hold. Ghost traps work only marginally better."

"Why the hell even bother?"

Ingrid crouched over the metal sheet, a dark look on her face. She almost touched the lines—almost, but not quite. "Because the operative word is powerful. Power always tempts, even those who know better. But there's a bigger problem with binding a ghost than disobedience." She stood to her full height and arched her back, stretching her arms out behind her. "The longer a ghost is bound, the more its personality bleeds into your own. Otherside strives for balance—even with us soothsayers."

Now that was the first time I'd ever heard that . . .

"It's cumulative, gradual," she added. "And barely perceptible to most. The power of the ghost, the discord with the soothsayer's own personality, all influence how quickly it happens. It's one of the reasons I interview my ghosts so carefully. And why I have so many. We're all quite similar. It's easier to bind ghosts who share my temperament—we have a more powerful connection, a harmony. That doesn't mean a ghost with opposite traits can't be bound, but it takes its toll."

I thought back to Richan. I wondered what toll Miranda took on his mental state? She was neurotic but good-natured, and Richan was an evil asshole. Did they make each other worse, or could they balance each other out? "So, if our soothsayer wasn't inclined towards serial killing before . . ."

She inclined her head. "That's one theory. And it does explain how Dane could be bound so well in the first place . . ." Ingrid trailed off.

A mind meld of serial killers. Fantastic.

I glanced up from Ingrid's drawings. She was staring at my notes, a peculiar look on her face.

"What is it?"

"It's odd. The style—it's familiar."

"Yesterday you said you didn't recognize it."

Ingrid inclined her head as she peered at it, looking more and more perplexed. "I don't—still don't. But now that it's reset, a few of these symbols and the way they were added . . ." She flipped back in her notebook to the drawings of the original trap that I'd made yesterday, while Katy's ghost had still been tied to the chair.

"They've been altered for another ghost," I said, hoping she wouldn't ask how I knew that. "Maybe there's something in the specification—the lure."

She looked up at me, eyes wide. "Yes—I think that might just be it." She sighed. "I need a better look under the binding's hood. Here, let me try something." She started to walk around the metal sheet in a slow circle.

My discomfort rose and I stood, acutely aware of all the Otherside around us and the trap's subtle glow.

"Ingrid, I don't know if this is a good idea. Not with the two of us—"

She continued her slow, methodical walk, staring intently at the trap as she circled. "I'm not going to touch it—but you know how ghosts are drawn to threes? So is Otherside. I just want to see what the trap does with the Otherside, that's all. Flush out some of the workings."

Sure enough, as Ingrid completed the first full circle, the trap and the Otherside around it glowed brighter.

Shit. I should have told Ingrid what Gideon had revealed about the trap being used on the living when I'd first shown him my drawings. "Ingrid, I *really* don't think this is a good idea. You said it yourself, we know nothing about what triggers this trap."

But Ingrid was intent. "A few circles shouldn't set it off, Kincaid. Besides, there are no ghosts in the room."

That was what I was worried about . . .

She completed the second circle. The trap glowed brighter and the Otherside pooling over it ignited like sparklers.

Okay, this was stupid. "*Ingrid!* Stop."

Ingrid didn't stop—her brow furrowed more as Otherside licked at her expensive shoes. "I'm not a ghost, Kincaid—it can't hurt me—"

Oh, screw Gideon. "It can. I think the trap works on the living."

Ingrid shot me an odd glance, continuing her slow walk. "Impossible."

I glanced over my shoulder. Where the hell was Stephan when I needed him? I turned my attention back to Ingrid. She'd almost completed the third circle, and though the trap itself only gave off a low glow, the Otherside in the room looked as if it was on fire.

I held up my hands. "Unlikely yes, but not impossible. You need to trust me—I have my own sources. That trap works on the living. I should have brought it up sooner."

Damn it. Stephan was right. Practitioners played their cards too close.

Ingrid had stopped short of completing the third circle—thank god—and was staring at the Otherside flickering all over the room.

Her eyes turned to the ground. "Fuck," she swore. "Kincaid, we're in trouble. Look at your feet."

I looked down.

I'd been so concentrated on the Otherside in the room, so worried about Ingrid, I hadn't noticed the Otherside strands licking at my own boots, and up my legs.

Leading straight to the trap . . .

My stomach bottomed out. "Ingrid, what was it you recognized about the bindings that made you decide to walk around them?" I asked, though I was certain I already knew the answer.

Slowly now, she was backing away from the trap, towards me, though considering how the Otherside from the trap pooled around my feet as well, I wasn't certain that was a great idea.

"It was a small binding added to the sheet metal—a simple one," she said, now standing beside me. The trap glowed again, but now it was seeping its own Otherside, which pooled our way as well. "But it was altered."

"*How?*"

"It was drawn to target the living. I assumed it was a call to my ghosts—or yours—a modification that meant a ghost affiliated with practitioners. They would be valuable to another soothsayer."

Her eyes went wide again. "That's why I probed it. I thought it was reaching for my bindings."

Shit. Two fucking practitioners in the room, how could we have been so *stupid*?

We'd assumed the ghost trap was for a ghost. Soothsayers trap ghosts. But we had a soothsayer, probably on the serial killer spectrum, who knew their shit *and* had just shown with Katy that they could trap a just-murdered ghost. Worse, they could guarantee ghosts . . .

I'd been focused on ghosts like Miranda—ghosts that could travel through time and collect lottery numbers, or ghosts who could sniff out lies. I'd been so wrapped up in the mystery of our soothsayer and what he or she wanted that I'd completely missed one of the most valuable ghosts out there: a ghost who could set bindings and pool Otherside, from a group who *rarely* became ghosts.

Practitioners and soothsayers.

Ingrid's eyes went wide as the Otherside collecting around the trap pooled in a ball that hovered over the metal sheet. It coalesced and began to unfurl like a blooming flower, and released more balls of ignited Otherside, which headed our way like mutant fireflies.

The first few landed on our skin, cold and icy. For a second I thought maybe I'd been wrong, maybe it was only looking for our ghosts.

And then the lines dug in, like barbs on a fish hook—painful, tearing.

"*Fuck!*" Ingrid doubled over in pain as the trap lines pulled.

I echoed the sentiment—and not just over the pain as I fought the Otherside line.

So many mysteries, so many layers, so many unanswered questions—the witches, the swamp, even Dane.

They'd built a perfect trap, all right, with just the right lures.

For *us*.

Ingrid had thought it odd they'd wanted us to find the trap. Of *course* they'd wanted us to find it. To get used to it, to become familiar around it, think of it as harmless . . .

The best traps are left in plain sight.

More of the fireflies landed on me, each one an explosion of pain as their Otherside barbs dug in—but there was no blood on my arm, there were no tears in my jacket . . .

The trap lines weren't targeting our bodies. They were digging into our *souls*, trying to drag them out while we were still living.

And from the feel of it, they were succeeding . . .

"Kincaid, look! Your arm!" Ingrid shouted.

There, in Otherside, for all the world to see, was a symbol, burning itself not into my skin but into the glowing layer of Otherside that rested just beneath. My life force.

Ingrid screamed. She was on her knees, and her bindings flared a brilliant silvery gold. She was trying to call her ghosts.

But no sooner did the lines shimmer than another pool of fireflies shot up from the trap, landing on Ingrid and eliciting another round of screams. One by one, the soothsayer symbols carved into Ingrid's flesh were smothered out, and new lines attached.

I watched as she tried again, but this time the brands didn't even flicker. "It's no use—I can't break free and I can't call my ghosts. I can't even feel them because of the swamp. I'm cut off!" She sounded panicked.

Understandably, my own panic was setting in at the gold brands still etching on my arms, binding me before I was even dead. Even as I fought the pain from the barbs, I felt a surge of anger. Like hell was anyone going to bind me.

I tore at the lines, ripping their anchors. It was no use—the more I fought, the more I tried to stop them, the quicker and deeper they dug.

Ingrid screamed again.

First things first, Kincaid. Ghost binding 101 from the manual: How do you stop a binding? Break the lines before they set.

I was sure there must be an eloquent, smart way to do that. I was almost certain, if I'd been more willing to learn a bit of ghost binding from Gideon, I'd know what the hell it was.

When in doubt . . .

I took all the Otherside I'd pooled in my head and threw it at the ghost trap.

The Otherside vines lashed out at us. I hit the bindings on the metal sheet. Sure enough, the lines buckled. A few of the vines fell away and others snapped.

Ingrid lifted her head. Sweat was pouring down her face, which had turned a sickly yellow shade. Blood trickled from her nose as she tried to speak and instead fell into a coughing fit. Whatever fuelled this trap had a much stronger effect on her than on me. A side benefit from my connection to Gideon? I hit the trap again with a larger wave of Otherside, pooling more even as I released it. I ignored the nausea that crept into my stomach as I felt the lines loosen. I glanced down at my wrist—the brand had ceased burning into my skin.

"It's working, Kincaid. Do it again!" Ingrid rasped.

But even as she said it, the trap released another round of fireflies. They came straight for us, seeking us out.

It hadn't been enough. Everything I had hadn't been enough. And Ingrid couldn't pool Otherside.

Cold sweat collected on my forehead as I strained to pool and throw more Otherside.

Before it reached the trap, I started again, and then again—each wave bigger, loosening more lines. The projection of Otherside that had bloomed over the metal sheet kept spewing its fireflies, like a poisonous flower.

It wouldn't be enough . . .

Ingrid screamed and clasped at her neck. A collar. I glanced back down at my wrist—the binding had etched another line.

Take more.

Fantastic. The last thing I needed was the presence—swamp or otherwise—weighing in with its hunger.

Go away, I thought at it.

It refused. *Trade. Bargain*, it insisted.

And, perhaps sensing I was running out of time and options, it didn't wait for my answer.

The pit in my stomach roiled, but not for food—for Otherside. A hunger I hadn't known was inside me.

Feed. Feed your hunger.

And with that, the presence was gone.

But the hunger—the hunger fuelled me. I started to pool more Otherside, drowning the hungry pit in my soul. Otherside filled it quickly, but the sickness that always followed was gone.

I pooled even more, pushing it deeper. More and more . . .

I opened my eyes. The world around me wasn't ghost grey—it was gold, a swirling mass, Ingrid and I golden bright spots in the sea of gold fog.

So much Otherside. And all, all of it, for the taking. I'd never held this much—and I'd never wanted more, not like this.

But through my hunger, I managed to focus on my real target. The trap.

I breathed out, my breath mixed with the gold Otherside now. And I sent everything at the trap.

It rattled, once, twice, and lines dropped and fizzled. The ones that remained pulled taut. Ingrid screamed beside me.

I held on, sending more Otherside at it. More and more—and then it shuddered.

The explosion hit me full force in the chest, sending me back against the wall.

There was shouting, running now.

I tried moving, but my limbs and brain weren't on speaking terms. A horrible thought struck me. "Ingrid?" I called out, my vision blurry.

She moaned. Then vomited, the smell cutting through the Otherside cold.

I closed my eyes, willing them to go back to working. Thank god, Ingrid wasn't dead, I hadn't killed her in destroying the trap.

A functioning part of my brain noted that I felt . . . fine. A little cold and dizzy, but that was par for the course. What the hell was going on?

"Kincaid—Ingrid—what happened?" It was Stephan—and there was genuine panic in his voice.

"Stay back by the door. We set off the trap."

He ignored my warning and rushed over, trying to help me up, but I shook my head.

"Get Ingrid first—she's much worse off, the trap almost got her. And send someone to get Liam."

He frowned but nodded, and turned to Ingrid, who was slumped on the floor.

I looked around the room and checked the pool of Otherside still sitting in the pit of my stomach. It wanted more. *Now*. I could feel it.

In a sec, I told it, as I pushed myself up to sitting and began checking the room for any remaining Otherside fireflies.

I saw that Stephan had handed Ingrid off to someone else and was heading back for me.

"No!" I shouted, my voice clear of the dry, raspy sound that much Otherside use should have produced. "Wake her up and get Liam!"

I started to stand. The dizziness threw me, but with the help of the wall I was back on my feet. I realized the air around us was already chilling.

Stephan froze, and looked at me. "Strange, what the hell is going on?"

I met Stephan's hazel eyes and pushed off the wall. Ingrid was looking the worse for wear, but she was awake. I caught her eyes, and though she didn't say anything, she nodded grimly.

"Stephan, that trap wasn't reset for ghosts, it was reset for practitioners—me, Liam, Ingrid." I shook my head at his confused expression. "Explanations later—if we live." I gestured around the small room and readied to pull more Otherside. "We have incoming."

"Everybody out of sight," Stephan shouted to the FBI and forensic people hovering in the barn. "Get into the vans!"

There was a cold breeze now, stirring my hair, chilling my neck.

I searched the ground, but with no idea if the trap was finished for good, I didn't dare risk a pentagram—or moving.

I waited until everyone except for Ingrid and Stephan had cleared out of the barn proper. "Stephan, please go get Liam."

"Is the trap resetting? Kincaid, get out of there."

I turned in a slow circle as the gust picked up, trying to pinpoint where he would appear. "Not resetting, Stephan, but we're about to see part two."

Stephan looked around the room at the black, scorched metal, warped by the force of Otherside and sorcery gone wrong. "What the hell else do they plan to do? Make sure the bystanders are dead?"

"No." It was Ingrid who answered this time, from the doorway. She was leaning on the frame, pale and weary. "To make sure the job is finished," she added.

Maniacal laughter filled the room. We were out of time. I turned to Stephan. "Please run," I shouted over Dane's cackle.

Stephan wavered.

I reached out and touched his arm. "Staying is brave, but getting Liam might actually save us. And you're one of the few people here with real Otherside experience."

He nodded—and then he slipped past Ingrid.

The wind stirred the dirt and dust into a cloud. It stung my eyes, but I didn't dare close them. "So, how exactly do soothsayers deal with a poltergeist?" I asked Ingrid, carefully backing up towards the door.

Ingrid inclined her head. "With the help of a lot of ghosts." Which we didn't have. "What about practitioners?" There was actually hope in her voice.

"Ah, yeah—pentagrams—a mirror, lots of sage . . ." None of which I had with me.

The dust and dirt was spinning in a slow funnel. Otherside coalesced, and at the centre of it I could see a pair of glowing red eyes. They were fixed on me.

"Fantastic. So we run, then?" Ingrid said.

"Hell yeah." And the two of us bolted out the door and into the main barn as Dane, the most powerful poltergeist I'd ever encountered, launched a chrome chair after us.

No ghosts to speak of and not a single tool in my arsenal.

"You're on your own, Kincaid Strange. Better make the run count."

And that's exactly what I planned to do as Dane bellowed his rage behind us.

CHAPTER 17

SCAPEGOATS

"Out of the way! Poltergeist!"

We both shouted it as we bolted into the field and towards the vans. Dane might be a powerful poltergeist, but he still had to see us to kill us.

I always find it interesting how screams of "Poltergeist!" separate the brave from the stupid, even in a highly trained paranormal unit. The brave remember their training—don't run, walk, protect your head, keep quiet, and get the hell out of sight. Granted, wisdom went out the window when you were the direct target . . .

Running full speed through the field, I was impressed just how many techs and agents took the time to back away slowly to their cars or ducked under equipment tables, heads covered. One bright fellow out in the open dove for the tall grass—smart thinking in my books.

The dozen or so who ran every which way—towards the forest, the road, yelling for help—were less confidence-inspiring.

Stephan was making quick work of the stragglers he could reach.

Luckily, Dane wasn't focused on them—he wanted me and Ingrid. Speaking of which . . .

"Chair!" Ingrid shouted.

We both dove into the grass as the chair sailed overhead, landing a few feet away. I checked behind us, but Dane had disappeared once again.

"I hate hide-and-poltergeist." I searched the field—most everyone was out of sight. Where the hell was Liam?

The grass stirred around us.

"Let's go," I hissed. "One, two, three—"

The two of us were back up and running as something thudded into the grass behind us.

"Rake," Ingrid said, out of breath. She stumbled and I caught her under her arm.

"Fantastic, we're on to garden tools. Only a matter of time before he finds the pitchforks," I said, half-carrying, half-dragging Ingrid towards the vans.

Ingrid shot a glance over her shoulder and shook her head. "Really wish you hadn't said that. Go left!"

I did, and narrowly avoided the pitchfork that landed in the grass.

If Dane wanted to kill us, there were faster ways to accomplish that.

He didn't want us dead. "Ingrid, something is up. He's running us down, not killing us."

"Part of the sport. Please stop, I need to catch my breath!" I stopped running and Ingrid doubled over, breathing hard. The trap had taken more out of her than it had me.

It was possible this was Dane's version of fun, but I didn't think that was it. I think he wanted to make sure we couldn't use Otherside.

Once we reached a car, I would be able to set up some decoy bindings to distract him—maybe hide us in a pentagram until we could get away.

Please say these people leave the keys in their cars . . .

Shit.

I skidded to a stop as the air a few feet ahead of us wavered gold. A second later, Dane coalesced. The pastel-pink twin-set and tennis shorts had been replaced with a white T-shirt, jeans and running shoes, though the red baseball cap was still covering his receding hairline. Soccer dad attire.

Clowns, handymen, now soccer dads were relegated to the nightmare-forming section of my brain. Thanks a bunch, serial-killer poltergeists . . .

He smiled at me, congenial, non-threatening—*kind*, even—except, that is, for the glowing red eyes. "Why hello, ladies. Fancy seeing you here. You weren't supposed to walk away from that, you know."

I cringed. Dane really had the neighbourly, unassuming demeanour down. It was even more disturbing than yesterday's tennis attire.

I glanced over at Ingrid and whispered, "First rule of poltergeists and serial killers?"

"Keep them talking," she said, not taking her eyes off Dane. "Kincaid, draw him away from me."

If Ingrid wasn't a soothsayer, I'd be inclined to say I liked her. "I really hope you have something good up your sleeve," I whispered, then shouted to Dane, "Well, can't win them all, Dane. Better luck next time?"

His grin widened and his eyes glowed brighter. "Oh, I'm not complaining, though the boss is going to be pissed. Ah, ah, ah—" he added, cutting Ingrid off as she tried running right. "The boss doesn't like surprises." His lips turned up in a feral grin as he dove at Ingrid, forcing her to duck as he flew around her, chilling the air. "But I do. More fun for me."

"What do you want?" Ingrid shouted as Dane swirled around her, corralling her back towards me.

"Besides us dead?" I figured I might as well state the obvious.

But Dane laughed. "Who said anything about dead?"

"The explosion?" If I could keep his attention . . .

But he kept us both in his sights as he laughed. "Incapacitate, not kill. I'm to bring you in alive."

We were playing right into Dane's game, and we needed one of our own. I started to pool Otherside—just a little, to see if he'd notice.

He flew at me and I ducked. "Oh, a little cranial bruising, a coma or three, mayhem, terror. The usual." He held his arms and another gust of cold wind hit us, forcing us to our knees, frosting the grass around us. "I got to admit, though, I didn't think I'd find either of you conscious. The boss isn't going to like that." His red eyes drifted between the two of us, and his lip curled. "Which one of you was it?"

Which one of us was it? *Shit* . . .

Ingrid grabbed my arm. "Kincaid," she whispered. "I'm going to try and call my ghosts."

"I have rules about my toys talking," Dane shouted at us, and there was glee in his voice. We had to be quick.

"I thought you said you couldn't," I hissed.

"We're away from the barn," Ingrid replied. "The barrier fluctuates. If I can reach even one, that's all it takes to set a pentagram. I'll only need half a minute."

Well, it wasn't airtight—but if the pentagram earned us a breather, even for a minute . . . "You go left, I throw Otherside," I said. I hadn't had a chance to run Dane through his paces yesterday.

Let's see how easily distracted this poltergeist is by Otherside, Kincaid, shall we?

I waved my hands at Dane, and Ingrid bolted to our left. "Hey—asshole," I shouted as I strode towards him. Poltergeists hate confrontation—it offends them. "I'm the one who clusterfucked your boss's trap. What's it to you?"

But Dane didn't take my bait. Instead, he fixed his glowing red eyes on Ingrid and sneered. "Looks like we have a runner. You stay right here, I'll be back in a jiffy," he said to me with a wink, then took off after her.

Not so fast . . . One, two . . .

I threw every bit of Otherside I had at him. It hit him square in the back, and stopped him with a jolt.

He turned around, slowly, his face no longer pantomiming cheer. "You shouldn't have done that . . ." he growled, all semblance of the genial soccer dad gone.

"What are you going to do about it? Kill me?" I *tsk*ed. "We're on to—what?—the second try? Performance problems, Dane? Can't get the old murder ghost up?"

From the low growl, I'd hit a nerve. "If I had my way—"

"But you don't, do you?" I hoped Ingrid was making headway. "Because you're bound. You answer to someone else now. Tell me, Dane—do you get anything out of the deal? Was killing Katy Price a bone thrown your way? I mean, look at you! I'm right here."

"He didn't say you couldn't be missing a few parts. We can start with your tongue, then your eyes—" He stopped mid-threat, as if just realizing what I'd been doing. He swore and searched the field for Ingrid.

Ingrid had stopped thirty feet away and was standing in the grass. Otherside swirled around her. I caught glimpses of a ghost darting around Ingrid as her lips moved.

How the hell had she got a ghost through with all the interference?

Dane spotted Ingrid and raced towards her. A silvery Otherside wound around her then flared bright silver as Dane crashed into it. He screamed with frustration.

Blood. That's how she'd pulled her ghost through and set the working so fast.

Dane was livid. He pummelled the silver Otherside. "Why, you— You're supposed to be playing fair, girls—*I'm* playing fair. I even gave you a head start!"

Ingrid might not be an Otherside-wielding practitioner, but she knew her poltergeists. She smiled and gave him both fingers.

Now all I had to do was get myself over there . . . inside the pentagram.

Dane must have come to the same conclusion. He vanished and reappeared a foot before me, hands bunched at his sides, the baseball cap clenched in one ghostly fist.

I stumbled back and pulled more Otherside in. How much Otherside had I used today? No headache, no illness—I wasn't even winded, though I'd be feeling the bruises from the explosion tomorrow.

Something to worry about after the poltergeist was gone . . .

"You *really* shouldn't have done that, little practitioner."

The disdain, the inflection . . . Only one ghost called me that. Had Dane seen us at the swamp?

I faltered pulling in Otherside, and it fed Dane's confidence.

"Congratulations. You just moved up in the field."

"That so?" I pulled faster, hoping I would have enough before Dane's patience ran out.

"Don't look so smug, girlie. You're out of Otherside." He leered at me, sniffing the air. "I guess I get it. Why they want you alive. You're interesting, all that Otherside sniffing around you like a dog looking for a bone."

He'd discarded the red baseball hat and replaced it with a baseball bat—a real one.

"Though mistakes happen," he said.

I frowned, but not at Dane.

Ingrid was still moving her lips. And Dane, well, he was concentrated on me. Stupid, stupid thing to do—for Dane . . .

"Batter's up . . ." Dane swung the bat over his shoulder and I readied to let loose what Otherside I'd managed to pool at him. The bat stalled and Dane stared at me, confused. The bindings around his neck flared gold.

Never turn your back on a soothsayer. I saw my opening and ran for Ingrid.

I made it halfway before the frost on the grass warned me.

"I think we got off on the wrong foot yesterday," Dane said, appearing in front of me, still carrying the baseball bat. I skidded to another halt. So close . . . "You think I'm a crazy serial killer, and I thought you were an easy-pickings practitioner. Potato, tomato."

"Who's pulling your strings, Dane, hunh?"

Dane ignored me. "I'm much, much more than that."

"You mean you posed your victims like the zombie Cleavers?"

A glimpse of anger, a waver in his apparition as he tried to control his temper—or the bindings did. "No one got it. I wasn't just killing people. I remade degenerates back into something wholesome."

"Katy Price wasn't a degenerate. She was seventeen."

Dane twitched his nose. "You'd think that, wouldn't you? But you're one of them. A *degenerate*. I can smell the Otherside on you, the *taint*. I can remake you too, Kincaid."

If you've got something up your sleeve, Ingrid, now would be the time.

Dane dove for me. I tried to run around him.

The baseball bat hit me in the stomach. I crumpled to the grass.

"Strike one," I heard Dane whisper.

I couldn't see him anymore. Or the baseball bat.

"Pssst." The sound came from behind my ear. I readied to throw Otherside. "Woah, K! Me, dude."

"Nate! What the hell?" I said, as I tried to spot Dane—or figure out where he would come from.

"Asshole—I mean Gideon—sent me. I've been trying to get through for hours."

"It hasn't been hours." Come on, Dane . . . where are you? And what the hell was Ingrid up to?

"I'm a ghost—I can't tell fucking time anymore. Oh, shit— poltergeist! Fucking asshole—I knew there'd be a fucking catch. Gideon was way too nice when he offered to send me over."

The air chilled and Nate vanished as Dane appeared and took a swing at me once again.

"Strike two, Kincaid," Dane growled with glee.

The bat hit me in the back this time, knocking the wind out of me—and maybe a kidney.

Nate reappeared—right beside Dane. "Yeah, K's not really a sports person, so . . ." He grabbed the bat and took off for the woods.

"Ahhh!" Dane roared. He was losing what little composure he'd had. He looked between me and Ingrid, still in her pentagram. "Stay right there," he growled at me before taking off after Nate.

I was not looking a gift horse in the mouth. I bolted for Ingrid's pentagram. I just hoped Nate dropped the bat and got away.

I used Ingrid to slow down, almost knocking the two of us out of the silver pentagram.

"What the hell have you been doing in here?"

"Trying to strengthen the pentagram as much as I can, thank you very much." Ingrid bit her lip, and a bead of sweat ran down her forehead. "Couldn't you have distracted him a little longer?"

"He hit me with a baseball bat—twice! And what are you strengthening it against, exactly?"

"That!" she said, as Dane slammed into the pentagram.

I had to hand it to her, it held—the first time and the second time. The third time, Dane's knuckles almost came through. "Here, kitty kitty," he crooned.

Ingrid buckled as she tried to hold it. I didn't need to be a sooth-sayer to see she couldn't hang on for much longer.

"Where does the Otherside feed in?" I shouted at her.

She nodded at the ground, where a small patch of blood near her feet glimmered with a silver sheen.

Right. Reinforcement . . .

I threw all the Otherside I'd collected and pooled more, feeding all of it into Ingrid's pentagram, which flared silver once again. Just in time to block Dane. He stopped his assault and pressed his face up against the barrier.

"Thought you'd be out of Otherside by now," he said. "No problem. Mom always said I was a problem solver." He vanished, and in his place Nate appeared.

"Is he gone? Did he give up?"

"No—" I started to answer, and saw the first purple ball drop from out of nowhere, bounce on the grass and roll to a stop.

Oh, nuts to this—we were all going to die . . .

"Nate, ever play dodge ball?" I said, and grabbed Ingrid as the second purple ball dropped to the ground.

"Fucking hated it—the jocks had a betting pool to see how many stoners they could hit . . ."

"Taking that as a yes—want to help? Figure out a way to stop him!" I shouted as three more purple balls dropped out of the sky. Dane reappeared, this time dressed in a phys. ed. teacher's shorts and polo T-shirt.

"Catch, girls!" he shouted, and launched one of the balls.

"What the—" Nate looked in time to see the first purple ball passing right through him. And into the pentagram.

"Duck!" I yelled, and dragged Ingrid down. Ingrid's pentagram would stop a ghost, even a poltergeist—but not an object. That kind of barrier would require sorcery—which neither of us had.

Worse, unlike a normal dodge ball, this purple ball didn't fall harmlessly to the ground and bounce away. It stopped mid-air and flew right back at us. I yelped as it smacked hard into the side of my head, and tried to block it with my arms, to minimal effect, as it boomeranged. I got down on my knees and curled up into a ball, both arms protecting my head from the demon dodge ball. Ingrid yelped—and a moment later she was curled up in a ball beside me, protecting herself.

The remaining three balls rose off the ground and hovered a few feet away.

I could see the coroner's report now: *death by poltergeist dodge ball* . . .

"You know, girls, this would be a lot easier if you dropped the pentagram. Come on now, for once in your outsider lives, try to be team players!"

The balls suddenly stopped their assault. I peeked up to find Dane floating around us, testing the borders.

"I can do this all day. Come on, what do you say?" he said in that irritating, cheerful voice, encouraging us as if we were Little League players upset after a bad game. He pantomimed strangulation. "It's fast, quick and painless—you won't feel a thing . . . well, not much." He let loose a battle cry and launched himself at the pentagram, red eyes glowing.

I flooded the pentagram with more, so much more, Otherside. I could have kept it up if all six dodge balls hadn't launched at me.

I screamed and ducked, but not before I saw the tips of his fingers pass through Ingrid's barrier.

"Batter's up, asshole!"

I heard a dull thud, and then another, and the assault lessened.

I glanced up. Nate was hovering outside the pentagram with the baseball bat. He was hitting the dodge balls into the swamp—well out of Dane's visual range.

"Why, you little—" The rage built up in Dane. "Now, now—stealing isn't very nice, little ghost."

Nate glanced at me. "Make it good, K, this is all I got left." He held up the bat. "You mean this? You want it back? Come and get it." Nate vanished back to the Otherside, taking the baseball bat with him.

Dane, for all his control, couldn't resist. "Now stay there, girlies, I'll be right back," he said, and vanished himself.

I got off my knees and took stock of things. Nate had just saved us, but with the swamp and carrying around something as heavy as a bat—he was right, he wouldn't be able to get back to help us, not for hours. I was amazed he'd got this far.

I still had Otherside, and I could keep the pentagram going—but still it faltered.

"What's wrong? I'm the one powering it!" I said to Ingrid.

She shot me a dirty look. "I still have to concentrate to hold it here. I'm having trouble keeping my ghosts this side of the barrier, and they're terrified of Dane! And probably dodge ball." Ingrid winced. "I don't think I can hold it much longer—neither can my ghosts."

Ingrid was almost done; the strain of controlling her ghosts and keeping the pentagram stable against Dane's onslaught was too much. Eventually, he'd get the bat from Nate or give up and come back. We needed a plan beyond holding him off. Dane wanted to wear us out—and it was working. Unless we flipped the tables.

"Kincaid! Ingrid . . ."

Shit. I turned to find Stephan racing towards us. He thought we'd got rid of Dane. He was doing exactly what he was supposed to under the circumstances: get the living out as soon as the coast was clear.

I raised my hands to ward him off—Dane would be back any minute.

But Stephan was shouting at us and waving.

"I think he's saying duck?" Ingrid offered.

The air chilled and we heard the singsong falsetto. "I'm baaaack!" We spun, trying to pinpoint where he would materialize . . .

He didn't waste time, picking a weak point and slamming into it. Ingrid couldn't hold him off. She faltered, and Dane's ghostly hands wrapped around her neck—just as they had with every one of his victims.

I'd have to drop the barrier, but I could still hit him with Otherside— *Crack*.

The gunshot sounded before I could act. I covered my ears and dropped to the ground. Dane let Ingrid go, his face enraged as he turned to see who had shot him.

"Back off, witch pup. It's not your turn yet. Ladies first," Dane growled, and launched a retrieved dodge ball at him, which Stephan narrowly avoided.

Dane threw himself at the wavering pentagram with more force.

I wanted to scream at Stephan—he couldn't see Otherside, let alone use it. But I didn't. Shooting Dane was nothing short of brilliant.

Ghosts, even a bound one, can't escape an obsession with their own death. Dane had been shot down outside a gas station by cops.

I stayed on the ground and pushed Ingrid to do the same as Stephan lined up another shot. It dawned on me then that, despite not using Otherside, despite resenting the secrets, Stephan knew what the hell he was doing.

It worked. Dane stopped his attack and faced Stephan. "You're being a very, *very* naughty witch boy." He spat the words.

Stephan shot him again, this time through the head. That had to hurt the poltergeist's ego.

But, despite his visible rage, Dane didn't abandon us and charge Stephan. He just floated there, between us all, as if he couldn't follow through . . .

Jesus Christ, why hadn't I thought of that sooner?

"Stephan," I shouted as I pooled and got ready to throw more Otherside. "Get in the pentagram—now!"

He shook his head, a slight movement, but enough for me to see. Normally he'd be right—don't put the fish in a barrel for the poltergeist.

"Stephan, please!" How to get Stephan to listen before Dane figured it out? "Remember the stick? The one Nate could only throw at me?"

I don't know if it was the pleading in my voice, or maybe he realized Ingrid was about to collapse. He fired at Dane as he ran at him.

Dane leapt out of the way, roaring and screaming, and Stephan squeezed into the pentagram with us.

Dane was shaking with rage—but he didn't attack. "Why, you— *you*—" Slowly, he floated towards us. "Clever, clever, clever," he chided, *tsk*ing as he fixed his sights on Stephan. He vanished and reappeared, this time with a pitchfork in his hands.

It dawned on me—the swamp stopped Dane from hurting Stephan, but Ingrid and I were still fair game. Just as Nate had been able to throw the stick at me, Dane could throw the pitchfork at the two of us. "Ingrid, grab Stephan!"

She got it and wrapped her arms around his neck. Stephan had picked up on my strategy and wrapped his arms protectively around me. All in the name of not dying by poltergeist.

"Otherside sluts! That's what you are!" Dane screamed. He was livid. He plunged the pitchfork into the ground. "You shouldn't be able to do that," he said, wagging a finger at us. "Of all the lousy— Oh, will you three break it up. You look like an Otherside whore sandwich!"

Well, Dane had been one hell of a prude for a serial killer.

I turned my head around and blew the poltergeist a kiss.

That did it. He screamed. The wind picked up leaves and debris around us, swirling like a brewing storm. Our breath condensed as the air chilled.

"Performance problems, Dane?" I shouted. "Maybe if you stop thinking about it—"

Dane threw his head back and laughed. It wasn't even close to a sane sound. "Oh, that's cute—you think you're real clever. But it isn't me you should be worried about—you *surprised* them."

Yeah, I surprised a lot of people . . . "Who's them, Dane? Your boss?" Or bosses?

He pressed his face against the pentagram. "That's it, yuk it up—I'm just a bound ghost. But take it from someone who's been there, Strange. Surprises never end up well with the unwholesome folks pulling the strings. They put a real damper in my mojo, and they'll put one on yours as well, mark my words."

And with that, he vanished, his words leaving a chill in me that wasn't entirely Otherside.

We'd surprised them. *I* surprised them, I corrected myself. And good thing, too, since the plan had been to take us alive.

I was one hell of a lucky practitioner. So was Ingrid.

We were still wrapped around Stephan, gripping onto him for dear life. As people were re-emerging from the proverbial woodwork and their cars . . .

Oh, hell.

We both let go of him at the same time—my face burning. The fact that it had been a completely innocent, life-saving strategy . . .

I managed to glance up at him, uncomfortably, certain my cheeks were bright red. For his part, Stephan looked resigned and more than a little embarrassed as he surveyed his co-workers—and subordinates.

"There is no way anyone is not going to talk about that, is there?"

"Two female practitioners wrapped around you in what probably looked from a distance like an Otherside orgy?" Ingrid smirked. "No, Stephan, no one here is going to let you forget that. Ever." She coughed. "Excuse me, please—I need to find Liam and make sure he's okay."

I turned back to find Stephan watching me. People were whispering and glancing our way. I sighed. "Yeah, she's right. No one is ever going to let you live that down. Thank you, we wouldn't be alive without your humiliation."

I swear to god, Stephan almost laughed—it was there, I was certain. He covered his mouth at the last minute.

"Tell them you're a dead zone," I suggested.

He regarded me, his expression serious again.

"It's not lying," I added. "You *are* a dead zone—here, anyways. But under the circumstances . . ." I trailed off. "I'll back you up—so will Ingrid. Liam too, I imagine, once she gets through with him."

Stephan looked as if he was going to say no. I knew he hated lying. Then he rolled his eyes. "Dead zone it is. God, Gran is going to love this."

"Speaking of Bergen."

He nodded. "Let me clear things up with my boss—and try to explain . . . everything to him. And Aaron is going to have a field—"

"I don't work for the Seattle PD anymore, Stephan, I'm freelance. You don't have to tell Aaron anything at all."

Stephan looked momentarily uncomfortable.

I sighed and decided to let Stephan off the hook. "Go," I said. "Try to salvage your dignity—and career."

He nodded and headed across the field.

I did not envy the man the explanation he was going to have to spin. And hoped they wouldn't try to replicate it the next time a poltergeist struck.

As I watched Stephan meet someone I assumed was his boss, he stood tall, nothing to indicate he had anything to hide . . .

Somehow, I figured he could handle himself.

My phone rang. I checked the number, half-expecting Aaron, and swore at the name that popped up. Of course, the son of a bitch hadn't taken me seriously.

I answered before the sane part of my brain could stop me. "Kincaid Strange."

"Let me guess. Trouble with the dead again?" Marks said, his voice full of derision.

I almost hung up right there and then. He wanted an update?

He could call the FBI. But, like it or not, Marks had a stake in the case and clearly hadn't taken my resignation seriously. He'd only keep calling. Besides, after our heart-to-heart last night, it would piss him off much, much more if I didn't stoop to his level.

I gritted my teeth. "You'll have to be more specific. Trouble with the dead is pretty much my job description. Will disputes, haunt-ings, poltergeists—"

Marks lost it. "Why the hell isn't Dane bound yet, you degenerate!"

He shouted it so loud I momentarily pulled the phone away from my ear. First point to Kincaid Strange. He must have an informer on site to have got news this fast. And he was the second asshole to call me a degenerate in one day. What do you know, Marks and Dane the poltergeist had something in common.

I sighed. "Unethical opportunist, freeloading con artist, Otherside degenerate . . . Make up your mind, will you?"

"Our deal was that you'd bind Dane," he said, managing a mod-icum more composure.

"We have no more deal. And the arrangement was to *stop* a poltergeist, not bind one. The two are mutually exclusive."

Marks snorted. "Oh, really? Did you tell that to everyone there?" The smug satisfaction . . . he knew something I didn't.

I glanced up in time to see more than a few people intently trying not to listen. Including Stephan.

"Bet you they're all asking themselves the same thing—why you and the soothsayer didn't bind the poltergeist. Why you two idiots decided to leave a serial killer loose . . ."

I watched the faces. No one was saying anything, but they were shooting me looks.

Son of a bitch. Somehow the captain had got the gossip mill going.

"I made the right call," I said quietly.

"Enough to bet innocent lives?"

I stuffed my desire to hang up or run and hide. Instead, I raised my voice so anyone who wanted to could hear. "Here's the deal. We're not binding Dane because it's not safe. We still don't know how he was bound. We've had one explosion." I left out the small detail that it was Otherside-triggered and I was the source. "We don't need another one, not until we know more. It's reckless. I don't want any deaths on my hands."

Here's the thing about people not speaking up when a bully like Marks is involved: eventually, some people start believing them. Others start to whisper and wonder if there's something they missed. Soon enough, they're all looking at you, wondering why you were the target in the first place. Maybe it really is you.

It's a universal truth that a crowd loves a witch hunt. Especially when things take a turn for the worse.

As far as practitioning goes, a paranormal killer is as bad as it gets.

Slowly, the looks turned interested rather than accusing. I'd made my point. Binding Dane could make things worse. I got a very subtle but encouraging nod from Stephan. I'd done enough—for now.

"If he kills someone else, this will all come down on you," Marks said, more irritated, less confident.

I smiled at that. "Well, since he made it clear I'm his target . . ."

I didn't get the chance to hang up. Marks did it for me.

Asshole. I ought to send Nate to haunt him—nothing serious, just a few misplaced keys, cutlery in the wrong places . . .

My haunting fantasy was interrupted by someone clearing their throat. I glanced up to find none other than Liam, standing behind me, looking sheepish. "Kincaid, I just wanted to say how sorry I am—" He coughed, covering his mouth.

I didn't let him finish. All my frustration with the captain had a brand new outlet.

"Tell me *that* isn't what you thought was going to happen today, Sinclair," I spat.

"Ah—I thought Dane might appear, but you have to believe, it never occurred to me . . ." Liam shook his head and stared at his feet, his shoulders slumped and defeated as he trailed off.

"That what? That someone would try to kill us? Or that—gasp—you wouldn't be able to help?"

Liam's brow furrowed for the first time. I'd hit a nerve. For a moment it looked as if he might defend himself, but the moment passed. He put his head into his hands and sighed. "You're absolutely right. I have no business being here on this case."

I agreed, though I didn't say it. Would I be any better in Liam's situation? Probably not.

Ingrid took her cousin's arm and shot me a fierce glare. "He would have helped if he could have. It's not his fault Stephan couldn't wake him." Her voice was low. She, at least, was cognizant of the crowd.

I was too. I just didn't care. "It *is* his fault. He knows he's too sick to be here, and I'll say it if no one else will—he's putting everyone here in danger, and for what?"

"If it wasn't for Liam, you'd be dead—or worse!"

"That's not the point—"

"Ingrid?" Liam's voice cut through our own raised ones. "I think I've had enough for the day," he said.

Ingrid ignored me as she helped her cousin back to the Audi, though I wasn't certain which of the two of them needed assistance more. She was still in rough shape. We all were, though comparatively I was okay.

Ingrid stumbled and Liam tried to catch her, doing his best to help. The problem was, he was in no state to be helping anyone.

The crowd dispersed—all except Stephan, who leaned against the barn, making it clear he had something to add. Once people were out of earshot, I headed over.

"What?" I said, closing my eyes.

"You were a little rough on him. She has a point—he's one of the best practitioners in the country. And," he added, as I opened my mouth to argue, "he did request backup. They wanted you. Because Katy asked for you, but . . ." He trailed off.

I made a face. He was right. They'd brought me down to see what Katy's ghost would do, but there had been a practical angle as well. They'd needed another practitioner to help Ingrid when Liam couldn't.

"You're right, but I'm not wrong." Stephan didn't argue with me. He lived with enough Otherside folks to know better. "Tell him I apologized . . ." I left it there. I was too exhausted to put together a coherent excuse.

Ghosts branded as slaves, intricate traps, manipulated poltergeists—at least we knew now why so many practitioners had been lured here and the appeal of Dane, even if we didn't know what had happened to all of the other missing ghosts.

"Stephan, the soothsayer reset the ghost trap for practitioners—*living* practitioners. They were after Ingrid, Liam and me, and I think I know why. What kinds of ghosts does a soothsayer covet?"

Stephan frowned, still not sure where I was going. "It depends on the soothsayer. Ghosts who skip through time, ghosts who can tell the future. Some of them are idiots who just want a slave to fetch things—"

"But the special ghosts, the rare ones—those are the real valuable ghosts, no? Like the ghost of a practitioner."

I watched Stephan pale as he realized where I was heading. "Jesus—but that's insane. You'd have to find the practitioners, then kill them, and you still wouldn't be guaranteed a ghost—"

"But the soothsayer *can*, because he has Dane. Dane had a ghost coefficient of one hundred percent while he was alive. *Every* person he ever killed became a ghost." I rushed on. "*What if* the traits that make valuable ghosts, like the ghost of a practitioner, rare *also* make them less likely to become ghosts in the first place? If your goal was to make practitioner ghosts, ghosts who could set bindings and do workings for you, how valuable would a poltergeist like Dane be? One who could guarantee anyone he ever killed became a ghost."

That was why the ghost trap was only meant to knock us unconscious: Dane had to be the one to kill us in order to guarantee we became ghosts.

"People murder for a lot less," I said. How could we have been so stupid? "Whoever the hell is pulling Dane's strings didn't want practitioners here so he could outwit us publicly in a huge ego stroke. He wants to harvest us," I said.

I could see the wheels turning behind Stephan's hazel eyes. "Katy, the Portland ghosts—they were practice, testing."

"And a lure." We'd been the targets of this show, not Katy. Three experienced, powerful practitioners, and the soothsayer had used a murder, missing ghosts and the FBI to lure all of us to the exact place they'd wanted. One giant shanghai . . .

"It still doesn't explain what they wanted with all the ghosts of Portland," Stephan said. "Someone this good didn't need hundreds of ghosts for trap practice. There has to be something else going on."

I shook my head. "I didn't say I had all the pieces. But the ones that are falling into place?"

It was as if Dane was born for the job. He was happy to kill people who used Otherside—

"*Shit.* Stephan, Dane doesn't just like killing people who use Otherside. He said he could smell it on us."

I watched as the ramifications sank in. Liam was a bona fide practitioning celebrity, and Ingrid by association, whereas I was moderately infamous in practitioner circles—not only for being the gatekeeper for one Nathan Cade, but also for our recent paranormal disasters up in Seattle. I'd made headlines twice in as many months. We were easy to find. Practitioners are guarded, usually secretive, like Stephan's grandmother, Bergen, and for good reason.

The soothsayer could use Dane to find practitioners in hiding.

"We—all three of us—were the fucking proof of concept." The soothsayer might even have buyers lined up for our ghosts already. Hell, Richan might be planning on buying me. I broke out in a cold sweat under my layers as the panic over being Richan's, or any other soothsayer's, slave set in.

Worse, there was no running back to Seattle. Dane was only powerful enough to beat us in the swamp, but there was no doubt in my mind that the soothsayer was trying to rectify that—and then? He'd be unstoppable.

"Get in the car," Stephan said, and started for his sedan. "We need to talk to my grandmother. Now."

I slid into the front seat. He was right. If the soothsayer knew about the swamp and its ghosts, they had to know about the witches. And if they hadn't known about Stephan's relationship with the swamp and witches before, they'd figure it out when Dane told them how Stephan had stopped his attack.

And then there were the rest of the practitioners the FBI contracted with. "You need someone to contact every decent practitioner in the public eye."

Stephan nodded, his face still determined as he pulled out of the swamp.

I checked for Ingrid's Audi in the lot, but it was gone. I called her, but it went to voice mail. As quickly and succinctly as I could, I told her what I'd figured out. I would have to trust that she and Liam would be fine on their own for a few hours.

As we headed down the road to Spalt and Bergen's strange deli, I recalled Gideon's words about the witches knowing more than they let on.

I was going to make Bergen talk. Not only did any chance of finding the missing ghosts depend on it, so did my life.

CHAPTER 18

FAST RIDE

To say Bergen wasn't happy to see us would be putting it mildly.

She was waiting for us on the deli's porch, formidable arms crossed over her chest, standing guard in front of the door.

And my Otherside senses were on high alert as Stephan parked the car. As we'd driven into Spalt past the single-pump gas station and up to Bergen's Deli, I'd noticed a distinct drop in Spalt's already small population . . . and the number of cars, and homes, and even stores. I was sure I remembered spotting a general store up the street, but beyond a dirt road, nothing was to be seen.

Concealed. Just like the Danish witches had done during World War Two.

"Better let me handle the talking," Stephan said, shaking his head as he got out of the car and slammed the door. "Gran is in a mood."

And she was a hell of a lot more powerful than I'd anticipated . . . obscuring an entire town. I slid my Otherside sight into place and turned around. I squinted at the spots where I recalled there had been buildings before, and thought I caught glimpses of the witch's faint, vine-like bindings.

I didn't get a chance to finish. I took two steps out of the car and my feet froze. I glanced down. Two mosslike mounds of Otherside threads covered them. I tugged, but they only tightened.

Shit.

"I don't see a whole lot of ghosts with you, practitioner," boomed Bergen's voice. "I believe that was our deal."

At her words, more vines of Otherside threaded out of the ground, wrapping around me. It snuffed out the Otherside I was carrying—my Otherside sight, even the deep pit of Otherside I'd recently found. It wasn't gone, but try as I might, I couldn't reach it.

"We'll have none of that," she said. "You can have all your Otherside back when I say so—or when you leave." She snorted, and the grandmotherly facade vanished, replaced by this hardened woman.

There was power in her words—*witch* power. As she spoke, the vines wrapped tighter until I couldn't even feel my own Otherside. Panic set in. I'd never not been able to reach for Otherside, it had always just been there.

"Gran!" Stephan shouted, realizing from my rapid breathing that something was wrong.

"Pshaw." Bergen waved at me as I struggled. "Practitioners are always too attached to the Otherside." To me she said, "Stop struggling," as if I was an idiot. "The vines only tighten as you struggle."

I breathed, and forced myself to stop reaching, to stop trying to see. Sure enough, the witchy Otherside vines stopped. My Otherside returned, though this time I didn't reach for it, or slide my sight back into place.

I glared at Bergen.

She couldn't have cared less. "I'm going to need a promise from you, practitioner, before I let you take another step."

No sooner had she spoken than a compulsion to move overwhelmed me. I tried to take a step backwards and found I couldn't, my feet rooted to the dirt.

Bergen turned her attention on Stephan. "And aren't you sup-posed to be catching a serial killer? You'd better get to it. We heard the explosion all the way across the swamp. Spilled a pot of special coffee I was brewing."

Stephan frowned at her. "Let her go, Gran, we're just here to talk."

A broom, thick and wooded, *living*, with leaves and branches growing from the end, appeared in Bergen's hand, seemingly from out of nowhere. She slammed the handle into the porch with a resounding crack. "*Not* until I get her word on a few things."

Stephan had stopped, his brow furrowed. I wasn't certain he could move either.

Bergen turned towards me. Her face was mature but unlined and youthful, eyes the same bright hazel as Stephan's, and they were *alive*. The same way the broom, something that should be dead, was alive. Even her shorts and T-shirt had a life about them. Bergen, and everything she seemed to touch, was brimming with life—in a most definitely unnatural way.

I had *completely*, utterly underestimated her. I'd known she had to be more powerful than she'd let on, but I hadn't come close . . .

"First things first, practitioner," Bergen said, striding down the steps towards me.

"Do you swear you won't call your sorcerer ghost, one Gideon Lawrence, once I release you?"

The question was simple enough . . . and raised a whole bunch more. I felt the vines loosen, allowing me to speak. As she knew his name, there was no point in denying our acquaintance. "Depends what you're planning on doing to me."

That got me a faint, terse smile. "Provided you're innocent, we don't intend to cause you any harm."

"Why do I feel like this is a reverse witch trial?" The Otherside vines tightened once more, cutting me off.

"Yes or no, sorcerer's apprentice?" Bergen warned. "And you won't be able to lie—not while my vines have you. They make you speak the truth."

I ran through the options in my head. There were none.
"I won't call him—but if he thinks I'm in danger, you're on your
own. Can't stop him," I managed.

"Fair enough." The vines released slightly—enough that I could
move my neck.

I glanced to where Stephan was standing, watching me and looking disappointed. More Otherside secrets,—and I'd dragged mine,
a powerful sorcerer's ghost, straight to his family.

Bergen interrupted my thoughts. "Now, let's get a second look
at you. My, we're full of surprises, now, aren't we, practitioner? It's
always hard to tell who you can trust where Otherside is involved,
and you, my dear, have more secrets than most of us." She smiled.
It wasn't unfriendly, but it wasn't kind either.

Surprises. It occurred to me that I was completely defenceless,
rooted to the ground in the middle of what had to be an entire coven
of witches . . . and Bergen knew who Gideon was.

Despite Bergen's warning, I slid my Otherside sight into place,
just for a moment, long enough to see that the witch vines weren't
just wrapping around me—they were also leading to Stephan. Shit.

Bergen wouldn't use witchcraft on her own grandson, would she?

"Gran, she's looking," Stephan warned, and once again I felt the
suffocating compulsion, though this time it came from Stephan,
not Bergen. I stared at Stephan, open-mouthed. The vines weren't
wrapped around him—some of the vines were coming *from* him.
Stephan had been the one to tell me he wasn't a witch, and I'd
bought it, all of it, even though I knew witches could conceal things
on a scale greater than any practitioner. He'd seemed so resentful,
so sincere, so unable to see Otherside . . .

The look on my face must have said it all. He shrugged, uncomfortably. "Sorry, Kincaid. Too many things didn't add up." He
sounded apologetic, but he didn't look away.

"You ass—" The vines tightened before I could finish.

Bergen *tsk*ed. "Plenty of time for that in a moment. The boy's
almost as good a liar as he is a witch."

I waited until the vines let me speak once again. "Don't tell me you're the one behind the ghost traps, Bergen."

"No," she said, exchanging a glance with her grandson. "Are you?"

"What? No, of course not!"

Another guarded look between the two of them. Stephan was no longer standing by the sedan. He was walking slowly, warily, towards me.

"Then why is the ghost trap of your master's making?" Bergen said.

"Woah—wait just one minute. Boss, not master, and sort of. It's stolen—trust me, he's pissed."

"Does he kill people often with Otherside?" Stephan asked. "What's he doing at our swamp?"

They'd discovered the ghost trap was of Gideon's making. Now here I was—his apprentice or, as Bergen seemed to think, accomplice.

I shook my head. "For fuck's sake, does everyone call me to a crime scene now because they think I'm a suspect? Seriously?" I sighed and forced myself to calm down. "Look, I see your logic. Katy calls for me, I show up, you find out the trap is Gideon's—I get it. Only problem is, it's *not* me. I was lured here. And the trap isn't just stolen—it's been altered. Between you and me, I think that pisses Gideon off more than the theft. He has rules about killing people with Otherside. I'm being set up."

Seconds ticked by, Bergen studying me as the vines rooted me in place. Just when I thought I had finally reached the end of the line, the vines let me go.

"Well, she's telling the truth."

"Same," said Stephan.

As soon as I was free, I pulled up my Otherside sight and searched the two of them. The faintest lines ran over them. I rubbed my neck.

"Sorry about that, Kincaid Strange," Bergen said. "But we had to be certain. Truth vines were really the only way. After the explosion today and what Stephan told me you said about the ghost trap, well, I had to be certain. Preferably before your sorcerer showed up. I've done what I can to keep him out of my swamp, but he's a powerful one."

"How did you find out about Gideon?"

Bergen stepped off the deli porch and headed for me, shaking her thick grey-blond hair, looking weary for the first time. "You'd better come inside, Kincaid Strange," she said. "For that's one of the things we need to discuss."

Like hell was I following them inside. "You can tell me just fine here."

Bergen gave me a withering look. "Oh, you mistake me. You need to *see* her."

*

The familial resemblance to Bergen and Stephan was obvious. She had Bergen's thick blond hair and height, and the hawk-like features of Stephan. Her eyes were too ghost grey to tell whether they'd been the same hazel shade, but I suspected they'd match. She was young, too—barely out of her teens, dressed in an early twentieth-century calico print dress. She sat in the centre of the room, on one of the tables, cross-legged, rocking herself.

"Lawrence, Lawrence, Lawrence," the ghost whispered in threes—over and over again, just as Katy had. "Lawrence, Lawrence, Lawrence."

Well, despite my indignation, I could see where the confusion came from.

"Who is she?"

"An ancestor of mine," Bergen said. "Not a witch, but she was one of the first ghosts taken. She's no longer bound, but that's all she says," Bergen said. "She showed up half an hour ago."

"Right after our latest altercation with Dane," Stephan said.

I shook my head, examining the ghost girl. "Someone released her." I crouched down in front of her while Stephan and Bergen had a quiet word. "Where did you hear the name Lawrence?" I asked her.

That got her attention. She ceased repeating Gideon's name over and over and shook her head. "From him. You're his problem."

I held my breath. Part of me knew I should wait for Bergen and Stephan, but what if she stopped talking—or, worse, was re-bound and pulled away?

"Whose problem am I? The soothsayer's?"

She shook her head, sending her ghost-grey hair cascading. "Gideon Lawrence's." She glanced furtively around the room, as if only now noting her surroundings, looking like a frightened animal. She found Bergen and Stephan and focused on them while she spoke. "I haven't long. I'm to deliver a message to you, Kincaid Strange." She turned her eyes back on me. "A bargain, one they're not to know about."

"What is it?" I asked, my mouth dry, knowing I should call out to the witches, but unwilling to risk it.

"Leave. Leave now. Leave the swamp, leave the witches, and leave Gideon Lawrence, and you can keep your life."

"Who told you—" I stumbled. Bergen hadn't told me the ghost's name. "Who sent the message?"

But the ghost only shook her head, and focused back on her descendants. "You can't trust them, you know. They mean well, but his parents are among the missing ghosts. If you don't do what my master asks, he'll bargain with them next. They won't say no. He's doing this for Gideon. To help him see what a problem you are, since he can't help himself—"

Her hands flew to her throat as she began to choke, eyes wide.

"Leah?" Bergen called. She and Stephan pushed me aside to reach the ghost. But it was too late. My stomach sank as the telltale bindings flared around her neck and she began to fade.

"I thought you said she wasn't bound?"

"She wasn't—I was certain of it." Bergen and Stephan both raised their hands, the same witchy Otherside vines dancing at their fingertips.

But too late. The ghost vanished without a word. Her resignation to her fate stuck with me. Sent to deliver a message, used as a tool . . .

I felt Bergen grab my shoulders. "What did she say to you?"

I shook my head. The soothsayer knew Gideon. What's more, if the ghost was to be believed, Stephan's parents would be used as leverage next. "Nothing—or nothing I could make heads or tails of." The lie tasted foul in my mouth, but I didn't see any other way.

The soothsayer knew Gideon. What's more, he wanted me out of the way. But because he was convinced I was somehow bad for Gideon, or because I had surprised him by escaping the ghost trap? Warning or not, I wasn't leaving, though I did need to speak to Gideon as soon as possible—alone.

"Right through our hands." Bergen spat on the wood floor. "And we're no closer to knowing who's behind this. First our ghosts, and then the ghost trap, and now Stephan tells me they're after practitioners. Turning us into witch ghosts is likely next." Bergen shuddered. "That suburban nightmare of a poltergeist left a ghost trap in town," she said after a moment.

"What?" Stephan said. "When? Why didn't you—"

"Last night," she said, and turned her steely gaze back on me. "I'm at my wits' end with that singing poltergeist. I've tried kicking him out of the swamp more times than I can count, but something has bound him to it as surely as any of our ghosts. Trying only embeds him further, makes him more powerful. And there's a strangeness about it now, an unfamiliar taste that was never in the swamp before. It stinks of soothsaying and sorcery. Why I suspected you and your master."

I sighed. "He's not—"

Bergen ignored me. "You can tell him my intentions were never to test you," she said in part apology. "The first time I made Stephan bring you here, I only wanted a good look, thinking it odd the girl's ghost asked for you. After a little light reading, I thought you might be able to find our ghosts. I don't like to waste opportunities—it's not our way." She paused. "I spotted all the handiwork you're sporting, and told Stephan to keep an eye on you. Then we sensed the sorcerer's ghost poking around our swamp, and then the trap showed up last night, and Leah repeating your master's name, over and over . . ." She shrugged. "You understand, I had to be sure it wasn't you. To Stephan's credit, he didn't think so, but . . ."

Did I understand? No, not really, but saying that wouldn't help things along.

"This soothsayer almost had the entire paranormal community at each other's throats," I said. And keeping all of us on the defence.

"Celeste's missing ghosts? Aye, they may have had a hand in that as well. Celeste and I don't get along so well, never have. We both like to get our own way—runs in the family. She's a great-great-aunt of mine."

Now that Bergen mentioned it, they did have an uncannily similar gruffness.

Bergen arched her eyebrow. "She didn't mention that, did she? Never mind. I ignored Celeste and I was wrong to, though no sense in apologizing. No one holds a grudge like the dead, and that woman . . ." Bergen shuddered.

I was not getting between a witch and a zombie queen. No way, no how.

Bergen got up and headed into the kitchen, returning with three steaming cups of coffee. Stephan took his while I eyed mine. There were bindings all over it.

"You have my word all they do is cut the acidity and save your stomach from ulcers. Like your sorcerer, my word is one of my currencies."

I thought about refusing the cup, but I needed the coffee. Besides, I was already at the witch's mercy.

"The soothsayer keeps luring us in and throwing Dane at us. We need to go on the offensive," I said.

"Set our own trap? I'm all ears," Bergen said, taking a seat at her table.

Great question. How did we lure Dane and the soothsayer out? What would tempt a soothsayer bent on acquiring valuable ghosts? Besides dead practitioners—or Gideon?

It hit me: the swamp. They wouldn't be able to resist taking control of the swamp.

"Bergen—the strangeness of the swamp. It feels alive." She gave me an odd look and I searched for the right words. "I think I've felt it since Seattle—as if it's seeking me out. It's almost as if it's talking to me. It feels hungry, famished, jealous."

"And sick," Stephan offered from the doorway. The two of them exchanged another glance. It was Stephan who shrugged. He hedged his answer as he sipped his coffee. "It's not alive," he said. "It doesn't think or feel anything, but it reacts. It's an ecosystem, like a forest, but—"

"Dead?" I filled in. In a weird way, it made sense. A reflection of the afterlife of a forest.

"The soothsayer has been eating at my defences for weeks. That and stealing the ghosts has damaged the balance, made my swamp sick. That's what you've sensed," Bergen said.

I looked up at the two of them. "If the soothsayer wants it so damn much, I say we use the swamp as bait. Bergen, can you drop the defences? Or pretend to? Just enough so the soothsayer thinks he's won?"

"Maybe," she said. "For a short time. But what about the poltergeist? I can't keep a soothsayer at bay *and* handle a poltergeist."

I shrugged. "Dane hates me, and I imagine he feels similarly towards Stephan. I'm sure we can keep Dane entertained." I crossed my fingers that once the soothsayer was out of commission, Dane would become manageable. Regardless, I doubted Gideon would protest the risk if it meant catching the soothsayer that was misusing his traps.

"If the poltergeist is distracted, I might have a way to tie up the soothsayer," Bergen said, nodding thoughtfully. "But first we need to find him. He's well hidden. The only practitioners I can sense in the swamp are you three."

"Gideon may be able to help." Bergen looked dubious, so I added, "It can't hurt to ask. We can use all the help we can get."

"Provided your sorcerer can be trusted."

"You can trust he wants whoever misused his traps more than fighting with a coven of witches."

Bergen chewed her lip and searched the far wall.

"I think we have to consider it, Gran," Stephan said. "At this point, I'm willing to try."

"All right, Kincaid. Tell the sorcerer's ghost to come see me. Maybe we can drag this soothsayer out of my swamp—preferably kicking and screaming."

Yeah, Gideon probably preferred something like that as well.

I pulled out my compact and held it up. Carefully, I traced Gideon's name into the glass along with a quick message.

With witches—they need to talk to you.

I waited, but there was nothing.

Frowning, I tried Nate. No response.

I looked up at Bergen and Stephan, shaking my head. "I can't get hold of either of them. The swamp's been interfering ever since I arrived. Back at the hotel, I should be able to contact him. I'll send him here, I promise."

"Make it fast, Kincaid," Bergen said, getting up from her chair and collecting the empty coffee cups. "If we're going to set our own lure, I want it sooner rather than later. Before the soothsayer smells the wind changing. In the meantime, what do we do about the other two? The celebrity and his assistant?" Bergen said.

"I think we involve them—better bait, more firepower," Stephan said. "I don't see how they could be behind it."

"I'll leave it to you," Bergen said to her grandson.

We started for the door, but Bergen gripped my arm, stopping me. Stephan, already on his phone, gave his grandmother a wary glance.

"Go," she said to Stephan. "I just need to talk to Kincaid—about her sorcerer."

With one last glance between his gran and me, he nodded. "I'm just outside," he said before leaving.

I waited until the door had shut. "You don't want to talk about Gideon."

"But I wanted to talk to you alone, without Stephan's ears." She reached up a weathered hand and tapped my chest. I felt the power in the gesture, her strange Otherside coursing through me. I was ready to reach for my own, when she said, "There are strange things about you, Kincaid Strange."

I tried to shrug it off despite the blood rushing through my head. "At least the name is appropriate."

"Oh, I don't just mean the sorcerer's workings, though there are plenty of those." She peered intently at me with her brilliant hazel witch eyes. "You have much more of it now—the Otherside. It's easier, isn't it?" she said, not unkindly, but with certainty.

I swallowed. My silence was all the confirmation she needed.

"It happens sometimes. Those who are closer to the dead than they should be, well, the Otherside rarely leaves them alone. Given half a chance . . ." She paused, reconsidering whether to say more.

"Closer to the dead?" I was bewildered by her revelation, and more than a little confused. "Ah—do you mean that I hang out with ghosts? Use too much Otherside?"

"Better you ask that sorcerer of yours. Tell him to come find me, and let's hope he's as powerful as they say. And be quick about it—I sense the winds here changing fast. It won't be long before the soothsayer knows we're after him—and then?"

I found Stephan waiting for me on the porch, on a call with what sounded from my end like his boss. There had been a foreboding in Bergen's voice that left the hairs on my arms standing up. I followed Stephan back to the car, an urgency in my step as I strapped myself in and decided to try Ingrid.

I got her voice mail. Not wanting to leave a voice message, I texted for her and Liam to call me as soon as they could.

Stephan finished his call and we drove in silence for a good ten minutes, until I couldn't take it anymore.

"You lied about not being a witch," I said.

"You lied about being a sorcerer." His voice was matter-of-fact and unapologetic.

I sucked in a breath. "No—I omitted that part. And I'm an apprentice. Big difference. And not a lie."

"How'd it happen? The apprentice part?"

I laughed out loud at that. "Oh no, I've learned my lesson about sharing."

We reached a stop sign and he took a moment to glance over at me. "I meant to tell you—we did. We just had to make sure . . ." He trailed off.

That I wasn't the soothsayer serial killer ghost thief.

"And I was telling the truth about the Otherside secrets. I hate 'em."

"You still use them." Like everyone else, including me. Still, I didn't see what harm it could do. They knew about Gideon. "Long story. It involves a few dozen too many Otherside hangovers and a deal I couldn't refuse."

"I highly doubt that's all there is to the story. Maybe you'll tell me the rest of it. Sometime."

I sat there with my eyes fixed on the road. Maybe, but not today.

"So, it's really over between you and Aaron?"

The question caught me so off guard I did look over at Stephan. Who kept his eyes on the road. "That's none of your bus—"

"Aaron called me. Said he was following a lead down the coast today. He asked how you were handling the case, but he gave me the impression . . . things were not well."

I kept my face neutral. "I'll bet he did." Stephan could fish all he wanted, but if he thought I was giving him information like that . . .

"Captain Marks also called my boss."

I swore. Of course he did. "Let me guess. I suck, you should fire me?"

Stephan smiled at that. "Only slightly more tactful, but that was the gist. He ignored it."

I sat back in the seat. "I need to learn to beat him to the bottom of the barrel."

"Or you could try being better."

I gave him a wry smile. "With people like Marks, that usually doesn't get you very far. The loudest blowhard wins."

He inclined his head. "I didn't say not stick up for yourself. I said take the high road. With less snark."

I had no answer for that. The last ten minutes of the drive were silent, though not as awkward. When we reached the hotel, Stephan parked the car and walked me to the elevator with the agreement that he'd look for Liam and Ingrid while I contacted Gideon and passed on the invitation from Bergen and the witches.

"I meant what I said about telling you—Gran and I both," he added, before I stepped out on my floor. "If there had been any other way . . ."

I took a good look at him. He looked hopeful, sincere. Despite the deception, I still liked Stephan . . . I didn't have a lot of friends—not the living kind—and none since Max died who had a hand in the Otherside. I could use one.

Everyone on the Otherside keeps their cards close to their chest, Kincaid. Witches more than the rest . . .

Still, it couldn't hurt to try. "Apology accepted," I said, before the elevator door closed.

✳

As soon as I was safely back in my room, I tried to get hold of Gideon.

Witches want to talk. They think they can help us catch the sooth-sayer but they need your help.

If that didn't get Gideon's attention . . .

Next on my list was Nate. I tried to summon him with the compact, but he didn't answer. That didn't surprise me—he'd run enough interference with Dane to put him out of commission for a few days. I imagined he'd come looking to make sure I was alive—hopefully soon.

I started the coffee pot and checked the bathroom mirror. Still nothing from Gideon. Where the hell was he?

As soon as there was enough coffee for a cup, I poured one and sat on the edge of the bed, closing my eyes while I sipped, taking a much-needed breather as I waited for someone to get back to me.

Anger, rage, hunger, sickness—

I sat perfectly still. The pull of the swamp was unmistakable. Had I triggered its attention with my own exhaustion? Or was it something else?

I warned you to leave.

The voice. It wasn't the swamp—Bergen and Stephan had confirmed that. Or my imagination. The soothsayer, then? Using the swamp to communicate? He knew about Gideon. I closed my eyes and reached down, tapping the Otherside. Immediately, I felt the reservoir that seemed to permanently rest inside me now. Was that what Bergen had meant? The strangeness?

"Who are you?" I whispered back, throwing the Otherside behind my words.

You were warned.

The voice vanished and the sensation changed. I felt it slowly, the sickness, seeping into my thoughts. I tried to stop it, but it held on, feverishly.

"Stop it!"

I tried, but my reluctance, my attempt to chase it away, egged it on.

I needed Stephan. I tried to reach for my phone, but my fingers wouldn't move. *Shit.*

There was a knock on the door. I sensed the voice's startlement. I cut off contact, letting the barrier go.

I stood and shook my head, as someone knocked again.

I peered through the keyhole, and to my surprise, Liam stood there. He looked paler and weaker than he had even earlier today. In fact, he didn't look well enough to be standing at all.

Despite being unsure on my feet, I opened the door.

"Liam . . ." I searched down the hall, expecting to find Ingrid.

He gave me a wry, slightly pained smile. "Ingrid is back in her room, plotting with Stephan." He frowned at me then, his famous green eyes reminding me a bit of Bergen's, brilliant in his otherwise drawn face. He arched an eyebrow and covered a cough, leaning on the door frame as I struggled with my own light-headedness. "Bait? Is that really the best we can do?"

"Yes, we—" I stopped and closed my eyes as I tried to shake off the last dregs of the swamp.

"It's a gutsy move, putting the three of us in the middle of the swamp, bow tied for the soothsayer to come and kill us. I'll give you that it might work, Kincaid. Though I debate the wisdom."

"Yeah—" I started, then winced. The swamp had really done a number on me . . .

"I'm about to head downstairs for dinner while I let my cousin plot. Would you like to join me? I'm certain we can find bacon of some sort on the menu, and we can talk about this plan to lure the soothsayer out that Stephan just told Ingrid and me about and is so desperate to throw into action. I could use the company, and after today you must be famished . . ." He trailed off and peered at me. "Are you all right?"

"Perfectly." Lie. The headache was getting worse by the second. "Look, Liam, I appreciate the invitation, but what I need right now is rest. A lot has happened." And I'd had to use a lot of Otherside.

He took that in his stride, though I detected disappointment—or maybe confusion. My head was pounding so hard, he could be grinning like an idiot and I'd still see a frown . . .

I held my hand up to my forehead, for once happy it was cold. "As to the wisdom?" I said, suddenly desperate to be alone. "I learned a long time ago that the difference between wise and foolish is a lucky gamble. Good night, Liam," I said gently, and shut the door.

I sighed, leaned against the frame and closed my eyes. My god, I felt awful. I needed a shower—and to try Gideon again. Where the hell was he?

"Pssst."

Startled, I reached for Otherside before my eyes opened. Astrid's translucent face was inches from mine, and she was grinning like a cat who has swallowed a mouse.

"We need to talk."

CHAPTER 19

RICH-GIRL BLUES

Oh, for Christ's—

"Beat it, Astrid, I'm not in the mood." Just the effort of dealing with her right now . . . I walked straight past her and into the washroom.

"No word from the scary ghost yet!" Astrid chimed, following me. "I know, I checked. See? I'm helpful."

I shook my head and checked anyway. Still no reply. Despite myself, I was starting to worry.

"Kincaid." Astrid's voice was peevish. "I've been very patient with you. It's time for you to pay attention to me!"

I refilled my coffee—then stopped. I was exhausted. The last thing I needed was more caffeine . . . I changed my mind and poured myself a glass of water instead. Astrid stayed right beside me.

"Astrid," I said, barely holding my temper in check, "feel free to take this the wrong way, but you need to get lost." I checked the time. It was only six-thirty, but the way I felt, it might as well be 2 a.m. "I need my rest."

Astrid pouted but didn't seem to take offence—or care. I sucked back a glass of water and filled it again. Willing Gideon to show up—Astrid would leave then . . .

"It's not what I want from you, Kincaid, it's what I can do for you." Before I could stop her, Astrid vanished and reappeared beside me. I felt the chill as she leaned in close and whispered, "I know something, Kincaid—something you *need*."

Despite my exhaustion, I whirled on her. "You're way out of line, Astrid—and there is nothing . . ." I stopped short. I meant to say she couldn't possibly have anything I needed—but I wavered and had to cover a yawn. Through my fog of exhaustion, I found myself wondering if maybe Astrid really did know something?

Astrid's grin turned feral. "But *I* want something first." She reached out an icy finger and stroked my cheek. "And you're going to give it to me."

The chill from her fingers snapped me out of it. That was it, I was putting a stop to Astrid's antics now, and I didn't care if she ever made her way back, her parents' retainer be damned. I tapped the barrier. "Time to go, Astrid."

The first flicker of fear crossed her face. "Wait! Okay, fine—*fine*. I know who's behind your murder—all of it, the trap, the murder, the ghosts! And I'll tell you, but I need something first."

I shook my head. "No, you don't," I said, and slid on my track pants and shirt. I needed sleep.

Astrid's movements got more frantic. "I do! Stop and listen to me!"

I had to grab the dresser as a wave of exhaustion hit me. I stared at myself in the mirror. There were dark circles under my eyes, and my face was shockingly pale. I slid my Otherside sight into place and peered into the bathroom mirror, with half an idea to send her through it, willing or not. Astrid was floating behind me, but what was that coming off her? They looked like golden threads. I blinked, and they were gone.

What the hell is happening to me? There is something seriously . . .

This time, when Astrid whispered in my ear, I didn't have the strength to send her away.

Her voice turned hungry. "I'm sticking up for myself, like I never did when I was alive! See, ghosts can change!"

For Christ's sake, maybe if I heard her out, she'd go away. It was the lazy way out, but I needed to sleep. "You've got until the count of three. One, two—" I yawned.

She shook her head, sending her thick, grey-black, ghostly hair cascading. "Bargain first—or you get nothing."

I stumbled again. There were those threads again in the mirror, emanating from Astrid. And they were attached to *me*.

I spun on her and almost fell over. "What the hell are you doing to me, Astrid?" I was shaking now. I wouldn't be able to stand for much longer.

Astrid's cool hand caressed my cheek. "Shhhh, is that better, Kincaid?"

"What do you want?"

"Simple, I want us to be friends—good friends. Better friends than you and that horrible has-been rock star. Or the scary one. I'm much nicer than the scary one, don't you think?"

Shit—this had to be bad. I tried to move. Astrid pushed me down on my knees. She was still speaking to me.

"And just think, once we're very good friends, *best* friends, there's so much more I can tell you, Kincaid. All the secrets of the Otherside . . ."

I opened my mouth to say no. Not a sound came out. Her translucent red lips broke out into a Cheshire cat grin and she leaned her face down and pressed her lips onto mine. I struggled, unable to breathe.

I was vaguely aware of the air around me chilling.

"Okay, party's over!" Nate shouted as he coalesced behind Astrid and gave her a hard shove, sending her floating back. She yelped, her focus broken.

Along with the hell spell she'd woven.

I pushed myself up on shaky legs.

As I blinked, my head foggy, Nate stood guard between us, clenching his ghostly fists, ready to throw a punch.

Astrid regained enough composure to look indignant. "I was just having a conversation with Kincaid about my parents—they have her on retainer."

I frowned, the fog not entirely gone yet. "No, we weren't—" I started, but Nate cut me off.

In his hand had appeared a ghostly baseball bat, which he slammed on the coffee table, making a gentle thumping sound. Astrid leapt back once again, this time holding her arms up in defence. Nate waved it in front of her like a light sabre.

"This is not the music festival you were looking for, princess. Now scram," Nate said, in mock Jedi fashion. He smacked the coffee table again.

Astrid appeared to be genuinely confused. "*Excuse* me?" She tried looking at me again, but this time I noticed the pull, the influence tugging at me through faint resonating gold lines. What the hell were they?

Shit. Astrid, a new, seemingly powerless ghost, had seriously whammied me.

Nate waved the ghostly baseball bat in front of her face, once again distracting her from looking at me. "This is my house, ghost. Be glad you're dealing with me and not the other asshole."

Astrid threw her hair back, hands on hips, rolled her eyes and made an exasperated mewling sound. "I was just—"

"Save the show, sister, I've got your number. 'Oh, I just need to crash for a day or two—really, it's so hard being dead,'" Nate said, doing a rather good impression of Astrid's affected way of speaking. "You think a dozen other freeloading ghosts haven't tried to creep their way in here? Find another couch to surf."

I winced as Astrid pulled the thin threads, trying to regain her hold. I tried reaching for Otherside to fight back with, but felt a dizzy spell coming on.

Nate saw what she was doing. "Stop it!" he shouted, swinging the bat. But though Astrid screamed and ducked out of the way, she didn't disappear. And she didn't let go.

"Kincaid, please! You have to help me! I didn't mean any harm,

I promise—it's all a big misunderstanding, an accident," Astrid cried, the ghostly baseball bat thumping against the furniture.

The buzzing and needling made my head feel thick, my movements slow.

I did the only thing I could think of. I reached for my compact on the coffee table. I held it close to my face while Nate chased Astrid around the room.

"Gideon?" I whispered, and hoped to hell he showed up this time.

So bad was the pain and fog in my head, I almost missed the drop in temperature. But Nate felt it—and so did Astrid.

They both halted, Astrid searching the room, wary. "Who's coming?" she asked, as Gideon coalesced.

I closed my eyes. Thank god.

"Oh, you are so in for it now," Nate told her. "Should have bailed when I said, ghost babe."

Gideon appeared in modern dress and took a quick look at the two ghosts in the room, and then his eyes settled on me. His mouth set in a hard line before he turned his attention to Astrid.

"What do we have here?" he said, arching his eyebrow.

She threw back her hair and stared right back at Gideon, the frightened-little-girl act gone. "Why, nothing at all—" she started.

Gideon *tsk*ed. "You've been a very, very naughty ghost," he said as he slowly made his way across the room, circling her. "You didn't learn this yourself," Gideon said, and to my surprise lifted one of the thin gold lines of Otherside that ran between me and Astrid. "Not this quickly." He loomed over her. "Who taught you?"

The line snapped and Astrid winced, but she stayed quiet.

Gideon snapped another of the lines, then another. The third time, she yelped in pain and scrambled to stop him.

Astrid looked up at him, her eyes rimmed red. "Honestly, I didn't know I was doing anything wrong!" She leaned around him and focused on me. "I'd *never* hurt you, Kincaid, you have to believe me!"

The act was flawless—contrite, pleading, begging for help. But this time I saw it for what it was: a performance. Astrid wasn't sorry. Not one bit.

"Interesting loyalty for a hungry ghost. And futile. Don't think for a moment your friend will save you. She won't. She can't." Gideon looked at me and his eyes narrowed. "We need a change of scenery," he said, crouching down where Astrid was seated. "Kincaid—Kincaid's ghost—I will be back in a moment." He grabbed Astrid around the waist. She shouted and struggled, but she couldn't break his grip. Gideon spared one last glance at me. "This will likely hurt, apprentice," he told me, and disappeared.

"Oh, I do not like the sound of that one bit—"

A sharp, stabbing pain ricocheted around my skull, and the buzzing between my ears intensified. And then my consciousness dove into the deep pit that waited for me. Inviting dark, promising relief.

"K?" Nate shook me, but I felt only a slight chill on my shoulder. Nate had used up all his energy chasing Astrid. "Hungry ghost, K," Nate said, and I felt something cool on my forehead. "I thought I smelled one. K, they're bad. Like, *real* bad."

I laughed—loudly. I'd thought Astrid was young, spoiled, someone to feel sorry for. Jesus, look where that had got me.

Gideon's words came back to me: *Who taught you?*

As I sank into the darkness, I wondered what answers would be waiting for me when I woke.

CHAPTER 20

HUNGRY GHOSTS

It was the sound of voices that roused me. Or, well, Nate's voice. That, and the scent of burning sage, and a powerful need to cough.

"And then, she just left. I mean, who does that? Runs up a tab and then disappears with some bad-hair zombie guy out the back door?"

Gideon's long-drawn-out sigh was unmistakable. "Every woman who's ever wanted something from a man without having to pay for it. Dear god, you make moments feel like an eternity."

The disdain, the lack of interest, the snide tone—Gideon was in good form, even if I was not. It was a talent, being that disagreeable.

My head and back hurt—and I was lying on something hard and uncomfortable . . . Goddamnit, the ghosts had left me unconscious on the floor. Nate was going to get an earful. I kept my eyes closed on account of the throbbing headache, but forced myself to sit up.

I paused until I was certain I wouldn't puke before opening my eyes. Gideon was waiting.

"Little practitioner, we need to talk," he said, then stared at Nate.

"Oh, you mean without me." Nate looked at me. I waved at him to go. I didn't have anything to fear from Gideon right now—and I wanted answers.

I stood up and slowly helped myself to a glass of water.

Gideon motioned for me to sit in a chair, and once I was seated, he circled it, examining me.

"That, Kincaid Strange, was a hungry ghost. Consider yourself lucky you're still alive. They're what you might call real assholes. They cling and claw at the living until they find someone they can sink their strings into. And once that happens? There is usually no getting rid of them."

"I mean, I've heard of hungry ghosts. I thought they were—"

"Myth? A folk legend?" He shook his head.

In areas of Southeast Asia, feeding hungry ghosts is part of the funerary rites, to dissuade ghosts from malicious haunting. It's what the food at Astrid's raising was for—sort of . . .

"That's because the real ones are rare. Incredibly so, and it's a good thing. They're as cursed as the undead can become. It's mostly their own fault," Gideon said. "I had relegated them to the realm of myth along with dragons, manticores and unicorns myself. A South Asian fairy tale preserved in religion and story. That is, until I met one. In Singapore."

He paused, his eyes searching my limbs meticulously. Then they drifted to my desk. Where the journal lay.

Oh shit.

But if Gideon was angry with me, for once he didn't show it. A silence fell between us, only interrupted after he'd finished another few passes around me.

"I'm making sure her entanglements are gone. I believe I caught them all, but you can never be too careful where a hungry ghost is concerned," he said.

Gideon was silent while he examined me. I fidgeted as the silence turned uncomfortable.

"I was in Singapore with an apprentice of mine—Johnathan, whom you are no doubt now familiar with. He worked with the East

India Trading Company as a translator, he had a gift for languages, much like you have a gift for freehand Otherside work."

Again my eyes drifted to the journal, and I swallowed.

Gideon ignored my discomfort. I felt a shot of pain in my neck as he snapped a thread.

"There's one. Johnathan was an asset—as a translator and a practitioner. Through his position in the company, I had more access to the world that existed outside Europe than I'd ever dreamed of. It was mutually beneficial. I expanded my own network and acquired new workings, and he had the assistance of a sorcerer in some of the more . . . inhospitable places the company went. That is, until Singapore.

"Johnathan and I only met once or twice a month, whenever he had a new translation or collection of bindings for me. On one such visit, I noticed he looked ill. I assumed it was due to malaria, a common-enough malady. With no interest in finding a new apprentice, I decided to help, and for a while he got better." He paused and peered at my right arm. "Ah, found another one. Clever, she left some thin threads. To find her way back at a later time, I imagine. Hold on."

Gideon flicked his wrist, and I flinched at the sharp, needle-like pain.

"Hold still. It hurts less the faster I can find and sever them. Where was I? Oh, yes, Singapore," he said, his voice distant. "The fever returned, and I realized it was not the malaria that had struck the traders. Still, it appeared to be a minor illness and Johnathan looked to be in no danger, so I let him be, to recover. A month passed. I was waiting on a series of translations so sought Johnathan out, only to find him bedridden. Except I couldn't find a thing wrong with him—no disease, no festering wounds. And that's when I saw her." Gideon looked up, his lips curling into a sneer. "The ghost, weeping by his bed. Her name had been Ming. She fled as soon as she saw me, but the damage to Johnathan was already done. She had sucked the very life out of him."

"Jesus!" I yelled as one of the remaining lines was ripped off my neck. "Seriously?" I glared up at Gideon as I rubbed it.

He made a face. "Sorry. My temper got the better of me."

I shook my head as I processed Gideon's story. Ming, Johnathan's lover, had become a hungry ghost. "How did she end up a hungry ghost? Why her?"

Gideon seemed to consider that. "Ming was . . . an interesting choice. She was a vapid young thing who depended on her beauty and favours. She'd died during the malaria outbreak a month before. She'd come back as a ghost and—without my knowledge—Johnathan let her stay, thinking she was no more trouble than any other spirit."

He glanced up and gestured for me to stand and turn around.

"But she wasn't a normal ghost. She was *hungry* for the pleasures she'd so freely and selfishly partaken of while alive: food, drink, sex, even the simple compliments on her beauty and demeanour. She hungered for life, the one thing out of her grasp. With no family of her own to mourn her, she clung to Johnathan, and he, a sympathetic lover and practitioner, felt sorry for her. So she stayed." Gideon made an irritated *tsk*ing sound. "And fed on Johnathan's life until there was nothing left but a man on his deathbed decades too soon and a ghost crying beside him." His eyes turned a glittering black as he spoke, and the sneer returned. "Not out of despair, or guilt, or any sense of loss for the man who'd taken pity on her, mind you. The pathetic creature cried because she was hungry. *Famished*. Devouring Johnathan's life force hadn't sated her—it had fed her hunger. The locals knew how to deal with her. They hung wards in their windows and over their doors to keep her out. But the other foreigners from the East India Trading Company? She seduced them—in their dreams, through their windows. When I finally caught her, ten more men were dead and dozens more struck down with the strange wasting sickness . . . All right, I've got them all." At the look I gave him, he added, "I am certain."

I nodded and rubbed my forehead. To think how close I'd come . . . Johnathan had had no idea. "How did you stop her?"

Gideon shrugged. "By the time I found her, she'd drunk down so many lives she was mad with hunger." His eyes glittered at the memory and he smiled, for the first time in recounting the story.

"I stuck her in a deep, dark pit. Some of her victims recovered, and those who didn't have the fortitude died. Her lack of control, her ignorance was her demise. She couldn't resist and paid the price."

Gideon's price. Though, considering everything, I wasn't sure I could fault him. "And Astrid?"

"Another dark, deep pit." He glanced up at me once again. "She's dangerous, Kincaid. She can't be trusted. She wants to feed. You can't help her. I doubt anyone of the living could, not knowing now what she can do."

Gideon was right—I had no cogent counter-argument. But despite what Astrid had done, despite the obvious danger she posed, I still felt sorry for her. "It's a curse."

"In more ways than one." Gideon paused. "When I dealt with the hungry ghost in Singapore, she was a broken, sad thing, barely aware of her own power, acting solely on instinct. But Astrid? No." He shook his head. "Someone showed her what to do."

That got my attention. "Who? Why?"

Gideon paused. "I don't know, but I suspect the soothsayer had a hand in it, directly or indirectly. A hungry ghost, a bound polter-geist, my *ghost* trap—however disconnected they may seem, it's all too coincidental."

"I think you and the soothsayer know each other—or at the very least, he knows an awful lot about you," I said, and filled Gideon in on the voice and what it had said to me, both about Gideon and warning me to leave.

"Not good for me." Gideon snorted, then his eyes landed on the journal once again and his expression turned dark. "Well, he's not wrong about that."

"Gideon, it's not what it looks like. Or . . . it is what it looks like, but not for the reasons you think—"

But Gideon cut me off, not taking his eyes off the journal. "I should be furious," he said as his features shifted—anger, bitter-ness and sadness, or something resembling it. "Where did you find it? It's been missing for years." He held the journal up. "You found it to read up on me."

It was a statement, not a question. I nodded.

A flicker of the dark anger as Gideon turned his dark eyes on me. "To find a way to cheat me again?"

"No! I swear, I'm not trying to cheat you. I might not be as reverent as some of your other apprentices," I said, waving at the book, "but I've kept to the letter of our bargain—"

"And no more." His eyes were still dark as he shook his head.

I started again. "I'm just trying to understand why you're—"

He turned on me. "What? Angry all the time? Because I am the ghost of a very angry and vengeful man whose life was stolen from him for vanity, and I've spent a thousand years trying to get even!" Gideon shouted. He managed to compose himself. "I care about power, Kincaid, little more. Why you've been pushing for answers . . ." He made an exasperated sound and gestured between us. "I am not another undead friend for you, Kincaid Strange. Not like that excuse for a ghost, Nathan Cade. You are my apprentice because I *need* one, and this"—he held up the journal again—"Johnathan's musings will not give you any more meaning, they offer no insights."

He spat the words at me, and I realized for the first time that Gideon wasn't angry at me—or no more than he usually was. He'd expected me to research him, he probably knew about my library visits . . .

Jesus, he misses his friend. That's what this is about.

"If I'd known I'd found your long-lost apprentice's journal, I would have given it to you. I bought it yesterday. You can have it. Please, take it."

Gideon didn't want to hear it. "Last warning, Kincaid. I *forbid* you from looking into my past again. If you need to know something to assuage your curiosity, ask me. Look into any other ghosts and zombies you like, but *not me*." There was a finality, a venom in his voice. But he picked up the journal.

I nodded. "I'm sorry. It won't happen again."

Gideon eyed me for a long moment before nodding. "I'm going to speak with the witches. It's not a bad idea, using them to trap the soothsayer. Keep your eyes open and your mirror closer. Maybe you won't end up dead."

He started to coalesce. This might not be the hill I wanted to die on, but I couldn't leave it at that . . .

"Gideon, before you throw that in a bottomless pit, you might want to read it," I said before he could disappear. "Johnathan thought of you as a friend. I'd hate to think it was so one-sided—"

And then he was gone.

And once again I was by myself.

I only wavered a moment before picking up my phone and dialling the number the Youngs had given me. Gideon had claimed that he'd stuck Astrid in a deep, dark pit . . . but he'd also said that hungry ghosts go after their families, and thinking back to the seance, Mr. and Mrs. Young had both looked under the weather.

Mrs. Young didn't answer. My call went straight to voice mail. Not surprising, since it was so late. I wetted my lips. There was no turning back now, and it was the right thing to do. "Mrs. Young," I said. "Please call me when you get this. We need to talk about your daughter."

After I hung up, I drank down another glass of water. Then, without getting changed, I lay back in bed and closed my eyes, hoping my worry for the Youngs was all for nothing.

It felt as if only five minutes passed before the phone rang. I sat up and fumbled for it on the night table. "Mrs. Young—sorry to bother you so late—"

"Kincaid!" I startled at Ingrid's voice. She sounded panicked. "I'm in trouble. We're in trouble. Can—can you come get us— *please*?" There was a sob in her voice. "We made a terrible mistake—" Her voice cut off with another sob.

So much for sleep. "What's your room number?"

"No! You don't understand. I'm back at the barn—I don't have much time. I came out here, I had a hunch. They have *Liam*."

I pulled on my shoes. "I'll get Stephan—"

"No! Don't! He won't know what to do, and I'm afraid . . ." She trailed off. "I need you. Please—you need to help me save him."

I paused. Come alone, we need you, vague danger—it was starting to sound suspicious. "Okay, Ingrid," I lied. "I won't call him."
I would. I'd call both Bergen and Stephan, and Gideon, as soon as
I was off the phone. If Ingrid and Liam really were in trouble, I'd
need them. If she was trying to lure me out . . .

Either way, I didn't want to be out there on my own.

I'd seen the rental cars out front. I could grab one of them and
be out to the farm in thirty minutes, maybe less. I didn't like the
idea of her waiting that long, especially if Dane was there.

"Please—just hurry."

And the line went dead. I checked the time: 4:30 a.m.

Shit. Dane had killed most of his victims in the early morning—
before the sun rose. If the soothsayer had Liam and Ingrid . . .

Head still pounding, I stumbled to my bag and grabbed my
compact. I scrawled *Nate?* as quickly as I could on the glass, then
added, *Check out the barn, please. Ingrid and Liam may be in trouble. Need reconnaissance.*

Next I went to the bathroom mirror. "Gideon?" I called.

No response. God, I hoped he was busy with the witches and
not off in some tiff . . . I picked up my china marker and started to
write a message.

Wait a minute. I didn't need Gideon—I had my own personal
witch. I called Stephan on my way out of the room and reached his
voice mail. "Stephan, I got a distress call from Ingrid— Oh, hell,
I'll just come get you."

I headed down the hall and up the stairs to his room on the floor
above. I banged on the door. "Stephan? Stephan, wake up." I waited
but didn't hear any sound, so banged again, harder. "Now! It's serious— Oh," I said as the door swung open.

Stephan stood there in the door frame, without a shirt, dressed
only in his boxers.

"Uh, yeah . . ." I managed, trying to not look and staring at him
anyway.

"Kincaid, please say you have a reason for banging on my door
at four-thirty in the morning."

"Ingrid just called me. She said the soothsayer has Liam at the barn. She wants me to go alone and help her save him, but—"

"You think it's a trap," Stephan said, and took my phone, no longer looking exhausted or irritated. He pressed Redial and held it to his ear. Only Ingrid's voice mail came back. "So do I," he said. He gestured for me to come inside. "I only need a minute," he said, and disappeared inside the bathroom.

A minute hadn't yet passed when he exited the bathroom dressed and looking awake and armed. And he was brighter. I slid my Otherside sight into place. Sure enough, there was the glow about him, not as strong as Bergen, but bright. Well, the witch secret was out of the bag . . .

"Please tell me there's some witch thing you can do—to stop him," I said.

He considered that as he palmed his keys off the entrance hall table, passing close enough that I could smell his cologne and felt the vital power emanating off him. Both were an intoxicating mix. I held my breath.

"Honestly?" Stephan said, his witch-bright hazel eyes boring into me. "Maybe. I hope so, but . . . You?" There was witch power behind his words, a compulsion for me not to lie or embellish.

"Maybe. Depends what throwing a lot of Otherside does," I answered truthfully.

"Well, here's hoping one of us can do something, otherwise he's about to add the ghosts of three practitioners and a witch to his collection."

I said nothing more as we rode the elevator down to the garage. As Stephan pulled out of the hotel and pushed the speed limit, I hoped to hell that Ingrid and Liam would still be alive and well when we got there, despite the fact that we were most certainly driving straight into the soothsayer's trap.

CHAPTER 21

GHOSTED

The moon was out and bright, so Stephan killed the car lights as soon as we turned onto the driveway. He hadn't been able to contact the officers who should have been on watch on his radio, and there was no sign of their car as we drove in. We found Ingrid and Liam's Audi, parked in the field, off to the side, in their usual spot. And there was the barn, lit with the flood-lights the FBI had installed inside, doors wide open.

I slid my Otherside sight into place and searched the field, the cars. Otherside fog was heavy in the air.

That wasn't out of order, but something felt more preternatural than usual this evening.

"You noticing what I am, Stephan?"

"It's too quiet. The swamp's alive with noise before dawn, even this late in the fall. Coyotes, birds." He scanned the empty, silent farm. "Not even the trees are rustling."

Silent enough to wake the dead. "Stephan, please say you can see more than I can with your witch sight," I whispered. "That would make me *very* happy."

"I can feel something's wrong with the swamp, but nothing *looks* out of the ordinary. If it wasn't for the silence . . ."

In other words, nothing useful. "No point prolonging the inevitable," I said, and carefully, quietly, eased the door open. No sooner did the night air hit me than an unnatural chill brushed against my shoulder.

Expecting to find Dane, I spun—and came face to face with Nate.

"Jesus Christ," I whispered. "You scared the shit out of me!"

He was shaking his head. "I tried, K, I can't get inside. I'm sorry—"

"Shit." We both turned towards Stephan, who had got out of the car more quietly than I had. I think it was the first time I'd ever heard Stephan swear.

"Something is wrong with the barn," he said, peering at it. "It's cut off from the swamp bindings entirely. I can see them around, trying to get back in, but . . . Even when we found Katy, it wasn't cut off."

"Meaning the swamp can't stop Dane attacking you anymore." Stephan wouldn't be immune. "Fantastic."

"I'm not defenceless," Stephan said, a touch indignant.

"No, I don't doubt that, but we just lost one hell of an advantage." I sighed. What do you do, Kincaid? Run in with Otherside blazing?

"K?" Nate asked, looking bewilderedly at his hands, which were blending into the swamp's thick Otherside fog.

"Go," I said, and waved our compact mirror. "Try to keep an eye out."

"Vamoosing," Nate said, already almost gone.

I kept my ears open for off-key show tunes as Stephan joined me. "What did Cade find?"

Good question—*great* question, in fact. "Something blocked Nate getting inside the barn. No sign of Dane and his twin-sets. I don't see anything here beyond the swamp fog that would prevent a ghost getting inside."

"There might be a barrier inside."

Yeah, that would be the smart thing to do. I shivered again at the silence—as if every living thing had been chased away.

A woman's blood-curdling scream pierced the night air.

I started for the barn doors first, but Stephan soon overtook me.

Before we could reach them, Nate reappeared—waving his arms wildly. "K—witch dude, everyone shoot the horsies!" He whispered loudly.

Stephan and I dug our heels in and skidded to a stop, as I caught the glint of a silver metal sheet peeking through the frost and freshly turned dirt, just past the barn door threshold. One that had most definitely not been there the day before.

"Like, seriously, don't move!" Nate whispered as loud as he dared.

I quickly figured out why. There wasn't just one silver plate. As my sight adjusted to the Otherside fog, I spotted at least three more over the threshold. Someone had laid the metal ghost traps all over the floor of the main barn. A quick look at the bindings told me they were the kind that killed the living.

Oh no . . . My stomach sank.

The nearest metal plate, the one Nate had narrowly stopped one of us from stepping on, was already a dull grey. The trap had been triggered.

"Kincaid," Stephan whispered, grabbing my arm. From the tension in his face, he could see or sense the traps as well. "Listen," he said.

I heard the sob coming from inside the barn and wished I could shut my eyes, to look away. Instead, I searched the rafters until I found her ghost. She was clinging to a wooden beam, hiding. Her copper hair was dulled by the ghost grey, and her fair skin was now a dead white. Even her blue eyes were shadowed ghost grey as she stared sadly down at us. And there, around her neck, was the same golden collar that ran around Katy's and Dane's necks.

I shut my eyes and pushed back tears. It didn't stop her weeping from reaching me—or Stephan.

Stephan drew in a ragged breath. "Oh, no—Ingrid," he whispered beside me. He started forward, anger emanating off him.

"Wait," I said, stopping him. "That's what they want. There are more traps past the fog, I'm sure of it."

He listened to me, but there was a sadness in his eyes and his fists were clenched.

Now open your eyes and focus on the room, Kincaid. That's where the answers are . . . She's not frozen like Katy, maybe there's something you can still do.

I looked at the barn, ready to read it.

Despite the thick fog, the bindings from the un-triggered traps glinted visibly through the dirt. Ingrid's ghost glowed softly as well. Where the hell was Liam?

Stephan had the same thought. "Ingrid? Where's Liam?" he called as loudly as he dared.

She bit her lips and shook her head at us.

"Ingrid," I said, louder than Stephan had, keeping my eyes peeled and my ears tuned for the slightest change, the merest sound that might indicate where her cousin—or Dane—could be . . . "Who did this to you?"

She hid further behind the rafter, shivering. "My ghosts are gone. They've all left me—every single one, not one stayed to help me."

Of course—her ghosts. As soon as Ingrid died and they'd been set free and left to their own devices . . . So much for her "friends."

Ingrid peered at me. "You shouldn't have come. I made a terrible mistake," she said, biting back a sob.

Shit—I wasn't going to get anything out of her in this state. I turned to Stephan. "She's not frozen, but something's not right—"

"I see them, the traps. We need to get inside, to the back room. If Liam's here, that's where he'll be."

And if Ingrid was dead, I didn't hold out much hope Liam had escaped the same fate.

I searched the ground just inside the barn.

Three traps—no, make that four. There had to be a way around them.

"Follow me—exactly," I whispered to Stephan, and took my first tentative step into the barn, carefully placing my foot where there should be no trap. Nothing happened. I took another, then another. Each time I put my foot down, I held my breath, hoping to hell I wasn't reading the ground wrong.

After we made it a few feet inside, Stephan touched my shoulder—gently—stopping me mid-step. "Kincaid, is it me, or is there more Otherside billowing in?"

I checked the ground. Sure enough, there was more, so much I could barely see my feet.

"We need to get out of here," Stephan said.

He was right. I knew he was right. But I couldn't move. What if Liam wasn't dead? Nate was still hovering outside. "Nate?"

He tried to come inside but was stopped by an invisible barrier. He shook his head. "No can do, K. It's got to be Otherside. Why the hell can't we see it?"

"No idea. Just—" I stopped. What exactly? I was out of my depth. I needed to summon Gideon.

I slid my compact out of my pocket and wrote Gideon's name with Otherside, and *trouble* underneath it in capital letters with exclamation points beside it. I waited—one, two, three . . .

Nothing. Not a damn thing. The letters faded without a response.

Liam had saved me from Dane once already—and here I was with a chance to maybe repay him.

"Kincaid," Stephan called again, while Ingrid continued to weep overhead.

Well, fuck.

I let out a breath I'd been holding while I wavered. "Just a quick look, in and out. I'll turn right around at the first sign of a polter-geist," I said, and before Stephan could stop me—careful not to disturb the ground any more than I had to, and checking ahead for more metal traps and their Otherside bindings—I leapt—and leapt again, staying on my toes in case I accidentally triggered one of the traps.

"Kincaid, get the hell back here!" Stephan swore—twice in one night—and I heard him coming after me.

"Stay there—one of us needs to be alive." Just because I was an idiot didn't mean Stephan had to be. "I need to see if Liam is still alive." I'd never forgive myself for not at least trying to help him.

"That's what the soothsayer is counting on."

Yeah, that wouldn't surprise me one bit either . . .

Another survey of the dirt floor, another careful leap.

I readied my Otherside, for what I didn't know . . .

And I caught my breath as Ingrid appeared a hair's breadth from my face, red-rimmed eyes still weeping. "Stop! Both of you, you don't understand—neither did I, not until this afternoon." She frowned. "Or was it yesterday? A week ago?" She searched the room, momentarily bewildered, before her eyes settled on Stephan. "My god, time really is strange to a ghost."

"Give us a name—*anything*, Ingrid," Stephan tried, still a few feet behind me.

But Ingrid gave him a sad shake of her head. "He's—" Her eyes widened, and her hand flew to her throat as the gold bindings flared. She gripped my shoulders with her icy hands. "Please, Kincaid—save Liam," she whispered. And then she was dragged backwards. Into the hidden back room. Dane's murder room.

"K?" came Nate's panicked voice. "Something's happening out here. There's a lot more Otherside!"

I looked back the way I'd come. More fog had seeped into the barn, covering the floor in a blanket of Otherside. Tendrils of it wrapped around Stephan's feet, licking at him as if he were some delicacy it was tasting for the first time. I couldn't see the traps behind me anymore.

"It's not the swamp fog—it's something else," he shouted, recoiling from the Otherside's touch. "It's trying to cut me off from the swamp."

Shit. Trap.

My fingers numbed as the fog rose up to my knees.

"Running would be a real good idea, K!" Nate shouted.

"I second the ghost," Stephan said, backing up, brightening, collecting more power as he did.

I spun around. "One problem: I can't see the traps anymore—"

"Kincaid?" It was Liam's voice—disoriented, weak. "Is that you? I can't move—please! I don't know when Dane will return. Ingrid . . ." His voice trailed off.

Damn it. I turned around.

"K, don't you dare follow that voice!" Nate shouted.

I stood there, frozen.

Liam called out again, "Kincaid! *Please!*"

I should run.

"Kincaid, I forbid you going in there!" Nate shouted. "Oh, for— Hey, witch boy, do something useful and talk some fucking sense into her, will you?!"

"Strange, listen to the dead rock star," Stephan shouted, the tendrils of Otherside still licking at him.

I frowned. He looked dimmer than he had just a few seconds before, even as the Otherside around us grew brighter. I checked my own pool of Otherside. There was still a bottomless pit, but there was less than I'd had even a moment earlier.

"The fog—it's draining my Otherside reserves," I called to Stephan.

"Mine too."

And once our reserves were gone, we wouldn't be able to see the traps . . . Shoulda, woulda, coulda . . . I took stock of the floor. The fog obscured the traps. I couldn't see a damn thing. And I was so close—a few feet more. Liam was *right there*. Three of us stood a much better chance than two and a wayward ghost. "I'm going after Liam—"

"Oh, for fuck's sake!" I heard Nate yell, about the same time as Stephan shouted, "Wait, will you?"

"It's your family's swamp. Figure out a way to clear this fog before it takes all our Otherside." And left us really defenceless.

"Oh, hell," Stephan said, and with a few more unintelligible words whispered under his breath, he held out his hands, face straining. Once more he took on the same "alive" energy as Bergen had, though nowhere near as strong as it had been before. The tendrils licked at him—but the fog started to dissipate, slowly but surely, as if a breeze had picked up. Enough so I could almost see once again where the traps had been laid.

I ran the last few steps and slid open the hidden door. It was dark inside, but the floodlights from the main barn illuminated it well enough that I could see Liam just fine.

"He's alive," I called back.

Liam blinked as his eyes adjusted to the light. He looked dishevelled—shirt untucked, hair mussed. Slumped in one of the kitchen table chairs, though unrestrained.

"Kincaid?" Disbelief and relief flickered across Liam's face, mixed with a heavy dose of confusion. With visible effort, he straightened. "You're . . ." He faltered. "Here I thought for certain you'd both . . . left. You both should have been . . . you should have left me." He stared at me, as if not certain I was really there.

"What happened?" I asked as I searched the ground, looking for more traps.

"I'm—I'm not certain." He started to stand, his arms thin in his dress shirt, his blazer nowhere in sight. "We were at the hotel. I fell asleep." He frowned and scanned the room with a look of confusion. "I have no idea how I ended up here." He struck me as disoriented but otherwise sound. There were no Otherside bindings I could see . . . only the scorch marks from the day before. "Where is Ingrid?" Liam asked, regaining some of his composure. "She was with me."

I didn't think now was the time to let him know she was dead.

"Come on, Liam," I said, catching him under the shoulder. "We need to get out of here, Stephan's waiting . . ." I said as I scanned him with my Otherside sight. No bindings on Liam, none on the floor, no traps. Had Liam just been left here?

I had no problem easing him towards the entrance. "I found him," I called to Stephan and Nate. "We're coming—"

"Kincaid!" Liam said before falling into another round of coughs.

Oh, no—more fog was settling in, creeping its way into the room.

"It's fighting me for control. There's nothing else I can do," Stephan called. "Move, Kincaid," and once again there was power behind the words. A bright burst of Otherside flooded me, and I could see more clearly through the fog, and the traps. I might be looking at Stephan's last push of witchcraft.

"Agent Wolf is here?" Liam shook his head, still leaning on me. "It's no use—we're trapped."

Not if I had anything to do with it. I wasn't about to let Stephan waste his last bit of witchcraft on me. Not willing to risk setting off one of the traps, I eased Liam back into a chair and began searching the walls.

"What are you doing?"

"Trying to find another way out." A loose panel, a hatch . . . anything I could kick down.

What about the stove hood? The air had to off-gas somewhere outside . . .

Jesus. I gasped, then covered my mouth.

"Kincaid?" Liam asked. "Did you find something?"

"Ah . . ." I hesitated at the finger Ingrid held up to her lips. "No, ah, splinter," I lied, hoping to hell I hadn't just made the worst mistake of my life. She nodded at the fridge, finger still firmly on her lip.

I checked my shoulder: Liam was focused on the fog, not looking my way. Carefully, slowly, I opened it—a little more than a crack— and sucked in a breath.

Inside, squeezed into the small space with her arms and legs bent at what would have been uncomfortable angles if she'd still been alive, was Ingrid. Her blue eyes wide open and staring unseeing at me, her expression more surprised than scared.

The thing that really stood out to me, though, was one of her hands, held up against the door. It should have fallen when the door opened, if Ingrid had only been dead a matter of minutes . . . Her entire body, instead, stayed perfectly wedged, frozen in place.

Rigor mortis takes a minimum of two hours to set in. Meaning Ingrid had been dead when she'd called me. And Liam . . .

"Kincaid, do you have a mirror? I may have a workaround. If I siphon off enough Otherside, between the two of us, we may be able to find the traps, make our way through."

"Ah—just a second," I said, and glanced back over my shoulder at him. He was still concentrating on the fog.

And Liam had been doing what these past two hours? Ram's Inn can knock someone out for hours. It was perfectly plausible he'd been left here unconscious.

I looked back at the fridge, to find Ingrid gesturing at her body, her eyes intense, fixed on me. There was an urgency about her movements.

What the hell does she want you to find? There's something here. Something I need to know.

I looked at her—really looked with my Otherside sight. Ingrid shook her head and slapped me—or, more accurately, ghosted me.

Not the Otherside . . .

She touched the Otherside collar around her neck.

And I saw the glimmer of the gold Otherside threads—*dozens*, just like the ones that had once attached Ingrid's ghosts to her. She touched one, and it reverberated like an elastic. All the way, straight to Liam.

Shit.

I searched, but Ingrid's ghost was gone. I shut the fridge. In the reflective red chrome surface, I watched a sentence scrawl itself out backwards in the condensation. *I'm sorry for my part, Kincaid. Truly I am.*

Whoever had bound Dane had to have sociopathic tendencies, like the serial killer himself. That's what Ingrid had said, and they'd get worse—travelling to some sort of equilibrium. Pieces fell into place in rapid succession: the opportunity to bind Dane, the desperation and switch from stealing ghosts to murder . . . But *why*?

Quickly, I pulled out my phone and texted Aaron. If the worst happened and Stephan, Nate and I didn't get out alive—or dead . . . He'd never get here in time, but he'd have the proof to get Liam for Katy, even if Liam went free for everything else. As soon as my text was done, I took a step back from the fridge, towards the stove.

"What gave it away?"

I spun to find Liam standing behind me. Weak, tired, but not nearly as vulnerable as he'd appeared a moment before, or in the preceding days.

I swallowed. "*Stephan—Nate*," I called, even as I sensed the chill.

Liam took his glasses from his pocket and cleaned them methodically with his untucked shirt, his piercing green eyes never leaving me.

"Get the car started. Now!" I shouted.

God, I hope Stephan has enough sense to do it.

"Honestly," Liam said, matter-of-fact. "I'm genuinely curious, Kincaid. It wasn't the witches, I've kept them busy. And Stephan's good, but he's not his grandmother. Please, tell me."

I licked my lips. First rule of serial killers . . . "Well, Ingrid was dead when she called me—"

"Ah, yes. I suppose that would throw a wrench in things," he said, taking another step towards me and giving a noncommittal shrug. "Must have been killed while I was unconscious. What else?"

I stood my ground. Dane loved a chase, and I was hoping that instinct had rubbed off on Liam. "The collar. The gold threads led back to you."

Another shrug, another step. "The soothsayer has a perverse sense of humour and bound my cousin's ghost to me while I was unconscious."

I'd run out of room soon—unless Liam was trying to corral me towards the traps. "Then there's Dane. We all discounted it because of the circumstances, but you were one of the only people to have direct contact with Dane's corpse, when his zombie tried to strangle you."

Liam clapped at that. "Contact with the corpse. Ghost Binding 101. Still not proof that would hold up in court."

"Oh, I agree. The symbol that Ingrid showed me on that chair there," I said, pointing at it. "You know, the one that kept Katy sitting perfectly still?"

"An old Victorian trick. What about it?"

I allowed myself a small smile and held up my phone, showing

Liam the text I'd just sent to Aaron, asking him to get a practitioner and check Liam's last studio. "Tell me, how many of those are they going to find on your guest chairs, the ones where your ghosts always sat? I always wondered how the hell you made the dead sit still while you droned on and on and on . . ."

Liam made a pained face. "I *knew* it. Ingrid got cold feet. She never should have shown you that. Even silenced, my dear cousin finds a loophole, a way. Do you hear that, Ingrid?" He raised his voice for the last bit. "I'm very angry with you."

I racked my brain for a way out of this. I'd written Liam off because he was sick, because he was dying. We'd all written him off. His illness hadn't made him harmless, it had made him desperate—though for the life of me, I still didn't see why.

Liam was dying. What the hell did he need with bound ghosts and dead practitioners?

"Why, Liam? Why steal the ghosts—why do any of this? You're—"

Liam's face twisted in rage. "*What*, Strange? Dying? Joining them soon?" He sneered at me. "You look at me just like everyone else does—a dead man walking. Well, not if I can help it."

Liam closed his eyes, and as I watched, firefly points of Otherside emerged as if from his skin, gold threads attached to them, just like the trap we'd set off.

What the hell? They were coming towards me. I threw all the Otherside I had at them, causing them to spark and fizzle out.

Liam flinched in pain, but when his eyes opened, rage was all I could see—as much as I'd ever seen in any poltergeist. "*How? How* can you see them?" Liam shouted at me, his fists clenched. "There's no way you should be able to pull Otherside—not after this afternoon, not with Dane, and certainly not after the fog in the barn. I made *certain* of it. It's not physically possible."

Liam didn't know about my Otherside sight . . . but he knew about Gideon—he'd said as much, hadn't he? More strangeness from the last few days clicked in place.

"You were meant to be easy—you've vexed and evaded me at every step. I know the witches aren't behind it. *How?*"

I opened my mouth to tell him that was my little secret, but more firefly threads were emerging from him, coming my way. I got rid of them as well and manoeuvred my back towards the exit.

It only made Liam more furious. "You have to run out of Otherside soon, Kincaid. No living person can keep this up."

I shrugged. "In that case, I'll be dead soon—so what's your rush?"

"You *will* tell me, Kincaid. If not while you're alive, then you can be damn sure I'll make you once you're dead."

More Otherside threads headed my way. Liam was like a spider spinning silk—not unlike Astrid had been. I took those out as well. Not even breaking a cold sweat . . .

"Did she know you were going to kill her?" I shouted back at him, watching for more of the threads. He was banking on tiring me out, but he'd eventually realize that wouldn't work. And for a dead man walking, Liam sure was packing an awful lot of Otherside. He *was* sick, he wasn't faking that. How was he still standing?

There was a trick I was missing.

"Ingrid knew what was at stake. *You* were supposed to die yesterday, Strange—not *her*. She helped you with the traps, didn't she?"

"Actually, I think she was trying her damnedest not to, Liam." Until she showed me the symbol on the chair.

Liam bared his teeth at me. "Soothsayers know the best lures. Still, I can't give her all the credit. She didn't redesign the traps.

"I will have you eventually. There's nowhere to run. This time I've made sure of it—"

A shot rang out through the barn, cutting Liam off. He ducked behind the table.

Stephan—he hadn't left. I glanced down. While I'd been concentrating on Liam, the fog around my feet had thinned. It wasn't gone, but I could see the ground through it. Enough to see the traps—every last one, bright silver and gold. Stephan had done it.

"You've got about five seconds!" Stephan's voice echoed through the barn. "That's it, Kincaid," he shouted, and fired again, keeping Liam behind the table.

I didn't waste any time.

"Stop, Strange—" Liam doubled over into a coughing fit, unable to finish.

I made it to the exit as the fog started rolling back in and found Stephan, unconscious on the ground. Shit, he must have overextended himself. "Nate?" I called out. Why the hell wasn't the car already running? I'd told them— For a ghost who prided himself on hot-wiring cars . . .

I reached down and tried to help Stephan up. The smell hit me—one I was all too familiar with. Sickly-sweet chloroform. And another scent mixed in. Formaldehyde and rotting flesh.

Oh, you got to be kidding me . . .

I looked up to find Nate gesturing wildly down at me, shouting without making a sound. He was trapped in a golden net of Otherside.

Fuck.

"An ill man's cough disarms them every time, Kincaid Strange," I heard Liam shout behind me, just as the sack closed over my head, reeking of chloroform.

I felt the cord pulling tight around my neck, even as I held my breath against the chemicals.

"I always get my men—and women," Captain Derrick rasped in my ear, to a chorus of undead laughter.

I couldn't hold my breath any longer, and with the bag, I couldn't see the zombie bindings to dismantle them. My last thought as the chloroform nixed my consciousness was that I hoped to hell they had something more in store for me than a quick death and whatever it was Liam had planned.

CHAPTER 22

HOOK, LINE AND SINK HER

When I came to, though my head was still covered I could tell it was dark outside and, even though there was still no snow or frost, a penetrating chill filled the air.

Well, I thought as I went through a mental checklist of body parts and living functions, making sure everything was there and doing what it should: whatever it was Liam needed me for, I'm not dead. Yet.

I didn't find that comforting, not one damn bit . . .

Despite the hood, I made the effort to push myself up. Despite the chloroform and the wooziness that came with it, it all came rushing back—Ingrid's death, Liam, the zombie ambush. I breathed in deep, testing the air. There it was: a tinge of ozone, the taste of Otherside, right alongside the last traces of chloroform. The chill, the dampness . . .

I couldn't smell the zombies, though I heard rustling and low voices, hinting that they were in the brush nearby. I also couldn't feel any Otherside bindings—just rope binding my hands behind me, my feet left free. That was a plus; it meant I could still use

Otherside, and provided I could get free, I could still run. Though that was contingent on me *getting* free.

"Pssst—pssst, K?" Nate whispered from overhead. "Come on, time to wakey-wakey real fucking fast. We're solidly in batshit crazy territory—"

"*Quiet.*" Liam's voice, commanding, and with its own tinge of Otherside. Sure enough, Nate followed the command and stopped talking.

I reached out and felt for the Otherside I could taste and smell. Hunger, anger, fear, desperation all rushed at me.

I knew *exactly* where I was.

I tested how much movement my legs had, and realized I was propped up beside someone. Stephan. He was warm, though he didn't respond to my kick. Out or . . . ? Relief hit me as I felt the movement of unconscious breathing. At least I knew he was alive.

"Ah, you're awake," I heard Liam say through the muffled darkness. The hood was removed and I blinked at a flashlight aimed directly at me, bright in the early dawn. Liam's face hovered less than a foot away, tinged with gold Otherside. "I'm sorry it had to go this way, Kincaid, I really am," he said, pushing up his glasses.

I kicked out with my bound legs and missed. "Someone else will figure it out, Liam," I said, and began inching my hands back and forth. If I could loosen the ropes . . . "You can't kill two practitioners and an FBI agent and think you'll get away with it—"

Otherside wound around me, stinging my arms with a chill that sank into my bones. I froze in place.

"Don't," Liam said, pausing to cough, a horrible, racking sound. "It only makes it hurt more. I did the workings myself." Rather than angry, he sounded more resigned now. "You really should have gone with your instincts. Once a soothsayer, always a soothsayer." His eyes narrowed. "I gave Ingrid one simple task: keep you distracted until the trap caught you. Instead, she showed you my bindings."

I cut him off. "You murdered your cousin, Liam. Don't blame this on her."

"Betrayal is the unforgivable sin in our family." He was quiet for a moment. "And she was powerful." He licked his lips, as if savouring the words. "Do you know how long I've been sick?"

I shrugged. "Months, I imagine."

He sneered. "Years. I should have died a decade ago. And it's all thanks to *him*."

"Who? Who helped you, Liam?"

Liam only laughed and shook his head at me. "You have no idea what's out there, Kincaid, do you?" He stood up and moved out of sight. "How did you find my traps, Kincaid? The metal sheet? How did you recognize them for what they were?"

I shot back with my own question. "Why Katy, Liam? I get why you targeted me, Ingrid, Stephan—we've got Otherside, we're valuable as ghosts. But a seventeen-year-old kid? Why did you send Dane after her?"

His voice floated over. "Convenience—to keep Dane in line, to test a theory, as bait to lure you down here, to sow confusion, to give myself and Ingrid an excuse to volunteer our services. The swamp as well . . ." I heard him breathe in deeply. "There are things at work outside my control. The barn was Dane's home base during his killing spree. He led me to it after I bound him. And then to the swamp." He stepped back into view. "Dane had been watching her for months. It was the first bargain I struck with him." He inclined his head. "I'm not a serial killer, Kincaid. I'm not like Dane. I'm—"

"You're what, then? In control?" I laughed, working the rope that bound my hands.

Liam gave me a wry smile. "Weak, actually. Morally weak, just like Ingrid was. It appears to run through my family tree. And I'm dying. That helps."

Pleasantries were over. "Tell me how, Kincaid. How you found all my traps, how you keep pulling Otherside . . ." Liam closed his eyes briefly, and the gold firefly points of Otherside erupted along his shoulders, arms, from his chest. And each one was attached to him with a gold thread. Jesus, there were more of them than before. So much like the ones Astrid had attached to me . . .

Except, unlike at the barn, these threads didn't reach out for me. The fireflies made a beeline for the swamp, and as they touched it, Otherside flowed into them.

Sickness, anger, fear, hunger.

The lines, somehow they were feeding Liam. As I watched, Otherside flowed up the lines to Liam. He brightened, taking energy from the swamp like a vampire.

Or a hungry ghost. Liam licked his lips, and I tried to inch away.

"Oh, I can't feed off you—not while you're alive. Ingrid knew that. She knew she was in no danger . . ." He trailed off. "She wouldn't listen." He crouched down until our eyes were level. "I don't know what *he* wants with you. He won't tell me, but I can smell the Otherside drifting off you."

"Who?" My mind raced.

"No ordinary man, Kincaid. One of the dead, more powerful than even you can possibly imagine." He stood, the hungry look still there. "Ask for forgiveness, not permission."

I closed my eyes. "Liam, what did you do with the Portland ghosts?" I asked, though I dreaded the answer.

He inclined his head. "I only needed a few at first—here and there. For my show, just to keep the worst of Ram's Inn away. And then I needed more, and more—and then I found this place." He lifted his hand, as if examining the gold threads. "If it weren't for the witches stopping my feeding, I'd have it all by now." He shrugged and turned his bright-green eyes on me.

"You ate them." He had figured out a way to eat ghosts and Otherside to assuage his disease. And, like a hungry ghost, he was getting hungrier. I swallowed. "You don't need my ghost because I can set bindings, do you?" It was worse, much worse than I'd realized.

He shook his head. "You—Ingrid—even Stephan, you all have more Otherside, so much more when you die. And now that I have Dane . . ."

If he had Dane kill us, we would become ghosts and he could feed on us. I felt my heart pounding in my chest. "Please tell me you haven't eaten Ingrid yet."

"Ingrid regretted them all, but she was more concerned about saving her own ghosts." He paused. "Though they cared little for her in the end. I don't enjoy draining them until they fade away. I really don't. But I hunger for my life. You were right, Kincaid, to never trust a soothsayer, but not for the reasons you think—they aren't all inherently evil. Ingrid had a kind heart. She was the kind of girl who chased after the ghosts of our dead pets so they wouldn't leave her." He looked me straight in the eye. "The dead corrupt people—you spend enough time with them and your moral compass falters."

I spat in his face, hoping he'd hit me, kick me, anything that would put him in contact with me.

All he did was wipe it off, coughing again. "I suppose I deserve that." Liam took a few steps back, well out of my range.

Damn it. I strained my wrists against the bindings. "Who, Liam—who the hell is he? The undead behind this?"

He continued to back up, and I felt the air around me chill and the unmistakable whistle.

Dane.

"Liam!" I shouted.

I didn't hear his response, not over Dane's laugh.

The poltergeist appeared, this time wearing a pink pastel–striped twin-set and white tennis shorts, with red shoes and baseball cap that matched his eyes. In his hand was a tennis racket—a real one. Though there was something off about it . . . I caught the gleam of metal. Needle-sharp spikes had been added to the netting. There were hoots from the forest—Captain Derrick and his zombies, angling for some sport.

"Why, looky here, folks! You're back for round two, are you, Kincaid Strange? And—oh my gosh, boss—is it my birthday?" He clasped his face with both hands. "You brought me a witch for dessert? Aw, you shouldn't have!" Dane feigned brushing tears away. "All this time, I didn't think you cared."

"Liam, this is insanity. You're not just eating dead people now, you're killing people so you can eat their ghosts."

"Like I often said on my show, Kincaid, dying brings out the worst in people. I'll tell everyone you both fought very bravely and how hard I tried to save you." His eyes drifted hungrily from Stephan to me. "I'm hoping a practitioner and a witch will give me a month at least."

He was batshit crazy. "Ingrid was wrong—you're not becoming like Dane, you're worse—"

"K, watch your six!" Nate shouted.

There was a sharp pain in my shoulder that sent me sprawling on my face, the needles and twigs digging into my cheek. I strained against the bindings to feel my shoulder blade and felt wetness. Damn it, that was going to leave a mark. It felt as if the spikes lining Dane's tennis racket had gone right through my jacket.

"Name-calling, Kincaid." Dane *tsk*ed, flying back over me, his eyes glowing red in the moonlight. "There's a penalty for that. In fact, I think you've racked up a lifetime of penalties, practitioner. Let's see what we can do about that, shall we?" he said, and lunged at me with the racket again.

Finally, my hands slipped the rope holding them. I thought about pulling a globe, but I didn't want to play my cards just yet, not if Liam didn't realize I still could, and not with Nate strung up over my head. I licked my lips as I pushed myself up on all fours, stealing a glance at Stephan. He was still unconscious. I turned my attention to Dane. "Martin. How's your evening going? Kill anyone yet?"

Dane squealed with poltergeist glee and whistled at me. "You broke a lot of my conduct rules yesterday, Miss Strange. More touchy-feely hands than I like to see in a good, clean game of dodge ball." He hit the racket into the palm of his hand. "I decided we'd play a penalty round of tennis first."

I dodged out of the way as Dane appeared and disappeared, singing an off-key rendition of a song from *Grease* and swatting the racket at my head in time to it. I swore as I dodged one only to be hit by a second.

"You better shape up, because I need you dead! And my heart is set on you!" He launched into the chorus, *"You're the one that*

I want," with feeling, landing two more blows on my back. There were hoots from the forest—Captain Derrick and his zombies, cheering him on.

I reached out to the Otherside around me—and felt the swamp. But instead of its usual tentative pleas, this time it licked at my thoughts, reaching in, more intense and focused than it had ever been before.

I tried to pull back, but this time the swamp wouldn't let me. It latched on to my thoughts.

Fear, worry, anxiousness, impatience.

I frowned, dodging another of Dane's blows as he sang, "*I've got chills.*"

It pushed again, harder this time, wanting to know *something*. It wanted to know about Stephan.

No—wait. It wanted to *talk* to me.

Pay attention. I can't talk through this thing long.

This time there was a voice, and it sounded like *Bergen.* How the hell . . . ?

The swamp? You can talk through the swamp? I thought back, not certain if it would work. Also distracted by Dane as he reappeared, this time holding the dodge ball—which he launched at my head. I ducked, but too late. It smacked me in the shoulder. He'd abandoned *Grease* and moved on to Blondie.

No, I can't. But your sorcerer knew a witch coven who could. We figured something out. Where's my grandson?

I sensed the worry—and fear over Stephan's well-being.

Here. Stephan's back was to me, so I prodded him with my toe. Nothing, though I could see his chest moving and his body was still warm. *Not conscious yet—but he's alive.*

A wave of relief came through.

Bergen—tell Gideon that the soothsayer is Liam. He's like a hungry ghost—only in reverse. He eats the dead—and your swamp. And there's another undead besides Dane I haven't seen yet.

I could have sworn she sighed through the strange link. *Gideon figured it was something like that, though he called Liam a leech.*

The sorcerer is trying to sever the ties between him and my swamp, but he needs you to draw the poltergeist away. The both of them are too tangled to do it now. Now, let's see if this works. There was a pause, and then, *All right, look at your feet—carefully. No need to garner the zombie's attention.*

There was a thin trail of gold Otherside, like breadcrumbs—barely visible, they were so mixed in with everything else. I followed it with my eyes. It led farther into the swamp, veering in and out of the trees.

For fuck's sake . . .

Asshole wants me to run and make the poltergeist chase me, doesn't he? What about Stephan?

I've got eyes on him—and Liam. But I can't do anything about the poltergeist.

Right. What did I have to lose, anyway? Oh, just my life . . .

Now, where the hell was Dane so I could get his attention? Shit—I ducked as Dane reappeared, singing, *"I'm gonna getcha!"* I threw Otherside at him. It sent him squealing, but not before he launched the racket at my face. I shut my eyes.

I opened them to find Liam with a hand outstretched towards Dane, the racket on the ground. I could even see the gold threads of Otherside strung between the two of them and the swamp. Tangled was right. And Martin Dane was livid, but not at me. He'd turned his rage on Liam. "Oh, for fudge sake!"

"That's enough," Liam snarled, and dismissed the poltergeist with a flick of his wrist. "You know what he said."

"Oh, come on, now. Play fair!" Dane whined. "Seriously, boss. All I ask for is a little murder and mayhem—"

Liam lost it. "You'll get your due, Dane!" he shouted. "When the time is right."

Dane seethed over me, but the racket went no further.

The swamp brushed my thoughts. *Now.*

I took one last glance at Nate and Stephan and hoped to hell they'd be okay. I'd have to trust Gideon and Bergen. I fixed my attention back on Dane, who was still seething over me.

Come on, Kincaid—he's just a poltergeist. You handle all sorts of poltergeists.

Here went nothing . . .

"Hey! Dane!" I shouted, and threw Otherside at him.

"Foul!" Dane shrieked, as the wave of Otherside sent him sprawling over the water.

I bolted after the Otherside trail, following the strange path Bergen had laid out.

Dane howled after me, even as Liam shouted after him to wait.

The path led right into one of the ponds, and the freezing water. Oh, hell.

"Kincaid? Yooohooo, where did you go? *You know I'm gonna getcha, getcha, getcha really good!*" he sang out.

Bergen, Gideon—if either of you are listening, you have a lot to learn about fucking hypothermia.

The line only flared brightly, more insistently. Pointing towards the water.

I braced myself at the water's edge, working up the courage to jump in as Dane crashed gleefully through the forest after me, singing as loud as he could, "*Not stayin' alive, not stayin' alive, ah-ah ah-ah, Kincaid's not stayin' aliiiiive.*" I winced as the poltergeist's falsetto cracked—badly.

And he was getting closer. I held my breath and jumped.

This had to be Gideon's idea, I thought, as the water closed over my head. Leaving me unconscious on a hard floor, having me jump in a freezing swamp—the dead are lousy at keeping the living alive.

I surfaced and filled my lungs, ready to curse Gideon for the damn cold—

"*Kincaid, Kincaid-Do, where are you? Why don't you tell me where Kincaid is so I can kill her!*" he sang, the new lyrics barely fitting with the old cartoon jingle.

I ducked my head back under the water just as Dane's bright-white shorts floated overhead. I could still hear him singing as he flew back and forth, searching for me.

Killed by a show tunes–singing poltergeist. Fantastic end. My lungs needed air, and soon.

I reached for the swamp and its Otherside. The problem was, even under the water, I couldn't pull a globe without attracting Dane. I was trapped—whether he knew I was or not.

I waited for a probe—a word—anything from Gideon or Bergen telling me what to do next.

Come on, Gideon. Give me something.

I felt a distinctly different sensation this time as the swamp reached out. Colder, more methodical, crueller. *By your feet, Kincaid,* came Gideon's distinct voice. I glanced down. Son of a bitch. On the bottom of the pond was a mirror, the bindings so familiar to me, even if I couldn't see the ghost-grey cast in the darkness. It was the mirror I'd been working on with Gideon. The one I'd hated. And the one that acted as a lure. How the hell he'd managed to get it here . . .

You know what to do. Now leave us to concentrate on the other one.

I grabbed a quick breath and kicked down, until I felt the mirror in my fingers.

I didn't wait until I reached the surface. I made a quick modification to the mirror so it would look for Dane, and flooded it with Otherside. It flared a brilliant gold, the Otherside feeding into the rings, turning it into a beacon. I swam back up, to find Dane hovering overhead, peering at me.

"Heya . . ." he said, racket still raised overhead. "What do you have there, Strangey?" His voice was far away, and a little dreamy for a poltergeist. I bobbed in the water, freezing my ass off, holding on to the ghost trap for dear life.

"Oh, you know," I said, matching the poltergeist's tone as he hovered, feeding more and more Otherside into the mirror. "A little mayhem, a little murder. Why don't you go take a look, Dane? I'll bet there's something fun inside."

"You know—you know—there's something else I'm supposed to be doing." He wagged a finger at me, giving me a red side eye.

"You're a tricky one. You're the kind of kid I have to watch out for. Never up to any good . . ." Dane did the equivalent of a ghost hiccup as he drifted closer. He looked and sounded drunk. He was completely mesmerized by the mirror. The tennis racket fell from his hand into the water.

"You know," Dane said, hands reaching for me now. The mirror reached out for him and began sucking him in. Dane either didn't notice or was too enthralled to care. "All I ever wanted was for things to be nice, wholesome. Back like they were in the good old days. Was that really too much to ask?" He hiccuped again, his voice and body fading, shrinking. "For girls like you to be a little nicer? Dress a little prettier? Smile a little more? Was that really so wrong for the world?"

I nodded. "Yeah, it was," I said as he disappeared into the mirror. No resistance, no struggle. The killing force that had been Martin Dane was finally gone, and the ghost trap snapped shut with a bright point of Otherside, locking him up for good, just as he'd done with so many victims.

Still holding the mirror, I crawled out of the water. Despite my shivering, I couldn't help but smile at Dane's poetic end. No great battle, no final threats. He'd been snuffed out, just the way he'd deserved.

It had worked. I took a breather and willed myself to warm up.

A gunshot rang out through the swamp, back the way I'd come. Shit, Stephan and Nate . . .

Holding the mirror, I pushed myself to standing. Hoping to god Bergen and Gideon had handled Liam.

Something grabbed a handful of my hair and pulled me back into the water and held me under until my lungs screamed for oxygen. Just as I thought it was over, it pulled me out.

I surfaced to find the ghost of a man, translucent in the moonlight. Shoulder-length brown hair framed his young face—attractive but cold, cruel. He was dressed in Victorian-styled clothes—but Victorian ghosts were all supposed to be gone . . .

His face was devoid of emotion as he regarded me, but there was something familiar about him—a presence, the predatory and cruel expression, even the set to his mouth. And then there were the deadened black eyes and the darkness that surrounded him. The ghost was devoid of Otherside, except for the glittering gold lines that fed into him from seemingly everywhere.

Gideon. With the sole exception of the absence of Otherside, the ghost's presence, his manner, the way he watched me with indifference, all reminded me of Gideon.

I tried to wrench my arm from his grasp. *Gideon, we have a problem!* I shouted silently through the connection I still had with the swamp.

The ghost dropped me unceremoniously. "Clever," he said, his voice icy, devoid of human inflection. "But Gideon can't help you. The witch swamp can't help you. No one can help you." He leaned in so close, the chill sent me shivering, his eyes black pits. "Except me."

He knew who Gideon was, he even *behaved* like Gideon, and the only Otherside that surrounded him were thin gold lines feeding the blackened pit that was his ghost. I swallowed. Ingrid said the chair binding Liam had used to imprison the ghosts on his show was a Victorian relic.

"Hello, Johnathan," I managed. "I'm guessing Gideon doesn't know you're here yet."

It was pure luck I managed to suck in a breath as he dragged me back under the water. "People are like rabbits," Johnathan's ghost whispered. "Too scared to run. You're not like that, though. You're *she*. Gideon's new apprentice." He spat the last word as if it tasted foul in his mouth, then pulled me back up to examine me. "I made Liam call you here, if only so I could get a good look at you for myself. I'm not impressed."

I was freezing from the swamp water, and shivering uncontrollably, but still I managed an answer between chattering teeth. "You're the ghost Liam talked about. The one who taught him how to be that—abomination."

He smiled, and though I didn't think it was possible, his smile was colder than Gideon's. "Oh, I only helped him along. Liam was well on his way to discovering that talent, though not in his lifetime."

"And Astrid?"

He regarded me. "My, you're a clever one. Gideon always had good taste in apprentices. You should have heeded me when I told you to leave." Johnathan's ghost shook me. "Now, *where* is Gideon?"

I reached out for the swamp, but though I felt it on the periphery, watching, waiting, it couldn't reach me. And I couldn't reach the Otherside. I was cut off.

Without a drop of Otherside to speak of, I went for the next best thing—I lied. "No idea. But he sure as hell wants to talk to you about the ghost trap you stole." I held up the ghost trap mirror, hoping it could hold a poltergeist *and* a very powerful hungry ghost.

The glass cracked, shattering to pieces.

Johnathan smiled. "Not to the advanced workings yet, I see. More's the pity for you."

"Fuck off—" He dunked my head back under and held me there for what felt like a minute before throwing me back on land as if I weighed nothing. I shivered pitifully in a heap, trying not to freeze to death as Johnathan hovered over me.

Coughing, I thought: *Gideon, Bergen, if either of you are out there, I have a serious problem.* No response came.

Johnathan hovered over me.

"What do you want, Johnathan?" I said, trying to put more space between us as I fought for time. "Liam, the murders, the ghosts— what was the point?"

"Revenge, initially. Though I'll admit this swamp has my interest now. With its power, Gideon will be no match for me. He doesn't even realize it's me who stole his trap."

"You were his apprentice. Why?"

Johnathan's face twisted in rage. "He *abandoned* me. Enough instruction to survive my death, but not nearly enough to escape my fate." He held out his arms, the gold threads waving in the Otherside swamp fog. "Did you think I wanted to become this? It took me centuries to master my appetite." I saw the threads coming for me and inched away. There wasn't much dry land left.

"Why didn't you ask for help?"

Johnathan snorted. "You really don't know anything, do you? Gideon really has got much smarter over the years, hasn't he? Who says a ghost can't learn a new trick. And you, with all your whining and brooding, are most definitely not what he needs."

How the—

Astrid. Gideon said she had to learn control somewhere. Who better to teach her than another hungry ghost?

Johnathan's Otherside threads licked my face, as if tasting me. For the first time, he smiled. "Oh, now I see why Gideon chose you. Pity I have to kill you. You're interesting. Valuable, more than Liam realizes. It will hurt Gideon if I take you away from him."

"Trust me, if it's revenge you're after, Gideon won't care if you kill me. He doesn't care about anyone except himself."

Johnathan brought his pale, beautiful face close enough for me to feel the cold hunger. "Haven't you wondered *why* you've such an affinity for the dead, for Otherside, Kincaid Strange? It's because, for a brief time during your life, you *were* one of the dead."

Despite his evil intentions, I knew in my heart Johnathan was telling me the truth. As I knelt there, a memory in the background of my ghost-filled dreams resurfaced. We'd lived near a field with a pond. I'd liked to go out there at night when my parents fought. I vaguely remembered families of raccoons and large frogs. And ice in the winter, which used to crack under my feet.

My mother told me I'd fallen through the ice, that was why I hated the cold so much. I'd been lucky it was winter, since hypothermia had set in once I'd gone under.

It was a vague memory. I'd been so young.

"And to think Gideon thought to pass you off as another useless practitioner. Help me, Kincaid Strange. Help me get my master back."

Johnathan wasn't just obsessed with hurting Gideon, he wanted him back. He'd gone insane with hunger for his old life.

"Not a chance in hell. Deal with him your—"

My throat clenched again. There was a flicker of glitter in his eyes—not the gold I often saw in Gideon's, but red. Poltergeist red.

"Help me take this swamp and I will show you how to break your deal with my old master."

I swallowed. I wasn't planning on agreeing to anything with a hungry ghost—but I also didn't want to have my head shoved back under the water. Or die.

Johnathan glanced around him, as if sensing something, and said something under his breath that might have been a curse, before pulling my hair back and hissing. "Know this: if you decide not to help me, there will be consequences. Maybe not here, not today, but soon. I swear it." His dark eyes bored into mine and a sole gold thread floated my way, lashing at my face before the cold burned my cheek. "*You* are not the apprentice he needs," Johnathan whispered in my ear. "And I'm most certainly the apprentice he deserves."

He vanished. I crouched there, trying to comprehend what had happened.

And then the shouting reached me. Nate and Stephan. Shit. I pushed myself back up and set off at a run, hoping to hell no one else was dead.

*

I found them in the same clearing, and the scene was not confidence-inspiring. Stephan was awake and had his gun trained on Liam, who was nursing his shoulder, though he was still standing, and Nate was no longer in the cage.

"K! Thank fucking god! K, he's trying to eat me— Get them off! Get them off!" Nate kicked at the gold threads that clung to him now, attaching him to Liam. My stomach sank as I saw the Otherside draining, feeding Liam.

I threw Otherside at them, severing the lines. Liam screamed.

"Vamoose, Nate!" I called.

He checked his wrists and hands, looking for any more gold threads. "Don't have to tell me twice. The son of a bitch tried to eat me!" he said, and vanished from sight.

Now for Liam—and whatever the hell he was.

"You took my poltergeist. I felt it," Liam said.

"Liam—" I tried.

"I had no choice! Both of you would have done the same thing if circumstances were reversed." Liam narrowed his eyes at me, still nursing the bullet wound.

Maybe, but I hoped to hell not . . . "It's over, Liam. Dane's gone. It's just you."

He took a step back. I glanced at Stephan, who still had the gun aimed at Liam. I tried to stay out of the line of sight.

Liam smiled, and nodded at Stephan. "Tell the witch to shoot," Liam said. "I won't come quietly." He raised his hands, as if in triumph. I glanced at Stephan.

He didn't look at all happy.

Liam let out a broken laugh. "He won't shoot me, Kincaid. Otherwise I'll be bound to this swamp as a ghost." There was a madness in his eyes. "And you can be damn sure I'll be hungry."

I didn't need to ask Stephan. I knew it to be true.

Liam reached into his jacket and pulled out a gun.

"Drop it, Liam," Stephan shouted.

"Or you'll what, Agent Wolf? Shoot me? Please do," he said, and turned the gun on himself, a mad gleam in his eyes.

Shit.

"I know more tricks than you can imagine." Liam laughed. "I don't want to die, but as soon as I do, I'll devour this entire swamp, then come after you. Now, into the pentagram, Kincaid Strange— and you too, Agent Wolf." Liam cocked the gun and held it to his temple. "Or I shoot and eat your souls."

I glanced to where the pentagram lay. Intricate, ornate. Oh no. It was Gideon's ghost trap, the one that worked on the living in Otherside gold relief.

Both ways, I die, I thought.

Almost, I heard Bergen whisper, though perhaps it was my own fear speaking now. *Look*, she said, and nudged my thoughts towards the ground. Liam had etched his pentagram in the soil. It was touching the swamp . . .

Yes, I heard Gideon this time, whispering through the link. *It means Johnathan's made a mistake.* Gideon had figured out that his former apprentice was behind this. *Trust me,* came Gideon's thoughts. *Step inside, both of you, and before he catches on.*

Here's hoping you're right, Gideon. I didn't know if they could talk to Stephan—but when I glanced at him, he nodded. I took a big breath and stepped inside.

Otherside singed the air around me as soon as my foot touched the soil inside, and it only intensified when Stephan joined me. And then the pentagram lit up with fireflies—and they headed straight for us.

I don't care how much affinity I have for the Otherside—there is only so much one person can take at once. It was as if the swamp, all of it, wanted to feed me Otherside through the pentagram all at once. Ozone in my nose and cold Otherside flowed down my throat.

So much Otherside—just waiting. Stephan must have felt it too, because he reached out and took my hand. I squeezed it, glad someone else was there with me.

A moment longer, Gideon whispered, his words clearer than they had been a moment ago, now that the swamp was being funnelled into the ghost trap.

Fear, hunger, anger—

Not Gideon or Bergen this time, but the swamp itself nudged me, as if it sensed nearby prey, catching the scent of a weed left too long.

Liam shouted in pain, drawing my attention off the pentagram and the swamp. The lines of Otherside that had been rooted into the swamp were now severed and swaying around him as if in a breeze. They tried to touch the swamp again, but were repelled. Liam was cut off. Bergen and Gideon had done it.

Liam swore, in visible pain. He raised the gun, pointing it at Stephan. "What did you do, witch?"

Stephan only regarded him and shrugged. "I'm in a pentagram. Not even witches can cast spells in a pentagram."

Liam's eyes were bright green as he came closer, the threads of Otherside swaying in anticipation, waiting for our ghosts to emerge so they could feed. "I may have lost Dane and this swamp, but I'll be feeding off your souls for months."

The pentagram flared, and more fireflies emerged from the ground. I touched the pentagram—it sparked and I drew my hand back.

Stephan squeezed my hand as Liam raised his hands. "Stay still," he whispered beside me.

I hazarded a glance his way. "Please tell me you know what they're doing."

Stephan didn't nod, but he kept his eyes on Liam. He pulled me close to him as the fireflies floated our way. Liam stood there, waiting to feed off us.

I readied Otherside, but Stephan said, "Wait." I did, as a firefly came closer and closer to my face.

"I really hope the plan isn't for all of us to die and live in the swamp forever, Stephan. I would be very disappointed." I barely breathed as the firefly lighted on my nose and another on Stephan's cheek, waiting for the pentagram to kill us.

"Never, ever, try to work Otherside in a witches' swamp," he whispered, then closed his eyes. I closed mine as the bindings reached out with Otherside for me.

Now, came both Bergen's and Gideon's voices in my head.

Now what? The answer came a moment later. Stephan opened his eyes and lifted his hand. The fireflies stopped, hovering in place. Then they switched direction. Just a little at first, churning over each other, the gold threads that bound them all a tangled mess.

Liam screamed. But Stephan wasn't done yet.

Hold very still, apprentice, Gideon said, and another jolt of Otherside coursed through me. *And try to keep your eyes off the witch and on the soul-eater.*

The Otherside kept coming, filling the bottomless pit inside me until it was overflowing, until it felt as if every cell in my body was filled with Otherside. And it burned so hot for a moment, I thought I'd die. I could feel the entire swamp and every nook and cranny of Otherside that permeated it.

"Hold on, Kincaid," Stephan whispered, his face strained with pain as well, the Otherside fireflies and threads from the trap mixing with the vines of the swamp, winding around him. He was stalling the trap, somehow using witchcraft to stop it from killing us.

Well, now I knew why we weren't dead yet. Liam screamed again, this time in rage. Stephan distracted the fireflies and their life-leeching lines, while I absorbed the trap's Otherside. It was working, but we couldn't keep this up much longer.

Now, look at the pentagram, Gideon whispered. I did, except now I could feel it too, an extension of the swamp. *Move it under the soul-eater. The witch will help you.* I glanced at Stephan, who nodded.

Move an entire pentagram . . . I'd never even attempted something like that. Setting a binding freehand was one thing, but moving an entire working? But I could feel it, all the edges. Carefully, I teased them out of the earth while Stephan held off the onslaught. I detached the last anchor of the pentagram, the ghost trap tangled inside, and held it hovering over the soil, not entirely sure what the hell to do with it.

Another squeeze from Stephan's hand. A path of Otherside swamp vines crept from his feet all the way towards Liam, who was still launching his soul-eater attacks, trying desperately to leech Otherside from the swamp and us.

I reached for the vines. They were like railroad tracks, or a lifeline, a way to move the working.

I knew what would happen next: the trap would kill Liam. Unwillingly, Johnathan's words came back to me: *Help me take this swamp and I will show you how to break your deal with Gideon.*

For a moment, a hair's breadth of a second, I stalled. I could move the trap. I didn't just see how to do it, I could feel it through the swamp. But killing Liam with Otherside . . .

Understanding, sympathy, remorse . . . all three flowed through me from the swamp.

It's the only way, Kincaid Strange, I heard Bergen's voice in my head. *Move the trap. My grandson will do the rest. Liam will never hurt another soul, living or dead, ever again.*

Now, apprentice, came Gideon's less patient, more insistent thought. *Before Johnathan or his soul-eater catch on.*

I glanced from Liam to Stephan, who was really straining now to hold whatever witch working he and his grandmother had wound. But he looked resolved. As if sensing my trepidation, he hazarded a glance at me with those bright hazel eyes. "Hundreds of ghosts, Kincaid, maybe thousands," he managed through clenched teeth.

All the ghosts in Portland, Dane's victims, Katy—and Stephan and Bergen's family . . .

He was right. I took hold of the trap and moved it.

Liam realized something was wrong when the fireflies all left Stephan's vines—and aimed at Liam. He tried to move. Otherside vines from the swamp crept up and wound their way around his feet. Liam's eyes went wide in panic as I slid the trap the last few inches and reconnected it to the earth. The fireflies hovered around the trap and their new target, waiting, anticipating.

Liam watched them with pure terror, a look I well imagined reflected on every ghost he'd consumed. Horrible and karmic.

"You can't—that's impossible," Liam wheezed. Blood was pooling from the gunshot wound in his shoulder. The Otherside fireflies danced frantically, searching for a way out of the trap, the one Liam had built and I had moved. They sparked as they hit the pentagram's wall. "I—" Whether he realized the how or why I don't know, but he fixed on me. "I'll give you anything you want, Kincaid Strange. Fame, wealth—I can give you all that and more."

I shook my head. How many ghosts had begged just like that?

Anger replaced the panic. "He'll come after you for this! I'm not alone, Kincaid Strange."

I was certain Johnathan would.

Finish it, apprentice.

It was time to set loose all the Otherside I'd consumed back into the pentagram and the ghost trap. *Gideon, Bergen, I don't think I can stop a hungry ghost.* For I had no doubt that as soon as Liam was dead, that's what he would become.

You do your part, and Stephan and I have the rest covered, Bergen replied, and sent along a wave of comfort, thanks and trust.

I met Liam's bright-green, panicked eyes one last time. Despite everything he'd done, I couldn't help feeling a little sorry for him and what he'd become. "It didn't have to be this way, Liam," I said, and flooded the pentagram.

The last thing Liam did was scream as the fireflies and the ghost trap held by the pentagram consumed him. For a brief second I saw his ghost float over his body and eye me hungrily. The swamp caught him, and wound a cage over and over itself while the hungry ghost screamed. And then Liam was gone, stuck in the swamp, his body discarded on the ground, the trap no more.

Blood rushed to my head as silence once again filled the night air. The ground wavered under my feet. If it hadn't been for Stephan, I might have tried sinking into the swamp myself.

"What happened to Liam? Did the swamp . . ." I couldn't say *kill him*.

Stephan shook his head and took my face in his hands, forcing me to look at him. "He's contained. He'll never get free, not in a thousand years. He's gone. You did the right thing."

I laughed and closed my eyes. The right thing. "How come with me the right thing always ends up a dark grey?"

"If life was black and white, there'd be no monsters like Liam," Bergen said, not thought.

Oh no. I opened my eyes. There was a sole ghost standing in front of me, with piercing hazel eyes.

"Bad luck, I'm afraid," Bergen's ghost said.

"Gran—" Stephan cried out, more shocked than I was—and hurt. "You swore the workings were safe—"

She stopped him with a raised hand. "I lied, Stephan. Don't look so shocked, I've done it before, I'll do it again. The sorcerer warned me it might happen. He kept his word—it's not his fault. Or hers," she said, nodding at me. "Fair is fair and all that." At the pain in Stephan's face, she added, "I'm sorry. But I have my swamp back, and the darkness is gone. And now I can help the others." She looked around. "Whoever is left. The swamp is empty without our ghosts. If I need to be the first to fill it, so be it."

And with that, she disappeared.

"Gran? Gran?" Stephan shouted, his fists clenched by his sides. She didn't return.

He turned on me, the pain still raw. "Did you know that would happen?"

"I—no, I had no idea—" I started, but Stephan, normally so controlled, lost his temper in his grief.

"The sorcerer—he *made* her—"

"No." The force and certainty I said it with surprised me. "Gideon is a lot of things, but he always keeps his word. And he doesn't kill people."

Stephan looked away.

"Stephan," I said, but he shook his head.

"Save it, Kincaid Strange." He held up his hand and I felt the power of the swamp behind it. The man who'd tried to comfort me a moment before was gone, in his place a powerful witch, in command of the swamp, warning me.

I stepped back and raised my own hands.

"We're square, but there is *nothing* you can say that will make this right."

I felt the cold beside me, and thanked god it was Nate who appeared, not Gideon. "K—" he started, then stopped, hovering beside me, his eyes on Stephan, consumed by his grief.

I didn't know what to say—or how to help. He had trapped a dangerous man and lost his grandmother in the process. It wasn't a fair trade.

I heard one last whisper from Bergen in my ear. "Give him some time. We witches are a strange lot when it comes to our loved ones." I thought I caught a glimpse of her in the Otherside fog that swirled around me, but I could have been mistaken.

"I'm sorry, Stephan," I said, glad Nate was beside me.

"I am too," Stephan said, and turned and headed out of the swamp. Leaving me there with my ghost of a best friend and Liam's corpse.

I should have followed him. Stephan knew the swamp like the back of his hand. But I'd just channelled more Otherside than a living person is supposed to. It finally hit me, and I sank to the damp swamp floor, shivering in my wet clothes. Ah, there was the nausea, coming back with a vengeance.

"K? I don't *think* he meant to ditch us here with a corpse. I get the impression these witches are a weird bunch. Aw man, please don't upchuck. I can't take any more shit tonight."

"Where are the zombies? Derrick and his men?" Fresh brains, alone in a witch swamp? It'd be well-nigh irresistible.

"Took off as soon as the cops started showing up in force."

That was a relief. Despite my stomach's threats, I kept its meagre contents down.

I heard someone call my name and a flashlight passed overhead. "Over here," Nate shouted. I heard voices nearby, and saw lights. I thought I heard Stephan tell someone I needed help, though that might have been wishful thinking. I lay down on the ground and took my phone from my pocket. With shivering fingers, I texted Aaron, just in case I didn't wake up for a while.

Finished with the case. Liam and Ingrid did it. Dane is gone. Trapped in a broken mirror, never to be seen again. A fitting end. I was thankful for the darkness that prevented me from seeing Liam's open, dead eyes.

And then I closed my eyes while Nate cajoled me to get up. I ignored him. The dead get to sleep, and after tonight I deserved a good sleep too.

CHAPTER 23

THE DEVIL I KNOW

I was vaguely aware of FBI agents carrying me out of the swamp and back to the barn, where they'd arrived *en force*. A female agent, whose name I promptly forgot, helped me out of my wet clothes in the back of a police van and draped a blanket over my shoulders before handing me a hot Thermos. I sat there until the shivering abated, almost dozing off once or twice.

I caught sight of Stephan once. He looked at me for a long moment before disappearing into a car with other agents. I also saw them carry Liam's body out in a black bag, which disappeared into another van.

The Otherside was gone, the ghosts Liam had taken were all gone . . . well, save one.

She appeared beside me as I huddled in the back of a car, while everyone was busy with Liam's body, dressed in track pants and a T-shirt, just as she was in most of her photos.

"Hello, Katy," I said. "Are you the only ghost left?"

She shook her head, staring at the ground, not making eye contact with me.

"Some of them say we have you to thank. For saving us." She looked at me then, and all I saw was the shock, and pain, and more than a little accusation.

"I can't find my parents—what if they're—" Her ghost choked off the last words and a tear slid down her cheek, falling on my hand.

For a moment, I thought about giving her my usual spiel, about how her death wasn't fair, she hadn't deserved it but she needed to make the most of her afterlife . . . She'd been through enough. "I don't know if your parents are waiting for you on the Otherside, Katy, or somewhere beyond. But I do know you'll never find out if you don't go and look." After a moment I added, "And if you find yourself on the Otherside, and need someone to talk to, come find me. Ask Nathan Cade, he'll point you in the right direction."

When I looked beside me again, she was gone. I hoped that was a good thing, and that she'd manage to find peace somewhere on the Otherside.

Someone drove me back to the hotel, where Liam's last victim appeared in my bathroom mirror.

"Thank you," Ingrid whispered.

I wanted to scream, let my anger loose . . . Despite my best intentions, I had begun to like Ingrid.

I did the next best thing: I reached for the mirror bindings. Before I could unravel them, she said, "There's a laptop in an airport locker, 2211, my birthday. The key is waiting for you at the hotel's front desk. It's paid up for a month. Everything is there . . . I'm sorry," she added softly, as I unset the mirror and was left staring at my own reflection.

I slept in the warm, comfortable bed until late that afternoon, my dreamless slumber a welcome relief.

When I woke up, there was an envelope slipped under the door with a generous cheque inside, and a thank you for assisting the FBI. Signed by Stephan.

That he hadn't delivered it in person hurt more than a little. Inside was a ticket back to Seattle for that evening. Part of me wanted to push, make Stephan talk to me, but the smarter part stashed the cheque and checked in online.

Stephan had my number, he could call any time. Bergen had said to give him time. I'd leave him to his cases, the swamp and the rest of the witches. But I was sorry for the loss of a friend; I didn't know a lot of people who lived in the world of the Otherside and weren't already dead. I'd started hoping . . . what? For something more? Maybe.

Back home in Seattle that evening, there was an e-mail from Aaron, professional and to the point. Clarifying details on the case only, for which I was grateful. I settled back in with coffee and a BLT, and sat down to look at the bag I'd retrieved from the airport locker. I'd send it to the FBI eventually, and let them know a ghost had found it for me. I needed my own questions answered first.

True to Ingrid's ghost's word, she'd outlined the whole story and confessed to her part in it. Liam had been feeding on ghosts for a decade. No wonder none of the guests on his show had ever gone back to haunting their families—he'd eaten them.

Ingrid hadn't known about Johnathan, though he had to have been in the picture for just as long as Liam had been feeding on ghosts. All that anger and vengeance—over a hundred years obsessing over his former master.

*

"I can feel the temperature drop," I called out a few hours after I'd arrived home.

I turned to find Gideon in my kitchen, Johnathan's journal sitting on the table between us. We stared each other down.

"I thought you hated witches," I said.

Gideon made a face. "Hate is a strong word," he said. "Dislike is more accurate. And under the circumstances, we all concluded our business amicably."

"Was Bergen supposed to die?"

"The workings to extract the soul-eater and his poltergeist from her swamp were difficult, and she was not young. She accomplished what she set out to do. I helped save her grandson and reclaim the swamp. In exchange, they used the swamp to prevent you from dying. It was a fair bargain." He trailed off, and a silence stretched. "You met Johnathan, didn't you? It was him, leading the soothsayer, reworking my trap. I didn't recognize him at first . . . He's changed."

Gideon didn't say anything more. I sighed and headed to the sink. If he was going to sit there chilling up the room, I might as well boil water.

"Johnathan was not like that while he was alive—jealous, hungry, vindictive, corrupted by the dead," he finally said. "He was kind, sympathetic, curious." He stared at the table, lost in his own thoughts. "He's dangerous now, Kincaid. He's broken rules of the dead that should never be broken, and his recent antics—Liam, the swamp, I suspect the Jinn and wraith—have attracted attention."

"Whose?" I asked, shaking my head.

Gideon gave me a wry smile. "Even the dead have our politics. He knows I am hunting him now."

I took that in. "He said I was useful. That I'd been dead before." After my return, I'd confirmed it with the hospital in Vancouver. As a child, I'd been dead for a full minute before being resuscitated.

Gideon nodded. "Yes, you have a greater affinity for Otherside because of it. You're safe enough from him, for now." He glanced up once more. "Read his journal or not. Our lessons and your work-ings are suspended for the week."

Gideon vanished.

I left the book on the table while I steeped my tea, wondering whether I should open it, if I really wanted to know. My curiosity won out. I flipped to a page that had been bookmarked with a black ribbon, one of the ones Gideon had revealed.

Rest assured I am of sound mind and body, but the story
I am about to tell you will put your faith in that to the test.
For this story is not mine but that of Gideon Lawrence, a
powerful sorcerer's ghost, and my mentor, teacher, and I dare

say friend for these past two years. A cursed soul who carries the anger of a poltergeist wherever he goes.

But that is not where his story begins. It all started in 1052 in a kingship in Northern Denmark, where Gideon fell into the service of a local warlord who wanted to be king . . .

CHAPTER 24

HUNGRY HEARTS

I got approved for my federal licence almost a week after arriving home. It was waiting in my mailbox. They'd rushed it—a special request from Agent Wolf of the FBI paranormal unit. Aaron had also vouched for me, I saw, despite Captain Marks's threats. Aaron was on a well-deserved leave of absence. I didn't know where he'd gone or what he was doing. He hadn't told me.

But the pang in my heart was small, barely an echo of my former heartache, and I was happy for him. Hoping that he was out of Captain Marks's manipulative web, and out of mine as well. Maybe we'd patch things up one day, but not without fixing what was wrong with ourselves first. It wasn't just Marks's meddling that had poisoned us. We'd both had our hand in that as well.

I took Nate to Damaged Goods to celebrate my new licence.

"K," Nate said as he nursed his beer thoughtfully, "something Liam said still bothers me."

"What's that?" We hadn't talked much about our trip to Portland. The fact that Sinclair had tried to eat Nate was still a sore spot. It was too close to being bound. Ghosts aren't meant to face their biggest fears; that's what the living do.

"He said something about how the dead, no matter how good-intentioned, always corrupt the living?"

I laughed and opened my mouth, intending to tell him that all the proof he needed was the new pile of video games and game consoles he'd convinced me to buy him after the FBI's cheque cleared. After almost being eaten, he'd deserved the bonus.

But the serious, disturbed expression on his face stopped me. "I don't know, Nate. Can the dead corrupt?" I shook my head. "I don't think they can do it any more than the living." I mean, if you spend all your time hanging out with thieves, are the chances good you'll become one? Sure, there are enough wayward under-cover agents across the law enforcement spectrum to demonstrate that spectacularly. But ghosts, the dead in general? I doubted it.

Nate made a face and stared into his beer as Lee moved around the room, serving her undead patrons. The decor had changed once again. The white lanterns decorated with pink-and-red blossoms had been replaced with light-blue lamps decorated with dark-blue and navy stars and snowflakes. Even the beaded curtain that hung just inside the saloon doors had been replaced with beads of icicles. She'd found them online, though where the hell she'd had shipped them to . . .

She was trying something new. Seasonal, she'd said.

"Okay, K. Here's my New Year's resolution," Nate said, placing the empty glass down on the counter with a solid thud.

"You're six weeks off."

"Chances are I'll forget by the time we reach New Year's if I don't say it now." He made a show of straightening up on his bar stool. "I'm swearing off white lies. In an effort to not have you turn into an evil ghost binder, or a self-centred, C-list, TV celebrity practi-tioner, or, you know, Gideon—"

I made a face. I had told Nate about Johnathan, Gideon's last apprentice, but not about Gideon's curse. I don't know if it made me like Gideon any more, but I understood him. A bit. That might even be the same thing.

"I'm taking one for the ghost team." He took a deep breath. "Starting with the chrome table." He looked at me, a little embarrassed. "I totally didn't find it in a dumpster. I paid, like, 350 bucks for it at a vintage place, a guy who's a huge fan of mine."

I swirled my beer. "I know, Nate. I found the sticker on the edge."

"And I may have sabotaged the legs of the old one after you glued it together. I mean, in my defence, it was hideous—and I hated it. Hate me for wanting nice things in my afterlife."

I sighed. I knew it.

"And what is with this 350 bucks? I mean, twenty years ago you'd find them in the alley all packed up for the dumpster." I shook my head as Nate continued. "Anyway, he let me give him a down payment—even delivered it to your place for free. FYI, I hate your front-door lock. How do you live with it?"

Maybe open and unfiltered honesty with Nate wasn't the best thing . . .

"Oh, and I still owe him 200 bucks. Speaking of which, I need the cash."

I finished my beer. "Give me the name of the shop. I'll drop it off and take it out of your piggy bank." Otherwise, some of that cash would likely find its way nowhere good . . .

I stood and left cash on the counter for Lee. I had a potential case waiting for me in New York, a financial adviser who had died of a heart attack—and *then* absconded with all his clients' money. He was reluctant to tell his partners where he'd hidden it.

It was a refreshing change from serial killers and paranormally tainted murder sprees.

As I walked through the streets of the underground, the frost crystalline on the ground and even a few more lights hanging in windows for the upcoming holiday season, I found myself whistling. And not even minding the cold.

Instead of rain, there was snow in the air. Cold but dry. It looked beautiful in the lamplight, reminding me of Otherside.

I had died, when I was very young, and it had left a mark on me, an affinity for Otherside and a paradoxical hatred of the cold.

Maybe even my talent for freehand. I was okay with it—it was a missing piece I hadn't known I'd been looking for. It gave me peace.

My good mood followed me all the way home, even past my unwieldy lock. So much so, I didn't notice the two missed calls until I was through the door. Mrs. Young. My elevated mood vanished as I called her back. Gideon had told me Astrid was locked up where she couldn't hurt anyone else.

"Hello? Mrs. Young?" I answered. "I'm so sorry I didn't pick up—"

Mrs. Young cut me off. "It's Astrid. Please—we need you to come immediately. It's—" There was a muffled sound on the other end as she spoke to someone else—presumably Mr. Young. "I'm so tired—and my husband. Please, make her stop!" Her voice cracked at the end.

My stomach sank as I grabbed my helmet and supplies, balancing the phone under my chin. "I'm on my way. Use the sage I gave you and lock yourself in a room, hang the spirit wards on all entrances. Leave the food and joss paper outside—that should distract her," I hoped. I'd explained the problem with Astrid in Portland, and the fact that the Youngs hadn't been visited by her after Gideon had dragged her off had left me hopeful. How the hell had she escaped?

Question for later, after I had her trapped.

As I stopped in the bathroom, there was the telltale chill of Otherside. "Nate?"

"*You. Wouldn't. Listen.*"

Astrid.

I spun and found her standing behind me. She looked terrible. Her face was pale and red tear–stained, and her hair was dishevelled and dull.

She clutched herself, still appearing in the designer clothes she'd worn on her last visit, though they too appeared the worse for wear.

"Astrid, how did you get out?" I said, backing away.

She shook her head. "I've done something terrible, Kincaid," she said, her voice a whisper, her eyes a pure black as she watched me hungrily.

She was worse. Which meant she'd fed. "What did you do to your parents, Astrid?"

She started crying again, bloody tears dropping on my white-tiled floor.

"This is all your fault," she said through a sob. "If you had just done what you were supposed to, I would be free. My parents wouldn't—" She choked off another sob and levelled an angry stare my way.

I went cold as her words hit me.

If you had just done what you were supposed to.

"How did you get by the wards?"

"I had to make a different deal with him because of *you!*" she said, her voice filled with venom. "I want you to remember that this was all your fault," she said, and threw a cloud of black powder at me. I shielded my face reflexively, but there was too much. It smelt of ashes and Otherside.

I lost my balance and gripped the counter. I was looking at myself outside my own body. Watching as Astrid slid inside, and with my own face smiled at me, patting my jeans and jacket down.

"Not great, but not bad. Nothing a little cosmetic surgery and a better wardrobe can't fix."

I ran at her—and was repelled. I couldn't touch her—I couldn't touch anything. I turned to face the mirror. It was me—I shimmered a blackened gold. Astrid had kicked me out of my own body.

Shit. I reached for the Otherside I knew was there, but only had a tentative grasp—it was fluid, more like water. Still, I threw it at her—at me, my body.

That wiped the smile off her face, and for a moment she looked terrified. She swatted at me, but my hijacked arms passed right through me. Her ghost began to leave my stolen body.

That's it, Kincaid, just a little bit more . . .

"He said you might try this," Astrid's ghost said with my voice through my clenched teeth as I pulled, trying to rip her out. With her own ghostly arms, she reached out and grabbed me. And shoved, straight into the mirror.

I landed on my back, hard.

I sat up and looked around. I was sitting on a stone street, there were lanterns everywhere, and houses, and though I couldn't see anyone, I felt them there watching me. There were murmurs, low and whispering, getting louder. I stood and turned in a circle, wondering where they all came from.

There were so many lights. It looked like a very old village, of indistinct origin, a mishmash of different styles and tastes—Asian, European, African influences. And the lights, they were all so beautiful . . .

"Kincaid?" There was surprise in his voice, and I turned to find Gideon standing behind me. But he didn't look like a ghost—he looked as solid as I did.

"Astrid, she showed up and threw something at me . . ." I trailed off as I spotted something in the window of a nearby house. It wasn't human—*at all*. It was red, with large ears and *tusks*. The face disappeared as soon as I saw it. I turned back to look at Gideon.

He lowered his head, shooting his own furtive glances at the windows and houses surrounding us. "We have a serious problem, Kincaid," he said.

Somehow, I didn't think that began to cover it.

ACKNOWLEDGEMENTS

Thank you Steve, Cindy, Wally and Whisky Jack for all the support (and or patience) while I edited this. Also thank you to my friends Leanne Tremblay and Mary Gilbert, who read each and every early draft chapter. I don't know if I would have finished this book, or any book, without all of your feedback and encouragement.

I also want to thank my agent, Carolyn Forde, who picked my first manuscript out of the slush pile and perked up when I described this new project. Also Anne Collins, publisher at Random House Canada. I will never forget the day Anne reluctantly admitted she "liked" my novel, with its voodoo and zombies. And a huge thank you to Amanda Betts for editing this manuscript and helping tease out story nuances. *Voodoo Shanghai* wouldn't be in nearly as good shape without her.

There are many other people who have mentored and encouraged me in my writing career over the past few years—thanks to all of you!

KRISTI CHARISH spent her formative high school years listening to a lot of grunge music. She has a PhD in zoology from the
University of British Columbia. She has worked as a scientific
advisor on projects such as fantasy and science fiction writer Diana
Rowland's series, White Trash Zombie, and is the author of *The
Voodoo Killings, Lipstick Voodoo* and the four books in the Owl
series: *Owl and the Tiger Thieves, Owl and the Electric Samurai,
Owl and the Japanese Circus* and *Owl and the City of Angels.* She
lives in Vancouver.

www.kristicharish.com